VISITATION

Carolyn Gillespie

Published and Manufactured by Softwood Books

EU Responsible person: Maddy Glenn
Office 2, Wharfside House, Prentice Road, Stowmarket, Suffolk, IP14 1RD
www.softwoodbooks.com, hello@softwoodbooks.com

EU Rep:
Authorised Rep Compliance Ltd., Ground Floor, 71 Lower Baggot Street, Dublin, D02 P593, Ireland
www.arccompliance.com, info@arccompliance.com

A CIP catalogue record for this book is available from the British Library

Paperback ISBN: 978-1-0681509-6-8
Hardback ISBN: 978-1-0681509-7-5

Praise for *Visitation*

"From the immersive and beautifully rendered 80s setting to the timeless themes of belonging and identity, Carolyn Gillespie's *Visitation* is a captivating exploration of loss, longing and difference. Gillespie perfectly captures the contradictory desires of adolescence through the brilliantly feisty Ella, whose spiky vulnerability stole my heart from the very first page."

– Louise Finch, Carnegie Prize Shortlisted author of *The Eternal Return of Clara Hart*

"A darkly atmospheric coming-of-age story – so haunting it kept me riveted until the very last page."

– Jane Hennigan, best-selling author of *Moths*

"Grief and bereavement, sexuality, mysticism and friendships are handled with subtlety and nuance. Gillespie demonstrates a real mastery of plot, setting and pacing, combining coming-of-age elements with knotty issues of grief, faith and belonging."

– Alice Tarbuck, author of *A Spell in the Wild*

"I devoured Visitation. A poignant reminder of what it is to be a teenager who doesn't fit in. The book's settings, from 80's punk rock in Dundee to the Maryan fantasies of convent schoolgirls, make for compelling reading. Ella is intelligent, lonely and raging with grief, but we are always on her side. *Visitation* is more than just a coming-of-age story – it also explores the nature of spirituality, the real and the fake. The pivotal scenes in the woods will stay with me for a long time."

– Julie Evans

"I couldn't lift my head, even to eat. Nothing distracted me, or at least I wouldn't let it. I was on the edge of my seat and if I wasn't reading an e-book, I would have quickly skipped to the end to make sure that Ella made it through okay. The only reason I didn't was because I was afraid to lose my place."

– Laura Macdonald

"A great story which is emotive and tender, funny, intriguing and brilliantly well written. I could really smell the musty dampness, smoke and stale alcohol in Mikey's squat; could envisage the unloved shabbiness of Ella and her Dad's home and reckon I could find my way to Our Lady's tree."

– Liz Rumbold

For David

"Have regular hours for work and play; make each day both useful and pleasant, and prove that you understand the worth of time by employing it well. Then youth will be delightful, old age will bring few regrets, and life will become a beautiful success."

Little Women, Louisa May Alcott

"I'm just going through a phase right now. Everybody goes through phases and all, don't they?"

The Catcher in the Rye, J.D. Salinger

Dundee 1983

CHAPTER 1

Oh! You Pretty Things (David Bowie)

The yellow bathroom smelled of mildew and neglect. Paperbacks, damp towels and empty Vim cartons littered the lino, and on the edge of a cruddy pink sink, an electric razor buzzed. Over by the toilet, a school blazer leaned back against the wall, retaining its form, as if the wearer had not so much taken it off as simply vanished while slumping to the floor.

Ella – the erstwhile wearer – took a pair of kitchen scissors from the pocket of her school skirt and dropped them into the bowl of the sink. She turned on the taps to drown out the hum of her dad's beard trimmer, and as the mirror clouded, she disappeared from view. With an open palm she wiped a circle clear of condensation and saw her face once more. Her mother's hair, her mother's eyes, her mother's nose, her mother's skin. Did any of it belong to her?

Taking her time, she brushed her long black hair, enjoying the

9

static bristle, the slow sweep down. When she was younger, she would sit on the floor while her mother combed her wet, tangled hair. Cross-legged, between Mom's knees, she had squirmed and resisted every stroke of the same Mason and Pearson brush that she now held in her hand.

She lifted the razor.

Do it, Ella.

The buzz travelled through her hand, and she struggled to hold steady. Peering at the smeared reflection she wondered where she should begin? If she started above her ear the rest of her hair would cover the shaved stripe. She could change her mind, and no-one would notice.

But she wanted them to notice. She wanted all of them to notice.

She pressed the razor to her hairline – a couple of inches to the left of the centre parting – and pushed back. Her eyes widened and she held her breath. But the long hair tugged in the guard and she couldn't force it through, so she grabbed the blunt scissors and hacked at a fistful of hair, throwing the hank to the bathroom floor. Then, still wobbling against the vibrations, she forged on with the razor, following the curve of her skull, over the top of her head and down to the nape of her neck, trying to keep the line straight.

She wiped the condensation away once more.

Fuck.

A stripe of scalp, sickly and luminous, drew attention like a white line in the road.

The second stripe was easier. There was less hair to negotiate and a clear path to follow, at least until she reached the crown of her head. She twisted, trying to see over her shoulder, but anything that was going on back there was largely guesswork.

As the shorn hair fell about her feet, she felt stronger than she had in months, and she worked faster and with more dexterity until the left side of her head was all but bald.

Switching off the razor she turned to examine herself in profile. From the right nothing had changed. She was still Ella. Poor Ella. But when she turned to the left, she was somebody new.

Laughing, she flicked her head back and forth. *Old Ella, new Ella, old Ella, new Ella.*

'Is everything all right in there? Those taps have been running a long time,' she heard her father call from the foot of the stairs. 'I know you're angry, but I've put your supper in the oven. Are you coming down?' A floorboard creaked as he shifted his weight, lingering for an answer he wasn't going to get. 'I'll be in my study if you need me.'

Where else would he be? Like the dancing figurines in her old clockwork musical box, she and Dad occupied the same space but skated past one another, on separate cogs.

Earlier tonight though, they had collided.

She twisted off the squeaking taps, knowing he wouldn't move from the landing till she did so. Then she listened for the study door to shut behind him before turning the razor on once more.

The second side of her head was quicker. Confident now, she tidied up the verges of the drills she had made, blurring the lines, smoothing the surface. Minutes later, all that remained was a thick mane of darkness running in a strip down the middle of her bone-white head. With the kitchen scissors she cropped it, shortening the length – a little more at the front, a little less at the back. And then she was done.

Standing barefoot on the lino, surrounded by the cast-off slough that curled around her ankles and clung to her toes, she heard the whispering voices of her grandmother and her aunts. 'So like your dear mother, all that beautiful black hair.'

CHAPTER 2
Goody Two Shoes (Adam and the Ants)

That night, it had been after seven when she got off the bus from Dundee. The last thing she'd eaten was a slice of toast at breakfast and she was nauseous with hunger. She'd grown accustomed to eating supper alone and kept a 'kitchen book' on the table for company. Her current companion, *Jude the Obscure*, would be open where she had left it, face down, waiting for her. Poor Jude, he was such a loser. That morning she'd left him standing on the hill-top, looking down over Christminster. *You're never gonna fit in, buddy, get used to it,* she'd thought.

Unexpectedly though, Dad was waiting. He was usually in his study by then. On the table, at the place where she always sat, a colourless chop, tinned peas, and a dollop of Smash cooled on a brown Hornsea plate.

'This came today. It's from the headmaster,' he said, passing a letter across the table.

She felt Dad following her progress as she scanned the lines, waiting till she reached the end.

She had wondered how long she would get away with it. She kept her head down and waited. But Dad said nothing. And when she finally looked up, he was staring at the papier-mâché longboat that gathered dust on top of the dresser.

Unbidden, a memory surfaced. Ella was standing where she stood now, showing him the model that she and Mom had so carefully carried home from school. Viking longboats, she had told him, were clinker-built, and with a combination of wind power and rowing power they had sailed all across the world, maybe even as far as America, where she and Mommy were from.

Against the backing track of kitchen noises, he'd sat at the table – where he was sitting now – listening while she talked, taking her as seriously as if she'd been one of his students. The memory, so sharp and sudden, hurt her, and she blinked hard and stepped back.

'What's going on, hey? You used to love school.' His elbows were propped on the table, a thumb and forefinger rubbing his chin through his sandy beard.

'Did I? Well, not anymore,' she said. Nothing was the same anymore.

He leaned forward and looked up at her through dark-rimmed glasses. 'Talk to me,' he said, 'Or at least sit down and eat something. You must be hungry. Mr Kelman sounds worried. Should *I* be worried, Ella? Should I?'

She turned away and rummaged in the cluttered sink. Tea bags and cornflakes clogged the plughole, and she clattered noisily through the stack of dishes until she found the least dirty tumbler, which she rinsed and filled with water.

'Kelman's not worried. He doesn't care about me,' she muttered.

'Oh, come on, you're not being fair.'

She huffed out a breath. '*I'm* not being fair?' Snatching up the letter she read aloud in the headmaster's Dundonian twang, '*We understand that family circumstances have been difficult.*' And crumpling it into a ball she threw it into the heap of reconstituted mash on the plate in front of her. 'Since when did *fair* have anything to do with it?'

Her father pulled himself straight and put his big hands flat on the table like he meant business. 'Look, Ella, I'm pretty easygoing. I let you wear what you want, go where you want and listen to your music – God knows that's not easy…'

She glared at him, and he turned away. It seemed to wound him when she looked at him these days.

'…but when it comes to your education,' he continued. 'I've got to take the school's side.' He retrieved the letter and shook off a blob of potato. 'From now on I want you to come straight home from school every night.'

Her jaw clenched and the sinews in her long neck tightened. Who was he trying to fool? He was useless at this, and they both knew it. 'What a joke,' she snorted. 'You're never here when I get back from school. And when you are here, you might as well not be. You're stuck in your study with your headphones on and your eyes shut. Don't pretend. You wish you were anywhere but here. Or with anyone but me.'

He jolted.

If he replied, his words were lost as Ella threw open the kitchen drawers, pulling out envelopes and photographs, bottle corks and bicycle pumps. Nothing was where it should be. Mugs gathered on top of the fridge, cereal boxes were stacked on painted chairs, empty milk bottles and sticky jars covered the table and the shelves of the wooden dresser were layered with books, books that blocked the bright plates and pretty teacups that now held only dust. They were drowning in detritus.

Finally, she found what she was looking for. She grabbed the kitchen scissors, slid them, blade first, into the pocket of her school skirt and headed to the bathroom.

'You don't know me at all,' she told him as she walked away.

***

The chill air on the back of her neck woke Ella early the next morning, and she reached up to touch her bare head, running her fingers over her freshly shaved scalp. For a moment she enjoyed the sensation of skin newly awakened to touch, but then she remembered the state of the bathroom. Her shorn hair was still all over the floor. She threw back the bedclothes to get to it before Dad.

But all evidence of last night's carnage had gone. There was no trace of the hair, the Vim cartons had been swept up and the towels were hanging almost neatly on the rail. Even the dirty washing had been gathered up and removed. It was as if last night had never happened.

And then she caught herself in the mirror. It had definitely happened. In the cold light of the November morning her scalp shone like a frost moon. Without her hair to soften her features she looked gaunt and haunted. The workings of her body seemed to have moved from inside to out: the sharp turn of her jaw as it rose towards her ear, the slash of her cheekbone, the hollow of her clavicle. Moving her chin up towards the ceiling she watched the shadows deepen around the sockets of her dark, hollow eyes, in the vacancy of her cheeks. All of her was open, exposed. She had never seen a girl who looked like this before. Not in the flesh anyway. And the thought of that almost made her smile.

She showered quickly and back in her bedroom she turned her attention to the strip of hair that ran down the centre of her head. It should have been spiked and vertical, but because it was freshly washed it was sleek and floppy, and this was a problem. She pushed at it with her fingers, urging it to stand proud and when this failed, she turned her head upside down and blasted it with the hairdryer, hoping that gravity would give it some backbone. Then, still upside down, she backcombed and sprayed it till it was slick with lacquer.

Upright once more, and lightheaded, she looked at herself from all angles. The effect was far from the pictures that Mikey had shown her. A Mohican, he'd called it. Right now, her hair looked more pony than punk but there was still no way you could miss it, or the lack of it, and that was what she wanted.

Her uniform was scattered on the bedroom floor, a map of her movements from the night before. Her shirt, stippled with hair, was nearest the door. She needed a clean one, but she didn't want to go downstairs before she was ready, so she shook it out and sprayed it with deodorant. Her skirt draped the back of the desk chair, and her tights lay concertinaed at the foot of the bed. She sniffed them, wondering whether they had another day's wear in them and decided that they did. She left the top button of her shirt unfastened and knotted her tie as wide as it would go. The navy-blue skirt stopped well above her knees and there were ladders in the black opaque tights. She laced her DMs and ringed her dark eyes with kohl.

Ready.

At almost six feet tall, Ella had grown fast and nothing fitted her anymore. At the end of the summer holidays her father had given her money for uniform. *Take Nicola*, he'd said. *Make a day of it.*

Nicola? What a joke. Dad knew nothing about her life anymore. The solo shopping trip had made her feel like a freak. They didn't make girls' school shoes in size eight and a half, the uniform that was the right length was too wide and the things that were the right width were too short. She already had 'short' things at home, so she bought a pair of DMs and spent the rest of the money on albums – The Cure, The Jam, The Clash. Dad never asked. He hadn't noticed when she came back with a bag from the record shop. Hadn't noticed how she looked on the first day of term.

But school had noticed, and battle had commenced.

On the way into assembly on that first day, Mrs Higginson, the Deputy Head, stopped her at the door. 'You stick out like a sore thumb, Ella Richardson,' she'd said, her voice a kazoo. 'Your skirt's far too short and as for those boots. You know fine well that you should be in sensible lace-ups.'

A group of girls tittered as they pushed their way past. 'I am in sensible lace-ups,' Ella said.

'Don't take that tone with me, young lady. Sensible, lace-up *girls'* shoes. See that you have more appropriate footwear tomorrow. The uniform rules are perfectly clear.'

But every day thereafter Ella had turned up in her DMs and every day fewer teachers bothered to complain. *Ella 1, School 0.* She had won that battle. She was ready for another.

***

On her way to the kitchen, she paused to pick up a new 'bus book' from a bookshelf in the hall. Mom's books. Ella was working her way through them, top to bottom, left to right. She always had a 'kitchen book', a 'bus book' and a 'bedtime book' on the go. *Mary Barton* was next. She pulled it down and flicked through the pages. There were notes in the margins. Whole paragraphs underlined. Mom had been big on social justice and had a taste for melodrama. Ella slipped the new 'bus book' into her satchel.

In the kitchen, Dad was sitting at the table and as she readied herself for his reaction her heart raced.

'Would you like porridge?' he asked, getting up to go to the cooker. 'I've made a pot.'

'Yeah, whatever.' She shrugged, waiting for him to notice.

They ate in silence, him reading *The Guardian*, her reading *Jude the Obscure*. It felt almost companionable, like old times.

And when they finished their breakfast, he collected the plates, put them in the sink and kissed her on the side of her shaven head. It was the first time he had touched her in almost a year.

'I like your hair,' he said. 'Your Mom cut off all her hair once. Can't remember why. She suited it too. Good bone structure and all that.'

CHAPTER 3
You're a Big Girl Now (Bob Dylan)

The streetlights were still lit as Ella walked up the main street of the village towards the bus stop. The morning had an aluminium tang and frost crystals on the leaves in the gutter winked in the sodium light. She scanned the shelter up ahead, as she did every morning, and by the shape of the huddle she determined its composition. Craig was leaning over Nicola, pressing her back against the shelter, partly for warmth and partly because they were 'going together'. A group of first years skittered outside the hut, windmilling their DFC schoolbags and shoving one another with the palms of their hands. It would be a couple of years before they earned the right to go inside. The fifth years were sitting on the bench, legs out in front of them, staking their claim. Sheila was smoking, pulling her mouth into a pucker that looked to Ella like the bum-hole of a cat.

As she got closer, Ella worked hard to control her breathing. One long draw in through the nose, three short puffs out through the mouth, pushing down on her diaphragm, steadying the fire that rose in her gut. Just as it did every day. But today was going to be different. She pulled her shoulders back and pushed her chin out, defiant. They weren't going to ignore her this time.

***

Ella had been just seven when they moved to the village, the American kid with the cute accent and the cool Mom.

'Sit with me at lunch, Ella?'

'Can I hold yer hand in the line?'

'Tak the end o' ma skipping rope, Ella.'

'Be my partner in gym after lunch?'

'Say tomato!'

'Say movies!'

'Say trash can!'

'Say gee!'

They had never heard anything like her. Except on TV. It was as if one of The Brady Bunch had stepped off the screen and into their world and they all wanted to touch her to make sure she was real. She was sprinkled with American stardust that they hoped would shake off onto them. Nicola and Joanne, Moira, Jane and Elaine had pulled her into their cluster, and she had liked it there.

But that was a long time ago. As she neared the bus shelter she saw the huddle stir. Nicola, looking over Craig's shoulder, was the first to notice. She did a double take, then pushed Craig to one side.

'Fuckin' hell, Ella. What's happened to yer hair?' Their eyes locked and for a second Ella felt a judder of connection.

They had been friends, once. Best friends even, but now, in

school, they adhered to an unspoken pact of forgetting. They nodded at each other now and again but seldom spoke. Ella couldn't remember the last time Nicola had used her name.

'Freak,' muttered Craig, pulling Nicola back with the crook of his arm.

All eyes turned to Ella, and she watched as their jaws dropped and their eyebrows arched, processing what they were looking at – who they were looking at. They weren't laughing, they were gawping, and that was just what she wanted.

'Cool,' muttered Sheila, exhaling smoke.

Ella shrugged, leaned back against the lamp post, and put her Walkman on. That way she could pretend she couldn't hear them.

'I cannae wait 'till Kelman gets a look at that, she's gonna be in the shite!' said Craig.

The anger, which often tasted like fear, felt like a power surge as it twitched through her body.

The bus which picked up kids from all over the glen was already full by the time she stepped on board. Usually she spent the thirty-minute journey to Dundee sitting alone in the front row, reading her bus book, headphones on to drown out the noise – the chanting, the shouting, the threats from the bus driver. 'Shut up, yooze lot. I cannae hear masel think. Oi, laughin' boy, sit doon or yer aff!'

But today, as she showed the bus driver her pass, silence, like a wave, spread from front to back. She was electrified to the fingertips and paused for a moment to look down the barrel of the bus. Everyone was staring, their pasty faces open-mouthed and gasping.

'Jings! Yer a wee bit late fur Hallowe'en, hen. That wiz last week,' said the bus-driver, breaking the silence. And suddenly the whole bus erupted.

Ignoring them all, Ella sat in her usual seat and rummaged in her bag for *Mary Barton*. But she had no intention of reading. Instead, she listened to the voices behind her.

'Fuckin' freak.'

'Eh think it's cool.'

'She's been hangin' oot wi they punks in the City Square.'

Ella allowed herself a tiny smile. For too long, she had existed in the blurred margins of their peripheral vision. Today though, she had stepped into the spotlight.

When the bus drew up outside the school, they were practically standing on top of each other to be first off, to spread the news. Ella took her time packing her things back into her bag, delaying, so that she was the last to leave the bus. By the time she reached the Form Room a group had gathered by the door, waiting for her. They jeered and cheered but she kept her shoulders back and her neck long as she crossed to her desk on the far side of the room.

Moments later, Mr Burrows' voice boomed down the corridor. '4JB! Stop that racket!'

She watched him as he stood in the doorway: his lip curled as he surveyed the scene, looking for the usual suspects. He was a mediocre man with a stupid moustache and breath that smelled of cigarettes and coffee. He'd never guess that the source of the uproar was her.

'Settle down. Settle down!' he shouted. 'You boys! Get back into your seats or you'll all be in detention. You are like a pack of...' His eyes settled on Ella. 'For the love of God... Ella

Richardson... what have you done to your hair?' He made his way to her desk and stood for a second taking in the full glory of the Mohican.

She smiled up at him.

Grasping the desk with both hands, he leaned in. 'This is not good.' He was so close now that Ella could smell him so she leaned back on her chair as far as she could go and stretched out her legs.

He looked around the room as if hoping for backup. 'We've got assembly in two minutes and Mr McLaverty from the Timex factory is giving a presentation to the Fourth Years this afternoon.'

Ella sensed his panic. As far as the headmaster was concerned, her hair would be Burrows' fault. Good. He was a shit Form Teacher, a timeserver, a bore.

'You will not attend that talk, Ella Richardson. We cannot have you representing the school looking like that. You're a... you're a... you're a bloody disgrace.'

She watched the beads of sweat gathering in his moustache. 'Gee whizz,' muttered Ella, still American when it suited her.

***

As 4JB processed into the Assembly Hall the collective intake of breath was audible, like the last sweep back of a tsunami before it crashes onto the shore. Ella stood for a moment in the stillness, staring at Kelman, waiting for his eyes to connect with hers. She had never felt like this before.

'Ella Richardson. My Office. Now.'

CHAPTER 4
Departure (Bauhaus)

'Well, would you look at that!' Mikey called as she made her way towards the concrete bench. 'Snow White's got hersel' a Mohawk!'

She'd been watching him as she crossed the City Square, hoping that he would look up and see her. And now that he *had* seen her, he couldn't look away.

He was at the centre of a jagged cluster of punks. His hair was bleached the yellow of the ferrets she had dissected in Biology and short spikes covered the surface of his head. His smile was a sneering curl of the lip and in the cold winter light his pale skin seemed ghostly. To Ella, Mikey was beautiful. The thought of seeing him had kept her going throughout the long day at school.

Stan, the smallest of the group, sat to Mikey's right, a red cockatoo's crest fanning from his head. And to the left sat Dek and Cass, Dek's arm hanging loosely around Cass's dog-collared neck.

Ella was fairly comfortable around Mikey, but she was still awkward with the rest of them. She never knew what to say or how to *be*. But a loud cheer went up as she approached, and she grinned when they held out their hands for her to slap.

'Fuckin' awesome!' said Stan, moving up so she could sit down. 'Wish I could o' seen the look on Kelman's puss.'

She squeezed in between them, wishing she wasn't still in her uniform. Stan smelled of stale beer and she pulled herself in tight, breathing through her mouth, leaning towards Mikey's legs. The concrete was cold beneath her thin school skirt and she jiggled her knee to keep herself warm.

'Yeah. Apparently cutting your hair destroys your future,' she said quietly. 'Who knew?'

***

That morning, in Kelman's office, she had sat up straight and faced his wrath head on. His red cheeks had flushed purple and the collar of his polyester shirt had become so dangerously tight round his wobbling neck that she suspected he might burst. Like a fat, sweaty berry. She had watched his mouth until it produced not words but the squall of an angry bird, a Berrybird, perhaps. In her mind she was drawing him with black Biro on lined paper. Long, groping claws, a squawking bill, and a purple berry belly that tumbled over an impotent holster belt. He was her mortal enemy, and she exploded him with a blink.

'I don't know what you find so funny, young lady,' he had cawed.

The room smelled of the Banda machine and Old Spice aftershave. Terrible artworks made from pins and silver string decorated the walls and a giant spider plant, heavy with offspring, spilled out from a bearded macramé potholder.

'It's just hair,' she told him.

27

'It's not just hair. It's a matter of respect. Respect for the uniform, respect for your teachers, respect for the other pupils and most of all respect for yourself, Ella Richardson. One thing leads to another, and before you know it, you'll have wasted your opportunities for the sake of a cheap statement. Is that what you want?'

She didn't give him the satisfaction of a response. She just folded her arms and stared back at him until he checked his watch and sent her on her way.

***

Although there was still some staring in the corridor, pointy fingers and whispering girls, by breaktime the buzz had quietened to a hum. The rest of her day followed her familiar routine. Break in the library, lunchtime on the move. Solitary and silent.

As she did most days, she had spent her lunch hour running. She had given up on the canteen at the start of her second year and saved the money for records. She missed neither the food nor the company. Instead, she would change into her running gear in the empty locker room, put on her headphones and head out. Dodging the potholes, she would drop down to Riverside and run by the edge of the water towards the new airport. Today there had been no wind, but the air was frigid on her bare head and the exposed tips of her ears. She huffed out clouds of silver breath and when she dipped under the bridge she stopped, crossing her arms to keep her flat chest warm, enjoying the pain in her fingertips, the ache in her nipples. She saw seals on the sandbanks in the great grey Tay and stood for a while watching, willing them to move. Then she checked her watch and headed back to school. Only two and a half hours before she would see Mikey again. Before he'd see her hair.

Mikey and his mates were older than Ella, though not by much. As soon as they could, they'd dropped out of school. Most of them had grown up in the Multis that formed the skyline of Dundee, but Mikey and Ella were from the village – the 'teuchters' Stan called them when Mikey wasn't there. Mikey had found a part-time job in Bruce's Records, just around the corner, but the rest of them were on the brew. They spent most of their afternoons on the same bench, drinking cans of Tennent's, smoking roll-ups.

***

Back in the spring, Ella had run into town during her lunch break. Usually she avoided the city centre, but she was looking for a record that she'd heard on John Peel. Avoiding homework, she'd been doodling at her desk when she heard the lyric from a track called Departure. She scrawled it on a scrap of paper and had rewritten it countless times since then. The words had been replaying in her head all day long.

She wanted desperately to feel the reassuring crisp, white sheets
Once taken for granted
To be back home, safe as houses, protected by walls covered in
Familiar patterns
But even wallpaper had become sinister to her.

Flipping through the vinyl in the Bauhaus section at Bruce's, she felt like a phony. She wasn't cool enough to be buying a record like this, and anyway, she wasn't even sure it had been released as a single. She couldn't afford an album.

'Ella, it's Ella isn't it?' She heard a voice behind her. 'Is this the kind of stuff yer intae? Ah didnae hae you pegged as a goth. You're more like some kinda crazily tall schoolgirl Snow White.'

She turned. It was Mikey. And he knew who she was. He remembered her name. Heat flushed from her neck to her cheeks and she dipped her head, shaking her hair forward to hide her face.

Words spilled out of her mouth. 'Yuh, I mean I'm not exactly a Bucks Fizz fan, if you know what I mean.' She shrank at the sound of her voice and carried on flipping the records, not looking at them anymore.

'More of an Abba groupie, are you?' He was standing beside her by now.

She laughed – a bit too loud. 'Yuh, that'll be right. Have you got *Departure*?'

'Aye. It's the B-side o' *She's in Parties*. Here it is. It's a bit shite though. Ah mean *Kick in the Eye* is okay n'all, but this one's kinda mainstream.'

He walked his long fingers over the tops of the singles till he came to the Ss, and pulled one out, handing it to Ella. 'You should hae a listen to this. Ah mean, it's old school, but you look a wee bit like Siouxsie. If a squint ma eyes. Mind, maybe Debbie Harry's mair your thing. What wi yer mum being American 'n' all.'

Mum. The word punched her in the stomach. Her mouth filled with saliva and her throat constricted. She was slipping into a black hole and had to scramble to gain purchase. Dropping the record, she bolted for the door.

'Ella, hey,' he called after her.

'I've… I've got to get back to school.'

'Hud oan. Ah'm on the four o'clock bus tomorrow. If you're on it, Ah'll tell you why yer taste in music is sae mingin.'

'Yuh… maybe… yuh,' she muttered, and sprinted down the street.

But the next day, she didn't take the school bus as she usually did. She walked into town to catch the four o'clock instead. And Mikey didn't seem that surprised to find her waiting.

'Here, this is for you,' he said, handing over a single. *Hong Kong Garden: Siouxsie and the Banshees*. 'It's her debut single.' He was talking to her like she was an actual human. Nobody did that anymore. She didn't want to screw this up. 'Thanks,' she mumbled.

On the sleeve a woman in a shapeless white dress seemed to be choking herself with a scarf that was wound round her head. Ella pulled the vinyl out of the sleeve and flipped it over to see the B side, *Voices*.

'It's nae a big deal. Ah get a discount. And Ah thought if Ah was gonnae start educating you about guid music, it'd be better to start at the beginning.'

After that, she met Mikey a couple of days a week. Travelling home together on the four o'clock bus, he talked to her about records and the gigs he'd been to at the weekends. Mostly, she just listened, but sometimes she showed him her sketches, and talked to him about books. He made her mix tapes – *Punk: The Origins; The Early Days*, that sort of thing – and she played them on her tape-recorder over and over in her room. Those bus journeys became the best parts of her week. She came alive when she was with Mikey, felt the blood in her veins and the air in her lungs. He didn't care if she was a weirdo, a misfit, a freak. 'It taks one tae ken one,' he laughed.

In the summer he had introduced her to his mates. They didn't know what to make of her at first. She didn't sound like them, and she certainly didn't look like them, but they put up with her because Mikey liked her. And she didn't say much.

***

And here she was in the City Square, eight months later, with her hair shorn off, hoping she had proved worthy.

Cass wriggled out from under Dek's arm and stood in front of Ella. 'Right. Nice one. First things first. Eh'm gonna gie you a few tips on they spikes.' She leaned over to size up the problem and prodded at the hair. 'They look… well… wilted. Why don't you come back tae meh place and Ah'll fix them for ye. Ye havenay been to meh hoose have ye?'

'No,' said Ella. She didn't really want to leave Mikey, but it wasn't every day that a girl asked her back to her house. 'Thanks. That would be cool.' She got up to follow Cass, putting to the back of her mind Dad's instructions to come straight home after school.

They walked together up the Murraygate to the new shopping centre. Cass, almost a foot shorter than Ella, was small and round. With her short-strided gait she was almost running to keep up. Ample breasts bounced like jellies and her biker jacket strained to harness them. Her short hair was purple and today she had styled it to look rough and jagged. Her nose was pierced with a silver hoop, connected by a chain to her ear.

A group of schoolgirls nudged each other as they passed, and an old woman in a headscarf tutted. Cass lifted her chin and linked her arm through Ella's so that they could keep pace. A couple of boys in drainpipe jeans and denim jackets whistled, and Ella couldn't help laughing when Cass stuck up her middle finger and wiggled her wobbly arse at them.

She and Cass hadn't spoken much before and Ella wondered if she would feel awkward now they were on their own. But Cass, breathless and rosy-faced beneath her heavy, purple make-up, had no such worries and talked without needing a response as they made their way up to the Hilltown.

'Ah ken yer dead brainy an aw, but Eh hated school. Ah couldnae wait tae get oot o' there. Ah left when Eh wiz sixteen and went straight intae hairdressing. Eh wiz a yopper. Ken whit a' mean?'

Ella nodded. Everyone knew about the Youth Opportunity Schemes.

'Och, it wisnae bad. Eh wiz mostly just sweepin' up hair and daein' the shampooin', but it wiz a laugh. They never kept me oan though.'

'That's a shame,' said Ella.

'Yeah. One day, Eh'd love tae hae ma own salon. Someplace really cool though, no one o' they Aunty Beany places.'

'That'd be great.'

'Wait till Eh'm finished wi those spikes.' Cass laughed. 'Ye might no think so then! Here we are.'

They had reached Carnegie Tower.

'Mum won't be back yet, so the hoose'll be full o' wains. Mind, don't look them straight in the eye or they'll be all over ye like a rash,' said Cass as they stepped into the lift. 'Press 18 for me, will ye. Most o' the time the lifts're oot o' order, but yer in luck. When Mum first moved in abody thought the lifts were the business, but no noo.' She pinched her upturned nose and laughed. When the lift doors opened it was so dark on the landing that Ella wasn't sure she wanted to step out.

'Dinnae worry. The lights get smashed oot by the dealers but you're okay at this time. Stick wi me.' Cass pulled Ella by the hand. She was on home turf and knew how to handle herself.

'Cass, Cass, whit's fir tea?' the kids shouted when they heard her key in the door.

Her brother and sister and two of their friends were in the living room watching Grange Hill: the boys on the floor on their stomachs with their heads propped up on their hands, the girls lying on the settee. Toothy school photographs in cardboard frames were arranged on the teak wall unit and the air smelled of Mr Sheen.

'Gie us a chance,' Cass called back, heading straight into a kitchenette which was small and clutter-free. Storage jars with wooden tops and orange leaf patterns were ordered by height, and the silver electric kettle was polished to a shine.

'It's really nice,' said Ella.

'She's a bit o' a fanatic, meh ma. Maks us rake the shag pile.' Cass raised her black eyebrows and pointed to the leaf rake propped in the corner.

Ella leaned back on the worktop, trying not to be in the way while Cass pulled a packet of crispy pancakes from the small freezer compartment above the fridge and put potatoes on to boil. A tin of beans had been left out, and a pan loaf and butter were on a bread board on the table.

'Tea'll be ready in half an hour. Yer pals need to get awa hame,' Cass called. She turned to Ella. 'Right, let's fix they spikes.'

Cass opened drawers and cupboards gathering her equipment: scissors, a Perspex bowl, a measuring jug, a wooden spoon. She poured a pint of boiling water into the bowl and tipped in half a bag of sugar, stirring till it dissolved.

'Bet ye never kent it was sugar water that kept oor spikes up! Sit there.'

Ella's head was tugged back rhythmically as Cass brushed out the spikes. She tried not to wince. Then, with a metal comb in one hand and her scissors in the other, Cass snipped away until she was satisfied. Using the end of the comb to separate out sections of hair, she soaked each of them in the sugar solution, then coaxed it into points. With a hairdryer, she stiffened them till they were solid as stone and sharp at the tips and when she was satisfied, she led Ella to the bathroom and turned her to face the mirror.

'Cool,' she said. The transformation made her heart race. 'Thanks very much.' She reached up to feel the sides of the Mohawk, bounced her fingers off the points.

'It's a wee bit hard tae lie doon. That's the only problem. Meh advice is tae pick one side or the other.' Cass laughed. 'Either that or drill holes in yer pillow!'

CHAPTER 5

Hong Kong Garden
(Siouxsie and The Banshees)

On the bus home, Ella watched her reflection in the dark window, barely recognising the girl who stared back. She looked hostile and hard and the people who got on must have thought so too because no-one came to sit by her, even though the bus was full. She thought about Dad who might or might not be waiting for her at home, about his useless attempts to control her, and about how she had left things that morning. Kicking the chair back when he told her that her mother would have liked it. Slamming the back door so hard that the blue paint had cracked. *What a joke*. He couldn't control her. He couldn't control anything. He was limp and pathetic and would never make anything right.

'Hello, Ella. You're late.' He was standing in front of the dresser, polishing his glasses with the corner of his t-shirt when she walked through the door. His face was different without his glasses, exposed. He looked almost like a child.

She headed past him to the fridge.

'Where have you been?'

Not a word about the spikes.

She grabbed a tub of Stork. 'Out.'

He pulled himself up to his full height and put his glasses back on. 'I told you to come straight back from school, and I meant it.' His tone was unfamiliar, firm. 'Tomorrow I'll be here at 4.30pm and I want you to be home by then. As I asked you to be.'

She pulled a thick crust of bread out of the waxed paper wrapper and spread it with margarine. 'Or what?'

'Or else I'll pick you up from school myself.'

She pictured their clapped out 2CV with the CND sticker on the bumper pulling up outside the school gates, and Dad emerging in his patched tweed jacket and flared corduroys. She stared at him in disbelief.

'I mean it.'

He turned away and drained some pasta through the orange enamel colander. 'I've made your favourite,' he said over his shoulder, conciliatory now.

The bolognese was thin and grey, but she was hungry and twisted the spaghetti round her fork, a skill of which she had once been proud. Her father carried on a one-sided conversation about Margo, a colleague in the Anthropology department who was having a baby. As if Ella cared. His voice hurt her ears, like nails in polystyrene, and she focused on the spaghetti, sucking it up fast.

'How was your day?' he asked.

You wanna know how my day was? Well, it's a bit late for that. What do you wanna hear? That I have no friends? That I'm a weirdo? A mute? A freak? I don't think you wanna hear that, Daddy, do you? She said nothing and ate her dinner.

When her bowl was empty, she grabbed her schoolbag. 'I've got homework.'

She climbed the stairs and he headed down the corridor to his study. She hadn't been in there for months. But she remembered it well enough. Inside, strange objects occupied every surface, evidence of a life spent deciphering the traces left behind. Buttons, shards of pottery, the stone head of an axe. She used to love watching his big, gentle hands turning over the artefacts. He understood them through his fingertips, knew them by touch. Her father found consolation in the refuse of the dead.

'I'll be watching telly later,' he called after her. 'Come down when you're finished. If you like.'

As if. She slammed the door behind her and leaning back against it, she covered her face with her hands, palms pressed to cheeks. She felt their cold comfort and dug her fingertips into the sockets of her eyes, pushing until the shapes behind her eyelids turned violet. She breathed slowly, then once her pulse had stopped racing, took her hands away, enjoying the suck as skin peeled from skin.

Her blurred room gradually returned to focus. Over by the window, the desk was barely visible beneath all the paper: layers of lined pages from exercise books covered with intricate ink drawings; envelopes scrawled with spidery words; bulging scrapbooks; photographs; newspaper cuttings; pictures from magazines. The paper seemed to creep beyond the desk and up the poppy-red walls; every inch was covered. Sometimes she imagined herself sweeping a hand across the surface, and the papers flying upwards and splattering the walls like blood from a gunshot wound. But some of the things on the desk mattered and she always held back.

Kicking a path through the clothes and books that littered the floor she picked up a small, framed photograph from the desk. Two faces were pressed together, cheek to cheek. Ella and Mom. Little Ella was rosy from the cold, her eyes watering in the wind and her mouth open and laughing. Her mother's black hair blew across her face and her eyes crinkled, almost shut, in a smile of pure joy. Mom, promising so much. Tricking her into trusting that everything would be okay, that there would be forever, a lifetime of happiness.

Next to the photo was a small statue of the Virgin Mary. It had been Mom's. Made from white soapstone, it was smooth, almost impressionistic. Wrapped in a mantle that tapered down to narrow ankles, only the small face and tiny hands of the Virgin were visible. Her head was tilted to one side, the eyes cast down and the hands held together in prayer. Ella picked her up: she fitted comfortably into her palm. The smooth surface always calmed her, and she clasped her hands around it. Her breathing slowed and for a second she connected with something that was no longer there.

On the desk, in the space where the statue had been, a pile of tiny torn-paper fragments blinked up at her, each covered in the same spidery handwriting. That morning, just as she did every morning, Ella had ripped a corner from one of her sketchbooks and scrawled a jagged note which she had added to the heap. She couldn't pick it out now – it was one scrap among many. She replaced the statue, like a paperweight, on top.

There was homework to be done but working at the desk was not an option. Sometimes she sat at the kitchen table, but she didn't want to be that close to Dad tonight. Instead, she would work, as she often did, on her unmade, single bed.

She sat up against the headboard and emptied the contents of her bag about her. Just as Cass had warned her, her new spikes dug into the faded headboard, so she propped a pillow behind her, and leaning back she thought of Mikey.

Before he had even left primary school, mums were warning their kids to stay away from him, as if his mettle was a virus that could be passed on through touch. Not *her* Mom though. Maybe it was because she was American and the patchouli whiff of Woodstock still hung about her, or maybe it was the warmth of the home she had created – the music and the colours, the chocolate brownies and fresh flowers? Whatever it was, misfits seemed to gravitate towards her. Other mums with their prams and toddlers looked away when Mikey strutted through the school gates, his graffitied canvas schoolbag slung across his chest and his middle finger stuck up in the air. But Mom would call, 'Hi, Mikey.' And he would wave back.

Back then, Ella hadn't waved. She too had looked away. She was scared of his mad eyes, and the way he hawked globs from the back of his throat, spitting with precision at the feet of waiting parents.

On their first night at Youth Club, when Ella and Nicola were just ten, Mikey had called them a pair of abortions. For weeks after that she had lain awake at night, tormented by the word she didn't fully understand.

She had been afraid to look at him, but one time she had dared herself to flick a furtive glance, and after that she found she couldn't look away. His movements were often erratic, like a jack unleashed from a box, but sometimes there was an intensity in his focus. She had watched him as he sat in the corner beside the

Calor gas heater. His long, white hand was steady as he drew Sid Vicious in Tippex on the back of his biker jacket. The drawings on his schoolbag were dark and intricate and Ella began to recognise his style. She saw evidence of his artistry all around the village - in the bus shelter and the bike sheds, on cable boxes and bins: dark occult symbols, Gordian knots, detailed portraits of the Queen with a safety pin through her bottom lip, newsprint lettering blinding her eyes. She didn't understand his drawings, but she felt their power.

A lot had happened since those days at Youth Club. To Mikey she was still just a kid, a wee sister at best, an acolyte at worst, but he liked her, and that was enough – for now.

She tried to get comfortable. Her spikes were digging into the pillow and her black tights were in a tangle. Reaching up under her skirt she hooked her thumbs under the top of her tights and rolled them down the long length of her legs. Her pants were caught in the crack of her bum and raising her hips off the bed, she reached a hand back between her legs to release the bunched cotton. Her thigh flopped to one side. Wiggling her hand out, she traced the edge of her pants with her fingers, stopping at the raised tendon that stretched like a bridge from her inner thigh to her pelvic bone. She pinched it between her forefinger and her thumb, digging into the hollows. Then, sliding a finger beneath the edge of her pants, she shut her eyes and thought of Mikey, feeling her slippery wetness.

CHAPTER 6
Lust for Life (Iggy Pop)

The threat of 'humiliation by car' was too awful to contemplate so for the next few weeks Ella came straight home after school. Her father was there when he said he was going to be, and every night they ate a dismal supper together, barely speaking. As they sat opposite one another in the cramped little kitchen, the noise of him seemed to overwhelm her. The slurping of water, the chewing of meat, amplified until she found it hard to eat.

With nothing else to do Ella threw herself into her schoolwork, rapidly making up lost ground. Mr Burrows even kept her back to tell her how pleased he was that she was 'knuckling down' and 'toeing the line', but his words meant nothing; she was empty.

When she wasn't doing schoolwork, she would scribble furiously in her sketchbooks and every morning she slipped another tiny note beneath the Virgin Mary on her desk. Silent on the bus and silent in school, whole days passed without her hearing her own voice. Sometimes, in class, she would look down at her hands and spread the bony fingers into branches. She flipped them over to see the veins in her palms and traced a blue line to her wrist, watched the throb of her pulse.

The black holes that had appeared after Mom's death were gaping once again.

***

In desperation one Saturday she asked Dad's permission to go into town and to her surprise he agreed. As long as she was home by seven, he said. He seemed relieved that he would have the house to himself. She waited until the late afternoon and took the bus into Dundee. It wouldn't be long before Mikey finished work.

'Hey, stranger!' shouted Cass as Ella made her way towards the bench. The square was busy and all around punks in bondage trousers and bum flaps were comparing Mohawks and competing for the longest spikes. Over by Littlewoods, a couple of skinheads were shouting their mouths off.

'What's their problem?' said Ella.

'Dinnae bother aboot they mad bastards. Park yer erse doon here,' said Cass, throwing an arm around Ella's shoulder. 'Whar've you been? We've missed you.'

'Just busy with school and stuff,' said Ella, cringing at the sound of her voice. She wasn't about to tell them she was in trouble with her dad. She flicked a glance up Reform Street to see if Mikey was on his way.

Cass seemed to read her mind. 'Have you heard aboot Mikey? He's moved intae one o' thon tenements that's due for demolition. There's aboot five or six o' them living there.'

'What?' Ella's voice was louder than she meant it to be. He'd left the village. How could she not have known?

'We wur there last night,' said Cass. 'You should see it. He's made it look pure dead brilliant. They've spray-painted the hale wall o' the sittin' room.'

'That guy could've gone tae art college if he'd wanted to,' said Dek.

Stan handed him a roll-up. 'What a talent. Aye.'

Ella had stopped listening. She was thinking about all those journeys on the four o'clock bus. Her finger drawing spirals in the condensation on the window while Mikey talked and talked. It was their time. And now it was over.

Just after five, she saw Mikey coming around the corner from Reform Street. His familiar gait – long strides, shoulders back, arms swinging wide – made her stomach lurch, and she adjusted her position, lifting one foot onto the bench, and clasping her arms around her knee to hide the speed of her breathing.

'Shove up,' he said, squeezing into the middle spot between Ella and Cass. He joined in effortlessly in the banter and Ella forced herself to laugh in the right places, nodding along, but her mouth was dry, and she said almost nothing. She had got the hair right and she knew she looked good in her black drainpipes, but she was nothing more to him than a mate. Just a mate, like Cass or Dek. Not even important enough to tell her that he'd moved.

A woman with a small dog walked past, looked over at the crowd on the benches, and scowled. Something about the blue lead reminded Ella of that summer when she turned ten, and of how much she had wanted to be like Mikey. 'What was up with you and that brick?' she asked him.

He laughed. 'Fuck. Brickdoag. Ah'd forgotten aboot him.'

'Brickdoag? What wiz that?' asked Dek.

'It was when ah wiz mates wi Mark Allinson, remember him? We used to muck aboot at school and he was always gettin' intae trouble. His mum thought it wiz meh fault, but the wee cunt wiz a nutter. Anyway. His mum decided he couldnae muck aboot wi me anymore. When a went roon tae his hoose and asked if Mark wiz cumin oot tae, play, ken, like we a did, Mrs Allinson started sayin' things like, "No, Mark's having his tea," or "Sorry, Mark's doing his homework."'

Mikey had Mrs Allinson's voice down pat and Ella saw that a group had gathered round their bench, encouraging his performance. He could be really funny when he wanted to be, which was rarely. Sitting so close she watched his mouth as he played out the parts. His presence seemed to fill up the square.

'Any road, a kent fine well that Mark wasnae daein hamework. The wee cunt couldn't concentrate on anythin for mair than a minute. So aifter a few weeks at school I says, 'Mark, whits goan on?' and he telt me, "Ma ma thinks yir mad. Ye ken, touched in the heid, nae right."

So, I thought tae masel, if Mrs Allinson thinks am no quite right, mibee I'll gie her somethin' tae think aboot. So a made the brick doag. Brickdoag I kelt him. I made him a lead an a'thin. Am no gonna lie, a got tae like the wee guy. And it was a right fuckin' laugh seeing those twats in the village doin' the old double take when I took him fer walkies. One day, Mark's mum saw me when I wiz oot wi Brickdoag.

"Michael," – she always called me Michael – "Michael, love, is everything all right?"

"Fine, Mrs Allinson," a said.

"Then why are you pulling a brick on a bit of string?"

I looked her square in the eye, then looked down at Brickdoag, and back up at her as if it was the stupidest question a'd ever heard.

'Well Mrs Allinson,' ah said, nice and slow, as if she was the mental one, 'Have you ever tried pushing one?'"

The group that gathered round the benches, exploded into laughter. They slapped Mikey on the back, cheering and howling, then spread out once more in a radio wave of high spirits. Ella turned her eyes from Mikey back to the square. Late Saturday shoppers stopped to see what was going on, wondering if it was a fight, used to that after the football on a Saturday. They watched the punks laughing then turned away, wishing it had been a fight. Laughter didn't match their expectations.

When the crowd settled, Cass turned to Ella. 'You comin' tae the hoose warmin' the night?'

'Oh no, I don't think I can.' Ella thought about Dad and pulled her shoulders up to her ears as if her head could be swallowed by her body this way.

Stan passed her his can of Tennent's. 'Go on,' he said.

Did he mean the beer or the party? She took the can but just swilled it around for a second and passed it on to Cass. She'd drunk alcohol before. Mom had been cool about that. She used to make elderflower champagne, dandelion wine, brown-bread beer, and Ella had tasted them. They were all disgusting.

'We'll get a poke o' chips on the way there,' said Cass, who was always thinking about her belly. She batted Ella's arm with the back of her hand. 'Go on.'

'No, I'd better not.'

'A keep forgettin' yer still at school,' laughed Stan. 'Off ye pop then, Snow White, back hame tae Daddy.'

'Leave her alane,' said Mikey, taking a swig. 'Do whatever ye feel like, Ella.'

By now, all of her consciousness seemed focused on the length of her left thigh, which was pressed against Mikey's. Maybe, at the party, they could be alone. 'I suppose I could come for a couple of hours,' she said.

'Great. It's a plan,' smiled Cass. 'C'moan, let's go back tae ma hoose tae get ready.'

Cass pulled Ella to her feet; she was a bit pissed and they linked arms and sang as they swayed along the street. Ella, sober, held her up.

***

Back at the Multis, Cass's mum was in the kitchen. She was dressed in a neon pink leotard with matching tights and an electric blue headband that pushed her permed hair off her face. She was chopping carrots for the mince that was simmering on a ring.

'Mum, this is Ella.'

'Hi, Mrs Clancy.'

'Ella, it's nice tae meet you. 'Scuse the rig out. Eh've just finished ma Jane Fonda. It's still in the box if you girls wanna hae a wee go.'

'Y'er aw right ma,' Cass laughed.

'Cass tells me you're a really clever girl,' said Mrs Clancy. 'See if you can knock some sense intae her heid. Most o' that lot she hangs aboot wi have'nay a brain cell to rub together.'

'A'right mum. Gonnae no embarrass me in front o' ma pal.' Cass rolled her eyes at Ella. 'Mums, what are they like, eh?'

Ella swallowed hard and Cass winced. 'Shit. What a stupid thing tae say. Ah'm sorry.'

But Ella was surprised to find that she didn't mind that much. Cass had called her a pal and she liked that.

In the bedroom Cass shared with her little sister, Ella had no trouble deciding which side of the room was which. On the left was a poster of Holly Hobby, hiding under her bonnet, perhaps shielding her eyes from the Buzzcocks poster opposite – *Orgasm Addict,* Ella read. Beside Holly, Laura Ingalls, pigtails flying as she careered across the prairie, smiled across the room at the writhing torso of Iggy Pop. Beneath Holly and Laura, a bed was hidden under a mound of soft animals, while every surface on the other side was covered with make-up pots, Kirby grips, and cans of hair spray.

Ella sat on the end of Cass's bed and watched as she got to work selecting her outfit for the night, pulling out t-shirts and skirts from her wardrobe. She customized her look with belts, chains and safety pins till she jangled.

Ella clapped. 'You look great.'

'Ta.' She bowed. 'Noo, whit aboot you? You're no goin' in that are you?'

Ella looked down at her baggy Angora jumper and her black jeans. She'd been happy with them earlier. 'I haven't got anything else.'

'Stand up. Let's hae a go wi this?' Cass began strapping leather thongs around Ella's thighs. 'The jeans are great, but ye cannae wear a jumper tae a party.'

Ella pulled her jumper carefully over her spikes. She was wearing a ripped black t-shirt underneath.

Cass stepped back, thinking. 'Right, we can do somethin' wi that.' Then taking some scissors from the top of the chest of drawers, she cut off the bottom of the t-shirt so that it finished just below Ella's small breasts.

'That's no bad. Put this shirt over it.' Cass gave instructions while she pulled things out of her wardrobe and Ella did as she was told.

'Aye. That's cool.' Cass said, tying the shirt in a knot just above Ella's belly button, 'Here, try on this denim jacket. I cannae shut it over ma tits these days.'

Next Cass did her own makeup. She painted purple lightning flashes on her eyelids and using wet black paint she lined her lashes with a thick rim.

'Noo you.'

Ella enjoyed the feeling of Cass's cool fingers on her face, the tickle of the make-up brushes, the smell of the lipstick. It reminded her of when she and Nicola used to play beauticians.

When she looked in the mirror, she liked what she saw. Normally her reflection was black and white, but tonight it was injected with flashes of green and yellow, complementing the black around her eyes and the dark purple lips.

'Yer' hair's growin' back fast, isn't it?' said Cass. 'Nae quite so baldie noo. Ye ken whit would look great – a nose piercing. D'ye fancy one?'

Ella gulped. What would Dad say? Or Mr Kelman? 'Okay then – go on,' she said.

'Ah'll hae to sterilize the needle first. Ah'll be back in a wee minute.'

Ella stared at her reflection while she waited.

What was she doing!? Cass was going to stick a needle in her nose! It was going to be agony. Right through her nostril. Cass might have been an apprentice in a hairdresser's, but that didn't exactly make her qualified. *She got sacked for fuck's sake!*

But Cass was back before she could chicken out.

'Here, hud this oan yer nose. It'll numb it,' she said, handing her an ice cube.

Ella felt sick. She pressed the ice-cube to her nostril till her whole head ached and water dribbled down her wrist and up the sleeve of the white shirt.

'No too far back, and no too high up, that's the perfect position for the piercing,' said Cass. And before Ella could think about it, Cass had pushed a piece of cork up her left nostril and was forcing the point of the needle into her flesh. The pain was exquisite, and her eyes watered instantly. She bit down on her molars forcing back the urge to scream, as the pain shot like white heat through her nose, up her sinuses and into her brain.

'Fuck! That hurt!'

'No pain, no gain,' chirped Cass cheerfully.

She's pissed, thought Ella. *What am I doing?*

'Best no tae think about it too much. Sit still and let me get the ring in. Ah've ge'en this one a guid wash in the TCP.' Cass pushed the straight end of a small silver ring into Ella's nostril and swiveled it until she closed the hoop. The pain soared to another searing climax and Ella writhed. Inside her DMs her toes curled tight and despite her best efforts a constricted groan forced itself through her windpipe.

Cass ignored her and twiddled the hoop once more. 'Eh'm no just sayin this, but that looks pure dead brilliant! There's a wee bitty blood, but no too much.'

Ella screwed up her eyes while the pain subsided, and Cass mopped her up with cotton wool and TCP. When she opened her eyes, Cass had brought over a hand mirror so that she could have a good look. She dabbed at a streak of black makeup. 'That's better. Whit d'ye think?'

Ella's nose was red and hot looking, but the little ring sat neatly, and she liked it. She grinned up at Cass. Yes, despite the pain, this was good.

***

Half an hour later they were standing outside Mikey's flat. A relentless beat pulsed from the open windows. It was a dark, drizzly December evening and although she was nervous about going in, Ella wanted to get out of the cold. Her nose was aching and her head was pounding. She hadn't eaten many of the salty chips, but her mouth was so dry.

'Just hae a wee drink,' said Cass, offering her the end of a can she'd opened on their way there.

The smell of it made Ella gag. And Dad would kill her if he found out.

As if she could read her mind, Cass pulled a bottle of perfume from her bag. 'Eh've got a' the tricks,' she said. 'Before you get the bus hame, Eh'll gie you a wee scoosh o' this right ontae yer tongue. Tastes totally fuckin mingin' but it taks awa' the smell. Honest.'

'Okay then,' said Ella. She finished what was in the can, tipping her head back to get the last of it. Its bitterness lingered like bad medicine and she shook her head, trying to dislodge the taste.

'You'll get used to it,' said Cass, pulling a second can from the six-pack she was carrying and handing it over. 'Come oan, let's get inside before the rain melts the sugar on meh spikes.'

Inside the music was even louder, and the smell of damp and

smoke caught Ella's throat. In the foggy room the only light came from an orange bulb in a shadeless standard lamp, and it took her eyes a moment to adjust to the dimness. There was no furniture, but the room was full of people dancing and drinking.

The goths stood in a huddle in front of a wall, spray-painted with a huge mural of The Sex Pistols. Most of them were art students or wanna-be art students and Ella liked their style. She recognized a few of them from the City Square – like the Peter Murphy look-a-like in the black fuzzy jumper, with the cheekbones and the fringe. Sometimes she had seen him looking at her from behind his hair, his chin down, glancing up through his lashes. He reminded her of Lady Diana in a weirdly sexy sort of way. Beside him stood a girl in a biker jacket with a spider's web drawn in black eyeliner on the side of her chalk-white face. She had sprayed and backcombed her long hair until it emanated like a black aura. She was pretty cool.

The Bauhaus fan with the Lady Di fringe was looking Ella's way.

'Cool place, eh no?' shouted Cass over the heavy clash of The Damned's *New Rose*. Slumped on a mattress in the corner was Dek, who had been drinking since early afternoon. Cass waved. 'Ah'm just gonna go over and say hi.'

Ella watched as Cass picked her way through the crowd, then she moved forward to the edge of the dance floor where the punks were pogoing, their arms straight by their sides and their feet close together, springing unpredictably with the force of pneumatic drills. A figure on the floor jerked spasmodically on his back, like a dying fly. The music was deafening.

She swigged the beer, holding her breath, trying to hide the taste from her tongue but she couldn't help screwing up her face.

'Look at you! Ah'm liking the nose ring. Pretty cool, wee sis.' It was Mikey. He was standing close and leaning in over her shoulder, shouting right into her ear. He had never been this close before. His breath on her neck and his lips brushing her earlobe jolted her nerve-endings until every sensation seemed amplified like the music. 'Disnae look like yer enjoying that. I'll swap,' he said, taking the can and handing her his mug, which looked like it had Coke in it. She took a gulp, desperate to get rid of the fetid taste of the beer.

'Vodka and Coke. Y'll hardly even taste the voddy,' he said, and she drank it down like it was pop. The pain in her nose throbbed less and Mikey brought her another one.

The Bauhaus fan was definitely staring, and when Mikey left to change the record, he pulled her into the centre of the room to dance. The thought of dancing usually terrified Ella. Her long, gangly limbs were hard to control and even alone in her bedroom, she felt awkward and ungainly. But all of a sudden she felt super-charged and when she moved to the frenetic, discordant music, its beat felt like a release. When the dance was over, she joined the goths, who admired her make-up and filled up her mug with more vodka and Coke. More vodka, less Coke. She liked it. A lot. The music was too loud for conversation, but she was laughing and smiling, free and loose. Why wasn't it always as easy as this?

Mikey came over to her. *He wants to dance with me*, she thought. *He thinks I'm hot with my nose ring and my bare belly and my purple lips.*

'Mikey,' she slurred, and reached up to his face. She touched his cheeks, his chin. She moved closer, smiling up at him. 'Mikey, you look so beautiful tonight.'

Mikey was looking at her purple lips, but he wasn't smiling back. His face was swimming. The room was moving. Her brain seemed suddenly loose inside her skull. It was veering off to the right and when she tried to move her eyes to keep up with it she staggered to one side. The happy feelings had gone.

'Right, come wi me,' he said, taking her hand and pulling her off the dance floor into a corridor. 'Here.' He pushed her into a dark, dirty bathroom.

'I feel right at home here,' she assured him, her brain swimming chaotically. She couldn't stop swallowing.

'Oh aye, posh girl. Am sure you do.'

He pointed her head towards the toilet bowl with seconds to spare, then knelt beside her and patted her back while she retched.

After a while she sat back on her haunches. 'Mikey,' she groaned, 'I'm not feeling so good.'

'Think it might be home time, Snowy.'

It was Cass who walked Ella to the bus stop and saw her onto the bus, but not before she reached into her bag and pulled out the bottle of *Poison*, which, true to her word, she sprayed directly into Ella's mouth.

On the bus Ella stared out of the window, motion-sick and reeling. Every time she shut her eyes she swilled and spilled until she didn't know in which direction she was pointing. The bus lurched forward in slow motion, stopping forever at the villages along the way. *Have there always been this many? Does it always take this long?* She opened her mouth and let her tongue loll, hoping that the air might carry away the smell of the toxic perfume which had now filled every cavity inside her head.

It was after eleven by the time she walked through the door.

The lights were on in the kitchen but no-one was there. She sat down at the table and put her head on its sticky surface. It smelled like dirty dishcloths. When she looked up a few seconds later, Dad was standing in the doorway.

'Evening, Ella.'

Her eyes wanted to slide off towards the window, but she forced them to stay on him. Standing there in his stupid Harvard t-shirt and baggy pyjama bottoms, his shaggy hair was sticking up like he'd been rubbing his hands through it for hours. He looked like he was trapped behind glass. *Was there glass?* She could shout and shout, but he still wouldn't hear her. If he wanted to, he could put his hands on the invisible pane and move them like Marcel Marceau until he found the edge. He could push his way through if he wanted to. If he wanted to. But instead, he was just standing there.

Why didn't he take her in his big arms? Wrap her in his body? He could fix this. Make it like it was before. But he was still standing there, his bare feet on the wooden floorboards. Just standing there, staring.

All of a sudden, the fire that she worked so hard to keep in her belly forced its way up and through her open mouth. 'Why are you just standing there?' she screamed. 'Why?' And the word became a noise that grew and grew, carrying her hungry pain out into the open.

Her father's face crumpled, and he put his hand on the door frame as if he needed help holding himself up. For a second she thought he was going to step forward.

'Go to bed now,' he said, instead. 'We'll talk in the morning.' And he turned and walked away.

CHAPTER 7
American Pie (Don McLean)

At the tail end of Sunday morning, Ella woke to find her tongue stuck to the roof of her mouth. White light from the window shot like a bolt through the dip in her temple and lodged, throbbing and petulant somewhere inside her skull. So, this was what a hangover felt like.

It was all coming back to her: dancing with the Lady Di lookalike, the mural on the wall, the chips with Cass, the vodka and Coke, and... *fuck*... her nose. She reached up and felt the nose ring, picked at the crust of blood. Mikey had said he liked it. She had felt his breath on her neck and his face in her hands. And then... and then... had she really told him he was beautiful? *What a loser. What a complete and utter loser.* And what had he seen, looking back at him? The sweat on her top lip. Her eyes, dipping in and out of focus. Had it really been him kneeling beside her while she heaved into that filthy toilet? She pulled the blankets over her head and wished she could be swallowed by darkness.

The nausea soon changed to an emptiness deep in the pit of her stomach and she realised she was starving. All she had eaten since breakfast the day before were a few of Cass's chips. She wanted toast and butter, bacon, greasy eggs, ketchup, a steaming cup of tea. She wanted the hollow in her belly to be filled and to bury the shame of the night before under a mountain of food. But then she remembered the howl in the kitchen. Dad would be up by now and she dreaded facing him.

Sunday mornings used to be different. Sometimes, on the way back from Mass, Mom would stop to buy ice-cream from Davey's in Lochee, and Ella would eat it in the car as they sang along to Mom's tapes – Joni Mitchell, Simon and Garfunkel, Don McLean – something like that. The two of them knew all the words to *American Pie*. That was their favourite.

As they parked the car outside the house, their music would give way to the Gregorian chant that spilled out of the kitchen window, open because Dad had burnt the bacon again. There would be fried eggs and ketchup, mugs of coffee for her parents and hot chocolate for her. And they would sit in the kitchen with the papers, reading out the funny bits. Ella would do her imitation of Father McIlvenney and Mum would relay the stories she had heard on the way out of Mass. About Moira whose husband was working offshore, and Isabelle whose mother was sick, about Pat whose son was getting on well at Glasgow University, and Shona who had taken up Taekwondo.

'I swear you find out more about a person in ten minutes in the queue for a toilet than most people would discover in a month of Sundays,' Dad would say, and Ella would watch him smiling at Mom like she was a perpetual, beautiful mystery.

There would be no bacon rolls today. But the thought of toast was enough to get her out of bed. In the bathroom she stuck her head under the tap and gulped in the fresh, cold water. The chill of it constricted her stomach and she heaved into the sink. Just water. There was nothing left to bring up.

A ghoul looked back at her from the mirror. Her spikes had flopped, her white face was streaked with black and green and the purple from her lips was smeared across her cheek. Running the cold water, she lathered up the soap until her palms were filled with a froth of bubbles. She brought her hands to her face and rubbed in a kind of frenzy. With the tips of her fingers she kneaded the suds into her eyes, feeling the sting and screwing up her lids in a battle against her own impulse. It hurt. And she was glad of that. As she rinsed off the paint with the icy water the chill woke her, and she shook her head to prolong the sensation.

***

Later, she stood by the toaster building a tower of toast until there was no bread left. Placing the giant tub of margarine and the pot of marmalade on the table, she set about working her way through the stack. She couldn't remember the last time she had felt so hungry. The toast and the tea were sucked into a vacuum, pushing out her stomach and giving her a satisfaction that felt like consolation. Then a door opened, and Dad's voice called down the hall. 'Morning, Ella.'

Shoving the last crust into her mouth, she kept her head down, focusing on the crumbs on the tabletop.

'I think it's time you and I had a talk.'

She bit her cheek. *Now he wants to talk.*

He sat down opposite her, his baggy green jumper worn through at the elbows, and crossed his forearms on the table, leaning in, bearing down on her. 'I didn't know where you were last night. You told me you were only going into town for a few hours.'

She pushed the crumbs around the table with the side of her hand. *And?*

'When you didn't come home for supper, I was worried.' He paused and she felt him staring. 'When you still weren't home by nine, I rang Nicola's mum to see if she knew where you might be.'

Ha. Shows what you know.

'She said she hadn't seen you in a while and that Nicola was at a party round at Elaine's. She said all the village kids were there.'

She snorted. *Sounds like fun. Gutted to miss it.*

'So, I went around to Elaine's house.'

She kept her head down and said nothing.

'And turns out you weren't there either.'

She worked at the crumbs, drawing them into a heap. *Nope.*

'And Elaine said that you didn't talk to any of them anymore.' He waited. 'And that you had new friends.' More waiting. 'And that she hoped you were okay.'

Ella looked out of the kitchen window. *Yeah, right.*

'She suggested I ask Mikey.'

Shit.

'So, I went down to Mikey's Mum's house.'

She put her head in her hands.

'I can't believe that she brought up nine children in that house. The paper is hanging off the walls.'

She bit her cheek harder. *Like our house is a palace.*

59

'Anyway. Turns out Mikey isn't living at home anymore. But you probably know that. Don't you?'

Silence.

'Don't you, Ella?'

She shrugged.

'She's worried about him. She said that he's in with a bad crowd.' He paused, and she felt his eyes on her again. 'And she said that his sister, Sheila, was at a housewarming at the new place. She didn't know the address, but she thought you might be there.'

He waited for her to respond.

Nothing. She gave him nothing.

'Were you, Ella? Is that where you were?' His voice was faster now, higher, and tinged with fear. 'Did you spend the evening in some sordid squat with those deadbeats? I mean I know that your mom saw something in that boy, but I'm struggling to figure out what. Is he responsible for the condition you were in when you got home?' The questions shot across the table, trapping her in her seat. 'I'm not even going to mention the state of your nose. Talk to me, Ella. You're still a child, for God's sake.'

She shoved the table away from her, pushing it into Dad's chest, scattering the crumbs. 'I'm not a child!'

'I need you to stay where I can keep an eye on you. You're grounded till the end of term.'

Ella pushed her chair backwards and ran out of the kitchen. Taking the stairs two at a time she headed for her bedroom and threw herself onto her bed. A stifled scream constricted her throat. She held her breath, willing herself to hold it forever, until the drive for survival forced an outbreath.

She sat up, took the sketchbook from her bedside table, and began to write. Angry words tumbling fast like scree in a landslide. She wrote without pausing for punctuation or paragraphs and in minutes her spidery handwriting had filled four pages. On the fifth page she drew. Quick and hard, her black Biro moving over the paper until a figure took form: a clown with a comic nose and a cone shaped hat. Black tears slid down his face and a wide, painted mouth streaked across his cheek. When she was finished, she tore the page from the book and fixed the sketch to the wall above her desk. On the top line of the next page she wrote a short note. She ripped it out of the sketchbook, folded it in half then placed it beneath the soapstone statue of the Virgin.

Ella was calmer then, and taking a blanket from the unmade bed, she headed to the living room where she spent the rest of the afternoon watching bad films while Dad hid in his study. As the day wore on, the nausea of the hangover lingered and by five o'clock she had begun to feel hot and a little dizzy.

Her head was swirling, and her appetite gone. She lay down on her bed to rest her eyes and when she next looked at the clock, it was eleven-thirty. Her curtains had been drawn and a blanket pulled over her shoulders. She thought of the scrap of paper she had placed under her statue – *I can't do this anymore. Please tell me what I need to do.*

CHAPTER 8
Big Yellow Taxi (Joni Mitchell)

The house was quiet when she woke the next day, and the light coming in around the edges of the curtains confirmed that she'd slept late. She turned to look at her alarm clock and saw a note propped against a jug of water.

She read: *I let you sleep. You're running a temperature so you should spend the day in bed. I've telephoned school to tell them you will be off for a day or so and I've asked Nicola's Mum to call in on you at lunchtime. I'll be back as early as I can. Drink plenty of water. Call me at work if you take a turn for the worse. The number's on the pad by the phone.*

She had spent a fitful night lurching in and out of dreams and nightmares, burning up one minute and chilled to the bone the next. She had seen her father's figure standing in the doorway, her mother at the foot of the bed, draped in a shawl, head tilted gently to one side. She had called out to her, she was sure. Now her head was throbbing and as she pulled herself upright to go to the loo, her eyes flashed with stars and a dark surge made her sit back down on the edge of the bed.

As she staggered back from the bathroom, she heard a voice calling from downstairs. 'Ella, it's only me – Mrs Stout, Nicola's Mum. Are you up the stairs, hen?'

She mumbled a reply and got back into bed. Before she knew it Mrs Stout was standing by her bedside looking down at her with concern. With one hand on her hip and the other reaching out towards Ella, the small round woman had the look of a teapot. Ella shrank back as she tipped towards her.

'Well, look at you. You're like the wreck of the Hesperus. It's no wonder you've come down with something, the state o' this place.' But there was no trace of shock or judgment in her tone; Mrs Stout was just saying it like it was. The house was in a state, and so was Ella. 'Let me see if you're hot?' She put her cold, plump palm on Ella's forehead. Ella frowned and pulled even further away. She didn't want this woman here, in her space.

'It's all right. I'm no gonnae bite.' Mrs Stout put her hand back on Ella's brow and rested it there for a minute or two. Ella looked at the wall.

Nicola's Mum was a nurse and everyone in the village knew it. They used her house as a kind of triage centre. It was nine miles to Dundee, and nobody wanted to take a trip to Dundee Royal Infirmary unless it was absolutely necessary. Once, Ella had fallen off a swing in Jane's garage, headfirst onto the concrete floor. Jane's Dad had sent them round to Nicola's house to get Mrs Stout to have a look. She had pressed a tea-towel full of ice-cubes onto the throbbing lump, given her a Wagon Wheel and a *Disprin*, and told her she'd be fine in the morning. Which she was.

There had been a time when Ella and Nicola were in and out of each other's houses all the time. They had secrets that they kept.

In their club-books they wrote down targets such as 'get a bra', 'have a period', 'kiss a boy'. Did Nicola know Ella was still waiting to tick that last one off the list?

Mrs Stout removed her hand from Ella's forehead. 'Not too bad,' she said, as if her hand was a scientific instrument. 'About 98 if I'm not mistaken. You'll live. But that nose of yours is looking nasty. Give me a wee second.'

Ella heard her walk into the bathroom. Soon the taps were running, and a minute later Mrs Stout was sitting on the edge of the bed with a kidney dish filled with Dettol and warm water, and a hand full of cotton wool balls. 'Lucky I brought my own supplies,' she said, matter of fact. 'There's no much in that bathroom cabinet of yours is there?'

She dipped the cotton wool in the warm solution and swabbed Ella's nose, inside and out. 'It's a wee bit puffy but nothing to worry about, not if you keep it clean. It's no your nose that's made you ill. Your Dad was worried about that. You've just got a wee dose of this flu that's doing the rounds.' She put the dish to one side. 'You need a couple of days in your bed. And when you're feeling up to it, try to get some fresh air. Put some colour in those cheeks. You're affy peely-wally. And wear a hat. Your baldy heid needs a wee bitty insulation!'

Ella was in no mood for jokes. She looked from the wall to the window, avoiding Mrs Stout's eyes.

'I'll bring you up a cup of tea before I go. I'd forget about food for the day. We'll try you with something light tomorrow. Some soup, maybe.'

***

For the next few days Ella drifted in and out of febrile dreams from which she found it hard to return. In them, Mom stood at the end of the bed, watching over her, listening to her breathe.

But when she was awake, the previous Saturday re-played on a continuous loop. For a while that evening, she had forgotten who she was. Who she wasn't. What she'd lost. The freedom of the dancing, the vodka, the Lady Di look-alike and Mikey. Mikey. Mostly it was Mikey. She was an idiot, a total loser. And Mikey must think so too. But they'd been so close she'd felt the breath from his open mouth and the heat from his damp skin; the pulse of the music beat through him and through her so hard it was like they were touching. It'd felt that close. And then she *had* touched him. She'd felt the dip of his temple under her fingertips and his cheek, rougher than she'd expected, beneath her open palm. And the touch had run through her like quicksilver. She could feel it now. And even if he did think she was a total loser, she wanted to feel like that again. If she could get back to the squat, dance with him maybe, perhaps there could be more.

***

Mrs Stout, who was working nights that week, came in every day about noon. The next day she heated up a bowl of broth, and on the third day she gave Ella a plate of stovies. Hot and buttery, they tasted like heaven. Ella ate the whole bowl and assured her she was feeling better and ready to get up.

'Just a wee walk around the village.'

'Mrs Stout...' Ella hesitated, struggling to say the words. 'Thanks... for looking after me. You know... just... thanks.'

Mrs Stout looked down at her and gently shook her head. 'It's no more than your mum would've done for Nicola if it had been the other way around.' She put her hand on Ella's cheek, pretending to check her temperature. 'Why don't you pop down for your tea sometime? Nicola misses you, you know.'

***

When she got back from her walk, Dad was home.

'You look better. You've got roses in your cheeks.'

'Yeah, I'm feeling better.'

'Another day or two and you'll be ready to get back to school.'

'Yeah, I guess.'

'Mrs Stout has been ringing me at work to keep me posted. She said she was hoping you'd pop round to see Nicola.'

'Yeah, maybe,' said Ella, and without missing a beat she added, 'Maybe Friday, in fact.'

CHAPTER 9

Exquisite Corpse (Bauhaus)

On Friday night, Ella was clearing the table when she brought up the subject of visiting Nicola again. 'Maybe I will go round to hers. Just for an hour or two.'

Dad looked so grateful that she was talking to him that he didn't risk shattering the fragile peace. 'Good idea. I'm glad you're feeling more like your old self again.'

She turned away. Had he forgotten that he'd grounded her till Christmas? God, he was a joke. 'Back by 10?' she said.

'Yeah. Sure.' He sounded relieved. 'Have a great time.'

Ella had spent all afternoon solidifying the peaks of her Mohican with sugar water and her scalp was tight around the base of the spikes. Upstairs, she widened the neck of a white t-shirt and stretched it over the jagged ridge that ran down the middle of her skull. She knotted the top in the gap between her small breasts, exposing her flat belly and the thrust of her hips. A crust had formed around the piercing in her nose again, and she picked it off before blackening her eyes with kohl.

As an afterthought she grabbed a mohair jumper from the top shelf of her wardrobe. But as she pulled, it caught on something buried at the back. A shoe box. She caught it just as it toppled off the shelf and held it for a moment in her hands. Clarks. It was heavy and bulging, and the lid was tied down with string. She didn't want to look at this now, she didn't want to see it, so she shoved it back into the black hole of the cupboard and covered it with clothes. The box was the last thing she wanted to think about tonight.

Pulling on the jumper she shouted goodbye and headed out the back door. Disobeying her father wasn't new, but this was a planned deceit. It fired her with adrenalin that made her pinkie fingers twitch and as she stepped out into the cold night air a vibrato giggle lurched out from behind her rib cage. Tonight could be the night.

Christmas trees flickered in the windows along the main street as she made her way down the hill. The gaudy lights seemed loud and jeering and their coloured fractals split the darkness of the frosty street below. They hadn't bothered with a Christmas tree since Mom died.

Instead of turning right to Nicola's, she continued to the bus stop at the bottom end of the village. On the far side of the shelter, she was hidden from view, should Dad decide to look out of the living room window. That was a laugh. He'd be in his study by now, headphones on, Wagner at fifty decibels. But nevertheless she felt furtive and tasted excitement on her tongue.

On the bus she put on her Walkman, but she wasn't listening. She was thinking about Mikey and his breath on her neck. She was thinking about his pale blue eyes, and the curl of his lip, and his hands. Sure, he called her 'wee sis', but when he looked at her – she knew it – he wanted her too.

It was only a short distance from the bus station to the squat, but it was a cloudless night and the temperature had plummeted, so she pulled the sleeves of her jumper over her hands and ran to warm herself up.

Her heart was pounding by the time she reached the derelict tenement and she stopped, listening to the music pumping out onto the street. Black ice hardened beneath the guttering and frost had begun to bloom over the bin-bags.

She was looking up at the open window, trying to pluck up the courage to go in, when somebody bumped into her. 'Sorry, hen,' an old man growled out the corner of his mouth, his lips pursed round a roll-up. 'Ah didnae see ye there.'

He and his dog were blocking her way. He lingered, relighting his cigarette behind a cupped hand. He clocked her Mohican and the nose ring and then his wet eyes settled on hers. She squirmed a little and moved forward to show she wanted to get past.

'If you're goin' tae see that bunch o' heid cases, ask them to gie it a break, will you?'

Ella shrugged, shivering now.

'That bloody racket hasn'ay stopped a' week. A've been on tae the council, but this place is gettin' pulled down in the New Year and they're nae interested.' He tugged on the little dog's lead and shuffled off. 'Tae think Ah've lived here a' ma days.'

She should have run straight up the stairs to see Mikey, but she didn't and she wasn't sure why. Instead, she watched as the old man and the dog made their way up the street, picking over the patches of ice. And suddenly, without thinking about it, she shouted goodbye.

The dog stopped to cock his leg on a lamppost and the man called back, 'Take a wee bit o' advice from an old timer, hen. Get awa' hame tae yer ma.'

Ella clenched her fists. *Not a possibility.* She waited until the man and the dog disappeared around the corner, then climbed the stairs to the flat.

The door was ajar, and she stood in the frame for a while, heart pounding, scanning the room for Mikey. The crowd was smaller than last week, and she could see just how decrepit the squat really was. Crushed beer cans, newspapers and takeaway cartons littered the floor and black mould spread across the walls from the corners of the room. Her eyes flicked over the faces but there was no sign of Mikey, and suddenly she wished she hadn't come. Then somebody called her name. Her heart lurched.

Over on the mattress, with a couple of punks she recognised from the City Square, Stan was waving. She didn't look at him, she just leaned on the doorframe like she wasn't bothered. She could pretend she hadn't seen him, just turn around and leave. But she had pinned so much on this evening that she couldn't give up yet. Mikey might be back any minute, he was probably just at the offie.

Stan was getting to his feet, shouting to her over the bass line that pounded from the amp. 'Hey, Snow White! You were really something last weekend! Totally goin' for it on the dance floor, weren't you?'

Shit. Had she made a total idiot of herself? Had they all been laughing at her behind her back? 'Yeah, whatever,' she shrugged.

'C'mon over,' Stan shouted.

She didn't want to talk to Stan but he might know where Mikey was so she picked her way towards him through the people and the rubbish.

'Cass said you were as sick as a parrot. Pair kid. Just nae used tae it, yet. Try some o' this,' Stan said, handing her a mug and slithering back down onto the mattress. 'Bacardi and coke. It'll go doon a bit easier than the voddy.'

'I'm not staying long. I just came to see if...' she hesitated, 'if Cass was here.'

'If you say so, Snowy. Go on, hae a wee snifter,' said Stan, his eyes swirling. He must have been drinking all day.

She remembered moving on the dance floor. She'd stopped caring what other people thought. And suddenly she wanted to feel like that again, so she took the mug and sipped.

'Nice, eh?' Stan gestured for her to keep drinking.

It really wasn't that bad. She drank more and slipped down to the mattress while the alcohol moved through her veins like a slow wave, down the backs of her legs to her toes, from her armpits down to her fingertips. A gentle vibration, numbing the edges. But her eyes remained fixed on the doorway.

'He's no comin',' said Stan after a few minutes. 'He's at a Subs gig in Glasgow, wi' Cass and Dek and some girl he met at Bruce's.'

Disappointment sank into her stomach like cement. Folding in on herself, she pulled up her knees and buried her head in the crossbars of her forearms. She should have known. Of course Mikey wasn't interested in her. He was never going to be interested in her. And she would never be one of his crowd. Even with the hair and the nose and everything, she wasn't like them. She wasn't like anybody. She was *Ella the Obscure*. Faint.

Undefined. They didn't want her. And her cheeks burned hot from the shame of it.

"Aw…" Stan reached his arm out across her shoulder and, feeling the steamy heat of him, she recoiled. She wanted to get up, but he was the only person in the room she knew, and she couldn't go home, not yet, not to that shell of a house. So, she stayed where she was. Moments passed, and Stan reached out to her again. This time she turned and smiled wanly.

'Any road, since we're here, we might as well hae some fun,' he said, his breath rummy and his grey front tooth catching on his bottom lip like a paperclip. She nodded and downed the Bacardi. He refilled her glass.

'Here's a wee plan that's gonna make your night a hale lot better,' he said, his mouth too close to her ear. 'E've got some mushies offay ma pal. How 'bout I brew us up some tea. You look like a girl that likes a nice cup a tea.' He stuck out his pinkie and mimed taking a sip.

'You're all right,' she said, trying to play it cool.

'They'll fuck you up,' he said. 'In a guid way. It's like yer mind literally explodes. Oh, man. The sounds, the colours. It's pure doss.'

She'd heard stories about magic mushrooms and the crazy things Mikey did when he was on them.

'A' that stuff in yer heid that makes nae sense, well, the mushies see through a' that shite.'

There was plenty of stuff in her head that made no sense, that was for sure. She was listening now.

'A' the stuff ye cannae deal wi'. The mushies tak awa' the fear. You finish yer drink, hen. Hae a wee think and Ah'll go and brew up the tea. You'll like it. Trust me.' He got up from the mattress and made his way across the dark room, pulling a small bag from the back pocket of his bondage trousers.

Ella watched him. What was she doing? Sitting on a mattress with the ugliest boy on the planet, waiting for Mikey who wasn't coming, who was never coming. Her life was a totally screw-up. Could it really get any worse?

And then Stan was coming back, with two mugs in his hands. 'Let's do this, Snowy! Just youze and me. Ah'll look after you, nae need tae worry on that count. Ah've done it hunners o' times and it's a' guid.'

'I don't know,' she hesitated.

'Come oan, Ella. If Mikey knows you've been on the mushies, he'd be dead impressed. Whit have ye got tae lose?'

Stan was right. What did she have to lose? Nothing. This was a good plan. 'Go on then,' she said, and reached out for the chipped mug.

The liquid was amber and steaming. Flecks of something solid floated on the surface and a bitter, earthy stench blended with the dampness of the flat so that if she shut her eyes, she could believe she was in a forest.

'We need to let it brew. Gee it another ten minutes or so. It's guid stuff – strong – well dried.'

They sat and waited. Over by the mantelpiece, in the candlelight, the art school goths were lurking. That girl with the spider-web eye make-up was wrapped in some sort of cloak. They had taken over the stereo, and the sound was loud and gloomy. She wished she was sitting with Mikey now. Next to her, Stan swilled his mug and sniffed it like a wine-waiter. Satisfied, he nodded to show that it was brewed. 'Tak it slow, we dinnae want you vomming again.'

In the orange light of the cold room, vapour rose from the tea and she drew it in through her nostrils. Then, tipping the cup just enough to let the hot liquid touch her mouth, she pulled in a draft, sucking it through her pursed lips to cool it down. She screwed up her face. It was foul. Way worse than Cass's beer. She groaned.

'Aye, it's no exactly a cup o' Tetley. Some people put in honey, but sadly, your majesty, this establishment isnae exactly The Ritz.'

'S'okay.' She forced it down as though she was taking medicine, swallowing the slimy slithers which had reconstituted in the water. Was she meant to chew them? Too late.

When she had drained the mug, she looked at the debris left in the bottom – leaf litter, mulch, grit, soil – and waited.

Life is but a dream. Life is but a dream. Bauhaus again. She leaned back and tried to focus on the room. People were talking, leaning into each other's ears or gesticulating with their hands to tell stories that couldn't be heard above the music. Over by the kitchen, a couple was pressed against the wall. He was grinding his narrow hips into hers, sucking a love-bite onto her neck while she puffed on a cigarette and looked into the distance. In the centre of the room, on the bare boards of the 'dance floor', a group swayed to music. Everywhere Ella looked, people were connected. She envied them. Even the girl with the cigarette seemed to be hooked onto the planet while Ella was crawling through life on her hands and knees clinging to the surface, terrified of falling off.

Nothing was happening.

Stan's brew was shit, just like everything else.

She had no idea how long she sat there, head back against the wall, eyes shut. The music was pounding, and the vibrations throbbed inside her until the whole room was pulsing in time with her breath. In and out. Slow and deep. When she opened her eyes, she was surprised to see that everything looked the same as before: the same orange light, the same groups of people talking and kissing and dancing. In and out. Slow and deep. More time passed and all she thought about was the breath. The insistence of it. Its ebb and flow. The letting go and the pulling back. And then, as she drew in, long and deep, the straight edges of the walls in front of her quivered a little. She laughed.

'You doin' okay there,' Stan shouted into her ear, and she nodded. She forced the breath out slowly, and as she did the verticals in the room, the edges of doors and walls and windows, began to vibrate like trees flickering in a heat haze. And then she saw that it was her breath that was moving the edges, that she was drawing in the walls through her nose. She breathed in again and watched as everything began to bow inwards, the ceiling was sagging, and the floor buckled in the centre. Then with the rush of her out-breath she pushed the lines back into alignment. In and out. She giggled. For the first time in so long everything was funny. She was in control. *In.* She pulled hard, really filled up her lungs, and the room sucked in around her, like elastic. *Out.* It pinged back into shape, strobing and juddery.

As the wall opposite surged towards her, she reached out to touch it and saw that her hands had begun to grow. Her fingers were stretching outwards like branches, her palms elongating like giant trunks. She turned them over and watched, riveted by the way the veins on her wrists undulated, snakes coiling under the bark of her flesh. And then everything began closing in on her again. Fractals of fairy lights burst like stars in the centre of the room, and beyond, by the mantelpiece, a woman in white was watching.

Ella blinked, expecting the woman to be gone when she opened her eyes. But she was still there, her head tilted to one side.

'Can you see her?' she shouted to Stan. 'Can you see her over there?'

'You're tripping, just go wi' it,' he shouted back, lost in his own space.

The boughs of her fingers stretched across the room towards the woman, green cordate leaves unfurling on the tips of the branches. The woman shrugged the mantle from her head and black hair, just like Ella's own, tumbled to her shoulders. Light shot from the palms of her hands as she stretched them out towards Ella's. She was smiling. She was mouthing Ella's name.

'Mom? Mom? Is that you?' she cried. 'I'm coming!'

But the room had filled with shards of light, needle-points, slivers of glass, and her path was blocked. She swiped and kicked, but her head had filled with noise and the noise was blue, and her mother was blurring. Blue noise, and rain and sirens. And crunching and red lights and white. White. White.

She covered her eyes with her hands.

***

And she is twelve again.

It's raining now, lashing, and she's wet with it. She's wet to her skin, and shivering. And she's standing on the side of the road in her thin Girl Guide uniform which has turned dark blue in the rain and is clinging to her thighs and her shoulders. She's waiting for Dad. And he's late. She's hungry and she's wondering if Dad will buy her chips, like he sometimes does on the way home. The rain is bouncing off the pavements which have been dry for weeks and the gutters, full of leaves, are filling up fast. A drip is tickling down the side of her nose and she wipes it away with the back of her wet hand. Dad's never late.

'Do you want me to run you home, Ella? It's a terrible night,' the group leader, Mrs Wilson, asks her, her Girl Guide handbook over her head to save her perm from the rain.

'It's fine,' she's saying. 'He'll be here in a minute.'

And then she hears them. Sirens streak past her, splashing water from the puddles. The ambulance. And then the fire-engine. And she is standing in the road. And Mrs Wilson is pulling her back. And she knows. She knows that it is him.

But it's not him.

It's her.

And later at the hospital, she sits on his lap, though she's too big to do that, and he's pulling her wet head very tightly into his shoulder when the doctor comes to tell them there was nothing they could do. That the impact of the lorry had killed her instantly and that there had been no pain. And, just like that, her father's breath stops. He is holding in something so big it will kill them both if he lets it out. She waits. But he is frozen.

'Dad!' she shouts and bangs her forehead on his chest until, at last, he gasps for air.

It doesn't make sense. None of this is right. And as he holds her head tight to his chest, her voice is muffled by the silencer of his shirt. 'It shouldn't have been her, Dad. Why was it her? Oh Daddy, it should have been you.'

She blinked. The lights were white, too white and too bright, and the figure in the corner was gone.

Stan was shouting. 'Ella, Ella, breathe. Chill out, you're just peaking.'

Vomit. She was going to vomit and needed to get outside. Pushing his arms away, she staggered to the door. The stairs rippled and she clung to the banisters, stumbling down, gulping for air. She wanted the coldness of the night on her skin and at the bottom of the stairs she lurched for the end of the passageway. Tripping over bin bags, she lunged into the street and, as she raised her head to the night sky, her foot slipped on a patch of black ice. Her legs shot out from under her and the back of her head hit the pavement like a clay pot on a tiled floor.

CHAPTER 10

Pretty Vacant (The Sex Pistols)

When she opened her eyes, the lights were still too bright and there was a dull dark ache in the back of her head. The air was antiseptic, the blankets tight and Dad was asleep in a chair by her side. She was in hospital. This was real. A cannula ploughed into a blue vein in the crook of her elbow and tubing connected her to a bag of blood that hung from a metal stand. The vein throbbed and slithered under her skin, and momentarily a serpent coiled down her arm and twisted around her wrist. She shut her eyes and when she opened them again, it was gone.

A nurse slowly made her way through the ward full of old women to Ella's bed by the window. 'Well, you gave us all a bit of a fright, pet,' she said. While her cool hand took Ella's pulse, her eyes focused on the small watch which dangled upside down above her breast pocket.

Dad stirred and pushed his glasses up onto his head. 'Ella, you're awake. How's the head?'

She reached behind her and felt thick wads of bandages. The spikes were gone. 'Sore,' she said, her voice hoarse.

'I'm not surprised.' The nurse patted Ella's wrist. 'That was quite a dunt you gave yourself. We had to shave the back of your head to get the stitches in.'

'I don't remember.'

'You've been out of it for a wee while, honey. You were unconscious and you'd lost a fair bit of blood by the time the lads got to you. By all accounts you were quite a handful when you came round in the ambulance. Like a banshee apparently. They had to give you something to calm you down. Any road, the back of your head was quite a mess. But don't worry, we've stitched you back together.'

Ella shot a glance at Dad to see if he was listening.

The nurse leaned in and spoke in a whisper. 'The doctors have had a wee word with him. They've told him they think you were on the mushrooms. I'll leave you two together for a minute or two, but then he'll have to get away home. He can stay till the breakfast trolley comes. It'd be a good idea to eat something, pet. There's nothing of you and you were really anaemic.' She pointed at the blood bag.

Ella looked at Dad. On the windowsill, just beyond his shoulder, a potted geranium was moving. The succulent stems wriggled along the white gloss surface, stretching like creepers, towards him.

'Dad!' she shouted, pointing, but as he turned the plant froze and she shook away the hallucination. 'It's nothing. Nothing.'

The movement made her head throb. She put a hand to the bandages again, imagining the line of jagged stitches that were pulled so tight her skin felt gathered'.

He was watching her, and his tired eyes blinked with disappointment. 'How are you feeling?'

'Fine. Yeah, fine.'

He looked out of the window, to the river and the lights of Tayport on the far side of the water. 'How did we end up here?' he said.

She turned away from him, and shut her eyes, willing him to leave her alone and wanting him to stay. 'I don't feel like talking, Dad.'

'Okay,' he paused, and she waited for him to push her. 'I'll let you get some rest. I'll pop into work and leave a note to let them know what's going on, but I'll be back later this afternoon.' He stood up and pulled on his coat. 'You probably don't remember, what with everything that's been happening, but Grandma and Grandad are arriving this afternoon. I'm picking them up from the station just after three. We'll come straight here.'

Fuck. She'd forgotten. She would rather be visited by demons, jeering classmates, the plague. Anything would be better than Dad's parents with their pity faces and their head shakes, reminding her just how miserable she was making their poor son. And here, trapped in this bed, wound up in bandages and plastic tubing, there would be no way she could escape.

She shut her eyes and pretended she hadn't heard while Dad lingered by the side of her bed. She wondered whether he would kiss her and whether she would shrug him off. But instead he pulled the blanket over her shoulder and tapped her on the back, as if she were a bomb and contact with her actual body might cause a detonation.

***

Sometime after breakfast a doctor, trailed by a line of students, appeared at her bedside. He looked like a duck followed by ducklings. He shone a torch in her eyes, wiggling it from side to side, and the light was so blinding she thought she might be sick. Instead, her stomach lurched in an inappropriate giggle.

Doctor Duck quacked questions at his students and they quacked their observations back. But Ella wasn't listening. It was as if an umbilical cord had been severed and she was floating off into space. If it wasn't for the headache hammering the back of her head, she might not have believed she was really there at all.

'The patient suffered loss of consciousness and significant head trauma.'

'Ataxia and hyperkinesis thought to be caused by ingestion of psilocybin, most likely from so-called magic mushrooms.'

'Headaches suggest concussion. Potential brain bleed.'

'Ella.' Finally, someone was talking to her. 'Ella, can you hear me?'

She nodded and the movement made her wince, so she put her hand over her eyes to hide from the pain.

Doctor Duck spoke to the ducklings, not to her. 'We'll keep her in for observation for a couple of days, at least until the headaches have abated.'

She spent what remained of the morning staring at the geranium, waiting for it to move again. She willed it to grow tendrils that stretched like creepers across the room to the geriatrics in the beds beside her, pulling them by the ankles and launching them out of the open window in their billowing floral nighties. The old women talked incessantly, rambling on about people who weren't there, calling for the nurses in plaintive voices, begging for bedpans and sweeties. She wanted to grab the vines herself, swing out of the ward and down the corridors, like Tarzan, out of the hospital and over the Tay, away from the catastrophe of her life. But the geranium did not so much as flicker.

And all the while she thought about what she had seen at the squat. Mom had been there. Standing on the opposite side of the room, stretching out her hands. If Ella had reached her, touched her, she could have caught her and held on. She shut her eyes and imagined the feel of her, willing her back into being. But her hands were too heavy, and Mom did not come and hold them.

***

At three o'clock, the ward began to fill up with visitors and Ella watched the doors, dreading the arrival of her own. How much would Dad have told her Grandparents? When the three of them appeared at the end of the ward, their grim expressions left her in no doubt that the Grandparents knew the full story. They looked old in their matching raincoats, Grandma clutching an embroidered handkerchief, ready to swab her puffy eyes. Spotting her, they locked onto their target and zoomed in, while Dad stopped at the desk to speak to the nurse.

Grandparents. Grimparents. Grindparents. Here we go. 'Hello,' said Ella.

Grandad leaned in to kiss her cheek. 'Ella,' he said. 'It's terrible to see you like this.'

Grandma's mouth twitched and her breathing was fast like she was struggling to keep her thoughts from becoming words. Reluctantly, she leaned in and pecked a lip-sticky kiss on Ella's forehead. 'Your poor, poor father,' she lamented with a small, histrionic moan.

Grandad shot her a look of warning. 'Jean, now is not the time.'

Dad joined them and arranged three chairs around the bed. 'Right, there's nothing to be too alarmed about, they're pretty confident everything will be fine, but there's a small chance that Ella's had a minor bleed on the brain.'

Grandma pressed her fingers to her lips.

'The head injury was quite serious and because of the length of time she was unconscious they need to keep her quiet and comfortable for a few days, until she's out of danger. So, let's keep it all nice and calm here, folks.'

Dad and the Grandparents conducted a stiff conversation about Aunty Judy and the dreadful cousins while Ella concentrated on her white hands, which lay like dead weights on the cellular blanket, holding her down. Her head was throbbing. At least they weren't staying for Christmas; they were going to Aunty Judy's. Dad's sister, Judy, lived in Birmingham with her chinless husband and her revolting offspring. Rupert and Toby went to some posh boarding school. The thought of them made her sick. She shut her eyes and the voices became just sounds. Bird calls, craawing, sharp, shrill. For a brief moment she imagined drawing them in heavy black Biro, but she didn't have the energy and shut her eyes.

**

Time passed slowly in the hospital. She did what she was told, ate regularly, sat up when Doctor Duck came to call and took walks down the corridors in her hospital gown.

'You've got a visitor,' the nurse said on the second day. And Ella's heart lurched, hoping it might be Mikey. But it was only

Grandma bringing a flannelette nightgown. Small blue rosebuds, frills round the neck and elastic at the cuffs. It was hideous and stayed in her locker.

On the third day, the headache became a background irritation rather than a full body-thumping immersion experience. She considered lying to the Doctor, telling him it was worse, just so she could stare at the geranium a little longer, chat to Ethel in the next-door bed, eat more hospital toast. It had to be better than going home to the Grindparents. 'The talk' was coming. They were just holding back until the moment was right.

On the fourth day Doctor Duck told her that her vital signs were good, that the psilocybin had worked its way out of her system and that there was no sign of a brain bleed. The headaches might continue over the next few months, but she could treat them herself with paracetamol. She was going home.

CHAPTER 11

Heart of Glass (Blondie)

Dad was on his own when he picked her up from hospital and for that, if nothing else, she was grateful. 'The talk' felt imminent. On the drive home her body tensed, ready to deflect whatever came her way. She bit down on her back teeth and clenched the muscles in her jaw, pulsing them.

But Dad said nothing and as they turned into the village she snatched a look at him. He was washed out – ashy – and his dark eyes seemed sunken behind his glasses. His mouth moved constantly. Teeth catching the small square of beard above his chin. Lips clamping together to hold back all he couldn't say.

The lights were on in the kitchen and through the window she could see Grandma and Grandad sitting at the table. The smell of home-baking hit her as she walked in the door. The kitchen was barely recognisable: the cooker gleamed white against the orange walls, the dresser had been cleared of books, and a batch of scones, fresh from the oven, had been arranged on a cake stand she hadn't seen for years. She could even see the pattern of the floor tiles that had been tacky with grease for so long she'd forgotten they were green.

'Wow, Grandma. I hardly recognise the place.'

Grandma smiled, proud of her hard work. 'Why don't you pop up to your bedroom. Put your bag down and I'll make us all a cup of tea.'

The whole house was brighter, more colourful, as if a veil had been lifted and she felt almost excited as she opened the door to her room. The sheets had been changed, the pillows plumped and the floor cleared of the layer of mess that she'd been wading through for years. She turned. Her chair was empty and her desk, clear. Totally clear.

The artwork that she'd spread up the red walls was gone and there were only two things left on her desk – the small, framed photo of her with Mom and the soapstone statue of the Virgin. But there was nothing beneath the statue's feet. All Ella's scraps were gone.

Panic rose in her throat and she lurched for the desk, pulling open the drawers, looking for the tiny scraps of paper. But the drawers were neat and tidy, pens in rows, paperclips in boxes, and the precious scraps were nowhere to be seen. For all that time, from the silence of her dead home, she had sent her words out to the universe, to Mom. She had scribbled the deepest parts of herself, the words she could not speak with her mouth. And now those words were gone.

She ran downstairs, past the Grandparents who were arranging plates on the kitchen table, out of the back door and across the garden to the bin. She lifted the lid, ready to tip the stinking contents onto the grass and rifle through them. But the bin was empty and smelled of bleach, and her secrets, her prayers, were lost.

A spitting rage coiled in the darkness of Ella's belly, raised its cobra head and shot poison up her windpipe and out of her mouth. Her scream shook her bones and reverberated through her skull and though she dropped to her knees at the side of the bin and held her head in her hands, the noise kept coming.

Grandma came first, running, wiping her hands on her apron. 'Ella, what is it? Whatever is the matter?'

'You had no right,' she yelled. 'You had no right to touch my things.'

Her grandfather was there too. 'Calm down, Ella. What have you lost?'

'My scraps. My scraps. You don't know what you've done!'

'Why don't we go inside. Grandma has worked so hard to make the house nice for you coming home.'

'Nice! Nice!' Ella's face contorted with rage. 'Those were *my* things.'

'It was just old rubbish that I threw out! Just bits of old rubbish.' Grandma was talking to Grandad, not her.

'They weren't rubbish to me. They were all I had.'

Grandma was crying now, rubbing her eyes with her apron. 'After all you've put us through. I only wanted to make it nice.'

'They were my things. They were my business.'

'But, Ella, your room was such a mess. People don't live like that. Not people like us.'

'People like us?' she scoffed. 'And what sort of people are we exactly?'

'Oh Ella, you know what I mean. Nice people. I only threw out the rubbish.'

Ella clutched her head. The pain was dark and visceral.

Her father stepped out into the garden with the shoe box in his hands. 'I saved this from the bin men,' he said. 'It was too late for the rest.'

He crouched down to where she was slumped and put his arm around her shoulder. He stayed like that for a long time, until her breath steadied. Then gently he lifted her to her feet and walked her back into the house.

In the kitchen he pulled out a chair and guided her into it. 'I'll put this back in your wardrobe. You have to take things easy, Ella, the Doctor was clear about that.'

She slumped forward onto the table, her cheek on the pine surface, and shut her eyes.

Grandad stood behind her and patted her shoulder. 'I'm sorry if we've thrown out something precious. Grandma only wanted to make things nice for you coming home. Why don't we all have a cup of tea and a scone, she's made them specially. They used to be your favourite.'

Dad came back downstairs and sat opposite her. He leant back in his chair and pulled off his glasses. With his thumb and forefinger, he pinched the bridge of his nose and squeezed his eyes shut.

The anger in Ella's belly slowly slithered back into its dark cave. She wanted to sleep away the pain in her head, to sleep until the world returned to normal. But there was no normal. Not anymore. And if she fell asleep, she wasn't sure she would want to wake up.

***

For the next few days Ella stayed mostly in her room while

Grandma and Grandad fussed about, cooking, mending, putting things right. The hoover hummed constantly, the washing machine rumbled, and she felt a tinge of nostalgia for the silence that had occupied the house for so long.

In the evenings, Dad and the Grandparents sat in the kitchen, Dad on one side of the table, the Grandparents on the other. It often sounded as if they were arguing and Ella's ears pricked up, knowing she was the source of the tension. Conversations ended abruptly when she approached and all she caught were fragments, words – *Rupert and Toby, continuity, opportunities* (Grandparents) *principles, elitism, separation* (Dad). She didn't like this. Something was up. But whatever it was, it was bigger than Dad. He was shrinking, day by day.

The only time Ella left the house was when Dad took her to the hospital to have her stitches removed. A nurse held up a hand mirror so that Ella could see the angry red scar that smiled like a clown's mouth across the back of her skull. Her Mohican had been shaved from the back of her head and what was left of it, on top, drooped to one side like a black horse's forelock. Elsewhere, stubble darkened her skull. *What a joke.* She was glad Mikey couldn't see her now.

Whenever she thought of him – and she thought of him a lot – he was with some blonde girl – normal height, normal feet. Just normal. In an arty, punky sort of way. Some normal girl, wrapped around him like a blanket.

CHAPTER 12

Christmas Wrapping (Waitresses)

Though tears were always just a sniffle away, Grandma was relentless in her effort to sound cheerful whenever Ella was around. 'Why don't we get the Christmas decorations down from the attic? That will brighten us up a bit. We could get it done before Dad comes back.' Christmas cards had been arriving over the last week and Grandma had been arranging them on the mantlepiece and the windowsills.

'If you like,' said Ella. 'I'm just going up to my room to read my book.' She had started *Jane Eyre* and things were not looking good for poor Helen Burns. 'Where's Dad anyway? I thought term had ended.'

'Oh, he just has something to sort out. He'll be back by tea-time,' Grandma said.

Mysterious. Perhaps he's planning a surprise present. Ella laughed to herself. *A pony? How perfect. All my dreams have come true.*

***

When she came down for supper Dad still wasn't home. Grandad had been out to Woolworths to buy a silver tree and they had decorated it without her. Coloured lights and tinsel. Ella hated it. It was everything Mom loathed and she could hardly bear to look.

The trip to buy the tree had been such a big part of Christmas, before. Every year Dad would say, 'This is the best tree we've ever had.' And he was right, every year it *was* better than the last. But now the old decorations looked miserable. The popcorn garlands were shrivelled and the cranberries had dried like raisins. The glittery bells Ella had made with Mom were dog-eared and pathetic and their stockings had been nibbled by mice.

'Isn't it lovely?' Grandad asked.

Ella could hear a tremor of uncertainty in his voice.

'We've left the fairy for you to put on the top.'

She took the fairy from his hands and straightened her sparkly crown. It felt like a lifetime since she'd seen her. Her feathery wings had been squashed in the box and Ella smoothed them out.

This was her first Christmas at home, without Mom.

She didn't like to think about the time after it happened. About those first days and weeks, when the curtains had stayed shut and the black holes appeared. She was afraid of the dark. She had bad dreams. And when she climbed into their bed, in the sleepy darkness, there it was, in the place where Mom should have been – a hole so black it almost swallowed her.

And Dad had been no help. He couldn't eat or sleep. He stopped answering the door, and the phone, and her, and she stayed in her pyjamas, eating bread and jam. And while he paced, she drew herself in, still and quiet, looking out for black holes.

The holes were sneaky, and she found them in the most unlikely places. In a notepad, on a coat hook, in a book. They smelled like lemons and lilacs and homemade brown bread, but you couldn't trust them, they were deeper than they looked. And Dad was not careful. She knew, even before she lost him, that one day he'd fall in.

Mom's parents, the Grampies, had moved in for a while. They were old, and sad, but they were the only ones who got dressed in the mornings. 'Why don't you come to Boston with us for a while?' they said. 'Daddy needs some time to get things sorted out.' And just like that, they had taken her away. Taken her from Dad, Nicola, her friends, and the new secondary school that she had started only a few months before. And he had let her go.

Across the ocean, in the emptiness of the Grampies' home she had skirted round the margins, with her back pressed to the wall. That first Christmas she had watched from somewhere far and high, like a spider on the bathroom ceiling. She saw their faces change when she came into view – the pity in their eyebrows, the sadness in their smiles.

She didn't even try to make friends at the school they sent her to in Boston. She kept her head down, still and quiet. Her bones became transparent, her face turned to glass. And when she finally came back to Scotland later the next year, nothing was the same. Nicola had made new friends and there was no space for her. Ella was different now, dark and silent; she couldn't be the girl who sprinkled stardust anymore. She was 'poor Ella' with a touch of gloom, the whiff of death about her. People turned away when she came too close. They didn't know what to say, and that was fine, because all her words had gone.

The last two Christmases, they'd spent at Aunty Judy's with the disgusting cousins and their piles of presents. The kind of Christmas Mom would have hated.

So, the last time she'd held this fairy it was Mom who'd handed it to her. 'Now you're tall enough to put it on the top, without me picking you up,' she'd said.

Ella swallowed hard. There should be music, the smell of pine, mulled wine brewing. This wasn't right. But all the same she took the fairy to the silver tree and placed her on the top. Ella shut her eyes. 'Happy Christmas,' she whispered.

'Happy Christmas, Ella,' Mom whispered back.

CHAPTER 13
The Bitterest Pill (The Jam)

They were just sitting down for supper when Dad got back and joined them at the table, complimenting them over-enthusiastically on the terrible tree. To his credit, he didn't say it was the best tree ever. That would have been a step too far. Grandma had made a chicken bake with green beans and potato gratin. There was no denying that the food had been better lately.

The Grandparents were tense and seemed to be waiting for something to happen. Ella stabbed a forkful of beans and shoved them in her mouth. *Here we go. The talk.*

Finally, Dad put down his cutlery and took a glug of the wine that Grandad had poured for him. 'Your Grandparents and I have been worried, Ella. I don't think you appreciate just how worried. We're so glad that you're on the mend, but...' His voice cracked and he paused for a second to take another slug of wine. 'But we could have lost you.' He wasn't looking at her. He was looking at his hands. Why couldn't he meet her eyes?

From the other side of the table Grandma nodded, urging him to carry on.

'You lied to me. You're only fifteen and you were drinking in that squat. But worse than that, those magic mushrooms… And the fall.' He stopped to swallow, his Adam's apple bulging under the coir of his neck beard. 'It could have killed you, Ella. I can't lose you. I just can't.'

Dad couldn't look at her but the Grandparents were boring into her with their eyes, willing her to feel bad. Heat rose from her chest, up her neck to her earlobes, but the Grandparents were still staring and she suddenly pulled off her jumper, dropping it onto the floor beside her. 'Okay. No need to get heavy. I know, all right. It was stupid.'

Dad looked up at her at last and there was something resolute in his eyes that scared her. 'I've made a decision. Your Grandparents and I have talked it through and we think it's for the best.'

'What? What have you decided?' She needed him to get to the point. He was worrying her now.

'You need a fresh start, Ella. I have to keep you safe.' He broke off his gaze, his index finger beating a slow retreat. 'I'm doing a pretty terrible job of looking after you on my own…'

'Dad?'

'So, I… we… I've enrolled you at a new school.'

'What? Where?'

'Up north, near Inverness.'

She couldn't believe what she was hearing. Or seeing. Grandma and Grandad were smiling. They were making stupid yoffling noises to show how pleased they were with what they'd heard. But none of this made sense to her at all. 'Well, how's that going to work? Are we moving?'

'No, Ella. It's a boarding school. That's where I was today, I went to meet the headmistress. It's all decided.'

'Are you joking?' Her palms were pricking and she scratched at them furiously. 'A boarding school? Dad. This isn't funny.'

'It's not a joke. It's for the best. The sisters will be kind. They know you've had a difficult time.'

'The sisters?'

'Yes. It's a Convent.'

Fuck.

'A famous one,' Grandma interjected. 'They have pupils from all over the world. You're a very lucky girl.'

'Their academic record is outstanding, and you'll have a chance to fulfil your potential. You're clever, Ella.' Dad reached over to take her hand, but she snatched it away. 'You can't just waste all that talent.'

'I don't believe this. You've decided, without even talking to me, that I should be sent away to a boarding school for my own good?'

'Not sent away, Ella,' Grandad butted in. 'This is a prestigious school. Lots of girls would give their eye-teeth for an opportunity like this.'

She ignored him, looking only at Dad. 'Is this a punishment? I'll do whatever you want. I'll come straight home from school.' Her voice was getting higher, louder now. 'Or I'll come to your office and wait there. You can ground me permanently. But not this, please not this!'

'It's not a punishment, Ella. I've thought about this long and hard. It's the only way. Your Grandparents have very kindly offered to pay the fees. They want you to have the same opportunities as Rupert and Toby. It's worked so well for them.'

'It's been the making of them,' said Grandad.

But Ella had stopped listening. She was on fire. 'You can't do this to me. You can't. I won't go!'

'Mom...' Dad stumbled, like he always did when he said that word. 'Mom... was a Catholic. You're a Catholic. I know that she didn't believe in private education, I don't either... or I didn't... but I think in these circumstances she would understand.'

'Don't you dare bring Mom into this! She would hate this! I hate this. I hate you. I hate all of you!'

***

For the next two days Ella stayed in her room. She timed her trips to the loo to avoid bumping into anyone and left the trays of food uneaten outside her door. She lay on her bed, in her red room, reading *Jane Eyre*, nursing her rage. She scribbled hard black rants in her notebooks, and re-papered the wall with sketches: distorted faces, clowns and ghouls.

From the window she watched as her Grandparents loaded their luggage into the boot of their car. She ignored the tapping on her bedroom door. 'Ella, we're going now. Please can we come in to say goodbye?' She listened to the car door slam and her father's footsteps on the gravel. And then the house returned to silence, once again.

On Christmas Day, Dad heated up the dinner that Grandma had left in the freezer – chicken, stuffing, roast potatoes – and she ate it on a tray in front of the television, while Oliver sang his pathetic blond heart out. 'Whe-eh-eh-eh-ere is love?' *Good question, little guy. If you find out, be sure to let me know.*

She considered making her escape, packing a bag and turning up at Mikey's flat, begging for a chance to sleep on that stained mattress on the living-room floor. But in her heart, she knew he wouldn't want her there. She thought about asking Dad to send her back to Boston to live with the Grampies, but she didn't belong there either. So she lay on her bed and traced the lines of the walls and the ceiling, round and round, hard and angry. She was stuck in the wrong life. She didn't fit in anywhere, not even beneath her own skin.

She shaved off what was left of her hair and stayed in her room, writing new scraps, hoping for a miracle, trying to persuade herself that her silent protest would soften Dad's resolve. If he could see her desperation he might care enough to relent. But he did not. The decorations were down before New Year.

Then one morning, early, Dad knocked on her bedroom door. 'I'm going into Edinburgh today, to get your uniform. There's a really long list, perhaps you'd like to have a look. There are all kinds of things I've never even heard of.' He waited for her to open the door, to acknowledge that she'd heard. 'It would be great if you could come with me. Have a look.'

He pushed a piece of paper under the door.

Saint Cecilia's Convent of Our Lady of Mercy
Uniform List

Suppliers: The school uniform must be obtained from the Outfitters at Jenners Department Store, Princes Street, Edinburgh.

Weekday Dress

1 x blazer, airforce blue flannel with black buttons and the school crest
1 x winter hat
1 x gabardine overcoat
1 x school scarf, navy blue with three white stripes at each end, woollen
1 x pair gloves, black or navy blue, woollen

```
2 x ties, red or gold, house to be allocated before arrival
2 x pinafore dresses, airforce blue, serge
6 x blouses, long sleeved, pale blue
1 x v-necked jumper, airforce blue, woollen for additional warmth (n.b.
elongated baggy 'sloppy joes' may NOT be worn.)
1 x cardigan, airforce blue, woollen
6 x pairs knee length socks, grey, woollen
6 x pairs ankle socks, white (summer term only)
2 x pairs garters
4 x pairs stockings, beige or black (Stockings should only be worn if
the girls are prepared to keep them immaculate.)
7 x pairs outer-knickers, grey
```

The list went on. This had to be a joke. What was she going to do with a tartan sash? Or a pinafore? And what the fuck were outer-knickers? This was 1983 not 1923. As for the garters – she'd seen pictures of the blue satin things that brides wore under their wedding dresses, but she was pretty certain they didn't mean that. She smiled for the first time in days. This was actually hilarious.

For a moment she quite fancied a trip to Edinburgh. She turned and stared at the closed door. Dad was out there. Waiting. He must be bluffing. He hadn't bought himself as much as a pair of socks in the last three years. There was no way he was going all the way to Edinburgh to buy… she counted… 81 items of clothing, most of which sounded like props for a play.

Half an hour later he knocked on the door again. 'I'm leaving in about fifteen minutes. Why don't you come?'

So, he wasn't bluffing. And her heart began to race again.

'We could go to that little Italian on Frederick Street, the one that you and Mom liked so much. Make a day of it. It's going to be hard getting all that stuff without you. I'm not sure of your size.'

'Forget it Dad,' she shouted at the door. 'I'm not going to that stupid school so there's no point wasting your time. Or your money.'

'I'm not going to change my mind, Ella. The decision's made. You can see sense and make the most of it, or you can go kicking and screaming: the choice is yours. Either way, you're going.'

She screwed up the uniform list, flung open the door and threw the crumpled paper at him. 'I hate you!' she screamed, slamming the door and kicking the bottom panel with her size 8 1/2 boot.

'Kicking and screaming it is then,' she heard him say as he walked down the stairs.

Moments later his feet crunched over the gravel and the engine of the 2CV started up. It would be a long, cold drive to Edinburgh with the heating on the blink and the windscreen wiper sticking with every swoop. *Bastard. I hope you freeze,* she thought.

CHAPTER 14

Say Hello Wave Goodbye (Soft Cell)

'Welcome to Saint Cecilia's. I'm Sister Hanrahan, the headmistress.'

The Irish voice emanated from a grey slab of a nun positioned between two pillars at the top of an impressive set of steps. She seemed cut from the same stone as the building, colossal and joyless. Through the rain, her flinty eyes set on Ella and Dad, who hesitated on the wet gravel below, unsure whether they should climb the steps to shake her hand. The nun's mouth turned down towards her undershot chin and disappeared somewhere in the fleshy wattle of her neck. Ella imagined drawing her in black Biro, scoring in the crags of the hanging chops, the flat nose, until the woman before her became a bulldog.

The nun's eyebrow twitched, indicating that a response was required.

'Good afternoon… em… Sister,' Dad said, nudging Ella with his elbow, as if she was five. 'Say hello, Ella.'

Tempting as it was to parrot, 'Hello, Ella,' right back at him, she sensed this was no time for humour. The Bulldog had her in her sights. Ella met the stony gaze with a hard stare of her own and their eyes locked, unblinking, for a moment. But the nun's eyes were penetrating, and Ella broke first. 'Hello... em... Sister.'

Ella squirmed with discomfort and looked down. She was wearing the ridiculous uniform that Dad had bought. A pinafore with pleats down the front made her look like one of those cartoon schoolgirls from the 1920s. He'd bought it too big and it hung like a curtain, cutting off mid-calf where it skimmed the top of her DMs. Her red tie was knotted sloppily, and the gabardine raincoat was unbuttoned, its sturdy belt hanging loose and lopsided. She looked up at the nun and tried to regain some ground, thrusting her chin a little in defiance.

The nun stood stock still while the silence matured. She looked Ella up and down, taking in the shaved head, the purple lipstick, the pierced nose. 'You'll lose that belt if you're not careful.' Her Irish brogue was slow and deliberate.

The waiting resumed: the nun up on the top step, Ella and Dad, down on the gravel, in the rain. Something about the nun's stillness indicated that she could wait for a hundred years if she needed to. She would never back down, ever. Ella blinked and tightened the belt of the coat, pulling it firmly, fastening it with a knot.

A smile flashed briefly over the nun's face and her eyes narrowed until they all but vanished. 'That's more like it,' she said and clapped her hands together indicating the start of round two. Ella flushed with the shame of defeat and fought off an instinct to take Dad's hand.

'You're the only new pupil this term so the other girls will be raring to meet you. The Lower Fifth are in the Sistine dormitory.

You'll have a cubicle to yourself. Sister Cullen will be along to meet you shortly. She's in charge.'

Pointing to her right the nun addressed Dad. 'Head a bit further up the drive. There's a parking bay on your right. The dormitories are set back, between the Mansion House and the Gym. We've left the door open for you. You can offload the trunk there. There's no point in drawing things out. A quick goodbye and get on your way. That works best.' Turning back to Ella, she smiled as if she was sucking on a nippy sweetie. 'You're very welcome at Saint Cecilia's,' she intoned. 'You'll be one of us before you know it.'

Ella and Dad watched the nun turn her back on them and disappear through the door. A heavy knocker banged conclusively. Their introduction to Saint Cecilia's was over.

'Come on, let's jump in the car, it's freezing out here,' said Dad.

Ella was shivering as she got into the front seat. The gabardine coat was soaked through and the tunic clung wet and itchy to her stockinged legs. She breathed deep, grasping the last few moments of familiarity. She hated this broken-down embarrassment of a car, but she would willingly have lived in it if that were an option.

They drove past the Mansion House and parked outside a building she guessed, by the lack of windows, must be the Gym. Then, lumbering under the weight of the trunk, they made their way down a wide path between the two buildings to a fire-door propped open with a fire-extinguisher.

They paused in the doorway for a moment, getting their bearings. To her right, at the far end of a panelled corridor, Ella noticed a painted statue of a monk balanced on a shelf. He was wearing a brown habit and a group of small plaster children were gathered round his feet. The top of his bald head glinted in the orange light of the stained-glass window behind him, and one arm was raised, as if he was waving. To her left, a statue of the Virgin Mary, crowned in stars, was poised on a pedestal. She was standing on a crescent moon and seemed oblivious to the huge snake that was coiled beneath her feet.

'There it is, Sistine, just like the Chapel,' said Dad nodding his head at an open door, opposite left. 'I wonder if Michelangelo painted the ceiling?'

'Shut up, Dad,' said Ella, cringing at the thought of being overheard.

It was the smell that hit her first as they entered the barn-sized dormitory: wax floor polish, singed dust, and the peppery ammonia of dried pee. There were no windows in the yellow gloss walls, but a series of dormers lined each side of the roof. Neon strip-lights hung from the rafters and the air was filled with an electrical hum.

The dormitory was divided into cubicles by partition walls which cut off at chest height.

'Here's your room,' Dad said, pointing to a nameplate on the first cubicle to the right.

There was no door, but an opening gave access to an area just big enough for a single bed, a small wardrobe and a chest of drawers.

'I wouldn't call that a room, Dad.'

They heaved the trunk onto the sagging mattress, but not before Ella had noted the dark ochre patches on the ticking. Clearly the last occupant had been a bedwetter. *Fuck*. This was even worse than she'd imagined. There was barely enough room for both of them to stand inside the cubicle, so Dad stepped outside. Everything bar the mattress had been painted in the same yellowy gloss paint. The walls of the stall, the chest of drawers, the wardrobe – all the same. Was he really going to leave her here?

He had kept up the chatter on the long road North, given her control of the tape player, and bought her a bag of liquorice toffees when they stopped to fill up with petrol. But he was tapping on the partition now, pale and swallowing hard. The dormitory was ice cold and their voices echoed.

'I wondered why there was a tartan travel rug on the uniform list. The lady in Jenners tried to sell me one but I said I'd find something from home. It's so cold though, maybe a woollen one would have been better.' He sounded like he was trying to keep the worry out of his voice, but a quiver betrayed him.

'It's a bit late now, don't you think?' she said. It was getting dark and they hadn't seen another person since that nun on the front steps. She had no idea what would happen to her if he left.

On the other side of the partition Dad stretched out his left arm, wriggling his wrist free of the cuff, and pulled it back to look at his watch. This gesture, so familiar, made her stomach hurt, and she looked at the hair on the back of his hand, the knobbly bone that protruded on the side of his wrist, and imagined what it would feel like to touch him. 'I expect they like to give the new pupils time to unpack,' he said. 'Maybe I'd better go. Let you get yourself sorted before the other girls get here. I'll only be in your way.'

'Don't go yet. I don't know where everything goes.'

'Best not draw things out,' he said, shifting his weight from foot to foot. 'Sister Hanrahan's right. I should head down the road.'

'Please don't go.'

'You'll get it all sorted. I know you will. You're a good girl, Ella. You just need to get away from. . . everything. Time to concentrate on your studies.'

Her chest felt constricted, her breaths short and tight. 'Dad...'

'Fresh start.'

'Please...'

'It'll be Easter before you know it.'

'I'll be better, Dad. I promise. It's not too late...'

He couldn't look at her any longer. 'It will all work out.'

She reached out for him, grabbing his wrist, making him look at her. 'Dad... you can't leave me here!'

He took her hand off his arm and stepped back. 'Give me a call in a week or so when you're settled in. Or you could write me a letter?'

Her voice was a whisper. 'Dad...'

He ran the flat of his hand over the surface of her shaved head and shut his eyes for a brief moment, then, turning, walked away.

Ella crawled into the corner of the bed, into the space between the trunk and the wall, and folded in on herself. She drew her knees under her chin and pulled her arms tight round her shins, making herself as small as she could be. Until she was a ball of flesh and fabric and leather and bone and blood and nail. She squeezed it all in until the pain was contained, and she could hold it there. Still for a while. If only she could squeeze a little harder, she might explode into shards of light that shot into the sky and travelled on, burning bright into eternity. But she was really here. She knew it even with her eyes closed, she could smell it.

CHAPTER 15

Mad World (Tears for Fears)

It was dark when she uncurled, and from somewhere along the corridor rubber-soled footsteps were approaching.

A withered woman in a nylon overall rustled through the opening to Ella's cubicle. 'Holy Mary, Mother of God, have you not even made a start?' The sinews in her stringy neck tightened. 'I'm Sister Cullen. And I hope you're not trying to be bold. We've no time for shenanigans here.'

Sister Cullen, barely five-foot tall, was bone thin, her pewter hair cropped in a short back and sides. She wasn't wearing the same outfit as the Bulldog. Instead a black skirt and jumper exposed themselves at the edges of her yellow overall.

Ella drew back into the corner, her arms tight around her knees as the woman approached the bed and looked in the trunk. The contents had not so much been packed as tipped in, and the nun sucked in air through her loose teeth. She placed a bloodless hand on either side of the trunk, and a large black crucifix swung out from her overall. It dangled for a second, like a threat, before she tucked it away to show she meant business.

'We haven't got all day. Up you get.'

Ella, suddenly dwarfed by the tiny Irish woman, stood up.

'Your day dress and your Sunday dress go into the wardrobe. There's a rack in the bottom for your shoes. Newspaper in the gym-shoes, mind. We'll not be wanting any unsanitary odours in the dormitory. Undergarments, grey over-knickers, white under-knickers, brazeers and stockings go in the top drawer of the chest. Sports clothes in the middle and your home clothes, such as they may be, in the bottom.'

Would this woman check she was wearing not only the grey over-knickers, but the white under-knickers as well? She wasn't sure she knew what under-knickers were, or *brazeers* for that matter, but whatever they were, she was pretty sure Dad hadn't bought them.

'Make up the bed and get that trunk up to the store before evening prayers. The monitors will help with that.'

Monitors? Bloody hell. Had she stepped through a portal and landed in some twisted version of *Mallory Towers*? Or worse, was this The Lowood School for orphans, where poor Jane Eyre was sent?

The tiny woman peered up at Ella and dropped her voice to a raspy whisper. 'And you'll wash that muck off your face before the girls arrive back. Make-up is not allowed. The bathrooms are along the corridor, opposite, first left.' She pointed through the double doors. 'Girls are permitted to wear one pair of stud or hoop ear-rings. As you'll have seen on the uniform list.' The nun waited for a response, but Ella, pinned awkwardly in the space between the bed and the chest of drawers, stayed silent. 'You'd do well to remember that Defiance is a sin. And so is Pride. We'll be having neither of those at Saint Cecilia's.' Her lips twitched as if she was relieving an itch in her nose. 'One pair of *ear*-rings mind, studs or hoops. Most certainly no *nose* rings.'

As the yellow overall exited the double doors, a cold draft of air swept in from the corridor. The grotesque little wasp woman had chilled Ella to the marrow, and she needed a jumper, a blanket, something to warm herself up.

In the trunk, out of place amid the drab of the uniform, she spotted a rolled-up tea towel. The cloth with its pattern of orange and brown flowers, ancient now, pulled her straight back to their kitchen at home and she lifted it out, meaning to smell it, to breathe in home. But something solid was wrapped inside, and she opened the tea towel like a present. And there was her statue, the Virgin, from her desk. Dad must have stashed it in the trunk at the last minute because she'd seen it there, just before they left, when she'd placed one last '*save me*' scrap beneath the base. Ella held the figure in the palm of her hand and ran her thumb over the smooth surface. She didn't belong here. She wasn't safe with that witch on the prowl, so she slipped her under a pillow, hidden from view.

Ella turned her attention to the contents of the trunk. How could there be so much stuff? Ignoring the Wasp-Witch's instructions she shoved the clothes into the drawers in the order which they came out. She hung up the spare tunic and the blouses and fiddled around trying to hang the kilt before kicking it into the back of the wardrobe.

Finally, she reached the bottom of the trunk. There, carefully folded and smelling of ironed cotton, was the patchwork quilt

Mom had made when they first moved to Scotland. She pulled it out and held it in her hands. Where had it been all these years? Here was a piece of red gingham from the Little Red Riding Hood costume that Mom had made for her when she was four, when they were living in Boston. And here was a scrap of the dress Mom had worn on her honeymoon; she was tanned and blurred in the Polaroid; her dress yellow as the sun. This was a piece of the shirt Dad had worn on the trip to San Diego Zoo, and this was the tablecloth they'd found in a flea market, too square and too small for the kitchen table at home. Snippets of life, cut into hexagons and joined with stitches as irregular as tally lines, counting down the days. She held the quilt to her face and breathed it in. In the tiny spots of blood where her mother had pricked her finger and cursed loudly, this quilt contained her, contained them. 'Richardsons contra mundum,' they used to say, clicking their knives like swords across the table.

She kicked the empty trunk onto the floor and made up the bed, laying Mom's quilt across the bottom.

Fuck 'em. It would take more than a Bulldog and a Wasp-Witch to beat her.

***

Ella was digging in her canvas satchel for the bag of liquorice toffees that Dad had bought her when she heard voices. Over the partition she saw two identical girls backing into the dormitory with their trunks. A hefty middle-aged man wearing margarine-coloured cords followed them in, holding the other end of both trunks. He was puffing and his glasses had steamed up. Ella ducked and sat back down on the bed.

'Steady on, darlings. Put them down for a tick and let Daddy catch his breath.' He sounded like Mikey's impression of a Tory wanker. And he looked like one too. Ella watched as he pulled a handkerchief from his pocket and wiped his sweaty forehead.

She pulled her feet up onto the bed, chewing her toffee, listening to the twins with their preposterous voices as they ran down the central corridor checking the name plates of the cubicles.

'Here's your cube, Bernie. You're next to Dizzy. Lu-cky.'

'Oh no, you're right up here. Next to Noids. Hard cheese. Hope you brought your ear plugs.'

Holy crap. She really had arrived at *Mallory Towers*.

As the girls ran back to their father one of them caught sight of Ella. 'Oh, hello. I didn't know we were getting any New Bugs. I'm Theresa and that's my twin sister, Bernadette – everyone calls her Bernie. She's a red, I'm a green.' She shook the bottom of her plait to show off her green ribbon and her twin flipped her red ribbon over her shoulder.

'Hi. I'm Ella.'

The girls stared at her, taking in the nose ring and the shaved head, so she stared back, absorbing the identical faces and the long mousy plaits. They reminded her of something. The poster above Cass's sister's bed. Holly-fucking-Hobby, in duplicate.

'Righty ho, girls. Let's get a wiggle on. Mummy will be wondering where I've got to.'

'Nice to meet you… Emma, was it?' said the twin with the green ribbons, but before she could answer two more girls ran screeching into the dormitory.

From the corner, Ella watched as fathers, taxi drivers and a couple of older brothers hefted luggage. Girls flew into one another's arms or tore up and down the dormitory, keen to discover which 'cube' they'd been allocated. Their voices were loud and braying, and she snatched a notebook from her satchel and sketched a donkey – lips rolled back, long teeth, wide mouth *eeh-awing* at a crescent moon.

'Best Crimbo eva'!'

Seriously, Ella thought. *People don't actually speak like that.*

'When does the airport bus get in?'

'Is Mhairi back yet?'

And then loud whispering. They were talking about her. 'There's a New Bug in cube two?' somebody said.

'Is that actually a nose-ring?'

'Is she poorly? I mean, she's totally bald!' They definitely meant her.

She sat very still, hoping her stillness would render her invisible and watched as the girls said goodbye to their parents. Two kisses, one on each cheek, before they turned back to the dorm with what looked like relief.

Nobody spoke to her; they were too swept up in the excitement of reunion. From the corner she observed them, and scribbled more donkeys, short fat ones like those Thelwell ponies, knobbly ones, ones with ribbons in their manes. She looked on as they hugged, draping their arms around each other, totally at ease. This place, Ella realised – this school, this dormitory – was where they lived. They had not been sent away. They were coming back.

'Did you see Dizzy's ballgown at the Shoestring?'

'Droopy and Brown, I bet.'

'Is it true she lost it to Jamie H-B?'

'Under the billiard table, I heard.'

Interesting. These girls looked so innocent compared to the Dundee crowd, but maybe they weren't quite as 'Chalet School' as they'd seemed.

From the doorway a sturdy girl with orange hair and spots was keeping watch. Every minute or so she craned her neck down the corridor, until eventually she shouted, 'Mhairi's here!'

Seconds later, a tall girl with ripples of loose chestnut curls stepped into the dormitory. Her neck was long, and her head tilted back slightly. She swiped a feathered fringe back from her face and slipped into the knot of girls.

From the corner of her cubicle, Ella watched. Their queen, it seemed, was home.

'Mhairi and I are in the big double on back corridor,' a tanned, blonde girl drawled.

'Lu-cky!' the crowd replied.

'Come see.' Mhairi's voice was slow and confident as she looked down her nose at her minions. 'We're unpacked already.'

Ella heard the swarm follow Mhairi's clicking footsteps to the far end of the dormitory. A door swung open. Slammed shut. Then silence. She wondered for a moment if she was completely alone, but soon enough the noise of drawers squeaking resumed. Other girls had been left behind.

It had been hours since she and Dad had stopped for bacon rolls at a café in Tyndrum. She was starving and the toffee had made her thirsty. On top of the chest of drawers there was a stack of red plastic: a washing up bowl, a bucket, a jug and inside the jug a small red beaker. Grabbing the cup, she headed out to find the toilets.

In the wide corridor, coloured light spilled onto the floorboards from the stained-glass windows at either end. The two painted statues that she'd seen earlier were now silhouettes, backlit from bright lights on the other side of the glass.

The toilet block was empty. A strip of cubicles faced a row of white sinks; there were no windows, and no baths or showers as she'd expected. Sitting on a cracked wooden toilet seat, she listened to the sound of her pee and dug her nail into the plastic beaker. The Izal medicated toilet paper was hard and shiny and the flush was attached to a high cistern. When she pulled the long chain the noise felt deafening.

She picked a basin with a mirror and turned on the tap. The nun, the Wasp-Witch, had told her to wash her face, but she was not doing that. Everything about her felt bare, her head, her hands, her heart, all open and on show, and there was no way she was taking off the make-up. In the absence of paper towels, she dried her hands on her tunic and filled the cup. Then she downed the icy water in one, and refilling, drank again.

Back in the dorm the girls had returned and were unpacking. Here and there they stood on their beds, chins and hands resting on stall walls, sharing stories about the Christmas holidays. Ella put on her headphones and slotted in one of the mix tapes that Mikey had given her. She was unwrapping the black foil of another liquorice toffee when a figure appeared in her doorway.

'You're the New Bug, aren't you?' It was the spotty orange girl who had been on lookout. Clearly a master of deduction. Ella ignored her.

'Eliza, isn't it?' the girl said, her lip curling slightly as her eyes settled on the nose ring.

She took her time to respond. 'It's Ella.'

'Okay. Whatever. I'm Tibby. I'm a blue sash.' She indicated the wide blue ribbon she wore across her chest, knotted at the ample hip. 'That means I'm a Lower Fifth monitor. The purple sashes are the Upper Sixth prefects. Watch out for them. Sister Cullen's asked me to look after you for the next few days. But don't worry, I'm not going to babysit you. I'm sure you won't want to be hanging round with me all day long.'

'Yeah. That sure suits me,' said Ella, her old accent resurfacing as she struggled to find her voice.

Tibby's eyes widened. 'You're American?'

'Something like that.'

'Ok. Well, heads up, Walkmen are banned and you'll be in trouble if Sister catches you with tuck in the dorm. Stash them in your tuck box and bring it down to the Form Room after breakfast.' Words shot out of the girl's mouth, hard, like tennis balls and Ella caught a whiff of cheese and onion crisps. 'I wouldn't say no though, if you're offering.' The orange girl held out a hand and reluctantly Ella passed her a toffee.

'The trunks need to be in the Steading before prayers. It looks like you're pretty much sorted, so I'll grab mine and we can head up there now. I'll see if some of the others are ready. It's pretty creepy up there so it's better if we go in a group.'

Tibby flicked back her long fringe. Ella had seen the girl called Mhairi make the same movement earlier. Ella knew all about that, girls crushing on other girls, copying their hair and their mannerisms. For a while, some years ago, she'd been the one they had copied. She remembered hearing Mrs Stout tell Nicola to *stop putting on that American accent.*

A few minutes later, Tibby and the twins paused in the doorway, clutching their trunks, and indicated that she should follow them. There was nothing left in Ella's trunk and it was surprisingly light, if unwieldy. Turning it on its end, she carried it like an awkward dancing partner. The three girls went out of the door that she and Dad had come through earlier and Ella had no choice but to follow them. Blindly. Like a stupid sap.

Outside, a white light on the side of the building illuminated the path which led to the main drive. But they didn't turn towards the Mansion House where the Bulldog nun had stood to greet her; instead, they went right, towards the woods and the darkness.

Tibby and the others walked fast. With the trunk obscuring her view Ella was scared she might trip, making herself look an even bigger idiot than she already felt. She hated being so utterly reliant on these girls who seemed to have forgotten all about her, but she followed the sound of their donkey laughter and the scrunch of the gravel.

'That was the Gym, back there,' Tibby called over her shoulder, remembering her duty. The wind had picked up and she was shouting. 'We're going up to the Steading. We have some classes up there, but mostly it's just used for storage. We keep our bikes there in summer.'

Away from the spotlight the grounds were unlit, and it took a minute for Ella's eyes to adjust to the moonlight. The woods were on their left and in front of them tumbledown farm buildings emerged from the shadows. The girls stopped under a wide archway that led into a central courtyard and Ella put her trunk down for a second and stepped forward to get a better look.

Tibby called after her. 'Stay close, okay? You don't want to be on your own up here. Not at night anyway.' Ella clenched her back teeth – she'd had enough of being bossed around by the orange girl. In the dim light she picked out a tractor and a few pieces of farm machinery. Closer, some broken goal posts and a couple of benches had been stacked against a wall. As she stepped into the middle of the courtyard the sound of the girls behind her deadened and her own footsteps echoed. Suddenly she didn't like it at all. As she turned to go a flicker of light at the far side of the courtyard caught her eye. A curtain twitched behind a grimy window and a shadow retreated into the darkness. Ella shivered and folded her arms across her chest.

'Does someone live here?' she called back over her shoulder, cringing as her voice bounced off the stone walls.

The twin with the red ribbons dropped her trunk. 'Why? Did you see something?'

'Don't be stupid. Of course she didn't,' shouted Tibby. 'Come on, Emma. We all want to get back to the dorm.'.

'It's Ella, E.L.L.A..' She didn't look at Tibby as she picked up her trunk.

The storeroom, illuminated by a single bulb, was full of metal shelving, stacked floor to ceiling with trunks. The wind howled through a gap in a rotten sash-window and Ella loitered by the door, not sure she wanted to venture further in.

'Up there,' said Theresa, the twin with the green ribbons, pointing to a gap. And together they heaved the trunk onto a top shelf.

'Hurry up. Let's not hang about,' said Bernie, who had linked arms with her sister.

Tibby put her hands on either side of her face and gave a ghostly howl. 'Not with the White Lady on the prowl!'

'Shut up, Tibs,' said Theresa. 'You don't want to scare the life out of the New Bug on her first night.'

Great. She was stuck with these stupid posh donkeys. And now there were ghosts. She hated the dark and she hated ghost stories. But she sure as hell wasn't going to let them know that.

⁂

Back in the dorm, Ella sat on the edge of her newly-made bed while Tibby barked orders. She couldn't wait to be alone so that she could shut her eyes and pretend she wasn't here.

'Okay. You take the jug down to the bogs to get water and bring it back here to wash. Afterwards, pour the water from the basin into the bucket and take it down to the bogs to slop it out.' Tibby pointed a nail-bitten finger at the side of the chest of drawers. 'Hang your flannel on this hook and your towel on this one. Got it?'

'Does anyone really give a shit where I hang my towel?' Ella demanded.

'You're not going to get very far with that sort of attitude,' said Tibby. She turned to leave. 'I'm only trying to help.'

Without Tibby, Ella didn't even know how she would eat. And as much as she hated being so useless, she needed this girl's help. 'I'm sorry,' she said, the words sticking in her throat, and echoing in the empty space above her head.

Alone at last Ella washed and changed into her nightdress. She thought about taking her Walkman out of her satchel, but she didn't want to risk having it confiscated and grabbed her book from her bag instead. That morning she had pulled down half a shelf-full of books from Mom's bookcase and had started *My Ántonia* in the car. Pioneers, bitter winter and the unfreezable nature of the pilgrim soul – it had seemed like a good idea at the time.

But now, curled on the hard bed, in the gloom of the dormitory, the words wouldn't go in. She kept thinking about Dad. He would be home by now. He'd be sitting at the kitchen table. She shut her eyes and imagined the smell of him. Pears soap and woolly jumpers. A sob caught her throat, surprising her, and she turned on her back, squeezing her eyes shut. At the far end of the dorm, a small handbell tinkled.

She stood up and watched the others stepping out into the corridor, holding their buckets. Copying them, she turned her bucket upside down and sat on it like Oor Wullie. Sister Cullen, the Wasp-Witch, took the central position on a raised platform at the far end of the dorm.

'Good evening, girls. I trust that you celebrated the birth of our Lord with much reverence. But it's back to work now. Let us lower our heads in prayer.'

The Wasp-Witch's teeth clacked as she motored through a litany of prayers. Most of them were unfamiliar to Ella. She used to go to Mass with Mom and she knew the *Our Father* and the *Hail Mary*, but beyond that she was lost. From her position by the double doors she watched and listened as thirty girls hurtled through prayers and rose in unison to make the sign of the cross.

'No talking now. Disobedience is a sin.'

When the lights went out and all was quiet, Ella lay on her bunk and listened to the sounds of the dormitory. She was in the dark, surrounded by strangers. The pipes groaned, the wind rattled the dormers, and somewhere, a girl was snoring. Up at the Steading that curtain *had* twitched. She had seen it. Was that the White Lady? At home if she was scared, she would have switched on the lights and reached for a P.G. Wodehouse. *Right-Ho, Jeeves* was her go-to comfort read. It was in her satchel. But without a torch, reading wasn't an option. She had no choice but to stay in the darkness.

And then she heard a rustling.

Something was coming closer.

She wasn't imagining it. She really could hear breathing and now it was right beside her.

It was looming over her.

'Fuck!'

It was the Wasp-Witch. 'We'll have none of that language here,' she hissed.

The nun put down a candle and a small plastic font on top of the chest of drawers and picked up Ella's wet flannel as if it were a dead mouse. She hung it on the hook, then, tutting, thrust the font at Ella.

'Lord Jesus Christ, son of the living God,' she muttered. Ella was unsure what was expected of her and stared at the nun who stared right back.

'Lord Jesus Christ, son of the living God,' the nun repeated. If Ella was meant to say something back, she had no idea what it was.

The nun leaned in closer, her breath blowing in Ella's face. 'Have Mercy on me, a sinner. Repeat it. Then Bless yourself.' Ella mumbled the words, dipped her finger in the wet sponge and made the sign of the cross.

When she was gone, Ella lay on her back and stared at the ceiling. She watched the zigzag of the candlelight as the Wasp-Witch made her way, girl by girl, down the dormitory, and disappeared into the darkness. Of all the crazy fucking things that had happened in her lifetime, this was, without a doubt, the craziest fucking freak show of them all.

CHAPTER 16
House of Fun (Madness)

Ella woke before first light to the sound of the Wasp-Witch chanting prayers from the far end of the dorm. She listened to the sleepy responses of the girls who were stirring in their beds and the squeaks of the springs as they arose. Bodies wrapped in dressing-gowns, feet slippered to keep out the cold, shuffled past her cubicle.

'Get your jug, and head to the bogs,' Tibby barked on her way past. Putting her bare feet on the ground Ella felt a draft swirl up through the floorboards. She shivered. Dad had packed neither slippers nor dressing gown and in the dark chill of the January morning her nightshirt did little to insulate her bony frame.

Grabbing her jug, she followed the crowd to the toilet block where lines had formed behind the row of sinks. Girls from other dormitories, older and younger, converged in a shivering mass. She counted twelve sinks, seven or eight girls in every line, ninety-odd pupils queuing up for water. Her feet began to turn blue on the flagstone floor and balancing on one leg she flattened the sole of her right foot down the inside of her other calf to warm it up. Then she swapped legs to warm up the left.

The queue was quiet, the girls still half asleep, but now and again someone broke the silence. 'Fuck-a-duck, it's freezing arseholes in here,' the figure in front muttered through chattering teeth, to no-one in particular. Ella woke up a little.

'And those bloody Bubbers have nicked the hot water again,' shouted Theresa who had already reached the sink.

'They've no respect,' Tibby chipped in. 'When we were in the Upper Second, we had to wait 'til after the seniors to get our water. It's about time those Bubbers learnt their place.'

Back in her cubicle, Ella did her best to lather up enough soap to wash her face. Icy water dribbled down her front, running over her hard nipples that ached from contraction. Shivering, she rubbed herself dry with a towel, trying to heat her goose-pimpled flesh, wishing she could erase herself.

She felt like some pathetic baby, mewling and helpless. She couldn't even speak the language in this bloody awful place. The uncontrollable shivering wasn't just about the temperature in the dorm. Where was she supposed to go to eat breakfast? How would she find the classrooms? What was she meant to wear? She peered over the top of the partition. Where was the spotty orange girl when she needed her?

She waited until the first girls emerged, fully dressed, from their cubicles, then put on the same ridiculous St Trinian's costume as they were wearing and tried not to think what Mikey would say if he could see her now. Just as she was doing up her red tie, Tibby appeared in the doorway accompanied by the twins. 'Not ready yet? Get a move on. We haven't got all day.'

The girls gave Ella a cursory once over. There was no mirror in her cubicle, and she hadn't put on any make-up, but her nose ring was still in place and their eyes lingered on the Docs and her closely shaven head. She was glad about that. Their disapproval made her feel less pathetic and she pulled herself up to her full height and stuck out her chin.

'Good luck getting past Mrs Short with that thing in your nose,' Tibby said, as they headed out into the corridor.

'And wait till she sees your shoes,' said Theresa cheerfully.

'I'm not sure I'd call them shoes exactly,' muttered Bernie.

'Yeah, well, ballet pumps ain't exactly my style,' Ella said, hamming the accent. But no-one was listening.

Up ahead, Mhairi, the Queen Bee, had just walked out of a side door with two of her handmaids, and joined the throng heading towards breakfast.

Tibby lengthened her short strides and rushed ahead, trying to catch up. 'Mhairi. Mhairi. Wait up,' she called, but if Mhairi heard she didn't let on, and Tibby was left behind, looking foolish. As she waited for Ella and the twins, she turned on a group of small girls who were walking arm in arm along the corridor. 'Oi, you lot. Bubbers! Keep to the right or I'll take your Note. And spread the word – if you lot nick all the hot water again there will be an early rise for the whole of the Upper Second.'

'Sorry, Tibby,' they replied in unison, standing aside. When the smallest girl caught sight of Ella her mouth fell open in shock. She stared and nudged her friend to make sure she'd seen too. Ella grinned and winked and the little girls giggled.

'Move it!' Tibby shouted, and the Bubbers shifted further over to the right, standing back to let her pass. Ella had no idea what

Note Tibby was going to take or what an *early rise* was, but the little ones knew. Sure, back at the Leven, the older kids had a kind of power over the younger ones, but this was something altogether different.

As they walked into the dining room, Ella heard the whispers and felt all eyes upon her. She kept her chin up as Tibby pulled her through the crowd, depositing her at what was clearly the designated spot.

'Six girls at every table, one from each year group in the senior school,' Tibby whispered. 'I'm at the table over there. Watch me and don't sit down until I give you the nod.'

An ancient nun sat in a tall wooden pulpit. She waited until the girls were in place, then creaked to her feet and spoke the grace into a crackling microphone.

Ella was about to sit down when she caught Tibby glaring at her. 'Wait…' Tibby mimed, and Ella froze. Girls took their seats at the table in order of seniority. Ella was fourth in line.

The Upper Sixth girl at the table wore a thick purple sash across her chest. 'Seems everyone is talking about you this morning.' Her lips hardly moved, as if it was too much effort to fully form the words. 'If you want some advice, keep a low profile. Fit in or fuck off. That's our motto.'

Ella nodded slowly. She wanted to fuck off. She wanted that very badly. She just wasn't sure how to go about it when she was two hundred miles from home.

The Upper Sixth girl pointed around the table. 'Ginny, Primmy, Dobber, Hattie and me, I'm Bunny.'

Ella snorted a laugh but Bunny, finding nothing funny, stared at her across the table, a sneer distorting the perfect bow of her upper lip. 'Where are your napkins?' she asked, pulling out a drawer in the side of the table and handing napkins to each of the other girls.

Napkins? 'I… em… I haven't got any,' she said.

'Thought not. Ask Mrs Short if she's got any spare. Find her at Soup. She runs the uniform shop.'

'Soup?' Ella asked.

'Breaktime.' Bunny pointed to the double doors. 'We have soup and bread in the foyer just out there.'

Bunny and Ginny, the most senior girls, sat opposite each other in the centre of the table, talking about their Christmas holidays, but for the rest of the girls the meal of grey porridge and runny boiled eggs passed in silence. Ella could hardly eat, even though she was hungry. The food made Dad's cooking look palatable and she wished again that she was at home. She looked around the dining room. One minute she wanted to laugh at this ridiculous place and all the donkeys in it but the next, the reality of it seemed to swallow her like a new kind of black hole.

When the meal was over, Bunny put out her hand and each of the girls rolled up their napkins and handed them over. 'Starting tomorrow, you four will take it in turns to make the toast. Lower Fourther, you'll go first.' Bunny turned to Ella. 'And Eleanor, shadow her. She'll show you how to do it.'

'It's Ella…'

But the girls were already making their way to the door.

As they swarmed out of the dining room, Ella saw Tibby fighting her way against the crowd to reach her. Together they returned to the dormitory to brush their teeth. 'Dorms are out of bounds now 'til after prep,' Tibby explained. 'So, make sure you bring everything you need down to the Form Room or you'll lose your Note. Okay? Now hurry.'

What the hell was this Note she was in danger of losing? She threw *My Ántonia* into her canvas satchel and trailed after the blue ribbon that bounced off Tibby's hip.

***

The Form Room, Ella imagined, might be somewhere warm and relaxing, somewhere she could read or listen to music, that sort of thing. She pictured an open fire, some squashy settees, a bookshelf full of novels. But the minute she looked through the doorway, she was disappointed.

The Form Room was as cold and dark as everywhere else at Saint Cecilia's. Who was Saint Cecilia anyway? The patron saint of miserable places? To be fair, it wasn't quite as dark as the dormitory. At least it had windows you could actually look out of, even if they were barred. But there were no sofas, just twenty wooden desks arranged in four rows of five and twenty hard school chairs. Hard times, indeed. This was Gradgrind grim.

On one wall, small, padlocked boxes (*these must be the tuckboxes*) were stored neatly on shelves, but there was not a book in sight, or a record player, or a fire. The only decoration was a poster of kitten dangling from a branch. *Hang in there*, the slogan read.

Fuck.

Ella stood in the doorway while a ruck of girls tussled over who was sitting where. The voices became louder and increasingly strangulated. Arms flailed. A sob. A shout. A shove. A flying dictionary hit one of the girls on the back of the head: hardback, Collins School edition. *Nasty.*

She couldn't just walk in and pick a seat, not now, while the argument was raging, so she leaned against the doorframe and watched. From the eye of the storm, centre desk, second row from the back, Mhairi, the Queen Bee, was watching too. She fiddled lazily with a small silver medal that she wore on a chain round her neck. Her eyebrows were thick, like Brook Shields in *The Blue Lagoon*, her green eyes, upturned as if the ruckus had nothing to do with her. But it was Mhairi's mouth that held Ella's gaze. Her lips were slightly parted as if she was about to speak and the pink tip of her tongue slithered over her full bottom lip, making it glisten. Ella had to force herself to look away.

On Mhairi's left a small sporty girl with a cropped bob was sitting on a desk, her foot on the edge of Mhairi's chair. On her right the tanned blonde that Ella had seen last night, was filing her nails, an extra sweater draped round her shoulders. *The Holy Trinity.* At the centre of the triumvirate the Queen reigned supreme. The other girls in the Form Room were fighting to be near her. That made sense, Ella supposed. The further they were from the centre, the more vulnerable they would be. It was a matter of survival. She had spent enough time on the outside to understand about that.

Just as the frenzy reached its peak, Mhairi spoke. Her voice was slow and silky, like she had all the time in the world. 'Catriona, little Kit-Kat, sit back here with me. On the other side of Bells.'

A spectacled girl on the front row – Ella guessed this must be Catriona – looked up from her word search. Startled to hear her name, she seemed dazed to find herself in the room at all.

'And Noids,' Mhairi called to the girl who'd thrown the book, 'Come and sit behind us on the back row. You're so clever, you don't need to be near the front. We can always do with some help back here.'

Noids, the book thrower, blinked as if she had just emerged from darkness and sniffing, wiped her nose on the back of her hand. 'Tanks, Mhairi,' she said, her voice thick with snot.

'Grunty, you have the seat next to Tibby on the front row. You two are such great friends.'

Calling them by name, bestowing a special significance to every seat allocation, Ella watched as Mhairi arranged the girls into the remaining seats like flowers in a vase. And like saps, the girls did just as she told them. *What's the matter with them?* Ella thought.

And then, when only one seat remained, to the right of the sporty girl, Mhairi turned to Ella like she'd known she'd been there all along.

'Why don't you have the place next to Dizzy?' Her voice was so quiet that Ella moved forward to hear her. 'It will be lovely to get to know you a bit better. We're so pleased that you've joined us at Saint C's. It's Ella, isn't it? I love the nose ring by the way. So… edgy.'

This seemed like such a kindness in an unkind place that Ella's shoulders dropped, just a bit. Without even thinking about it, she took the seat that she'd been given and stashed her canvas bag in the flip-top belly of the desk.

The noise in the room settled to an ambient hum. *Why did I do that?* she thought. *Why did I do what she told me?*

Tibby called to Mhairi from her desk on the front row. 'It's almost nine. Sister will be here soon. I'll keep *cah-vay*.'

Dizzy, seeing Ella's confusion, leaned over and whispered, 'I had no idea what that meant when I was a New Bug. C.A.V.E. It's Latin for 'beware' or something. Basically, it means she'll tell us when a penguin's coming.'

'Em… thanks.' Ella was unsure how to respond. The girl seemed nice. Friendly even. Her rosy cheeks and turned up nose reminded her of Cass. And then she caught herself. This game was bullshit – the smart thing to do was to keep her distance until she understood the rules. Or at least until she could find a way of getting out of here.

One thing was clear though, Tibby was the gatekeeper. Positioned in the seat by the door it was her job to sniff out intruders. Protect the Queen. Report back when necessary.

'Cave,' Tibby mouthed to the class. Like robots, the girls drew their feet together on the floor in front of them and placed their hands on the desks, loosely clasped. And when the nun stepped into the classroom, the girls, as one, pushed back their chairs and stood to attention. Dizzy kicked Ella's chair leg and motioned for her to stand up. Just in time. The nun stood in front of the group, smiling, her hands tucked into the wide sleeves of her black habit.

'Good-mor-ning-Sis-ter-Gagn-i-er,' they chanted.

'Good morning, mes chères filles. Please, be seated.' The nun smiled, her accent lightly, deliciously French.

Sister Gagnier's little face was framed by the white wimple that drew attention to her tight jaw and high forehead: if it was possible to wear such a garment well, she was doing that. Ella looked more closely. How could someone that young, that lovely, be a nun? Sister Gagnier's eyes were bright and lively and she scanned the room taking in every one of the faces that looked towards her.

'And we have a new girl I see. Ella, welcome to Saint Cecilia's.

I am sure you are going to be very happy here.' She smiled broadly and Ella found herself smiling back.

The remainder of the form period was spent copying down timetables and while the others filled in their small blue diaries, Sister Gagnier called her forward to sit by the desk. She seemed unhurried, as if all her attention was focused upon Ella. And something about her reminded Ella of Dad, or of how Dad used to be, before.

Slowly, carefully, Sister Gagnier explained the shape of the school days, the classes Ella would attend, and about the mysterious system of *Notes*. All girls began the week as 'very good' but Notes, she explained, could be 'taken' for bad manners, lateness, the usual stuff. At assembly on Fridays the headmistress handed them out.

'Only rarely,' Sister Gagnier put a small hand on her heart to show her distress at the thought of it, 'have any of my girls been 'fair', and never, ever, has one of my girls been 'indifferent'. Non, ma chère, my girls are *good* girls.' She winked. 'Or even better, *very* good girls, and I know you are going to be one of them, Ella. You will not let me down.'

Ella found herself smiling back, enchanted by the gentle voice, the sophisticated accent, the enigma of this pretty woman who had chosen a life like this. Sister Gagnier did not recoil from the nose ring or the shaved head, instead she looked straight at Ella. Eye to eye. And Ella had the strongest sensation that she was being seen for who she really was. Whoever that might be.

***

On the way to the first lesson Ella noticed that the girls stuck with the others from the row they'd been assigned. Tibby led the front line, looking back to check that Ella was heading in the right direction. Ella's group, the third row, seemed to observe an even stricter hierarchy. They formed a v-shape, like the Red Arrows, with Mhairi out in front. Behind her, and a little to either side, walked Dizzy and Bells. And behind them, Ella and Catriona instinctively fell into line.

'We've got Biology next,' said Bells looking back to Catriona and Ella, the outliers of the phalanx, making certain they understood.

Ella was unsure how she felt about being drawn into the colony, but she had no idea how to get to Biology without them, so she decided to play along. Besides, she'd rather be with this lot than with Tibby. There was something ruthless about the orange terrier that was beginning to set her teeth on edge.

For the rest of the morning she was swept along to classrooms scattered across the campus. She couldn't believe how big this place was and how different it was from the Leven. There were classrooms up spiral staircases, in grand ballrooms and Nissen huts. And it took them ten full minutes to walk from the science block to the dusty Geography room. The girls called out greetings to each other and to the teachers as they passed. Everything was old and shabby. The corridors were decorated with posters that spouted motivational messages and pictures of old men in costumes that she suspected might be popes.

At breaktime – Soup – they headed to the foyer outside the dining room.

'Watch out for Shortie, she's always on the war path at the start of term,' warned Dizzy, the chattiest of the group. As they turned into a narrow corridor the girls shifted position without anyone saying a word. Suddenly Ella was in the middle. 'Head down,' Dizzy whispered. But Ella, even with her head down, towered above the girls who stood on either side.

'New girl!' a woman called.

They kept walking.

'Stop at once!'

They pretended not to hear.

'Fenella Douglas-Cook. I know you can hear me. Bring that new girl over here this instant or I will take your Note.'

'We'd better do as she says. Sozzer.' Dizzy, or Fenella or whatever-the-fuck she was called, pulled her across the stream of girls heading for Soup to a small office lined with shelves of folded uniforms. Mrs Short was waiting for her beneath a framed photograph of Margaret Thatcher. Blue suit. Frilly blouse.

Ella wondered about offering a salute, but Mrs Short was not one for preliminaries.

'No, no, no. This will not do at all.' She shook her head and looked despairingly at Ella as if she didn't know where to start.

Her accent was clipped and emphatic. It was the first Scottish voice Ella had heard since she arrived. 'The hair. Well, there's nothing I can do about that. A wig is out of the question. It will grow I suppose. But the nose. In all my years at Saint Cecilia's, this is a first. The nose will have to go.'

'The nose, Mrs Short? Surely you're not going to confiscate her nose?'

'Don't be fresh with me, Fenella. You know fine well what I mean. That thing. That earring in her nose. It's got to go. Take it out right now. What's your name?'

134

'Ella. Ella Richardson.'

'American. That explains it.'

Mhairi and Bells had disappeared, but Dizzy and Catriona stood stock still and silent. 'I'm waiting. Take it out.' She clicked her fingers and opened her palm.

Ella stared back, defiant. 'I can't take it out. The hole will close up.'

'That's exactly what I'm hoping for. Come on.'

Ella bit her lip. She wasn't going to win this one. The narrow corridor was crammed with girls and there was no escape.

Mrs Short clicked again. 'I haven't got all day. Your soup will be cold at this rate.'

Ella would do what this woman asked but only because she had another nose ring in her satchel. In fact, she had a whole bag of them. Cass had sent them to her for Christmas. It was the best present she'd received. She would put a new one in as soon as she could. Fumbling, she took out the hoop.

But Mrs Short wasn't finished. 'Your tunic is far too long and as for those boots. What do you think you look like? We have young ladies at Saint Cecilia's, not yobbos. Dignity and Decorum. That's what we expect. Dignity and Decorum. And you'll get on much better if you remember that.'

Dizzy held out her hand to one side and Catriona slapped it as if some silent wager had been won.

'What size are your feet, Emma?'

'It's Ella. And they're eight and a halfs.'

'Jeezy-peeps, they're enormous. I don't think I have a spare pair in that size, but I'll see what I can do.'

Ella dropped her nose ring into the middle of the outstretched palm and the woman's nostrils flared as she picked it up with a thumb and forefinger, pinkie outstretched, as if she was carrying something toxic. 'Into the bin it goes. Right. Off you go and get your soup, girls. You'll be needing something to warm you up. It's raw out there today.'

CHAPTER 17

The Milkman of Human Kindness
(Billy Bragg)

'Are you settling in okay?' Catriona fiddled with the cap of her shampoo bottle.

It was bath night and she and Ella sat on the top step of a narrow spiral staircase, towels over their arms, waiting for their turn. There were rotas for everything at Saint Cecilia's, even bath-times. Three baths per week. No showers after games.

Ella felt dirty all the time. She couldn't strip wash in her cube with the constant stream of people going past her open doorway and at night under the covers, she hated the smell of her own body – feet and sweat and period.

Her bath nights were Tuesdays, Thursdays and Sundays, same as Catriona's. They had a middle slot: after a Bubber, before an Upper Sixther. Ella was catching on with the lingo.

'Yeah, I suppose so,' she shrugged.

At hockey that day Catriona had spotted that Ella didn't know how to play. She'd picked her as a partner and was patient when

Ella fluffed the warm-ups. Another girl might have made her feel like an idiot. Catriona didn't.

'Not many girls lose their Note in the first month. You're practically famous.'

For the last few weeks Ella had been locked in combat with Mrs Short. Every time she saw Ella, she made her take out her nose ring. And every time Ella took one out, she replaced it with another. Her supply was starting to run low.

Catriona had short mousey hair and pale blue eyes that were magnified by her glasses. She was quiet when they were with the third row, but now that it was just the two of them she had much more to say. 'I hated this place when I first came. I wasn't a Bubber, but I still cried myself to sleep every night for a month – and nobody likes a cry-baby. I got used to it eventually. It gets easier, honest. I expect you're missing home dreadfully.'

Ella thought of her echoing house – Dad in his study, the kitchen piled high with plates. She hated it, but she missed it so much that it hurt. 'I suppose.'

'It's normal to be homesick. Now it's the food I miss the most. That and Indie, our black Labrador. Do you have a dog?'

'No. No pets.'

'Oh, that's a shame. Still, one less thing to miss I suppose. I bet you're really missing your home friends. Have they written?'

Friends. Who were they? Not Nicola, not anymore. Cass and Mikey? Cass had sent her the nose rings at Christmas, but she wasn't even sure if they knew she was here. 'They're not really the writing sort,' she said.

Catriona tipped her head, listening. 'Sounds like your Bubber has pulled out the plug. Don't wallow too long, Felicity Walsh is in after you. She's a Purple Ribbon and a total bitch-face. She'll take your Note if you make her wait again.'

The bathroom contained a chair and a giant enamel bath with claw feet and huge brass taps, a tiny mirror, nothing more. On the back of the door a notice read:

Rules for Bathing
1.   Girls are not permitted to lock the door.
2.   Baths must not exceed six inches in depth.
3.   Ablutions must be completed within 5 minutes.
4.   The bath must be washed out as a courtesy to the next user.

Fuck that. This was the first time she'd been on her own for days. Ella locked the door.

Water flowed fast through the ancient pipes and within minutes the room was foggy. She lay in the bath with the taps still running and the water closed in around her white body, until the islands of her hips, her belly and her breasts were submerged too. She thought of Mikey and the last time she had seen him, about her fingers touching his jaw. And shutting her eyes, she ran the soap over her nipples, down her belly to her pubic mound, imagining his fingers on her.

The door rattled. 'Oi! This door's locked. What are you up to in there?' Felicity Walsh was pulling on the handle. 'Right, that's it. I'm taking your Note.'

***

A few days later, after a hockey lesson, the PE Teacher, Miss Johnson, called Ella to one side. 'You're tall,' she said, as though Ella may not have noticed. 'And you were pretty fast up the wing once you got the hang of it. But it's too late for you to get into a decent team - these girls have been playing since they were seven or eight. You've the makings of a runner, though. Cross country might be your thing. We've got some fixtures in the calendar later this term.' She dug in her kit bag. 'Here's a map of the circuit. We call it the Pilgrimage. And this is a permission slip, in case you need it.'

Ella folded the pieces of paper and put them in her pocket.

When the afternoon lessons finished, and the girls were heading to the dining room for a snack, Ella slipped back to the dorm to change into her kit.

She wasn't meant to be there, she knew that, but that made it all the better. An illicit run. The light would be fading soon, and she wanted to get out before it got properly dark. She pulled tight on the laces of her trainers, put on her headphones, switched the volume up to max and felt the thrill of escape power her limbs.

The rain turned to sleet as she headed down the drive towards the village of Belgaddie. The shock of the cold drained blood from her extremities, and she shook her white fingers to bring back the circulation. She had missed this. It was good to run again, to stretch out her long legs and feel the pounding rhythm jolt through her frame, to put distance between herself and the school. To shake it off her back.

As gravel gave way to tarmac, she speeded up and her breathing became deeper and faster. She had a running mixtape that she had recorded herself. Stuff off the radio. From the charts. *Kids in America. Start me up. 9 to 5.* She'd die if Mikey ever found out that she listened to this shit, but it was good to run to. It kept her going.

Images, like snapshots in a viewfinder, registered with the blink of an eye: a church, a post office, a pub, a campsite, an army barracks. And by the time she was hammering through muddy furrows, the village far behind her, hot blood was flowing once again.

As she approached the hill – Ben Drum, Catriona had called it – the sleet stopped, and a fog descended. Ella had seen the hill from the playing fields, imagined climbing to the top, but today the summit was lost in heavy cloud, so she stuck to the route that skirted around the bottom before looping back towards Saint C's.

She stopped to get her bearings. Her wet aertex clung to her shoulders and she cooled down quickly as she checked the map. There was the school, the sprawling outbuildings and the Steading where she'd stored her trunk. The huge granite weight of it squatted in the mist, flattening the earth like a hunkered toad. It had been flattening her too. But now, from this distance, she was free of it and could breathe deep.

The light was fading as she rounded the playing fields and made her way towards the woods which stood between her and the dormitories. The narrow path was lined with fir trees whose height and girth obliterated the last of the daytime. She could smell their piny-ness and behind that the odour of mould, mud and decay. The ground underfoot was thick with needles and her footsteps landed softly as if she was running on carpet. She counted the steps between the trees. Fifteen long strides. *Not too fast, keep it steady.*

But soon the trees were closer together and it was harder to pick out the path. In the gloaming she tripped, twisting on a root, righting herself just in time. Her chest was heaving now, and breath condensed on her nose and mouth. She wiped her face with the back of her hand. Beneath her feet a tangle of brambles slowed her to a stop.

She looked around and a surge of panic caught her chest. Where was she? Heat radiated from her in a steamy cloud, and she put her hands on her hips, tilting forward to find her breath. She switched off the music. And then, in an instant, the darkness lifted. Between the trunks of two giant redwoods, the moon, a thumb nail of silver, shot light through the branches.

Encouraged, Ella pushed away boughs with her hands until she broke into a clearing. Right in the heart of all that thick woodland, a glade opened out, like something from a storybook, and she ran into the centre to take it all in. Long and oval, the grassy clearing was surrounded by tight bushes, rhododendrons mostly, and other smaller shrubs. Both the setting sun and the rising moon were visible, at either end of the glade, and the space in between filled with cool winter light.

Like a needle on a compass, Ella turned, stopping dead when a single tree caught her eye. It was a redwood, standing tall in the centre of the northern edge, the ground around it clear. She made her way over to take a closer look.

Just above head height, a painted statue of the Virgin Mary, garlanded with roses and haloed by the moon, had been fixed to the corky trunk. Ella stood for a moment and looked at it, but the eyes seemed to be staring and she turned away, disquieted. She was cooling down quickly and pulled her arms about her, looking over her shoulder to check she was still alone.

Beneath the tree, poking up through the leaf mould she spotted the first green blades of snowdrops and knelt to take a closer look. Reaching out to pick a white flower she spotted something that made her hand shoot back as if she'd touched a live wire.

Small and bleached white, a tiny cross pushed through the grass. And then she saw that there was not one cross, but dozens. All made from sticks and bound with dried grass or strips of bark, some no bigger than her thumb. The crosses encircled the base of the tree. And in amongst the crosses there were skulls. A mouse. A crow. And something bigger. Unidentifiable. A chill wind disturbed the leaf litter and icy water seemed to run down Ella's spine. Was this a shrine? A burial site?

From somewhere in the woods the gurgling kraa of a raven warned her off. Whatever this place was, she shouldn't be here. She had to get away. And fast.

She sprinted through the woods, stumbling on tree roots and rocks until, at last, she saw the security light outside the dormitories, flooding the path and the side of the mansion house. Leaving a trail of muddy footprints she sprinted towards the dorm and into her cubicle where she bumped straight into Tibby and the twins.

'There you are! We've been looking for you everywhere,' the orange terrier snapped. 'The dorm is out of bounds 'til after supper. Why are you so muddy? You'll be for it, if Sister catches you.'

'I was running. Miss Johnson told me I could.' She hated the sound of her own simpering voice.

'Running? Well, why didn't you tell somebody? We've wasted an hour looking for you.'

'Well, ta-dah, here I am.' Ella stretched out her arms like a magician's assistant. 'I didn't think I needed your permission.'

Tibby pursed her lips. 'That's the trouble with some people, isn't it? They just don't think.'

Ella glared back. She imagined sketching Tibby in Biro – a wiry terrier, head-first down a rabbit hole, shaking her orange arse. She couldn't help smiling at the thought.

Tibby, unnerved, took a step back. 'Well, what are you waiting for? Get changed. We're going to be late for supper at this rate.'

CHAPTER 18
A Town Called Malice (The Jam)

On Fridays the whole school gathered in the Gym for Notes. The girls sat in rows on either side of a wide aisle, facing the centre, and the Bulldog sat behind a desk in the middle of the stage, the teachers and penguins arranged about her. Forms were called forward one at a time, and the girls waited in a line down the centre until their Note was read out by their form teacher.

Ella stood with the rest of the Lower Fifth turning over a ten pence piece in the bottom of her pocket. *Heads: kick-ass Ella who doesn't give a shit. Tails: poor little Ella who wants to run and hide.*

'Ella Richardson,' Sister Gagnier's voice wobbled, 'Fair.'

There was a collective gasp as the Note was called. And kick-ass Ella made her way up the steps. She had her nose ring in, her boots were laced in red, and she ran a hand over the velvet of her head. Everybody would be staring at her. Her hair – like moleskin now – was the only thing anybody wanted to talk to her about. Even Catriona had asked if she could stroke her head last night.

Ella didn't look at Sister Gagnier, she'd heard the disappointment in her voice. Instead, she fixed her gaze on the headmistress, whose flinty eyes stared back.

'Thank you so much, Sister,' Ella said, flashing a fake smile and plucking the yellow Note from the nun's plump grasp.

Returning to her seat, she squeezed along the row of girls.

'Okay?' Catriona whispered.

'Yeah,' she whispered back.

There was a knot in Ella's stomach that never went away, its energy vibrated, and sometimes she liked doing things that made others feel it too. Their shock felt almost like connection. She looked at down at the small rectangle of cardboard, at the word that read, 'Fair'. It wasn't hard to shock them at Saint C's.

***

On Sunday night, Ella was lying on her bed reading *My Ántonia*. The pioneers' adventures out on the prairie – dug outs, wolf attacks, snakes, and pumpkin pies –reminded her of the Laura Ingalls Wilder books she had read so long ago, and she was lost in the story when Catriona burst into her cube. 'Sister's on the war path,' she warned, 'and there's smoke coming out of her ears.'

Seconds later the Wasp-Witch appeared, lips twitching beneath the tip of her pointed nose. 'Does this belong to you?' she said, holding up a red laundry bag.

Ella and the others had gone straight to the dormitory after supper. Sunday night was laundry night and Tibby had given her a pencil and a check list to tick off her washing as she put it into the bag. It had seemed simple enough. 'Maybe. Did I do something wrong?'

'Well how, may I ask, are we expected to know that this

laundry bag is yours, since neither the bag, nor any of the items in it are labelled? No name tapes at all. Not a single one.'

Ella wasn't really sure what she was talking about. But she was used to that.

'Open these drawers.'

'Sorry?'

'The drawers. Open them.'

Ella pulled open the top drawer of the chest to reveal an assorted jumble of clothes.

'In the name of all that's holy, will you look at this,' the nun hissed to an invisible ally. 'You were told, were you not, that the top drawer is for undergarments?' She pulled out an aertex and looked on the inside of the collar. Then, tugging open the remaining drawers, she sucked air through her teeth. 'Just as I thought, not a single item is named. Not a one. It plainly states on the uniform list that all items must be clearly labelled with Cash's woven name tapes.'

The nun dug around in the drawer and pulled out a bundle of white strips held together with a twist of wire. 'These will be the name tapes. They're not going to be much use to anyone sitting here, are they?'

Ella had found the bundle when she'd unpacked the trunk, but unsure what to do with them she'd buried them with the giant grey knickers that she'd never worn.

'What makes you so special, eh? Your father should have taken care of this. Or does he think there's one rule for him and another for everyone else?'

Ella jolted at the mention of Dad. She could say what she liked about him but the Wasp-Witch had no business talking about him like that.

'Nothing to say for yourself. I thought as much.'

Ella was so close to this woman she could smell the carbolic. It was anaesthetising her.

'Lay out uniform for tomorrow and bring the rest to me. You'll be off games until everything's labelled.'

'Off games? You mean I won't be able to run?'

'No, you will not. Now gather up the whole lot. And bring it to me.'

'All of it? You want me to bring *all* of my clothes to you?'

'And the duvet covers, the towels, the lot. Bring it all up to the dais and leave it beside my stool. The girls should see just how selfish some people can be.'

While the girls chatted in clusters along the corridor, Ella went back and forward to the raised platform at the far end of the dorm, piling her belongings in a heap. The more enormous the pile grew, the more exposed Ella felt. Her belongings were on display for all the world to see, and she shrank at the thought of it.

At prayers, the light was adjusted to shine upon the heap, to bare her shame beneath the spotlight. There was no mistaking the judgement in the other girl's glances. And when Mhairi pushed past her without a 'goodnight,' she knew she was in trouble.

Sitting on the toilet with her head in her hands, Ella felt very far from anything that made sense. Why did anyone care about name tapes? What had she done that was so wrong? She was so different from these posh girls with their flicky fringes and their plummy voices. She didn't understand them, and would never fit in. Not here. Not anywhere. Mom had said, *be yourself. The world doesn't need more followers. It needs people who dance to the beat of their own drum.* And she'd tried. She'd tried so hard to do that.

But sometimes she felt so achingly lonely that she didn't think she could breathe.

'Ella? Is that you?' a little voice whispered through the stall wall. It was Catriona.

'Don't worry about them, Ella. They're only pissed off because they were planning a midnight walk tonight and now that Cullen's sewing on all those labels there's no chance of sneaking out. She'll be at it till midnight for days. But don't worry, they'll get over it.'

A midnight walk? Seriously? The girls here all seemed so stuck-up and sanctimonious, she never thought they'd break the rules. There was a lot she still didn't know about this place. But at least some of it made sense now. No wonder they were pissed off with her. She'd spoilt their fun.

'Thanks, Catriona. I didn't know about the labels.'

'Didn't your mum have time to sew them on?'

Ella sat for a second. She'd never said the words out loud.

'Ella?'

'I… I don't have a mum. She died when I was twelve.'

***

Night after night the Wasp-Witch sat on her stool, her false teeth clacking as she sucked her way through Ella's toffees, making herself a martyr. She creaked as she walked and at prayers petitioned Our Lady for the mortification of the flesh. Hunched low over her needle, eyes straining to see, her head appeared to have dropped to the middle of her torso. And while the heap seemed to get no smaller, the constant presence of the nun put the girls on edge and made Ella feel like public enemy number one.

Without her kit, she was signed off games and condemned to

spend every afternoon indoors in the designated classroom. Noids was there with a handkerchief and a hot water bottle that she'd been given by Sister Forsyth in the San. Reading was forbidden during 'off games'. Instead, the crypt-keeper of a nun who was wheeled out for such sedentary duty, instructed them to pray for the truly sick and those in peril on the sea. It was unbearable.

By Tuesday Ella had come up with a plan.

'Sister, might it be possible for me to say my prayers in the Chapel?' She tried to sound like she was gripped by devotion. Catriona had told her that the penguins were always on the lookout for potential recruits. 'It's so beautiful and the Great Window really lifts my spirits.' She sounded so sycophantic she thought she might be sick.

The ancient crone sat up a little straighter in her chair, 'Of course, my child. I remember when the Great Window was installed. Back in 1925. I was a young nun then, of course, but what a blessing…'

Ella interrupted her. 'Oh Sister, I would so love to get to the Chapel and get started on my prayers.' *Gag.*

'Go, my child. Go.'

The Chapel was deserted and Ella stood for a moment in the nave, looking at the abstract stained-glass window. It formed the whole of the rear wall behind the altar. In front of it, a wooden Christ was crucified on colossal iron girders which stretched from wall to wall and ceiling to floor. In the low winter light, the Chapel was flooded with shards of colour that reached out towards her like jewelled fingers. Her hands were illuminated, one red, one green, and she turned them palms up and let the light spill through her open fingers.

Today, Ella wanted to be hidden, to discover a quiet corner where no-one would find her, and she crossed to the Lady Chapel over on the right. Here, two creamy candles provided the only lighting and the air was thick with the smell of wax and incense. Sliding along a pew she pulled her feet up on the bench and, using a kneeler as a back rest, leaned against the wall. This felt like a place of safety, an escape from the ever-present company of girls.

At the Leven she was an expert at avoiding people, but here there were so few places to hide. The girls made it look easy – friendship – like it had been with Nicola, once. She couldn't deny that it was nice, sitting on the stairs with Catriona, and Dizzy was pretty decent too. They didn't seem to care about the name tapes. But Mhairi, and Bells, were still ignoring her. And she missed them. Kind of. No. It was better to be on her own. Safer.

She pulled a book from her satchel. She'd finished *My Ántonia* and had selected an old copy of *Little Women* from her stash. She'd smiled at the idea of reading it at Saint Cecilia's, where the little women were everywhere. Most of them were Amys. She'd read it before, of course, more than once. It was Mom's favourite and when she read, it was Mom's voice she heard, smooth and liquid like there was no effort in the words.

And as she read her tight jaw slackened, her body relaxed for the first time in weeks and she curled up her legs, losing herself in the story. She was Jo, of course, not bound by convention, and she was delighting in Mr Laurence's library, when she heard the music. Gentle tinkling, almost like a harp. At first, she thought she was imagining it, but after a moment she realised the sound was coming from behind her. She'd never heard anything like it before.

She straightened in her seat, afraid that if she looked round the music would stop, and she didn't want it to end. But curiosity got the better of her and, turning very slowly, as if sudden movement might startle the birds, she saw a girl – or was it a woman – bent over an instrument partially hidden by the pew. She wasn't a Saint C's girl, she was older than that. Her long black hair was covered by a white mantilla – a beautifully crafted triangle of lace which looked old and fragile. Ella had been given one when she made her First Holy Communion, but hers looked nothing like this, it was more like a triangle cut from a net curtain.

Looking up from her playing, the woman saw Ella and fluttered as if she was about to take flight. Ella held her breath. Like a dream that disappears the moment you waken, the music evaporated, all trace of it gone.

'I should not be here,' said the woman, in a tiny, accented voice that chimed like her instrument. 'It is forbidden.'

'Don't go,' said Ella, taking her feet off the bench. 'I'm leaving in a minute, and your playing is... so beautiful.'

The woman settled a little and dipped her head in a gesture of humility. 'Thank you,' she said.

Ella usually avoided speaking to strangers, but for some reason she didn't want this woman to leave. 'What instrument are you playing? I've never heard it before.'

'It is a lyre,' she replied uncertainly. 'We brought it from Hungary.'

'It's lovely. I think that might be what it sounds like in heaven,' said Ella, emboldened.

'When I play, I *am* in heaven,' said the woman. A smile broke through her shyness, simple and honest as the snowdrops that had been placed upon the altar.

'I'm Ella, by the way.'

'And I am Magda.'

The following day, while the others were at games, Ella took her book to the Lady Chapel in search of solitude again. But, just as before, she was soon joined by Magda. The same happened on Thursday. On Friday, Ella made her way there as swiftly as she could, hoping Magda would be there.

Slowly, tentatively, in the stillness of the candlelight, they became acclimatised to each other's company, comfortable sharing the same space. They spoke little. And Ella liked it that way. She read while Magda played, the music seeping into her through the cracks and chinks, her long legs stretching out along the bench.

***

On Saturday, before lunch, Catriona took Ella to the menagerie in the shed behind the science labs.

'I can't believe you've not been before. I love it here. You're looking a bit happier. Told you it wouldn't take too long to settle in,' said Catriona.

She was a bit happier. She supposed. Saint Cecilia's felt like a different world to the one that had Mikey in it – the squat, the City Square, the punks. On the outside people had been angry about everything – seatbelts, Maggie Thatcher, the Falklands war. In here, all that stuff seemed to pass them by. The girls talked about taffeta, Duran Duran and eightsome reels, and nobody seemed angry about anything much. It bored Ella rigid.

Catriona lifted a rabbit out of its hutch. 'The Bubbers keep their pets here; it makes them feel a bit less sad.'

'They bring them with them?'

Catriona nodded.

Ella fed the rabbit a chunk of carrot while Catriona stroked its ultra-soft ears.

'I had a rabbit,' Catriona said. 'We called him Jet, because he was jet black.'

'Imaginative,' said Ella.

'Yeah,' Catriona smiled. 'I loved him.'

'Do you still have him?' said Ella, more gently now, sensing the story might not end well.

'No. Mummy gave him to our cleaner's daughter.' Catriona kissed the top of the rabbit's head and put it back into its hutch. 'She said he was pining for me and that it was unfair to keep him. That was probably an excuse, now that I think about it.'

Afterwards, as they walked back to the dining room, Ella asked Catriona about Magda. 'Do you know anything about a Hungarian woman who hangs about in the Chapel?'

'Who? No. I don't think so.' Catriona screwed up her nose, as she often did when she was thinking. 'Wait… Maybe, I do know who you're talking about. Bells told us about her, a long time ago. Bells and Mhairi have been here since Upper Second. They know everything. I think Bells said the girl and her mum came here years ago to escape from a revolution or something – all very dramatic.'

'Really? That sounds awful. I wonder how old Magda was when she arrived?'

'I don't know. I've never seen her. Or her mum. I'm sure Bells said they work in the vegetable garden or something like that. You know, to earn their keep. The young one – Magda you said her name was? – used to help with the Bubbers' gardening club. Something like that. Bells would know. The school and the

154

grounds are out of bounds for them, I think. There was a rumour that they live up at the Steading, I think. The nuns let them stay there for free.'

'The Steading?' Ella asked. 'That place where we keep our luggage? Where the mouldy Latin classrooms are?'

'Yes, that's the place. It's a dump isn't it? Creepy.'

Ella remembered her first night, the candlelight and the twitching curtain. Maybe it hadn't been her imagination after all.

***

It took the Wasp-Witch five long nights to finish sewing the labels onto Ella's belongings. It wasn't easy to get to sleep with all the clacking and sucking, the susurrations of her chanted prayers. 'She's saying a novena,' Bernie had told her. 'She's praying for your soul.'

Sister Cullen didn't need beads to say her rosary. The prayers had long since been committed to memory, and she counted the prayers by tapping her foot, leaving her dry fingers available for the needle and her rheumy eyes free to squint at the task. The nun may have been praying for Ella's soul, but the pain of the stitching and the hardness of the stool were a self-flagellation all of her own. The Wasp-Witch was saving herself, cleansing her own soul, one stitch at a time. And for what, Ella wondered, was the Wasp-Witch shriving? Wrath? Greed? Lust? Pride?

It was after midnight when the nun woke Ella. 'You can collect your belongings first thing in the morning. And put everything away properly this time. We'll have no more of your slovenly ways. *Whoever is lazy regarding his work is also a brother to the master of destruction.*'

And with that the Wasp-Witch retreated to her cell in the attic and the dorm belonged to the girls once again.

CHAPTER 19

Just What I Always Wanted (Mari Wilson)

By the end of February, the shape of Ella's days and hours had frozen into a kind of solid intransigence. The routines and the rules and the lack of privacy bore down on her like a giant thumb. And every day she felt a little further from home, from Dad and from herself.

To stop herself from vanishing she looked for the cracks, the chinks in the system that were just wide enough to squeeze through. She slipped in one of her nose rings whenever Shorty's back was turned and in the absence of any 'suitable' size 8½ shoes, the DMs stayed firmly on her feet. Her hair was growing, and she spiked it with her fingers into tufts. For every time she was sent out of class to wash the black eyeliner off her face, there was another when she dived into the loos to reapply it even thicker than before.

And she could run again.

Whenever she could, she put on her headphones and bolted through the front gates, filling her lungs with the cold, sharp air, and pumping her legs till they screamed. She ran further and harder as the daylight hours stretched, out past the barracks and up Ben Drum. And the more she ran the quieter the noise in her head became. She re-entered her body, felt the thud as her feet struck the earth, the in-breath and the out, the beat, the beat, the beat, until she was a living thing again, hot with breath and blood and spit. Nobody ever asked her where she went, so she made up her own rules. She ran until she was no more than a body, a working, heaving organism, connected with the earth and the air, in circuit. She was alive and alone, her living breathing self.

She stuck to the open, avoiding the woods with the creepy tree, but although she tried her best, every time she crossed the playing fields, and the school came back into view, her head filled up with noise once more. By the time she reached the dormitory, her heartbeat had slowed, and she was lost to herself again.

***

Every breaktime, once they had dodged Shorty outside the uniform shop and picked up their mail from the pigeonholes, Mhairi, Dizzy and Bells would disappear, leaving Ella and Catriona to have their soup alone. She preferred it when it was just the two of them; she never felt awkward when they were on their own.

She didn't get much mail compared to the others. Nothing interesting anyway. The other girls were always picking up letters from boys at posh public schools and parcels containing magazines, stationery and tuck. At first she had hoped there might be something from Mikey, a note from Cass. But nothing came, and gradually her disappointment faded. Last week, though, a parcel had arrived. A tin of homemade shortbread from Mrs Stout. She had shared it with Catriona and the girls from the third row, now that Mhairi and Bells were talking to her again, and for a few hours Ella had known what it felt like to be one of the gang.

Most days, there was a postcard from Dad in her pigeonhole. She had a stack of them now. Sometimes she didn't bother looking at them. She told herself it was because they were boring, that he never wrote anything worth reading, but in truth it hurt her to have him brought so close.

In the foyer outside the dining room, while Catriona collected the soup and rolls, she turned today's card over and looked at the picture. The University of Dundee, in glorious technicolour. Begonias in tight formation created stripes of colour in the formal beds, a sundial at the centre of the manicured lawn. Dad had written the word 'me' and drawn an arrow that pointed to a little smiley face in a third-floor window.

Mom's handwriting had been unruly and expansive, her looping gs catching the letters from the line below in their basket. Dad's handwriting was small and tight, like the begonias.

Hi Ella,

> *Hope everything's going well and that you've made some nice friends. I'm sure you're busy, but it would be great to hear from you. Everything's fine here. Margo's baby was born on Monday. It's a boy! They've called him Franz after Franz Boas, the American anthropologist. A bit hard to live with in Dundee, maybe(!) but who knows, maybe he'll be a Frankie. Anyway, it's good that the days are getting a bit longer. Hope you're eating enough – I bet the nuns are great cooks!*

> > *Much love, Dad xxx*

The old fire stirred in her belly and she swallowed hard, shoving the card into the front pocket of her satchel with all the rest. She wouldn't reply. This life that was happening here, was happening despite him, not because of him. He had abandoned her and deserved to know nothing.

Catriona handed her a plastic beaker and she took a sip of the tepid lentil soup. Hard pulses floated in carroty dishwater.

'Where do they go?' Ella asked. Not that she missed the rest of the third row. In truth, she was relieved to be free of them. Mhairi made her jittery, self-conscious. She acted differently around her. Everyone did. But she was curious nonetheless.

Catriona held the beaker of soup in two hands, warming her fingers. Her knuckles were red and swollen with the chilblains that plagued so many of the girls and which had appeared, hot and itchy, on Ella's bony toes.

'Where do who go? Mhairi and the girls?'

Ella nodded.

'Oh, I don't know. The smokers have their favourite haunts. Usually they go out into the woods, but in this rain, they'll be crammed into a bog somewhere.'

'You're joking! Mhairi's a smoker? She always seems so bloody perfect!'

Catriona leaned in and whispered conspiratorially, 'Smoking's the least of it! She gets away with anything because the penguins are all in love with her.' She looked over her shoulder to check no-one was listening. 'Her family are massive donors. The science lab is named after her granny or something.'

'Really? And what about you? Why don't you go with them?'

Catriona laughed as if the idea was silly. 'Me? Oh, I'm not part of their group. I mean, I know we're sitting in the third row and all, but we're only there as long as they say so, we're not Cecilians, and anyway, cigarettes make me cough. I tried one time at Dizzy's party, but I coughed so much I nearly spewed. Not cool.' She made a face at the memory.

Ella was just about to ask her what a Cecilian was, when a hand on Catriona's shoulder made them jump.

It was Mhairi.

'What made you puke, little Kit-Kat?' She tilted her head to one side and raised an eyebrow just a fraction.

Ella took a sip of her watery soup and tried to look like she wasn't ruffled, while Catriona squirmed to find an answer.

'Oh… Mhairi… we were just talking about what an idiot I am. Weren't we Ella?'

Ella frowned. Why did Catriona do that? Put herself down when Mhairi was around?

Mhairi cautioned them with a stone-cold smile.

Ella detected a faint whiff of cigarette smoke cut through with the stronger smell of *Poison*. Her mind shot to a different world: Cass and her top tip for disguising the smell of alcohol. *A quick scoosh tae the tongue.* Maybe the two worlds weren't so different after all.

***

Their next lesson, Religious Studies, was taught by a plain-clothed nun – a penguin in a paper bag, as Dizzy called them. She was unusual for a nun, by virtue of the sole fact that there was nothing unusual about her. The nuns, with the exception of Sister Gagnier, seemed to Ella an extraordinarily ugly bunch. Some were cadaverous with sunken eyes and skulls that protruded beneath the skin, others were corpulent and breathless, with massive chests that heaved under the tabards of their habits. As far as she could see they were a sisterhood of the aesthetically blighted, escaping the harsh judgement of society and taking their rejection out on the girls. But Sister Fraser, the RS Teacher, was absolutely ordinary. She had no discernible accent, her hair appeared to have been cut by someone other than herself, and her face looked familiar, like Nicola's mum. 'Sister Fraser has a car,' Catriona told her. 'She can even drive the mini-bus.'

They were learning about the lives of the saints, and a television on a metal stand with a video player underneath was wheeled in by John the caretaker, at the start of the lesson.

Sister Fraser shut the blinds. 'Make yourselves comfortable, girls. Take your shoes off if you like. I know it's in black and white and a bit old-fashioned but try to lose yourself in the story. Bernadette Soubirou was your age when the Blessed Virgin appeared to her. And now millions of people flock to Lourdes every year to see the shrine. Imagine that. An ordinary girl, like all of you.'

It took ages to untie her boots and by the time she took them off the rest of the girls had dragged their desks closer to the large television set and had laid their heads down on their arms.

'Come and sit by me,' whispered Catriona, pointing to a chair she had pulled up next to hers. Ella rested her head on the desk and Catriona ran her hand over the surface of Ella's head.

'I love the feel of it! It's gone from moleskin to guinea pig!' she whispered.

'You're crazy, you know that.' Ella smiled.

Sister Fraser had been right, *The Song of Bernadette* was old-fashioned, and hammy, at first. But the nuns in the film were heartless, just like the old crows here, and something about Bernadette, the girl who didn't fit in, captured Ella's imagination. There was no whispering, no note-passing and when the Virgin Mary appeared, Bernie and Theresa began to cry. Cynical as Ella was prepared to be, she sighed when the bell went at the end of the lesson.

'We'll finish it off next time,' said the nun, and Ella took out her small blue diary to see when the next RS lesson was timetabled.

'She was so beautiful,' said Theresa, wiping her eyes. 'Just like Sister Gagnier.'

'How wonderful to be chosen,' said Bernie, clasping her hands to her chest as if *she* was the chosen one, just because she had the same name as the saint.

Ella shook herself and put her diary away. God they were pathetic. If she wasn't careful she was going to end up as gullible as them. 'Maybe she just picked the wrong sort of mushrooms. It all seemed pretty trippy to me,' she scoffed, bending down to put on her boots.

Mhairi, who was walking away, clocked the reference and stopped. Dizzy and Bells nudged one another, and Ella got the distinct impression that she'd said something of interest, for once.

'What do you know about mushrooms?' said Bells.

For a second Ella was back in the squat. The walls were closing in and the lights were flashing blue and white. She blinked away the memory. 'Oh, nothing that you guys would be interested in. You're far too innocent.'

Mhairi draped an arm round Ella's shoulders. 'Don't judge a book by its cover, Ella. We should all be open to… new experiences.'

Something barely perceptible had shifted, Ella felt it in her fingertips. She wasn't exactly an expert on magic mushrooms, but they didn't need to know that. 'Let's just say, I have prior.'

'Interesting,' said Mhairi. 'We should talk. I like to keep my heart open to the mysteries of this world.'

Ella pulled the laces tight and threw her satchel over her shoulder. 'You can open your heart all you want. I'm gonna engage my brain, instead.' *Advantage, Ella.*

***

Later, after lights-out, Catriona tapped her on the shoulder.

'Mhairi wants to see us in her room,' she whispered.

Ella had been expecting the summons earlier in the day. It was a power play on Mhairi's part, to make her wait. But two could play at that game. 'You go. Tell her I'm sleeping,' she said, without looking up.

'She doesn't want just me. She wants us both together.' Catriona tapped her harder now. 'I've never been called by the Cecilians before and if I go on my own, she'll probably send me away. Please come.'

She sat up. 'What exactly are the Cecilians?'

'Oh, that's just the name for Mhairi's group. They're like a club, I suppose.'

'A secret society?'

'Well... sort of. I mean it's not a secret that they exist. Everybody knows that. But I suppose nobody really knows what they get up to.'

'And Mhairi's in charge?' she asked, propping herself up on one elbow.

'Yeah. But she didn't start it. There's been Cecilians at Saint Cs since it was founded, apparently.'

'Why is everyone so impressed by her?'

'Oh, you know…'

'No. I don't,' she said firmly. Though in truth, she did. Sometimes she caught herself staring at Mhairi and had to force herself to look away. There was something mesmerising about her.

Catriona shrugged and sat down on the end of the bed. 'I suppose she's the prettiest girl. She's from the richest family. She's got the longest connection to the school. That's just the way it is,' she said. She wasn't looking at Ella anymore, she was looking down, her fingers tracing the edges of the fabric hexagons on the quilt. 'I wasn't a Bubber like most of them. I came in the Lower Fourth. Bernie and Theresa, Dizzy and me were New Bugs together.' Her voice was slower now, younger. 'I thought I'd never stop crying. I missed home so much.'

'It must have been tough,' Ella offered. A picture of Nicola flashed into her mind. They were lying on her bed, laughing, their legs were entangled. She blinked her away. It had been so long since she'd been a friend that she wasn't good at this anymore.

'But that wasn't the hardest bit,' Catriona continued. 'Just before I came here… now I think about it, it's probably the reason they sent me away… Daddy left us. He went off with his secretary. She's my stepmother now.' She stopped talking and leant back against the wall.

Ella knew she should do something to make her feel better, take her hand, say something reassuring, but she couldn't seem to do either of those things, so she nudged her in the ribs with her big toe. It was as close as she could get to a hug.

Catriona carried on. 'One night I was crying, and the twins made me tell them what was wrong. You should have seen their faces. I might as well have told them Daddy was a mass-murderer.

They were so shocked. They told me that divorce was a sin and that he was going to hell – all the usual Catholic blah blah blah.'

Ella sat up now. 'Seriously? What total bitches.'

Catriona sniggered, covering her mouth with her hand to hold in the noise. 'I've been here long enough to know they were just spouting the rubbish they'd been taught.' And then she was serious again. 'But at the time I thought they were right, that Daddy was damned. And I might as well have been damned too. They sent me to Coventry. Completely left me out. It was pretty bad.'

She looked up at Ella, her face tinged green by the light of the fire exit sign above the door. 'It was Mhairi who stepped in and put a stop to it. I'm not sure what she said or did, but Bernie and Theresa have been sweet since then and they never mention the divorce. Mhairi made it all right and I'm grateful for that. She has a way of sorting things out. She's not that bad, if you stay on the right side of her.'

They sat for a little while in silence, Ella processing all she'd heard. She had known her place at the Leven – she existed in the farthest reaches of the Outer Rim. The difference there, was that at the end of the day everybody went home, and as rubbish as her home might be, it was better than this.

Catriona suddenly grabbed Ella's wrist. 'Imagine if Tibby was in charge!' she whispered. 'That would be so much worse!'

Ella laughed.

'Please can we go? I've never been asked before.'

She swung her legs over the side of the bed. 'Ok, I'll come. But for you. Not because she's summoning me.'

***

The room Bells and Mhairi shared, was at the end of a dark corridor. She detected a faint whiff of patchouli creeping out from below the door as they waited for a response to Catriona's knock.

'Yah. Come in,' called Bells.

Ella pushed the door open but she and Catriona hesitated on the threshold. The room was large and dimly lit and it took her eyes a moment to adjust to the twilight. For a second she was back at the squat again, looking for Mikey. A bedside-lamp covered with a silk scarf cast an orange glow. Regulations, it seemed, did not apply here.

Dizzy and Bells were top and tailing on the single bed furthest from the door, their legs crossed in the middle. Bernie and Theresa were on the floor beside them. The other bed was swagged with Indian bedspreads. Deep red and decorated with tiny mirrors, the fabric glinted in the dusky light. It was quite a contrast from Ella's stark cube. Or any of the others' cubes, for that matter. This place looked almost homey.

Mhairi sat in the corner with her feet curled up beneath her. The warm light cast shadows, drew eyelashes on her browbone, and Ella felt her heart speed up, like it used to when she saw Mikey.

'Hey guys, make yourselves comfortable,' said Dizzy.

But she didn't know where to sit. Bells' bed was occupied, and she daren't get too close to Mhairi. It felt safer to keep her distance. But Catriona took the lead, plonking herself on the floor by the door and leaning back against the wall. Ella sat down next to her.

She had made Mhairi think she was some kind of badass, but now that she was in the Inner Sanctum, she didn't feel so bold. Pulling her knees up, she wrapped her arms tightly around them and looked at the walls. They were plastered with photographs and pages torn from magazines, much like her room at home, before Grandma had wrecked it. But here the pages were mostly from Vogue and the photos were of pissed teenagers, arms thrown around each other, cigarettes poking from the corners of their mouths. Posh girls in puffy ballgowns snogged boys in tartan trousers who looked like Rupert the Bear. It was obvious the nuns never came in here.

Mhairi slowly uncurled herself from the shadows. Her feet in slipper socks slithered out from under a blanket. She made no attempt at conversation. The handmaids were watching her as if looking for a signal – for what, Ella wasn't sure.

It was Dizzy who spoke first. 'It must be so hard being a New Bug when you're the only one. I hope you're settling in alright.'

Catriona rested her head on Ella's bony shoulder.

'Oh yeah, it's swell,' Ella replied.

'Coping with life in the dorm?' Bells asked. 'Not too noisy, what with Noids snoring, and Grunty fudding herself stupid every night?'

Ella couldn't help laughing. She'd wondered where Grunty's nickname had come from, but she hadn't noticed any noises of that sort.

Bells continued, her smile shifting a little. 'You know, Ella, you're kind of hard to get to know. I mean you don't say very much and we hardly know anything about you. Where you live, what kind of family you're from.'

Ella narrowed her eyes. 'What kind of family?' She found it hard to keep the *what-the-fuck* tone from her voice.

'Yah. I mean, we like to know who we're living with. Obviously, you're American. But Mhairi's been asking around and nobody's heard of you, or any Richardsons for that matter.' Bells put her hands behind her head and gathered up her long blonde hair as if she was about to put it in a ponytail. She twisted it and piled it up onto the top of her head where she held it for a moment before letting it fall.

Ella said nothing.

'What school did you go to before?' asked Dizzy.

'The Leven, in Dundee. It was just an ordinary school.' She could be fairly certain they'd never heard of it.

Bells and Dizzy glanced at each other and Bells screwed up her nose as if she'd caught a whiff of something nasty.

'Well, that explains a lot,' said Bells. 'I mean... *Dundee*. It's so non-U.'

Ella's breathing quickened. 'Have you ever *met* anybody from Dundee? Apart from me.'

Bells scoffed. 'No way. Do you live in the actual – you know – city?'

'No, I live in a village half-way between Dundee and Perth.' Ella didn't know why she was even answering.

Dizzy sprang forward and actually clapped her hands. 'Perth. Why didn't you say so? Perth's so much nicer. From now on, when people ask, you should tell them you're from Perth. Dibber's from Perthshire, and the Bingley boys, and Sarah Dalrymple, Lady Sarah – you know her.' She was talking to Bells now, not to her. And all the while Mhairi watched from the corner, her chestnut hair pulled over one shoulder, her fingers gently twisting the curls.

While Bells and Dizzy talked Ella fiddled with her nose ring. She felt the weight of Catriona's body lean into hers and was glad of her proximity. She still had no idea what was actually going on here.

'Okay. Yah,' Bells said, looking down at them again. 'Well,

I'm sure we'll have oodles of time to find out all about you and your fascinating life in the village. I know we're just dy-ing to find out more about the nose ring and the hair and all. It's so deliciously grimy.'

Who the fuck does she think she is? Ella had had enough. Shrugging off Catriona's head, she pulled herself up from the floor, but before she could give Bells a piece of her mind, there was a knock at the door.

Tibby stuck her head into the room. 'I've just seen a Purple Ribbon head into the Bubbers' dorm.' Her tone was urgent. 'Better break it up in case she checks Sistine.'

Mhairi dismissed Tibby with a wave of her hand, swung her legs onto the floor and fixed her eyes on Ella. 'Don't pay too much attention to Bells. She likes you. We all do. We just want to get to know you a little better.' Her gaze made Ella squirm and she looked away. Bells was leaning back against the wall, her mouth puckered, her fingers picking at a hangnail. Yeah, it sure looked as though she liked her.

Mhairi smiled. 'But before we go any further, we need to find out if you have what it takes.'

'Have what it takes?' asked Ella.

'Yes. Do you have what it takes to become a Cecilian? We've come up with a little test.'

CHAPTER 20
Borstal Breakout (Sham 69)

The next morning on the way to Mass, Tibby leapt out at Ella and Catriona and pulled them behind the curtain of the big bay window on Silent Corridor.

'What the...?' Ella pulled her arm from Tibby's grip.

Behind the curtain the Queen Bee and her handmaids were waiting.

While the other girls slouched and flicked and shifted their weight, Mhairi held herself with composure and waited for them to settle. Her voice, when she spoke was honeyed, but her eyes were unblinking. 'I'm sure I don't have to remind you that what I'm about to say must go no further.' She paused to emphasise the threat. 'We plan to walk after midnight, tomorrow.'

'Yeah, and...' Ella couldn't help herself. She smirked at the cloak and dagger bullshit. What did this have to do with her? Unless they were going to invite her to come along, of course. Catriona shot her a warning look.

'There's a problem,' Bells whispered. 'And that's where you come in.'

This must be 'the test'. Ella had tried to laugh it off as she and Catriona had crept back to the dorm, but alone in her bed she hadn't slept well and all through the night the weirdness of the Inner Sanctum had replayed in her dreams. She had woken up that morning determined not to play their game. But now that she was standing there, she wanted to know more.

'Oh, yeah?' she said, trying to sound like she wasn't bothered. Catriona kicked her on the ankle.

'Bells…?' Mhairi indicated that Bells would do the talking.

'The new light. The one that shines onto the path between the dormitories and the Gym. You know the one?' Bells sounded sharp, smart even.

Ella nodded. She'd noticed it shining through the stained glass when she went to the loo at night.

'Well, it makes us too exposed – on our walks – and that's where you come in.'

So, they weren't inviting her to join them. Of course they weren't. They just wanted her to do a job for them, and for a second she was disappointed. But only for a second. Creeping about in the middle of the night was kids' stuff. She wouldn't have gone with them even if they'd asked. Mikey would piss himself laughing if she told him.

Bells continued, 'The penguins sleep in the attics of the Mansion House. Those dormers, the ones that jut up from the roof, are the windows of their cells. So, they've got a perfect view of the path.'

Dizzy giggled suddenly. 'Do you think they lie on their backs with their arms like this?' She held her hands together in prayer, pointed her upturned nose towards the ceiling and shut her eyes. Dizzy was funny, Ella had to give her that.

'Like the uncorrupted body of Saint Bernadette?' said Bernie, who had been obsessed since the film they'd watched.

'Imagine Sister H in her nightie! Do you think she wears fluffy slippers?' said Catriona.

Ella was surprised to hear her joining in.

'Slippers? I don't even think she's got feet,' said Dizzy. 'I swear she glides round on rollers. You never hear her coming.'

And Ella giggled despite herself.

Suddenly the curtains behind them swished open. The headmistress stood over them, her jowly face heavy with disapproval. 'Girls! What are you doing? You know there's no talking on Silent Corridor. Get along now, or you'll be late for Mass.'

It wasn't quite the bollocking Ella expected.

'I swear the place is bugged,' said Dizzy as they followed Mhairi along the hallway.

'Lucky Mhairi was with us, or we'd have lost our Notes for sure,' Catriona whispered to Ella.

'Does she never get in trouble?'

'Never.'

***

In Chapel, Ella sat wedged in the middle of the pew – Mhairi, Dizzy and Bernie to her left, Bells, Catriona and Theresa to her right. Pretending to pray, the girls bent so far forward that their heads were practically in their laps, and Bells carried on in a whisper. 'The four corner rooms are bigger, so obviously these go to the most senior nuns – Sister H and her cronies. The other three are ancient, but they're royalty in nun world.' Bells sounded like M debriefing Bond, and against her better instincts, Ella felt a rush of excitement.

They stood, recited the Gloria, then sat back down, bowing forward for the readings.

'So, which window is Sister Hanrahan's?' Ella whispered, caught up in the planning now.

Dizzy answered this time. 'Front left. You see her sometimes in the window. From that corner of the building she can see all the way up the Front Avenue, but she can also see the exit from the dorms. And that's our problem-o. That security light is going to make it tricky-dicky to get to the woods.'

Mhairi was sitting so close that her hair tickled the side of Ella's cheek, not contributing to the conversation, but in control of it, nonetheless. Bells carried on, 'I've traced the wiring from the floodlight to where it enters the Mansion House. It goes in through the wall in the north-west corner of the building. Ceiling height. Ground floor.'

Ella had taken her for a bully – a dumb, blonde, suntanned bully – but this was a side of her she hadn't seen before. She couldn't help being impressed at the detail of the planning. This wasn't just a glorified midnight feast.

'The lights are on a timer which is attached to the wall near the small, frosted glass window.'

Mhairi put her hand on Ella's knee. It was as if the girls had rehearsed it. 'And that's where you come in. It's really very simple. All you need to do is reset the timer so that we can walk tomorrow night as planned. Do you think you can do that for us? Are you up to the test?'

Ella spent the morning trying not to think about Mhairi's proposition and thinking about nothing else. What was it about this girl that made it so hard to say no? It wasn't just that she was beautiful. Ella felt herself being sucked in, just like the other saps, and now she wasn't even trying that hard to resist. She had to admit that it was exciting in Chapel. It had felt like fun. And it had been a long time since she'd had any of that.

But she wasn't a child. And this wasn't an Enid Blyton novel. I mean, sure, she'd sneaked out to see Mikey, but that was different. That was her decision. And she had been fuelled by hope. But look where that had got her. No matter how seriously Mhairi and her lot seemed to take this, it was still just a stupid game. Like the 'club' she'd had with Nicola when they were about ten. It was pathetic. Her mind was made up. She wouldn't do it.

But at Soup, when the Cecilians returned from their cigarettes in the bushes, Ella found herself asking, 'Where exactly is the room with the frosted glass window?'

Mhairi smiled, as if acknowledging a small victory, and raised an eyebrow at Bells, to indicate that she should respond.

'It's not far from the dorm. You can see the window on the left, half-way along the wall of the main building. But you can only get to it through the Great Hall.'

Ella pictured the entrance hall of the Mansion House. A wide double staircase swept up towards the first floor, splitting to reach both sides of a galleried landing. High above the marbled ground floor, a huge glass dome known by the girls as 'The Egg' flooded light through an oval opening.

'It'll be pitch dark, but that won't be your main problem.'

'What is my main problem?' Ella asked. 'The nuns? When do they go to bed?'

Bernie stepped in now. The twins had an auntie who was a nun, and consequently they were regarded as the authority on all things 'nunny'. 'The Sisters pray a lot,' she explained. 'More even than us. And we pray *a lot*. Though I guess they are married to Jesus. There's Lauds at 5am, then there's Prime, Tierce, Sext, Nones, Vespers and finally…'

'What?' Ella was losing patience.

'I was getting to it,' said Bernie, sulkily. 'Compline. Then bed.'

'And when's that?' asked Ella.

'Nobody knows exactly,' said Bells. 'But they're definitely in bed before midnight. The lights in the cells are always off by then.'

'So… the problem?' Ella asked again, her impatience evident.

'Your problem,' said Bells, 'is not the nuns. Your problem is the White Lady.'

Ella swallowed hard. She'd heard all about the poor wraith who haunted the dome. The legend of the White Lady was deep in the folklore of Saint C's and she'd already been told the story more than once. Her portrait hung in the Great Hall, larger than life-sized. Draped sideways over a chair, she loomed over the comings and goings. Her knees pointed to the right, but her gaze was cast over her shoulder, towards the front door. She wore a white muslin dress, Empire line, and her black curls were fixed with a golden headband, like a pagan goddess from Ancient Greece. A veil, gossamer thin, covered her head and shoulders and from beneath its opalescence her waxy face surfaced like a death mask. There was definitely an emptiness in her eyes that Ella found unsettling and she avoided looking at the portrait when she passed through the hall.

Thanks to Tibby's programme of indoctrination, Ella had learnt to side-step the cracked marble in the centre of the hall, and like everybody else, she never leant over the edge of The Egg. Those who did, Tibby warned, would feel cold breath on the back of their neck, and even a voice in their ear, urging them to jump. Lady Jane Scott, so the story went, was the only daughter of the man who built the Mansion House and when her fiancé was killed in the Napoleonic Wars she threw herself to her death from the gallery. Her restless soul now haunted the school. Ella didn't like to think about it. Especially not at night.

Dizzy was serious now. 'She doesn't like it when we encroach on her territory.'

Mhairi let the danger hang in the air for a second. Then she leaned towards Ella and whispered, 'We'll understand if you say no. Not everyone has what it takes to be a Cecilian.'

Ella looked her straight in the eye and lied. 'I'm not scared of some stupid ghost story. I just don't know if I can be bothered.' She didn't need their approval. She wouldn't do it. They could keep their Famous Five adventure.

'Don't decide now. Tell us before supper,' Mhairi said.

***

Later that afternoon, Ella and Catriona headed out to the pitches for hockey practice.

Catriona bit the dry skin on her chapped lips. She'd hardly spoken since breaktime.

'Are you okay?' Ella asked, wondering if she was jealous. 'I mean, it's a bit weird that they keep talking just to me.'

Catriona chopped at the grass with her hockey stick. 'I'm so stupid. I shouldn't have persuaded you to go to their room. I should have known.'

'What are you on about?'

'I've seen this before,' she said. 'Last year, I was friends with this new girl, Jo. They tested her to see if she was the kind of girl who'd do anything they asked. If you say yes to this, they'll start sending you on the fag run to the village shop, or to meet the taxi driver to pick up the vodka. Be careful. You can say no.'

Fags and vodka? This sounded like old times. 'I'll think about it,' she said, but she had decided already. Maybe Mhairi and her friends were fake and phony and manipulative, but they didn't know her. She could pass their test. She could be brave and fearless and up for anything. She could be anybody she wanted to be. Why the fuck not? Perhaps she would never fit anywhere, but at least now she had a chance to try.

After games she made sure Catriona was out of sight when she caught up with Mhairi. 'Okay,' she whispered, 'I'm in.'

The smile Mhairi flashed at her made Ella's heart race.

***

Before prayers, Tibby summoned Ella to the Mhairi's room.

'What about Catriona?' she asked.

'Not this time. It's just you.'

Without her friend by her side she didn't know where to sit, so she hovered by the door shifting her weight from foot to foot. The thrill she'd felt earlier was gone.

Mhairi watched from the shadows while Bells ran through the details. 'It's important that you do a practice run tonight. If it goes wrong, or the nuns suss that something's going on, we'll all be tucked up safely in our beds, and they won't be able to pin anything on us.'

'And I'll be the one who gets caught?' Ella shrugged. She was the patsy. Great.

'Yah. That's right,' Bells continued with no hint of apology. 'But you won't get caught. And tomorrow, by the time we walk, you'll have it down to a fine art.'

Dizzy handed her a torch and a hand-drawn map and smiled to reassure her. 'Wait until midnight before you set off.'

'It's a blue door. It'll be unlocked,' said Bells. 'We need the light to be off between half-past midnight and three o'clock. Don't screw up.'

'She won't fail,' Mhairi said, crossing the room to Ella and kissing her on both cheeks. She smelled like roses. 'You're going to be one of us. I know it.' Her smile was broad and dazzling, but her eyes were granite cold.

When she got back to her cube, Catriona was waiting.

'Are you doing it?'

'Yes.'

'Is there anything I can say to stop you?'

'No.'

'Then be careful, please.'

***

After lights-out, the girls in the dormitory chatted softly over the low partitions of their cubes. But Ella lay back with her eyes closed, stomach knotted, the Virgin Mary clutched in her palm. Gradually the voices faded out and snuffly noises of sleep commenced. Noids' snoring had become a familiar, even comforting sound to her. But not tonight. By the green light of the fire exit, she watched the juddering progress of the second hand on the clock, willing it to speed up.

Every sound in the old building seemed amplified, every creak and groan. Ella imagined the white gossamer dress billowing as Lady Jane fell to her death. The body rising from the marble floor and floating in the centre of the Great Hall. The hollow eyes, the arms stretched wide, the mouth agape and waiting. She pulled the quilt up over her head and squeezed her eyes so tight that violet fractals blossomed on her retina. She didn't want to do this. But there was no getting out of it now. Not without looking like a total wimp.

At five to midnight she put on her tracksuit over her nightdress and tucked the thin cotton into the waistband for warmth. She was tying the laces of her trainers when a floorboard creaked in the corridor. Throwing herself down onto the bed, she pulled the patchwork over her clothes and feigned sleep.

Soft footsteps entered her cube. Followed by a giggle. 'It's only me. I couldn't let you go on your own.' It was Catriona.

Ella gasped with relief and reached across the cube to squeeze Catriona's hand. *Woah!* She didn't do that. She didn't reach out and touch people. Not ever. But it felt right to hold Catriona's hand in hers. And her fear subsided just a little; enough to get her on her feet.

'It's gonna be okay. We'll stick together,' Catriona said.

Ella grabbed the torch. It was not forbidden to go to the loo during the night but there were two of them, and they were dressed in trackies, so they'd be in for it if they were caught. And nuns had a habit of appearing out of nowhere.

Tentatively, Ella opened the door that led onto the corridor.

Low on its hinges it scraped the floor and somewhere in the dormitory someone stirred. They froze, ears attuned to the slightest noise. Only when they were absolutely sure that all was quiet did Ella stick her head into the corridor to see if the coast was clear.

She looked across to the painted statue of the Virgin, backlit by the security light, then towards St Anthony at the other end of the hall. Just as they were about to make a run for it, a door creaked and Felicity Walsh, a Purple Ribbon and a bitch of one at that, stepped out into the corridor. Ella and Catriona dipped back into the dormitory and waited, pinned against the wall. When the door to the toilet block clicked, they tore off down the corridor, keeping their footsteps light.

Instead of heading straight towards the dining room, they darted through a maze of small passageways. At every corner they stopped to listen. The Mansion House was full of noises – soft scrapes, the scuttle of claws, and pipes that groaned like whales beneath the ocean. They hesitated, waiting for silence, then sprinted to the next junction. Their stop-start progress took them deep into the bowels of the old house.

At the final corner, Ella flicked on the torch to look at the map. Cold air circled her ankles, and somewhere distant, a door rasped on its hinges. Fear caught her throat and her heart pounded so hard she was sure it would give them away. But Catriona took her hand and squeezed. 'Just breathe. We're nearly there,' she said.

And then they were in the Great Hall, where the vast space swallowed them whole. The temperature dropped like a stone in a mill pond. Air eddied round the dome and whistled down the stairs and the hairs on the back of Ella's neck pricked to attention.

She had to beat the fear before it beat her. Shining the torch on the floor, she found the jagged rift in the marble, then holding her breath, she very deliberately stepped on the crack, squeezing her eyes shut as she did so. Then she waited. Nothing. Absolutely nothing. She breathed out and looking up to the massive glass dome, switched off the torch. Catriona, one hand clasped across her mouth, grabbed Ella's arm. It took a moment for Ella's eyes to adjust but then the weight of the blackness lifted and through the glass, she caught the glint of starlight.

'It's beautiful,' Ella whispered, suddenly braver. 'There's no ghost here.'

'Stuff the ghosts, let's go!

The two girls grinned at each other and Ella led the way into a passage hidden behind the stairs. Finally, at the end of the long creaky corridor, they found the blue door.

'I think this is it,' said Ella, matching the position of the door to the X marked on the map. She wrapped one hand around the mahogany doorknob and turned it slowly. It was open, as Bells had promised. Inside, the dusty cupboard smelt of paper and mildew. She would have known it was a book room with her eyes shut. The beam of the flashlight picked out shelves deep with ancient volumes. Ella could imagine enjoying being trapped in here for a few hours, discovering what treasures might be hidden at the back.

'There it is,' said Catriona, pointing to a metal box in the top right corner of the room, by the side of the frosted window, just as Bells had said. 'It's pretty high up.'

Ella gave the torch to Catriona then pulled the shelving to check it would hold her weight. Reassured, she climbed it like a ladder until she was level with the timer. Inside, the mechanism seemed pretty rudimentary. The wiring from the outside light was hardwired into a metal box which Ella opened to reveal a dial. A green arrow pointed to 5pm, the time when the light came on, and a red arrow pointed to 7am, when the light went off.

'It's simple enough,' she whispered to Catriona. 'Tomorrow, all we'll need to do is slide the red arrow along to 12.30am and the light will go off earlier than usual. That will give Mhairi her darkness. Then all we have to do is come back at 3am and slide the arrow back to seven.'

'We? Do you want me to come with you again tomorrow?' asked Catriona.

'Of course! I couldn't have done it without you,' said Ella, climbing down the shelves again. She brushed the dust from her hands.

'We did it!' Catriona squealed, and threw her arms around Ella, bouncing on tiptoes. 'Now let's go…'

They ran back through the corridors, hardly pausing to check if the coast was clear. Adrenalin surged through Ella's body. She'd done it! They'd done it! By the time they reached the dorm they were covering their mouths to stop the laughter escaping.

She hugged Catriona goodnight and threw herself down on her bed, drumming her heels on the mattress and punching her fists in the air. She hadn't had that much fun since primary school. Her heart pounded, blood pumping hard to every extremity. It was as if the central heating had come back on again. Like she had come alive once more.

CHAPTER 21
Wild in the Country (Bow-wow-wow)

Next morning, while Ella was queuing for the sinks, Tibby skipped the line and snarled in her ear. 'Did you do it?'

'Yeah.' Ella shrugged, keeping it casual. 'I've sussed out the timer. The light won't be a problem.'

Tibby's pink eyes darted around the washroom. 'Shhh! Little pitchers have big ears.'

***

Half an hour later, as Ella and Catriona made their way to breakfast, Dizzy and Bells ran up behind them and grabbed Ella round the waist.

'Darling! Tell all! Don't leave anything out,' said Dizzy.

'Run into the White Lady?' asked Bells.

Catriona slipped behind Dizzy's back and put a finger to her lips. Ella had almost forgotten that the Cecilians didn't know Catriona had been there too.

At first it felt awkward to pretend she'd been alone, but it also felt good to be the centre of attention. And soon Ella was making a story of the Purple Ribbon who'd nearly caught her at the start, the chill on her ankles in the Great Hall, and the long creaky corridor that led to the book room.

'The timer's a bit technical but we're all set for tonight,' she said.

Dizzy nodded in approval. 'We knew you'd do it.'

***

In RE, when the girls rearranged the desks for the final instalment of *The Song of Bernadette,* the Cecilians gathered around Ella. They'd set her a test and she'd passed. And for now, anyway, Ella could bask in their admiration.

Between lessons the third row adjusted its formation. Mhairi stayed out front as usual, but Bells and Dizzy linked arms with Ella, pulling her along while Catriona tagged behind, alone. Ella had envied the casual intimacy of the girls, the way they piled onto each other's beds and threw their arms around each other in the halls. And now it felt like she was one of them, and she didn't want anything to spoil that.

But at Soup, when the Cecilians left them, as usual, she felt ashamed of how she'd behaved. Catriona seemed quieter, smaller, her big pale eyes glistening behind her specs.

'I'm sorry I didn't tell them. That I let them think I was on my own,' Ella said.

'No. It's better that way,' said Catriona, both hands round her mug of soup.

'Why?'

'Because it was your test. Not mine.'

'And I'd have failed it if they knew you were there?'

Catriona nodded. 'Yes. They didn't ask me, remember. They'd be angry if they found out.'

Ella felt a ripple of discomfort in the pit of her stomach. 'That sounds kinda fucked up.'

'Yeah. But it's the way it is.'

'It shouldn't be, though. And I'm sorry we left you out, on the way to lessons. When Dizzy and Bells pulled me forward.' She pushed her hand over her scalp. The warmth she'd felt in her newfound popularity was dissipating.

'It wasn't your fault,' Catriona said earnestly. 'It's always like that with them. Sometimes you're in, and sometimes you're out. And when the sun's shining on you, you might as well enjoy it.'

***

After lunch, when Catriona and the Cecilians headed out for their hockey matches, Ella joined the cross-country team to warm-up for her first race. It was a home fixture against two Edinburgh schools, and all week Miss Johnson had been timing her. She had told her that if she paced herself, she could place in the top three.

It was a clear, crisp afternoon and the frost that covered the grass that morning had all but disappeared. The drive was full of parents' cars and Ella hung about on the gravel in front of the school where the cross-country runners were gathered. It hadn't even crossed her mind to tell Dad. Suddenly the lack of sleep hit her like a wave and while those around her buzzed with pre-match nerves, she fought an urge to lie on the front lawn and pull the hood of her tracksuit over her head. She felt slow, lethargic. She didn't want to run today. But minibuses had brought teams all the way from Edinburgh, and there was no way she was getting out of this.

The enthusiastic team captain gave her a nudge. 'Hey, Ella! Ready to give it all you've got?'

Ella shrugged and the girl, an Upper Fifther with a ponytail so tight her eyes stretched sideways, jogged over. 'I just need to pin these on.' Ella stood stock still while the captain attached a paper number to her red bib. Then, in a final attempt to rouse some team spirit, the captain punched the air, and called out just a bit too loudly, 'Go, Saint Cs, go!'

Fuck's sake... Ella turned away from the rest of the team and scuffed at the gravel with her trainer. She imagined drawing the captain in black Biro, a donkey with bulging eyes on either side of her skinny head, and a mane bound tight with a ribbon.

Sod all that ra-ra crap. She couldn't care less. But as they gathered at the starting line, her stomach tightened, and her mouth dried up. For the third time she checked her laces and casually, at the back, she joined in with the stretches that the ponytailed donkey led.

Miss Johnson came over. 'Do your best, girls.'

She put a hand on Ella's shoulder. 'This is your first race. Pace yourself. You're a runner, Ella – so enjoy it.' The other Saint Cecilia's girls clapped her on the back. And then they were silent, anticipating the gun.

When the pack took off, she found herself stuck in the middle. Some of them jostled her, pushing too close to her shoulders, their feet catching her heels. Her toes kicked the calves in front; she could smell their hot bodies, their panting dog breath. She gritted her teeth.

Once they had got beyond the village, she and a few others

surged ahead. Finally, she could breathe again. She could pump her arms without clashing elbows and stretch her legs without fear of tripping up. She found her rhythm and pushed harder. *You're a runner, Ella. You're a runner.* For the next mile or so she kept pace with the front runners. But then, from far behind, a nippy little girl from Mary Erskine's dashed past, splattering her with mud as she belted ahead. Within minutes she was so far in the lead that Ella could hardly see her.

And the battle for second place commenced. Ella's heart pounded in her chest and her legs burned as she pushed harder than she'd ever done before. As she crossed the playing fields and the school came into view, she knew she was breathing too hard and her muscles spasmed. But the finish line was in her sights and out of the corner of her eye she could see the Cecilians waving their hockey sticks. They were shouting her name. *Ell-a! Ell-a!* She gave it everything she had and shot forward. Second place would be hers. But just as she reached the home straight two girls powered past, leaving her to come in fourth.

Doubling over in pain, she grasped the back of her calves with her hands and spat out the bile that had risen from her stomach.

Miss Johnson rubbed her back. 'Learn to pace yourself better and you've the makings of a decent runner.'

Then the Cecilians surrounded her, cheering and jumping as though she'd won. They slapped her on the back and told her she was 'fabulous,' 'amazing,' 'super-bloody-sonic,' and in that moment, despite everything, she believed it was true.

Catriona was quieter. She patted her on the shoulder. 'Wait till you taste the match tea. It's the only good thing you'll ever eat at Saint Cs.'

And it was. Although Mhairi stood back and watched, the rest of them devoured mountains of egg sandwiches, slices of Victoria sponge and home-made scones thick with butter and fluorescent-yellow lemon curd. It all tasted so good. And Ella was ravenous.

But when the others headed back to the changing rooms, she slipped off to fetch her satchel from the Form Room and made her way up the spiral staircase to run herself an illegal bath. She needed some space. She pulled *Right Ho, Jeeves* out of her bag and slipped into the water. Her legs were stiff and aching and she lay in the warm suds, laughing at Bertie Wooster, wiggling her toes back to life. Today was a Wodehouse sort of day and nothing gloomy could spoil it.

In the chill of the bathroom, she rubbed her head with a towel and looked in the small mirror above the sink. The nose ring looked cool and her hair was growing back. She rubbed her fingers through it, making it look shaggy, choppy. No make-up, cropped black hair, roses in her cheeks. Old Ella, new Ella. Old Ella, new Ella.

Which Ella was she now?

***

Later, when she caught up with the others in the Form Room, it was already dark. Groups of girls were playing cards and flicking through magazines. At the weekend they wore 'home clothes' and there was an assortment of frilly blouses, pixie boots, knickerbockers and Peruvian llama jumpers on display. A mix tape was playing on a portable stereo. Abba. *Super Trouper.* Mikey would be sticking his fingers down his throat if he was here.

Catriona and the Cecilians were clustered at the back of the room.

'Over here, Ella,' Bells called to her. 'We've been wondering where you'd got to.'

Mhairi's long legs were crossed on the desk in front of her. 'We thought you might be having second thoughts,' she said quietly.

'No. I'm still up for it.'

'It makes us so happy to hear you say that,' said Mhairi, her stillness hypnotic. And the group nodded their assent. Yes, they were all happy. Yes, they were relying upon her. Suddenly, Ella felt bolder.

'What's this midnight walk all about?' she asked. 'What are you planning to do out there anyway?'

Catriona, whose face was still red from hockey, shifted uncomfortably in her seat. Mhairi straightened and her lip twitched.

'Oh, you know,' she said and flicked her hair.

'No, I don't,' said Ella. She knew she was pushing it, but at this precise moment she didn't care. And when Catriona kicked her ankle underneath the chair it made her all the more feisty.

'Well now.' Mhairi met Ella's gaze and didn't blink. 'You could think of it as a Marian devotion. Cecilians worshipping the Virgin Mary, out by her sacred tree.'

'Sounds freaky.' Ella snorted. 'Sacred tree? Is that the one in the clearing out in the woods? The one with all the little crosses planted all around it?'

Mhairi glanced at Bells and raised a sculpted eyebrow. 'That's the one. How did you find it?'

'By accident. I got lost when I was running and just sort of stumbled into it.'

Dizzy gasped as if Ella's words held some sort of significance and Bernie put a hand to the small silver medallion that she wore around her neck. All the Cecilians had medallions like that, now that Ella came to think of it.

'It's a sign,' said Theresa. 'Only true Cecilians are *called* to the tree.'

'It's a sacred place for us. We perform our rituals there,' said Mhairi, her voice so low Ella had to lean in to hear. 'One day, we might show you. If you're very, very good.'

Noids, the eavesdropper, butted in. 'Sacred rituals. Ha! Sipping sacred voddy, more like.'

'Oh Noids. We know how much you'd love to come, but you're just not well enough to be out in the cold night air. Think what it would do to your poor, weak chest,' Bells said, rolling her eyes at Ella like they were in on the same joke.

Catriona had moved onto the floor and was leaning her head on Ella's shins. Dizzy's elbow was on her shoulder and Mhairi had moved her feet from the desk onto her lap. Ella was in the centre of a nest of legs and arms. She smiled, glad that she had pushed Mhairi and that she had got an answer, of sorts. She was full of delicious food, warm and relaxed from the bath, and she wanted very much to believe that this was what it felt like to belong.

***

On Saturday nights the whole school gathered in the Gym to watch films that nobody really wanted to see. The nuns made wholesome choices, and the girls sat hunched on low benches, cramped and fidgety while the reels juddered onto a pull-down screen in front of the stage.

As they filed in later that evening, the Cecilians pulled Ella into the middle of their row. That night it was a more exciting choice than usual and there was an expectant hum in the audience as the credits rolled for *Murder on the Orient Express*.

Ella looked around. Catriona was sitting on her own on the end of a bench, a couple of rows in front. She pushed her way out and tapped her on the shoulder.

'Come back and sit with us,' she whispered.

'It's started. There's no room.'

'I'll make space. Or I'll sit here with you.'

'Sit down will you!' someone shouted.

'Okay, I'll come,' Catriona said.

As the two girls shuffled along the row, Ella could see a look of disapproval on Bells' face. She'd crossed some sort of line. But as she made room for Catriona in the middle of the bench, she didn't really give a shit what Bells or anyone else thought. It was the right thing to do and her confidence was coming back.

While the film flickered the girls passed bags of wine gums back and forward along the row.

'Don't take the blackcurrants, they're Mhairi's favourites,' Catriona whispered in Ella's ear, but she took one anyway and stuck out her tongue to show she wasn't afraid.

Ignoring the film, the group talked about the midnight walk in furtive whispers and scribbled notes in the back of their prep diaries.

And when Lauren Bacall raised her dagger and plunged it into a body, the audience squealed, but Ella was too caught up in the planning to care. They carried on whispering.

'Shut up, you lot! Some of us are trying to watch the film,' someone shouted.

The screeching soundtrack reached a crescendo and Ella looked up at the screen just in time to see Ingrid Bergman's beautiful face, half in shadow. *For their Daisy and mine. God forgive me!* Bergman wailed. The stabbing sounded like she was punching a lump of wet dough and the row of Cecilians exploded with laughter.

Later, as they brushed their teeth in the bogs, Dizzy raised an imaginary dagger and jabbed it into Bells' back. 'God rest the soul of my dear... dead... daughter,' she cried in the hammiest of French accents.

Ella was buzzing. She would have no trouble staying awake that night.

***

'Ella! Ella!' Someone was shaking her shoulder. 'Wake up!'

Wiping dribble from her mouth she blinked, and her eyes focused in the darkness. For a moment she didn't know where she was. The dorm. Catriona. 'Fuck! I fell asleep... shit... sorry... What's the time?'

'Shhh! Don't panic. It's just before midnight. Everything's fine.' Catriona was wearing her trackies and a woolly bobble hat. Under the patchwork, Ella was ready too.

Catriona waited by the door while Ella, as planned, tapped three times on the wall of Tibby's cube, to let her know that she was on her way. Tibby, in turn, would alert the others who had gathered in Mhairi's room, dressed in black, bags packed with their supplies.

Then, with the precision of a military operation, Ella and Catriona retraced their steps to the book room. This time they knew where to stop and wait, when to listen out for footsteps and where to run on tiptoes across the more exposed spots. Ella felt slick and stealthy. The theme tune from the Pink Panther was playing in her mind.

She stopped for a moment beneath the dome and switched off the torch to look at the sky. It was even clearer than the night before and the moon was huge. There were moon dogs. In her head she heard her father pointing out the bright spots on the frosty halo. She shut her eyes and, in an instant, she was wrapped in his arms again, bundled up for Bonfire Night, her very first in Scotland. And he was pointing at the moon dogs, telling her about Skoll and Hati, the ravenous wolves who race through the sky on a quest to gobble up the sun and moon. She was afraid, but she was safe.

Catriona pulled her on. They had no time to waste. Light-footed, they nipped down the corridor, avoiding the creaky floorboard, and Ella pushed open the door to the book room. While she climbed up onto the shelves, Catriona lit her way with the torch-beam. Re-programming the timer was simple. They waited a few minutes and right on cue the light outside the frosted glass window went out. They had done it.

And their adventure was nearly over. There had been no White Lady, no Purple Ribbons in the shadows, no nuns on the prowl. It had been easy. Too easy.

'Let's go with them,' Ella said.

'What? Are you mad? We can't just go with them!'

'Why not?'

'Because they haven't asked us. You don't understand how they work. They want you to prove yourself and then… if you do everything they want… maybe then you'll be invited to join them. This is just the trial.' Catriona's voice was squeaky with tension.

But Ella felt giddy with their success and didn't want the night to be over. She was invincible. 'You're wrong. We passed their test yesterday.'

'You don't know them, Ella. They're not as straightforward as you think.'

She didn't want to hear that now. 'Come on. It'll be fun. Why should they get all the vodka when we've done all the work?'

Catriona shook her head. 'We can't join them. We don't know the rituals.'

Ella made a face. Catriona was sounding kind of sensible and a little bit boring. 'Oh, come on. Rituals? That's not for real. It's just a cover.'

'I don't think so. They're pretty serious about the Mary stuff.'

'Well, that's just weird.'

'You have no idea.' Catriona's eyes were like saucers and Ella sensed genuine fear.

They crept back along the corridors towards the dorm. The statue of Mary, Our Lady of Grace, was in darkness. The security lights were most definitely off. Their mission had been a success and the Cecilians would be on their way.

Ella stopped. This was ridiculous. 'I know you think it's mad, but I'm going. I'm gonna to catch up with them.'

'Don't, Ella. You'll regret it.'

'You can do what you want, but I'm not being left behind.'

The fire door wasn't locked. It couldn't be closed from the outside and the others were out there already. Ella pushed it wide open and cold air flooded the hallway.

Catriona sighed. 'Then I suppose I'm coming too. There's no way I'm letting you go on your own.'

CHAPTER 22

The Wind Cries Mary (Jimi Hendrix)

As they stepped out into the cold night air a thick band of cloud passed in front of the full moon and plunged them into darkness. Ella glanced up at the Bulldog's cell to check that the light was off, then giving Catriona a nod, they crept to the corner of the Mansion House, hugging the side of the long granite wall. Fleetingly the moon reappeared, illuminating the drive, and they crouched low, waiting for more cloud cover before they sprinted across the road and into the woods.

She had only been to the tree once before, and then it had been at twilight and she had stumbled upon it by accident. To their left a bark path led to the playing fields, but they needed to go deep into the woods to find the glade. Minutes before, it had been she who had been the brave one, but now, in the dark, it was Catriona who led the way.

Ella's heart was pounding as she pushed into the dense undergrowth and she fingered the torch in her pocket, too afraid of what might be behind her to risk switching it on. Hidden roots, like damp hands, reached out from the leaf mould and the wind breathed cold on the back of her bare neck.

Catriona stopped. 'You can switch the torch on now, we're too far away for the penguins to spot us.' In the light Ella could see her friend smiling, her eyes wide and excited, but her own lips were so tight with fear that she couldn't force a smile. Catriona stretched out her palm. 'It's easier if we stay connected. Trust me. I know the way.'

Ella took the small, warm hand, and let herself be led through the woods. Catriona spoke reassuringly, her voice chirpy and encouraging. 'We used to go out to the tree all the time when we were New Bugs. But mostly it's the Bubbers who come out to the glade. They play horses, gallop around the paddock, you know. They got into the most terrible trouble last year about the graves.'

'They freaked me out. What are they?'

'The Bubbers bury little birds that have fallen out of their nests, dead pets, that sort of thing. Anyway, a whole bunch of them got their Notes taken to Fair at Assembly. It was really bad. They were all crying, and the nuns wouldn't even let us comfort them. All because a penguin caught them doing a funeral for a mouse.'

'What's so wrong with that?'

'Oh, you know, animals don't have souls or something. No, they don't go to heaven, that's it. Or is it a mortal sin to pretend you're a priest? Oh, I don't know. It's all so complicated.'

'But the crosses are still there.'

'Oh, yes. The nuns made the groundsmen pull them all up, but they hardly ever go out in the woods, and the Bubbers know that, so they just made a load of new ones and stuck them in the ground.'

Ella's teeth were chattering now, and Catriona stopped talking, concentrating on picking a way through the brambles. The trees became denser, and the darkness closed in once again. It didn't feel like fun anymore and Ella wished she was back in the dorm. 'Are we nearly there?' she asked.

'Nearly.' Catriona looked back over her shoulder. 'You look freezing. You should have worn a hat. We can head back if you like. We really shouldn't be here, you know.'

Ella hesitated. She could tell by Catriona's voice that she was scared, too. But it wasn't the darkness that frightened her friend. Catriona was afraid of the Cecilians, and that was just stupid. 'No, let's go on,' Ella said. 'We've come too far to turn back now.'

But for the crack of twigs beneath their feet and the sad cry of a barn owl coming from the direction of the Steading, the wood was silent. Ella watched the fog of their breath dispersing in the air and shivered.

Up ahead, a flicker of light made her snap off the torch. All her senses were alert, every sinew in her body tense.

'That's them,' Catriona whispered. 'The glade's just in front of us. We need to be really quiet now.'

A thick strip of cloud drifted clear of the moon and the glade before them flooded with watery blue light.

'What the absolute fuck?' Ella blinked, not quite believing what she was seeing. There, in the clearing, stood the Cecilians. Naked.

Stationed at five points around the edge of a circle, their bare bodies were luminous in the moonlight. Still, as though they had been turned to stone, their heads were bowed, and their arms were straight by their sides. Ella's eyes flicked from dark pubic mounds to pale rounded buttocks and budding breasts. Her blood rushed in her veins and her cheeks flushed hot with shame and excitement. 'They must be absolutely freezing!' she whispered.

Catriona squeezed her hand, her terrified eyes begging her to stay silent. A fire bowl flickered and candles burned. Ella struggled to focus as images, dark and shadowy, blurred then flashed into view, but in the half-light there was no certainty. Garlands shimmered, and pendants, like shards of broken mirror, splintered the firelight. In the centre of the circle the stump of a tree, an altar of sorts, was decked in branches. And around the circumference the Cecilians stood stock still, faces tilted towards the earth.

Ella jumped as Mhairi threw out her arms. She knew it was Mhairi – the chestnut curls, the body, strong and lithe – but there was an energy that she didn't recognise, something fecund and unrestrained. In contrast, with heads still bowed, the others began to circle the altar like automatons. And faintly at first, so faintly Ella thought it was the wind, a chant started up. Soft, monotonous, humming.

'What the fuck is going on?' she gasped.

But Catriona put her finger to her lips, begging her to be quiet.

As the Cecilians circled the fire, the pace picked up and the sound became louder until Ella could hear words, partly familiar, partly not.

'To thee do we cry, poor banished children of Eve.' She recognised the lines from the Wasp-Witch's late-night novenas, but the prayers had never sounded like this. 'To thee do we send up our sighs, mourning and weeping in this vale of tears.'

The voices were loud and deep and droning now, like they no

longer belonged to the girls, and Ella had to fight an urge to put her hands over her ears.

'Inspired by this confidence we fly unto thee, O Virgin of Virgins, our mother.'

Their steps became quicker and their chanting faster until they were spinning around the circle, birling, their loose hair flying as they rolled their heads in a wild, ecstatic dance.

'Virgin most powerful,' Mhairi chanted.

'Pray for us,' the Cecilians shouted back.

'Goddess Moon.'

'Pray for us.'

'Mystical Rose.'

'Pray for us.'

'Queen of the Night.'

'Pray for us.'

Out of the corner of her eye, Ella noticed a shadow. Outside the circle, a figure paced, beating a steady rhythm on an African drum.

'Look!' Ella pointed. 'There's another one over there?"

'It's Tibby,' Catriona whispered, her face as bleached as the moon.

The drumming got louder and louder. And then there was so much noise and flesh that Catriona covered her ears and squeezed her eyes shut. But Ella watched as the Cecilians gyrated, hips loose and mobile, hands riotously free, lost in the urgency of their chanting and the stamping of their feet. They were together and separate, one and the same. And the beat thumped in Ella's chest and deep in her groin. She felt what she saw. Something dark and sexual, out of time and place, primeval, like tribal dancers or the witches in the darkest places of her childhood imagination. That these were the same girls she had laughed at in their Alice bands and their frilly shirts seemed utterly impossible to her now.

Then suddenly they stopped.

The Cecilians took their positions at the edge of the circle. And Mhairi, their high priestess, threw back her head until her face pointed skyward. She was the leader in all the observances, throwing out her prayers to the Goddess Moon. 'To thee do we come, before thee we stand, sinful and sorrowful.' And the others joined her, incanting their devotions, sending them heavenward with a force that made the air vibrate.

'Mother Moon, Mother Goddess, Mother Mary, come!'

'Mother Moon, Mother Goddess, Mother Mary, come!'

'Mother Moon, Mother Goddess, Mother Mary, come!'

'We have to get closer,' said Ella.

'I don't want to get closer! We shouldn't be watching,' said Catriona, but Ella grabbed her hand and dragged her forward.

'Stop it! They'll see us.' Catriona wrenched her hand free and dropped to the ground behind a fallen tree. They sat for a moment with their backs against the trunk, staring into the blackness of the wood.

'We should go before it's too late,' said Catriona.

But as the noise grew, Ella was unable to resist looking again, and turning, she kneeled, leaning on the trunk as though it were a prie-dieu.

In the middle of the circle, Mhairi, her body ghostly in the starlight, picked up a branch from the tree-stump altar. Ella strained to see.

'Look,' Ella nudged Catriona, 'What the hell is she doing now?' Catriona knelt up and stared in disbelief.

Mhairi had a switch of some sort, long and supple, a fir branch maybe. She dipped it into a bowl of water and twirling like a dervish she doused the naked girls, who fell to their knees. And taking fir-boughs from the edge of the circle, the girls began to whip themselves, flogging their backs with the branches. First one side, then the other, ten, eleven, twelve times. And while their heads thrashed, and their hair flew, their groans grew more animal-like and unrestrained.

'Is this for real?' Ella whispered, but Catriona had screwed her eyes shut as if she wished there were things she could un-see.

In the centre of the circle, Mhairi raised her hands above her head and turned to face the full moon. Her whole body was stretching, reaching up to the night sky. On tiptoes – her legs taut with the strain of the stretch – she rocked, hips gyrating, every tendon extended. She seemed to be grasping at something invisible, grabbing high to bring it down, pulling with her hands like she was hauling on a rope. Whatever she clutched at, the moon, the Virgin, the goddess, whatever it was, she was drawing it into her breast. Her outstretched hands reached up again and again, sometimes open like a cup, willing the power to flow into her with her invocations.

And then she too fell to her knees. Ella watched, rapt, as she threw her head back, her mouth open in a kind of ecstatic agony. Mhairi's upper body began to sway as if she were dancing to a slow and sensuous beat that only she could hear. And then sound began to rumble from her mouth. There were no words Ella recognised. Although the cadences seemed like speech, the utterances were like no language she had ever heard before. Deep and guttural, rolling on a wave of Rs and Ss, ancient and terrifying.

'What's happening? I don't like this at all,' whispered Catriona, her lips deathly pale.

'I don't know, but whatever it is, it's seriously fucked up.' Ella's brain was crashing with sounds and images that made no sense at all.

And then, suddenly, Mhairi fell forward onto the ground. The sound stopped and her limp body twitched where it had landed.

Bells immediately rose and taking the blankets from the edge of the circle, draped Mhairi's shivering form. She continued around, placing a rug over each of the girls' shoulders. Then, moving to the altar, she filled five cups from a bottle of spirits and ripped a loaf of bread into hunks.

After a few moments Mhairi stirred and pulled the blanket around her a little tighter. She stood up, calmer now, and stiller, and her voice sounded more like her own. 'Our ceremony is over. Under the light of the full moon, we have thanked the Virgin Mother for the completion of our cycle and have asked her to bless us in the month to come. Now we close the circle and conclude the Rites of the Full Moon with our libations.'

The girls toasted each other with their plastic toothmugs and hungrily ate the bread. Then, refilling their glasses, they stepped out of the circle and ran to Our Lady's Tree where they pulled on the clothes that were piled on the grass.

A thick cloud covered the moon and darkness fell total and complete. Ella blinked, struggling to pick out the girls on the far side of the clearing now that they were dressed in dark tracksuits. From the pitch of their voices and the laughter that arose, it seemed they had returned to their usual selves. They were drinking and jumping about to warm themselves up.

'Do you think it's all over?' whispered Ella, unable to keep the tremble from her voice.

Catriona nodded, still blank with shock.

'Do you think we should… go over there?'

'No way,' said Catriona, emphatic now.

Ella's shoulders sagged with relief. 'Okay. Let's get out of here.'

As they stood up from their hiding place a muffled light shone on them from the bushes and heavy-footed, like an animal stumbling through the brush, a figure emerged. Catriona jumped back, terrified, and her leg caught on a bramble. She fell, pulling Ella down with her, and both of them thumped to the ground.

It was Tibby, routing them, like a beater flushing grouse. She stood over them, shining the flashlight into their faces, blinding them. 'You two! What do you think you're doing?' Her angry whisper contorted her mouth. 'What did you see? What did you hear?' There was panic in her voice.

Catriona shielded her eyes with her hands. 'Nothing, Tibby, we didn't see anything. We've just got here.'

Ella jumped in. 'I made her come. I felt left out while we were sitting in the book room and I wanted some of the vodka. That's all.'

The commotion had startled the Cecilians. Tibby, Ella and Catriona ducked low behind the tree-trunk and watched as the girls on the other side of the glade darted behind Our Lady's Tree, hiding themselves from view.

'What were you doing in the book room, Catriona? This was Ella's trial. Never mind. It's too late for that. Go back. Now!' Tibby jabbed a stubby finger towards the school. 'I'm going over there to Mhairi. I'll tell her the noise was just a deer. Do you understand me?'

Ella looked up at her dumbly.

'They must never know that you were here. Ever. Got it?'

'Yes, Tibby. Don't worry, we won't breathe a word.' Catriona understood instinctively what it took Ella longer to grasp. Tibby had one job, to make sure Mhairi was protected from intruders, and she had failed. But if the two of them sneaked back unseen, the Cecilians need never know that Tibby had failed in her task.

And in return, Tibby would keep the dirty secret, that they had stood and watched, like peeping Toms. That they had spied on something so intimate and dreadful.

'Not a word.' Tibby put her finger to her lips, then lumbered straight across the glade into the thicket behind the tree where the Cecilians were hiding.

'Let's go,' said Catriona.

'Wait, I've lost the flashlight.' With both hands Ella patted her way through the vegetation until she felt the cold metal of the torch. 'Here it is!'

She got to her feet and started back towards the school, but Catriona wasn't following. She hadn't even moved.

'Come on, let's get going, it's freezing,' Ella whispered. But still, Catriona didn't move. Her face was blanched and frozen, and Ella followed her gaze. On the right of the clearing, shafts of moonbeams sliced through the cloud-cover and circles of light, like stepping-stones, made a pathway across the glade.

And then Ella saw it.

A figure, soft and feminine, stepped into the brightness.

Ella blinked. Was the figure in the light, or was she the light? She was at once luminescent and insubstantial. An immaculate mantle covered her dark hair, draped over her narrow shoulders,

204

and fell, almost to her feet. Ella clamped her hand across her mouth, afraid to blow away the vision with something as real as breath. And in the liminal space between inhalation and exhalation the moment was all that existed. There was no past and no future. Only now.

Perhaps it was the pounding of her heart that gave them away, but the figure stopped and turned towards them. The face, she could almost see it, was soft, not dazzling, and comfortingly familiar. Ella was not afraid. She shut her eyes and shrank to the size of an infant as the brightness folded around her. It cradled her in an embrace that was secure and complete. She breathed in the light, until her lungs were a tree of white and a deep consolation settled on her. As if she was swaddled in the scent of lilacs, in a blanket as soft as love.

When she opened her eyes the figure had turned away and was crossing the glade towards the tree. She wanted to call out, *Don't go. I'm here. Can't you see me?* She reached out towards the figure, grasping through the darkness. She willed her fingers to stretch like branches across the glade. *Don't leave me. Not again. Don't go.* But Catriona, tears streaming down her cheeks, was pulling her back, begging her to stay quiet.

She stepped in front of Ella and grabbed both her hands. 'You're alright. Stay with me,' she whispered, and Ella gulped a lungful of air.

Over by the tree, the figure knelt to touch the little crosses and plucking one from the ground, she reached up to place it at the Virgin's feet. The moonlight caught her once again as she stood, and silvery light refracted from her fingers. Her hand lingered for a moment, then walking on a little, she stepped into the dark forest and was gone.

CHAPTER 23
Them Heavy People (Kate Bush)

Ella stood bewildered, clutching at fragments as they vanished into air. She could feel her feet on the ground, the cold through her tracksuit, but the things that she had seen did not fit with this version of reality.

A rustling on the other side of the clearing made her jump. The Cecilians were on the move and they were heading straight towards them.

'Quick!' said Catriona, pulling Ella into the thicket. 'We need to get out of here, fast!'

They dodged through the trees, ducking low branches, pursued by voices as shrill as bats. Ella felt damp breath on the back of her neck, imagined fingers grasping at her shoulders, but she was fast, and twisted through the undergrowth like a hare. Catriona stumbled alongside her, struggling to keep up, but Ella never let go of her hand, until breathless, they reached the safety of the dormitory, long before the others made it back.

In the doorway of Ella's cube, Catriona hugged her fiercely, her glasses pressing awkwardly into Ella's bony chest. 'The lady…' she gasped. 'Did you see her?'

Ella nodded. 'I think so… yes.' She did not pull away and they held each other until their breathing steadied, and their hearts, pumping through the nylon of their tracksuits, slowed.

'She was beautiful, wasn't she?' whispered Catriona.

'She was beautiful… yes… she was.'

***

All night, Ella lay awake, images clicking onto her inner eye like pictures in a slide show. Bodies, blue in the moonlight. Mirrors, fir branches, fire in a copper bowl. Noises replayed in her ears: drumming, chanting, that sound that had come from Mhairi's open mouth, which did not seem to belong to her. And then. When the woman had looked at her and she had shut her eyes. The comfort. The love. She had felt it. It was real. *Could it have been?*

She could not settle. The quilt twisted around her legs, the pillow lumped under her neck and nothing made sense. She was composed of her father and her mother in equal measure, the rationalist and the mystic, the academic and the artist, and all night long she flipped from one side to the other. There's no such thing as ghosts, her father had told her as he sat on the side of her bed, soothing her after a nightmare, pushing her sweaty hair off her face with the flat of his hand. They were optical illusions, or manifestations of the subconscious mind. But what she had seen couldn't have been something her mind had created, because Catriona had seen her too.

And as she lay in the darkness the night became liquid. Pictures and sounds swilled and melded with the last night she had spent at Mikey's. Her mother across the room, long hands stretching out to her, the familiar voice calling her name. Ella had wanted the touch of her so badly that she'd felt hands on her face, the coolness of fingertips pressing into her temples, soft palms cupping her chin. Maybe by just wanting things hard enough, she could make them become real.

***

The next morning, Ella and Catriona didn't walk to breakfast with the Cecilians as they usually did. Instead they kept their heads down and hurried on in silence. Last night in the woods, Tibby had told them both to lie, to tell anyone who asked that Ella had fixed the light, returned to the dormitory, gone straight to sleep and seen nothing. And Ella had promised Catriona she would do what Tibby asked. But now she wasn't sure she could manage it.

In the dining room, waiting for the nun to say grace, Ella's legs buckled under her and she had to grip the edge of the table to keep herself upright. Every time she blinked the lady was there, walking towards her across the glade. Ella's eyes darted around the room, finding the faces of the Cecilians. They were wan, like invalids recovering from a fever. They looked like she felt.

After breakfast she changed into her kilt and lay down on the bed. There was an hour to kill between breakfast and Mass so she slid Mikey's Mix Tape Number 4 into her Walkman, put on the headphones and pressed play. Wayne County and the Electric Chairs – *If You Don't Wanna Fuck Me Baby, (Baby, Fuck Off!)* – one of his favourites. She stretched her legs up the wall and scuffed the heels of her Docs in time to the beat, smearing a black smiley mouth onto the yellow paintwork. All around her girls were getting ready, polishing their shoes, braiding each other's hair. Some of them would be going out for lunch with their parents. For them, it was a Sunday morning, just like any other.

'Dignity and Decorum,' the Bulldog always said in assembly. 'That's the mark of a Saint Cecilia's girl. When we welcome the public into the convent, you become Saint Cecilia's public face. And we wouldn't want *her* to be looking a mess now, would we?' Mhairi and the Cecilians – the Bulldog's darlings – were such a bunch of hypocrites. Dancing naked around a fire one minute then fastening their kilt pins the next. They were full of shit.

She was staring at the neon light, watching it flicker, when Catriona came into her cube and tapped her on the shoulder. Ella budged over to the right and Catriona stretched out next to her, top to tail, Catriona's little legs under the bridge of Ella's.

They lay like that for a while, before Ella broke the silence. 'That was some pretty weird shit last night, huh?'

Catriona crossed her arms over her eyes. 'I'd heard about the stuff that they got up to on their night walks. I thought it sounded freaky. But I didn't ever think it would be like that. They must have been flipping freezing for starters. What did they think they were doing?'

'Calling down the Goddess or something? I've read about stuff like that.'

The Cecilians were real. Freaky, but real. She could talk about *them*. The other thing – the lady – she wasn't sure she could talk about that. Not yet.

'Mhairi wants both of you. Now!' Tibby barked from the corridor. Her eyes darted from one to the other. 'Remember, not a word about last night.'

As they followed Tibby to Mhairi's room, Ella's brain crashed through different scenarios. She could do what Tibby wanted – stick to the story, play dumb. But she was no actress and she wasn't sure she could pull it off. Why didn't she just tell them she'd been there? That she'd seen what they'd seen. That she'd witnessed it all. She wasn't afraid of them. She didn't owe them anything.

But Catriona grabbed her hand and squeezed. 'Please, Ella,' she whispered. 'Don't say anything. Let me do the talking.'

***

The Cecilians were lined along the edges of the two single beds, oddly formal with their feet on the ground and their hands in their laps.

'Morning, guys,' said Catriona, bubbly and bright, far better at acting than Ella would have guessed. 'You're all looking a bit rough. Big night was it?'

Bells spoke first, pulling herself up out of a slouch, asserting her authority. 'Yeah, something like that. It got a bit crazy. We need you guys to go out to the glade and check we haven't left anything behind. Empties. Fag butts, that kind of thing.'

Ella's lip curled involuntarily. Who did they think she was? Their servant?

Dizzy flashed a fake smile. 'We'll love you forever. It's just that we're feeling a bit fragile today, you know.'

Mhairi stood and turned to face the small, barred window, letting her deputies take care of the housekeeping.

'Sure,' said Catriona, 'no problem. It's a lovely day and we don't have anything better to do, do we Ella?' She was starting to overdo the chipper act, but nobody seemed to have noticed.

Bernie and Theresa were still staring at the floor, floppy and inanimate, like muppets.

Mhairi stirred. 'I want to get to Mass early.' Her voice was quieter than usual, and there was a stony detachment that made Ella uncomfortable. 'We'll take the front row. But I don't want to be in the middle as usual, I'll sit on the aisle today.'

***

They filed into Chapel a good ten minutes before everyone else and Ella sat in silence, looking at the veins on her hands, crunching her toes in her DMs. She felt the air thicken as the space behind them filled and sensed eyes on the back of her head. To her right chattering parents took their seats in the Lady Chapel and up in the gallery the nuns filed into position. Only Sister Hanrahan and the three most senior nuns sat in the body of the Chapel, at the edge of the altar, like four crows, behind a wooden gate.

As the Mass droned on, Ella, squashed in the middle of the pew, was uncomfortably aware of the proximity of the girls, of their bodies, touching hers. Shoulder to shoulder, thigh to thigh. Snapshots flashed again – hard nipples, buttocks, breasts, pubic mounds. And she tried so hard to squeeze away the images that stars burst onto her retina. The same girls who had danced naked in moonlight, chanting their incantations, now sat there in kilts and sashes, joining in with the prayers. Ella stayed silent. Nothing made sense.

Towards the end of Mass, Father Di Pono called them to stand for the Concluding Rite and drew his hands together in prayer. 'Hail Mary, Full of grace,' he began.

As the girls rose to their feet the low winter sun sliced through the long windows in the side of the Chapel. Ella turned to look and saw Mhairi, at the end of the pew, head tipped back, caught in the point of a triangle of light. The air around her was filled with flickering dust-motes, surrounding her like an aura. She seemed almost to sparkle, her hair burnished copper, her skin glinting like quartz. Ella wasn't the only one to have noticed. Dizzy clasped her hand to her mouth and the girls on the pew opposite turned to stare.

Slowly, Mhairi reached out towards the altar, then suddenly fell to her knees. The clatter of her fall startled the entire congregation and a murmur of concern swept through the nave. But Mhairi seemed totally unaware. A smile, warm and broad, crossed her face and she looked intently at something in the distance that seemed to fill her with joy. Ella looked over to see if she could see it too, but there was nothing there. Nothing except Father Di Pono, whose mouth was open as he stared at Mhairi. Her head was cocked, as if she was listening, and then she nodded in agreement with someone no-one else could hear.

Nudges passed round the congregation and soon pupils were craning their necks to catch a glimpse. Last night Ella had watched something intimate, and private. But here, now, everyone was watching and she felt too close to the centre of attention. She wanted to make it stop. She would push her way out of the row. Make a run for it. But when she turned towards the other end of the pew, Catriona had guessed what she was thinking and with the smallest of movements, she shook her head. There was no escape. Ella shut her eyes.

Bells and Dizzy sat down beside Mhairi, Dizzy talking gently, a hand on her friend's shoulder. Ella willed Mhairi to stop but rather than being stilled, she grew wilder and more agitated, throwing her head back, grasping at some invisible presence up on the altar. That strange language that Ella had heard the night before poured once more from Mhairi's mouth and a Junior from across the aisle covered her ears and screamed. Ella had to clench her fists to stop herself from putting her own her hands over her ears. *Dear God, let this be over*, she prayed.

Some of the parents stepped forward to find out what was going on, but, seeing Mhairi's ecstatic face, and hearing the low, rumbling noise, they hovered uncomfortably, unsure what to do. And Ella, who had remained on her feet, towering above the kneeling, seated, crying Cecilians, stood sweaty and awkward like a finger sticking up from the middle of a fist.

Father Di Pono shut his mouth and signalled for the organist to start the recessionary hymn. All around the congregation girls were looking up to the nuns in the gallery, and over to the crows on the altar, for guidance. The noise was getting louder and three rows of Juniors were in tears. Surely they were going to do something? To say something. To take Mhairi out. But the nuns were silent and implacable, hands held together, watching Mhairi with eyes that gave nothing away. Nobody moved.

In the absence of any adult direction, a few senior girls on the back row began to sing *Here I am Lord, is it I Lord?* And gradually other voices joined in with the hymn. Mhairi, meanwhile, continued to converse with a presence visible only to her.

Sweat poured down Ella's back. This was a fucking shit storm. And she was trapped in the middle of it.

At the end of the hymn the priest left the altar, followed by the Bulldog and the crows. As they walked down the aisle, the nuns, with their long flappy sleeves and tight, sharp voices, ushered the congregation out of the Chapel. 'Out now girls, out you go.'

But the Cecilians remained where they were, and Ella, trapped in the centre of the row, sat down. Every muscle in her body was tensed and she bowed her head, willing herself to become as small as possible.

Brisk footsteps approached from the back of the Chapel. It was Sister Gagnier. Ella's shoulders dropped a little, relieved that an adult had finally intervened. Mhairi mumbled on, and the nun knelt down on the ground beside her. The words were indecipherable, but Mhairi's smile was radiant, her eyes still bright. Sister Gagnier placed a hand on Mhairi's back then looking along the row she made eye contact with each girl in turn.

'Don't be afraid. Your sister is alive with the spirit. And who are we to disturb her?' Sister Gagnier held her hands above Mhairi's head, not touching her. 'Go now. There's nothing to worry about. I'll sit with her until the moment passes. However long that may be.'

CHAPTER 24

How Sweet It Is (To Be Loved by You)
(James Taylor)

Later that afternoon, after they'd been to the glade, Ella and Catriona were summoned to Mhairi's again. They'd done what had been asked of them. The paraphernalia was stashed in bin bags and all evidence of the previous evening had been erased.

Tibby stopped them outside the door, her mouth contorting with the importance of what she was about to say. 'I don't know what you saw last night, or what you think you saw, but you'd no business spying on us. Okay?'

'Okay, Tibby. We've been through this. We said we'd keep quiet.' Ella couldn't keep the irritation from her voice. 'I don't see why it makes such a difference, though. The whole school saw what happened this morning. Everyone knows something weird's going on.'

'You don't know what you're talking about. You shouldn't have been there, alright?' Tibby jabbed a nail-bitten finger at her. 'If you did see anything, you need to shut up about it. Got it?'

Flushed and trembling, she had a mad look in her eyes that prevented Ella from telling her exactly what she thought of her.

Catriona nudged Ella. 'We get it. Don't we?' Earlier, in the glade, she'd begged Ella to keep schtum.

'They're going to tell you some weird stuff, and you'd better act surprised when you hear it. Okay?'

Catriona nodded for them both.

Between them they carried the bin bags into the room and emptied the contents into the trunk between the beds: the silver bowl that had contained the water, the copper bowl that had held the fire, silk roses and lilies, candles, plastic mugs.

'We threw the empty vodka bottle in the skip behind the Steading and chucked the branches into the woods. Looks like you guys had quite a night,' Catriona said, still chirpy. But the mood in the room was dark and heavy. The curtains were drawn and all but the bedside lights were out.

'Thank you. Your loyalty is appreciated,' said Mhairi, her voice hoarse and faint. She uncurled herself from the shadows and flicked her hair. 'You have passed our test and now there are some things you need to know. Make yourselves comfortable.'

Ella and Catriona sat on the floor and leaned back against the wall.

'What I'm about to say is for Cecilian ears only.'

Ella felt Catriona's gasp. Was she addressing them as Cecilians? Did they even have a choice?

Mhairi continued. 'The Cecilians are a sisterhood consecrated to the service of Our Blessed Mother, Mary. Our ceremonies have been passed down from generation to generation. The Rites are written, in our sacred book.'

Mhairi nodded and Bells handed a small leatherbound volume to Ella. She felt the weight of it in her hand. A silver ribbon marked the place and the book fell open to a page where her name and Catriona's had been freshly written, in purple ink. A shot of excitement coursed through her. *Ella Richardson.* She traced her name with her fingertips then flicked back through the book. Pages and pages of names. And now hers was one of them. The last name on a list that must have run to hundreds. She was there. Part of something.

'Three generations of my family have been Cecilians. You cannot choose to be a Cecilian.' Mhairi stopped, for maximum dramatic effect, then continued. 'It is my honour to be the Priestess of this Ancient Sisterhood, and today, the Cecilians choose you.'

Ella snapped out of her dwam. Priestess. Ancient Sisterhood. Who was Mhairi kidding? This was like a bad movie. She passed the book to Catriona, not wanting the thing in her hands. She was horrified at the way she'd embraced her inclusion so quickly and unthinkingly. It was ridiculous! The school was only founded a hundred years ago so how ancient could this order be exactly? She pictured Mhairi's head flipping back and some deity with the face of a jackal wriggling from the open neck. She would sketch it when she got back to the dorm. This was too much. Lack of sleep and nerves made her giggle.

Catriona dug her in the ribs. 'Oh, Mhairi, we're honoured,' she intoned.

But Mhairi wasn't looking at them. Her eyes were fixed on some point outside the window. She carried on, 'Last night we performed our Marian Full Moon Ritual. We called upon the

Virgin to look with favour on our devotions and in return, she came to us in the glade and honoured us with her holy presence, beneath her sacred tree.'

'What?!' Ella's astonishment was real. 'You think you saw the Virgin Mary? Last night? Out in the woods?'

'We don't think. We know.' Mhairi was absolute. There was no doubt or hesitation. 'All six of us saw her.'

Ella's forehead crinkled with disbelief. 'You saw Mary, The Mother of God, at Saint Cecilia's, last night?'

The other girls nodded, mumbling their agreement. Yes, they had seen The Virgin Mary. In the glade.

Mhairi waited a moment, then rising a little from her position on the bed, she stretched her long neck and put a hand to her chest. 'And today, in Chapel, the Virgin came to me once again.' Her voice was so low voice it seemed to vibrate. 'She came in a vision. A vision of such beauty that I no longer knew where I was, or who I was. Only her presence mattered.'

'Did she speak to you?' Ella said.

'Oh yes, and her words were so gentle and reassuring.'

'Wasn't it frightening?' asked Catriona. 'I'd have been terrified.'

For a second Ella was back in the glade and the lady was standing in front of her. She hadn't been afraid, not one little bit.

Mhairi continued. 'She held my hands and told me not to be scared; she said I had been chosen.'

'Chosen? What for?' asked Catriona.

Bells cut in. 'She doesn't know yet. Don't bombard her with questions. Can't you see she's exhausted by it all?'

Ella saw Mhairi's shoulders drop, just a little, then she took her hand from her throat and sighed, right on cue.

'I'm sorry,' said Catriona. 'It's just so amazing. To think that you've been chosen. Here. In our school.'

'There's more. The Virgin has given her instructions,' said Dizzy. 'Mhairi's to go to the tree again tomorrow. And Our Lady is going to give her a message to share with all of us.'

Behind Ella, Bernie was sniffling quietly and Theresa was shushing her softly, urging her to stay calm.

'You'd better get your sister under control,' said Tibby from the doorway. 'We can't risk anybody else finding out. Got it?'

'But surely,' said Theresa, 'After what happened in Chapel, people are going to know. I mean she was having some kind of fit in front of absolutely everybody. How exactly can we keep that a secret?'

'Theresa. Speak respectfully,' Tibby barked.

'No, Tibby, they're right to be worried,' said Mhairi from the dark corner of the bed. 'We're safe enough for now. Sister Gagnier thinks I have a vocation. And maybe I have. She didn't ask too many questions and I didn't tell her what I'd seen. That's just between us Cecilians. We must keep this secret. Ella, Catriona, you are one of us now. Let us pray together and welcome you into the sisterhood.'

And Mhairi began the prayers that she had incanted the night before.

Ella bowed her head but she didn't join in. Did Mhairi believe that she'd been visited by the Virgin Mary? And was that actually any crazier than thinking you'd just seen your dead Mom?

CHAPTER 25

There's a guy works down the chip shop swears he's Elvis (Kirsty MacColl)

By the next day the strain of the secret was starting to show. The Cecilians were unravelling, it seemed. Bells and Mhairi clung together, leaving Dizzy on her own, waiting, picking the nail polish off her fingernails, gnawing on the inside of her mouth. Tibby was manic and could barely sit still. Even in lessons, her eyes flicked around the room and her foot tapped agitatedly on the wooden floorboards.

But it was Bernie who concerned Ella most. Her face was glazed and expressionless, and all through double Physics she sniffed quietly with her head in her hands. Ella watched Theresa watching Bernie and saw her quiet reassurance, an arm linked in as they walked down the corridors, a hand on the back as they waited outside classrooms. Theresa was worried about her twin, and her sister came first, no matter what Mhairi said.

At breaktime, while the Holy Trinity sloped off to smoke, Ella and Catriona waited with Theresa outside the loos.

Theresa tapped on the door of the stall. 'Come on Bernie. Let's get some soup. It'll make you feel better.'

'I can't face it. Go without me. I'll see you in Maths,' Bernie whispered through the door.

'We'll all go together. It'll be okay,' said Catriona.

And eventually Bernie emerged, her pale face marled with blotches.

Outside the dining room, the four of them formed a cluster, shielding Bernie from the crowd. Since Mass yesterday, the Cecilians had been under observation. The whispering stopped when they entered a room.

Tibby broke into their cluster and spat out a warning that smelled of mulligatawny. 'People are staring! Pull yourself together. Okay?'

'I'm sorry, Tibby,' whispered Bernie, wiping her nose with the sleeve of her jumper. 'I don't know what's the matter with me. I'm trying. Really, I am.'

Tibby turned on her heel and left.

'Who the fuck does she think she is?' said Ella, fire rising from her stomach.

'Be careful!' said Theresa. She put a finger to her lips. 'She might hear you.'

'I don't care; I'm not scared of her.' Ella felt bolder now.

'But you don't know what they're like.'

'Well, I'm starting to get a pretty good idea. And it ain't all lilies and roses, that's for sure!'

***

In the Form Room after lunch, Mhairi, Bells and Dizzy sat

with Bernie in the corner. To anyone else it looked like they were comforting her, but Ella could feel the threat in their proximity.

'She's just a teeny bit homesick,' said Bells loudly, to no-one in particular.

Dizzy put an arm round Bernie's shoulder. 'All you need is a bit of cheering up. And I have a bag of Kola Cubes with your name on.' She offered the white paper bag to Bernie who took one and popped it into her drooping mouth.

Someone was playing Barbra Streisand on their tape recorder and the girls in the front two rows were singing along to *You Don't Bring Me Flowers*. Ella winced. Dear God, had nobody told them that the 70s were over.

She sat with Catriona and Theresa, but Theresa's attention wasn't with them. Her eyes kept flicking to her sister at the back of the room.

'D'you think she's okay?' asked Catriona.

'I don't know. I really don't.' Theresa looked over her shoulder to see if anyone was listening. 'It was crazy out there. The dancing was bad enough, but then Mhairi went all weird and that was terrifying and then...' She stopped.

'Yes... then...?' Ella wanted her to go on.

'Then we saw her.'

'The Virgin?'

'Yes, The Virgin.'

'Are you sure that's what you saw?' Ella asked.

'I think so. I mean, we'd finished the voddy by then, so I wasn't sure, but Mhairi said it was her. And... well... she did look kind of like the Virgin Mary.'

'What, like in the school nativity? Blue dress, baby in her arms, that kind of thing?' Ella asked.

'Well, no. Not really. She was all in white.' She paused as if trying to remember the scene. 'Yes, white.'

'Maybe it was the famous White Lady?'

'Oh no, it wasn't her.'

'How do you know?' asked Catriona.

'I'm not sure. But it wasn't scary. She made me feel… peaceful. I didn't really see her face, but I could tell she was beautiful. I don't know how to explain it… I sort of couldn't take my eyes off her. It felt like looking at someone I knew, really, really well.'

'Yeah,' said Ella. 'She was so familiar.'

'Wow!' said Catriona, punching Ella's thigh under the desk and covering for her quickly. 'Maybe it wasn't Mary, though. Maybe it was just somebody walking in the woods. I mean what are the chances that the Virgin Mary would come here? To the north of Scotland?'

'Why shouldn't she pick Scotland? The other places she picked weren't exactly special. Guadeloupe? Fatima? We've heard all about them, and they were just ordinary places,' said Theresa.

'I suppose.'

'We went to Lourdes last summer and Bernie and I looked for her really hard. We prayed that we'd see her. But we didn't see a thing. And now. Now that we have seen her, it's all too much for Bernie.'

'I don't know how you can be so sure it was her,' said Ella.

Theresa shot a glance at the third row. 'You'd better not let them hear you say that. We Cecilians speak with one voice.'

'And that voice is Mhairi's?' Ella drummed her fingers on the desk.

'Girls,' Mhairi called from the other side of the room. 'Come back here and join us. We miss you.'

'We've managed to cheer up little Bernie-Boo,' said Dizzy. 'All she needed was a bit of sugar and some love.'

'Is that right, Bernie? Are you feeling better now?' said Mhairi.

Bernie pulled up one corner of her mouth in a twitchy little smile and blinked a couple of times. 'Yes, Mhairi. I'm feeling much better now.'

***

After games, Ella took herself down to the Chapel with her copy of *Silas Marner.* She hadn't been alone since Saturday and she was craving solitude. In the quiet of the Lady Chapel she drew her feet up onto the pew and tried to empty her mind of all that had happened.

Late afternoon light sliced in through the side window and she felt its warmth on the side of her face. She hummed to herself, softly, imagining she was rocking, on a swing, in a crib, a lullaby quietening the noise inside her head, soothing her still. And for a while she stopped thinking about the Cecilians and the ritual, the book with her purple name. She stopped thinking about the lady wrapped in the mantle too.

She felt the rise and fall of her stomach, the gradual unstiffening of her joints. She stretched her neck, hearing the crunch of sinew and tendon and tilted her head forwards and then back until it came to rest against the wall. And she breathed. Just breathed.

She shut her eyes and counted her breaths, as her mother had taught her. In for seven, out for eleven. Seven Eleven. That was a shop back home in America, before they had crossed the sea and come here, to Scotland. Seven Eleven, where they'd bought corndogs on a road trip to Niagara Falls, and a bag of chips so big her hands couldn't reach the bottom. She'd sat in the back of the station-wagon, listening to the songs on the tape Mom had made for the journey, and had fallen asleep to the sound of her parents talking, laughing, singing along. White noise, fragments of a dream: the words, the music, the crinkle of the chips.

And when she woke up it was dark in the Lady Chapel, the only light a flickering yellow from the votive candles. A lyre played softly, somewhere behind her. Magda. Ella had no idea how long she had slept or for how long Magda had been there, but it was comforting to know that while she'd slept, Magda had played, keeping vigil, in a way. She didn't want to break the stillness, but out in the corridor she could hear the sound of the girls filing towards supper. Catriona would be wondering where she was. She should go.

She straightened up and turned to the dark corner of the Chapel – the place where Magda played. Ella's eyes took a moment to focus. She could see the head dipped to the lyre, the black hair falling to the shoulders, the exquisite lace of the mantle that half obscured the face. There was such serenity in the sound, in the tilt of the head, and the movement of the hands, that Ella wanted to stay, to be bathed in the untroubled peace of it.

And Magda looked up, smiling through the gossamer fabric. Her smile was open, and beautiful, and Ella felt the warmth of it.

And suddenly she was back in the woods and the lady was standing right in front of her. Looking straight at her. The lady that brought such peace.

The lady.

225

The lady was Magda.

It was Magda that she'd seen.

And Magda had seen her. She'd looked straight at her.

Ella stood up, her heart suddenly racing. 'It was you. Out by Our Lady's Tree on Saturday night. It was you.'

Magda paused. 'I was there. Yes.' Her speech was thickly accented, and faltering, as if she was unaccustomed to using it. 'I saw you… in the trees. You… and your small friend.'

Ella sidestepped along the row in front of Magda and knelt on the pew to face her. She had never been this close to her before. 'And the others, the Cecilians, did you see them?'

Magda nodded. 'Yes.'

Ella swallowed hard. The lady was flesh and bone after all, and for a moment, she was disappointed.

Magda reached over and took Ella's hand. Her skin felt cold and rough, and Ella glanced down at the red swollen knuckles, the dried quicks of Magda's fingers. When she looked up, Magda was still watching. And her gaze seemed to pierce her.

'Your heart is sad. No?' she asked. Magda was half-hidden behind the mantle. There was so much Ella wanted to say that she said nothing at all. 'You were searching for something, in the woods?' said Magda.

'I don't know… maybe.'

'And did you find it?'

'I thought…' she hesitated. 'No, I don't think so. No.'

'And did they? Did they find what they were looking for?'

'They think they did, yes.'

'Then I hope it brings them peace.'

She kissed Ella's hand, and so quietly that her feet seemed

226

barely to touch the floor, Magda disappeared through the visitors' doorway.

***

Ella ran down Silent Corridor and into the foyer where the girls were milling before supper. Scanning the room for Catriona, she picked her out on the far side and waved her arms to catch her attention. 'Come with me,' she mouthed, and together they ran through the double doors to the courtyard outside.

The night air was so cold it took Ella's breath away and she could hardly get the words out. 'The lady... the lady in the woods... it wasn't the Virgin Mary... it was Magda.'

'What? Magda? Creepy Magda? Who lives up in the Steading with her mother?'

'Yes! No! Magda. It was her. She's not creepy. On Saturday night.' The words were tumbling out. 'It wasn't the Virgin Mary. Or the White Lady. It was her. The Cecilians have got it wrong.'

'Are you sure? How do you know?'

'I've seen her, just now, in Chapel...'

'In Chapel? Don't tell me you're having visions as well.'

'Don't be stupid. That's where I go sometimes, to read. And sometimes she's there, too. On Saturday, when we saw the lady, I had such a strong feeling that I knew her, but I couldn't see her face properly. And just now, when I saw Magda in Chapel, I knew. She's the lady. The lady from the woods.'

'And did you ask her what she was doing creeping through the forest in the middle of the night, dressed all in white?' Catriona raised an eyebrow.

Ella paused at last. 'No, I didn't.' She smiled. 'I probably should have, though.'

'That would have been a help.'

'But anyway. You see what this means? It means they're lying about all this Virgin Mary stuff.'

Catriona thought for a moment. 'Does it? I think they really believe it. I mean, we saw the lady too and we didn't know what we'd seen. I thought it might've been the Virgin Mary. Didn't you? Maybe they just want it so much that they actually believe it's true.'

'Maybe.' Ella nodded. 'I suppose a bottle of vodka and all that chanting might be enough to get you so off your face you'd actually believe you'd had a visitation from the Virgin Mary. It was pretty wild out there.'

Catriona shrugged. 'But what about that whole performance in Mass?'

Ella thought about Mhairi's face in Chapel. She had looked kind of… transfigured. If she was acting, it was a good performance. Was there any chance that Mhairi might be genuine? That she *had* seen something on the altar? She shook her head. No, she might not understand why Mhairi was doing this, but something was off. For Mhairi everything was about power – power and control. This was a game, and right now at this very minute, it was Ella who was winning. She knew something that Mhairi didn't, she had the upper hand for once.

'No, I'm pretty sure the *vision* thing's fake too,' Ella said. 'I mean, we know how manipulative she is. But this is nuts. She's got them all eating out of her hands. They actually believe that she's under orders from the Virgin to creep out on her own tonight.'

'Bloody hell, Ella. If you're right, this whole thing is pretty twisted.'

'I am right. I know I am,' said Ella. 'And you're not kidding, this is *really* twisted. You can see what it's doing to Bernie.'

'Yes. Absolutely.' Catriona paused. 'It's totally nuts.' She shifted uncomfortably and twitched her nose to push up her round glasses. 'But I'm not sure what we can do about it exactly. You're a New Bug. It's probably hard for you to understand, but in a place like this, the absolutely worst thing you can do is tell tales. If we told everyone that Mhairi's making it up, and that the woman they saw was Magda, our lives would be completely and utterly over.' She believed that. Ella could see it.

Whatever else she was, Ella wasn't a snitch. She'd have to think carefully about what to do next. 'Ok. We'll keep quiet for now. She's walking again tonight. Let's just see what happens. Part of me wants to see how far she's going to take this thing.'

'Girls!' a voice called from the doorway. It was the Bulldog. 'And why would you two be skulking about out here, when you should be inside having supper?'

'Good evening, Sister. Ella was just feeling a bit unwell and I brought her outside for some air,' Catriona said.

'A likely story. Be getting on with you now. Straight to supper. I have my eye on the both of you.'

***

Before prayers Catriona and Ella were called to Mhairi's. As they stood in the doorway, Ella's eyes flicked round the room, observing the dynamics. The Cecilians were gathered on the beds: Bernie was leaning on her sister, her eyes far away, her arms pulled tight

229

around her knees; Dizzy, in the shadows, hugged a pillow; Mhairi was composed and upright, the ashen look gone, her hair cascading in ripples once more. Bells sat stiffly at her side.

'It's been a difficult day for all of us. There's a lot to take in,' said Mhairi. 'I know it must seem as if I am the one who has been chosen, but never forget that we are all Cecilians and what happens to one of us, happens to all of us.' She looked at each of them in turn, ensuring she made eye contact. 'When I'm walking tonight, I'm only the figurehead. You are all with me in spirit. And I need you to stay strong.' She flashed the twins a stone-cold smile.

'We're behind you,' said Bells.

'Every step of the way,' Tibby chimed in from the door.

'We each have a role to play. Ella, I'll need you to do the light again tonight. Catriona, you should join her this time.'

Shit, the light. Ella had forgotten about it when they'd run back to the dormitory on Saturday night. It must be just as they'd left it, programmed to go off at 12.30am. But the Cecilians didn't know that. Last night it must have come on at 6pm as usual but gone off far short of the scheduled 7am switch off. She wondered if anyone had noticed. There was no need for them to go back to the book room tonight, the light would go off anyway, but she and Catriona would have to go along with the sham if their own secret was not to be revealed.

'Don't worry. You can rely on us,' said Catriona. She had developed skills to survive in this place and they were coming in surprisingly handy.

***

They went to the book room again that night, the route now

familiar, the darkness less terrifying. The lights went off at 12.30am, and all they had to do was wait for an hour, until Mhairi was safely back indoors and Ella could adjust the controller to switch off at 7am.

To pass the time they sat on the floor with their backs against stacks of class readers. They ate the jelly babies that Catriona had brought and talked about Mhairi and the Cecilians, guessing how the story might end. And then, as they relaxed into the darkness, they began to speak of other things – of home, and childhood, and happier days – things Ella hadn't spoken of in a very long time. They sat in the darkness and leaned on each other. Like friends.

CHAPTER 26

Bad Moon Rising
(Credence Clearwater Revival)

The next day when the smokers slinked off at breaktime, Ella and Catriona were dragged along too. A disused log store at the back of the Steading was clearly a favourite haunt: fag-butts littered the ground and the walls were covered with graffiti. The dank, foxy smell reminded Ella of the bike shed back home and she found herself scanning the walls for Mikey's tell-tale tags. Mhairi wasn't there yet, and in her absence, Bells took charge. She lit up and passed the cigarette to Tibby who puffed on it and handed it to Dizzy, bypassing Catriona. 'Not you, remember what happened last time,' Tibby said.

The circle of girls pulled tighter for warmth, white breath mingling with grey smoke. Dizzy passed the cigarette to Ella and she took a drag, trying to look casual, as if she'd done it before. Her head rushed and the smoke caught the back of her throat. She held her breath, controlling the cough that would give her away. Opening her mouth, a cloud billowed out, catching her eyes, making them water.

By the time Mhairi arrived the cigarette was almost finished, but Theresa handed it to her nonetheless. She took a long drag and flicked it to the floor, stubbing it out with the heel of her black pump.

Mhairi was in no rush and put out a hand for Bells to pass her the Bic lighter that she'd been flicking incessantly. Then she took a votive candle from the pocket of her tunic and lit it, placing it on an oil drum in the centre of the circle. Tossing her hair back, she looked up for a moment and closed her eyes. 'Oh Blessed Mother, present with us today, to thee do we cry, poor banished daughters of Eve. Let us pray.'

Ella rolled her eyes at Catriona. *Here we go again.*

She watched as the girls recited the *Hail Mary*, eyes shut, heads bowed. And when it was finished, Mhairi said the same prayer over, and over, the pace getting faster and her words more insistent until they had become a rhythm and poor Bernie was in tears once again. Theresa, looking up and seeing that only Ella was watching, put an arm around her sister to hold her up.

Seamlessly, Mhairi moved on from the frantic *Hail Marys*.

'Virgin most powerful,' she exalted.

'Pray for us,' the girls chanted back.

Ella didn't join in. She was afraid she might get caught up in the spell of the rhythm, and she needed a clear head.

'Goddess Moon.'

'Pray for us.'

'Mystical Rose.'

'Pray for us.'

'Queen of the Night.'

'Pray for us.'

Ella had to hand it to her, if Mhairi was a fraud, she was certainly convincing. It was almost as if she wanted it to be true. Unlike the Wasp-Witch who recited the prayers in a droning hum, Mhairi intonated every title with its full dramatic potential, each one building on the last until all of the girls, bar Ella and Catriona, were crying. Mhairi fell to her knees, just as she had in Mass, and the girls followed suit, joining hands.

When silence finally settled over the group, Mhairi reeled them in. Slowly, quietly, she began to tell the story they were all waiting to hear. 'Last night, the Virgin came to me by her sacred tree. She looked so beautiful, just like before, white and immaculate.'

Liar! Ella wanted to call out to tell the others they were idiots for believing her. But there was something so compelling about Mhairi's voice that she wanted to keep listening too.

'She held my hands, and called me her blessed child, just as she did in my vision. She said, "Mhairi, do not be afraid," and I wasn't. I just stood in her presence feeling the goodness of her heart.'

'And the message, Mhairi?' There was desperation in Theresa's voice. It had made her brave. 'Did she give you the message for all of us?'

'Theresa!' barked Tibby.

'No, Tibby, she's right to be impatient. She shouldn't be made to wait for such a blessing. And who am I to keep this good news to myself?'

Ella was as eager as the others to hear what was coming next.

'The message... yes... the message.' Mhairi shut her eyes. Her head swayed gently as if she was transporting herself back to the moment when the sacred dispatch was delivered. 'The message. Oh, Cecilians, her voice was so gentle, I wish you could have heard it. The Virgin looked at me as she spoke. She said, "I want you to come back to me once more to receive my final message. But for now, take this lesson to the girls: tell them that if they love something, they should set it free. If it comes back to them, it is theirs, forever. But if it does not, then it was never meant to be."'

Ella snorted a laugh, but a fierce look from Catriona made her put her hand to her mouth as if she were stifling a cough. She'd seen that crappy philosophy somewhere before – in a fortune cookie, a Hallmark card, on a stupid poster in the halls. Surely no-one was falling for this.

She looked round, expecting this to be the moment when the others would see this for what it was – a hoax. This was when Mhairi would reveal that she had fooled them. But instead the Cecilians remained motionless, their eyes fixed on their priestess with reverent devotion.

Dizzy spoke first. 'Oh, Mhairi, that's beautiful.'

Was she kidding?

'Maybe she is telling us we have no right to try to tame things that are truly wild,' said Dizzy.

'Oh! And to think that she gave us this message so close to the tiny graves,' said Theresa. 'It's such a perfect sign.'

Fuck. They've bought it.

Ella looked from face to face, incredulous, but she saw no trace of doubt or insincerity. These girls were enraptured by their Queen. She held them in the palm of her hand.

Tibby tapped her watch. 'Lessons in five. We'd better get going.'

The Cecilians had no time to recover before they were climbing the stairs to the tower, for French with Sister Gagnier. They were out of breath when they entered the room and were the last to settle down into their seats.

From the row behind her, Ella heard a sob. Bernie was in tears again. Tibby turned from her position by the door and scowled at the twins.

'Mon Dieu. Girls, what is the matter with dear little Bernadette? Child, what is making you so sad?'

Theresa spoke for her twin. 'Nothing Sister, nothing. Everything's fine.' She was twittering, unconvincing. 'It's just a touch of homesickness. Our Grandma's been a little under the weather, that's all.'

'Theresa, is this the truth? Our Blessed Mother is saddened when we shame her with a lie.'

At the mention of the Virgin, Bernie moaned, and the young nun stood up to address her. 'Bernadette, my dear one, come out here to see me.'

The third row tensed at the scrape of metal as Bernie pushed her seat back and made her way to the front of the classroom. Dizzy and Bells sat up straight in their seats and Ella saw that Mhairi's hands were clenched into fists beneath the desk. Ella's eyes flicked between Mhairi and Bernie who now stood with her back to the blackboard like she'd been called out for punishment. Heaving moans rose up from deep inside and her shoulders convulsed in time with the sobs.

Sister Gagnier stretched out towards her. 'My blessed child,' she said. As the nun's hand touched Bernie's shoulder the girl's legs buckled under her and she fell to the floor in a dead faint.

With a clatter of chairs, the Cecilians gathered around the prostrate figure. But Ella sat where she was, watching. This would be the end of it, surely. The farce would soon be at an end.

Sister Gagnier put an ear to Bernie's chest, listening to her breathing, while Tibby's eyes darted around the circle, her finger to her lips, reducing the huddle to silence.

After a few seconds Bernie stirred and the nun helped her to her feet. 'Sit down girls, sit down. She needs some air. I'm going to take her to the sanatorium. Theresa, come with us. Tibby, I'm leaving you in charge.'

As Theresa left the classroom, Tibby grabbed her sleeve and whispered something into her ear. By the contortion of the ginger-terrier's face, Ella guessed it wasn't something sweet and supportive.

***

Theresa and Bernie did not appear at lunchtime and when they failed to turn up for afternoon lessons the Cecilians started to fret. Before supper, Bells, Dizzy, Tibby, Catriona and Ella gathered outside the dining room. Ella pretended to listen while they exchanged theories about where the twins might be, but her attention was on Mhairi, who had distanced herself from the group.

Sitting alone in the centre of a bench the Queen Bee's gaze was fixed on a statue of Jesus – robed, arms outstretched, blonde hair, trimmed beard. Her legs were crossed to one side as if she'd been to finishing school and her face was a blank mask that Ella couldn't read. She didn't know why Mhairi was doing this, or what she had to gain, but one thing was sure, Mhairi didn't care about her precious Cecilians.

Word had spread about Bernie's faint and it hadn't taken long for the other girls to make a connection with the scene in the Chapel. At supper, while Ella forked her way through a gluey splodge of shepherd's pie, the girls on her table asked what she knew. Even Bunny, the Upper Sixther, seemed interested. But Ella had practised the party line. 'Oh, Mhairi thinks she might have a vocation, and Bernie's upset because her Granny's not well.' She wasn't fooling anyone, not even for a minute.

After they'd eaten, instead of heading to activities as usual, the Cecilians hovered while Bells spoke to Mhairi, over on the bench. Mhairi's face looked flushed, her forehead crinkled and for a second Ella thought she detected a chink in the immaculate facade. But Bells put a hand on Mhairi's shoulder and just like that she regained her composure and tossed her chestnut curls over her shoulder.

Bells came over to speak to them. 'Right. Mhairi reckons Bernie and Theresa are up in the San, so we're going to head there in a minute. Hopefully we'll be allowed to see them on our own. But before we go, Mhairi needs a word.'

Tibby's eyes darted, scanning for outsiders, and when the coast was clear they gathered around Mhairi.

'Sisters, we have been greatly honoured.' She was sounding more like Father Di Pono every day. But Ella noticed that there was an edge to her voice now. 'Sadly, though, it seems not all of us are strong enough to cope with the weight of such blessings. Our sister Bernie is weak. Perhaps she lacks the strength to bear witness for the Mother. But her weakness threatens all of us.'

The double doors to the courtyard blew open and a chill draft of air swept the foyer. Tibby ran over to push the doors shut while Mhairi carried on. 'If she draws too much attention, I might not be able to meet Our Lady, as she has requested. And her final message may never be delivered.' Mhairi paused, her cold eyes looking at each of them in turn. 'We must stop her from talking. You understand that don't you? We must do whatever it takes.'

The rest of the girls nodded, but Ella twiddled her nose ring and looked down at her DMs. How could she agree to something so wrong? It was time for this to be over; she was the one who could make it all stop.

But when she glanced up, Catriona was looking at her, willing her to keep quiet, bleached with fear. And although Ella didn't want to admit it, she was scared too.

Right now they were part of the group. It might be wrong. It might be twisted. But they were part of something. If she spoke out, she had no doubt that she and Catriona would become exiles. And she could remember all too clearly how that felt. She might be a coward, but she wasn't ready to cast them both into that particular hell. Not yet.

***

Outside the San, the Cecilians hung back as a steady stream of girls made their way through Sister Forsyth's door.

When the line finally petered out, Mhairi stepped forward and spoke for the group. 'Sister, we know that strictly speaking visitors are not allowed, but just this once, might it be possible for us to see Bernadette?' Mhairi inclined her head and smiled so sweetly that Sister Forsyth could not help but smile back, like a kind of involuntary reflex. 'She's very precious to us and we're so worried after her funny turn in French. We won't be long. Just five minutes?'

Sister Forsyth was a small, neat nun who smelled of TCP and

wore a white habit. Ella had come across her in the first week of term, at her medical. She had given her a butterscotch and told her to pay her a visit if ever she felt unwell. She seemed nice, in a gossipy sort of way.

'Well, that would have been just lovely, but it's out of the question, I'm afraid,' said the nun.

Mhairi was used to getting her own way and wasn't easily dissuaded. 'I promise we'll be quiet as little mice, Sister. You won't even know that we're there.' Again, the smile.

'I'm sure you would be. It's not that. It's out of the question, Mhairi, because Bernadette's not here. She left with Sister Gagnier and Theresa earlier this afternoon.'

Mhairi's lips pulled into a pursed little grimace and without responding she turned on her heel and headed down the stairs. On the landing she kicked the plinth of a statue of a pope and her tight mouth exploded in a volley of expletives. 'For fuck's sake! This was *not* supposed to happen.'

The Cecilians' faces froze. Ella had never seen Mhairi lose control before. For a moment there had been a flash of something real, something human beneath the marble.

In seconds Bells was by Mhairi's side. She put an arm around her shoulder, and they walked on ahead.

But Dizzy lingered behind with Ella and Catriona, no longer sure of her position in the ranks. 'I haven't seen her this rattled for a long time. I think the pressure's really starting to show.'

Ella nodded. Something about Dizzy's observation made her pause before saying, 'I can't imagine how hard it must be for her.' She sounded so much like a loyal Cecilian she almost made herself gag. 'I mean, the responsibility of being the chosen one… it's pretty heavy.'

'Yah. It's so intense. No wonder it's broken poor little Bernie. Mhairi's tough though. If anyone can cope with this, she can. She's made of steel, you know.'

'Is she?' said Ella, feigning surprise.

'Oh yah. You have no idea.'

***

At bedtime, Ella and Catriona were alone at the sinks. There was still no sign of the twins, and worry was etched on Catriona's face.

But Ella's fear had subsided, as it always did when Mhairi wasn't about. 'We should put a stop to this,' she whispered. 'We know it was Magda they saw in the woods.'

'But do *they* know that?' asked Catriona. 'I'm just not sure.'

'Okay. So let's suppose they all absolutely believe they saw the Virgin Mary out there. Fair enough. Like you said before, we weren't sure what we'd seen either. But, whatever happened last night, I think we can be pretty sure that Mhairi wasn't hanging out with the Mother of God. That message was bullshit. She's lying to them. And it's messing with their heads. Who knows where this will end if we let her carry on?'

'You're right. Of course, you're right. But we don't know what's happened to Bernie. Shouldn't we at least wait until we know?'

They didn't have to wait long. Bernie and Theresa reappeared during prayers. They avoided eye-contact and headed straight to their cubes as soon as the Wasp-Witch concluded Vespers.

***

An hour or so after lights out, just as Ella had drifted off to sleep, she was awoken by torchlight beaming into her face. Tibby held a finger to her twisted lips. 'Come with me. Now,' she whispered.

241

Tibby made her way down the dorm gathering Cecilians who followed the torch-beam to Bells and Mhairi's room.

In the dim light Ella could see Mhairi perched on her bed with Bells on her right. Hesitantly, Dizzy crossed the room and sat on Mhairi's left. Tibby pointed Ella and Catriona to Bells' bed, leaving Theresa and Bernie with nowhere to sit. They stood awkwardly between the ends of the beds and Theresa reached for Bernie's hand.

Mhairi began. 'There's no need to be afraid. We are sisters. And who knows better than you two about the love of sisters. We'd do anything for each other, wouldn't we?'

Theresa spoke for both of them. 'Yes, Mhairi.'

'And we always put each other first?'

The twins nodded.

'So, why don't you tell us what happened today?' Mhairi raised an eyebrow and waited for a response.

'Oh, Mhairi. I... I...' Bernie whimpered.

'Try not to upset yourself. Take some nice, deep breaths and tell us what happened.'

Ella wrapped her arms around her chest and shifted a little closer to Catriona.

Nobody spoke. Nobody moved. Ella could hear Catriona breathing, fast. Too fast. Her own heart was pounding too.

Mhairi was watching Bernie, whose mouth was moving but no words were forming. Dizzy and Catriona were looking at the floor. But Ella suddenly became aware that from the bed opposite, Bells was staring straight at her. Challenging her. Daring her to make a move. And why didn't she? Why was she letting Bernie suffer when she could stop all of this, now?

Bells only broke her gaze when Mhairi spoke again. 'Theresa, you're a little less… flustered. Since Bernie isn't up to it, why don't you tell us what happened?'

Theresa licked her lips and swallowed hard. She looked cold in her winceyette nightdress and Ella, who couldn't bear to look at the strain on the twins' faces any longer, looked at their bare feet instead. Bernie was rubbing the sole of her left foot over the top of her right foot, while Theresa rolled her feet outwards onto their edges as if she was trying to stop herself from running away.

'Oh Mhairi, it was all so upsetting. We went to the San and Sister Forsyth checked Bernie over and said that there was nothing to worry about, that she'd just got herself in a bit of a state.' She was talking quickly. 'It was empty in the sick bay, except for that little third former, Rose McGuinty, and she was asleep. Anyway, Sister Gagnier sat us down on the big sofas and Sister Forsyth brought us tea and toast. They were so kind, weren't they Bernie? You even stopped crying for a while, didn't you?'

Bernie wasn't crying now, she was just staring straight ahead, gripping Theresa's hand, her bony knuckles, white.

'And then?' said Bells, impatient now.

'And… and then Sister Forsyth left, and it was just Sister Gagnier. You know how lovely she is. She made us feel so safe, and she told us it was all right to talk to her. She said that whatever it was that was troubling us, she would understand.'

Mhairi's stony composure crumbled, and Ella saw the rage that had surfaced earlier, flash in her eyes once again. 'But you didn't say anything, did you?' Her voice was higher now, and faster. And for the first time, Ella wondered if the rage was laced with fear. 'You kept quiet? You know how much I wanted to speak to her after my vision, but I stayed quiet. I didn't blab. Please tell us you didn't blab.'

'It wasn't like that, Mhairi, really it wasn't. It didn't feel like blabbing. It felt like such a relief to tell her. To tell a grown up. It was just too much for us to handle on our own.'

Mhairi screwed her eyes shut and from her wide-open mouth came a scream so loud that Ella's ears rang. It ricocheted off the walls of the tiny room and reverberated down the corridor. The mask, it seemed, had slipped.

CHAPTER 27
Rabbit Fighter (T. Rex)

On the way to breakfast the following day, Mhairi and Bells walked ahead, while Dizzy, cold-shouldered, hung back next to Tibby. Ella and Catriona hovered in the corridor, waiting for Theresa and Bernie, but the twins, when they finally appeared, kept their heads down and limped past them.

All through lessons Mhairi stared ahead with her chin out, resolutely refusing to acknowledge the rest of them. In English, during group work, the Cecilians sat in silence. Bells dug her pencil into the woodgrain on the desk and Dizzy picked at the glue from the edge of her jotter-pad. There was a burning below Ella's rib cage that made her want to double over, a nagging, incessant fear that all this was her fault. Catriona, at the far end of the row, seemed to sense her anxiety and flashed her a tight smile that said, 'It'll all be okay.' But Ella wasn't so sure. There was a charge in the air that felt like an early warning.

At breaktime, Ella and Catriona were on their own once again. Since Sunday Mass, Mhairi and the Cecilians had been the subject of much speculation, but today the rumour mill had gone into over-drive. Everywhere the Cecilians went, eyes darted, fingers pointed, mouths were covered with cupped hands. And now, since they were the only two members of the group in the foyer, all this attention was focused upon them.

Catriona blew on her chicken noodle soup. 'You know Little Rose McGuinty?' she whispered.

'The Bubber who was in the San at the same time as Bernie?'

'Yeah, that's her. Well, I've heard she wasn't sleeping after all.'

Suddenly they were surrounded by a group of Lower Sixthers. 'So, is it true what everyone's saying?' asked a girl who had never spoke to Ella before.

Catriona jumped in, fumbling a lie. 'It's not true, no. I mean, no... I don't know what you're talking about. What are they saying? Who...?"

'Rose McGuinty. She says she heard Theresa and Bernie blubbing in the San. She said that you lot saw the Virgin Mary. And that Mhairi's been having visions or something. You know, like on Sunday, when she had that fit.'

'I don't know... I don't know anything about that,' said Catriona, floundering.

Ella feigned a laugh. 'Ha! Typical Chinese whispers. Looks like Rose picked up the wrong end of the stick. You know what Bernie's like. She was just a bit upset because we'd all watched *The Song of Bernadette* in RE. She got carried away.' Ella ploughed on. 'She's named after Saint Bernadette apparently. The film's pretty sad at the end – you know – what with the festering leg and everything.' God, what did she sound like? *The festering leg.*

The Lower Sixther raised an eyebrow at her friend. 'Come on, Tinks, I told you the skinhead wouldn't know any goss. These two aren't part of Mhairi's set. They're just hangers-on, like the rest of those Lower Fifth geeks.' The older girls turned away, looking for Dizzy or the twins, but Ella knew they were in the Form Room, hiding out.

'Looks like the secret's well and truly out,' muttered Ella.

'Seems like it.'

Ella scuffed the floor with the heel of her boot. 'Maybe we should come clean before this goes any further?'

'Maybe.' Catriona pushed a knuckle into her lip, biting on the chapped skin. 'But who would we tell?'

'I don't know. Sister Gagnier, maybe?'

Ella stood for a moment contemplating that thought. Yes, they should go and find Sister Gagnier. Tell her what they knew. Snitch. Blab. Wasn't that the right thing to do?

'We could try to find her after lunch?'

'If you think so. Maybe. Okay.' The burning in her ribcage flared. Since when had Ella Richardson – punk, rebel, liar, drug-taker and under-age drinker – been the person to do the right thing?

***

The whispering escalated over the course of the morning and by midday it was all anyone was talking about. But Ella couldn't help thinking about what they had to do. Find Sister Gagnier. Tell her what they knew. Dread seeped through her like an inkblot. She'd seen where snitching had got Bernie and Theresa. Was she really going there too?

At lunch, Ella evaded the questions that flew at her over the mince and by the time the nun in the rostrum said the concluding Grace, she felt totally nauseous.

Before they were dismissed the nun read out the usual afternoon notices. Ella never paid attention to these announcements – *Taxidermy club is cancelled; All girls who are litter picking should meet at 2.30pm* – whatever they were, they were never relevant to her. But today her ears pricked up.

'And finally, will the following girls go to Sister Hanrahan's office straight after lunch: Mhairi Campbell, Helena Cole, Fenella Douglas-Cook.' Ella's heart was thumping as she waited for her own name to be called. 'Tabitha Greer, Theresa and Bernadette McLeod.'

The nun switched off the microphone and stepped down from the rostrum. She and Catriona had not been summoned.

The announcement confirmed the rumours, and instantly the noise in the dining hall was deafening. Something big was happening. Big enough to involve a summons to the headmistress. While all eyes shot towards Mhairi, Ella and Catriona made a run for it. They pushed their way out of the dining room and bolted out of the doors, into the rain, past the Science block to the empty pet shed.

Inside, Ella shook herself dry. 'Oh boy. The shit's about to hit the fan!'

'Bloody hell!' Catriona wiped her steamy glasses on the hem of her tunic.

The shed smelled of sawdust, wet straw and turnips. Down the right side of the wooden building, hutches were stacked two or three high. A yellow ferret stirred at the sudden disturbance and a guinea-pig chattered, its nose pressed against the chicken wire, hoping for food.

Ella pulled herself up onto an old science bench at the far end of the shed. 'I don't know whether to be pleased or gutted that we're not in the room. I'd love to hear what's going on in there!' She twiddled the gas tap of a defunct Bunsen burner.

'Me too. But the best thing is, we're off the hook. The truth's bound to come out now. And there's no need for us to snitch after all.' Catriona opened one of the cages and pulled out a white rabbit. She stroked the soft fur between its flopping ears. 'You've no idea how miserable she would've made our lives if we'd told.'

She smiled. She seemed relieved, as if the monster she'd been running from had been caught and caged, and now, only now, was it safe to talk about it. 'Last year, there was this new girl, Jo. I told you about her before. She was fun and pretty, and super-popular with the front two rows. Everyone could see that Mhairi was rattled. So she started being really nice to Jo, pulling her into the circle. *Keep your friends close, keep your enemies closer* – that's Mhairi's motto.'

'Like some kind of mobster.'

'Yeah. Something like that. Anyway she started getting her to do little jobs for them. Nothing much at first. And then she invited her to a ritual. I don't know what it was about – I wasn't a Cecilian, and by that time Jo wasn't really talking to me anymore, but whatever it was, Jo freaked out and said she was going to tell. Said the Cecilians were sacrilegious.'

Catriona came over to the science bench and handed the rabbit to Ella. 'I brought some treats,' she said, and took an apple from her tunic pocket. Then she pulled open a squeaky drawer and pulled out a knife. 'Anyway, Mhairi made Jo's life so unbearable she was gone before the end of term.' She sliced the apple into quarters and held one out to the rabbit who munched its way down to her fingertips. 'Sister Cullen told us Jo was ill, but we all knew that was a lie. Mhairi got away with it, like she always does.'

'How does she manage it?'

'Oh she's clever. You can never pin anything on her. She's always so nicey-nicey. And that's the scariest thing about her. The nuns love her of course – all that crap about her having a vocation. But she's poison. You can see that, can't you? It might feel like the sun's shining on you when you're in her favour, but she twists things, turns people against each other.' She took the rabbit from Ella and put it back in its hutch. 'And when you're out of the light, that's a cold place to be. I don't know how she does it but we're all scared, you know?'

'Yeah.' She did know. 'She's a monster. And now everyone's going to see her for what she really is.'

Catriona shrugged, her frown deepening. 'Let's see.'

***

Later, when she was running, Ella tried to imagine the scene in The Bulldog's study: Mhairi in tears, confessing, the relief rippling through the rest of the group. She was glad that it was out of her hands, even if it meant she would never know exactly what it was that Mhairi had planned. The final message would remain a mystery, and there would be no more talk of night walks and rituals, visitations or visions.

But after her run, when she walked into the Form Room, one look at Catriona's face told her that things hadn't panned out like that at all. The Cecilians were in formation once again, Mhairi leaning back on her chair with her feet up on the desk, her handmaidens arrayed about her.

'Ella, come and sit with us. There's so much to tell,' said Dizzy.

Catriona, sandwiched between Bells and Tibby, peered up at Ella through her glasses, her face pale, her eyes enormous.

Mhairi spoke softly, but not so softly that the whole room couldn't hear.

'Our Lady works in mysterious ways. I have to admit we were a little lost at first, but our sisters, Theresa and Bernie, have shown us the right path.' The twins were sitting behind her on the back row. Ella glanced up at them. They were smiling. 'When something truly wonderful happens, it must be shared. We couldn't keep the miracle of the Visitation to ourselves. I see that now.'

Mhairi had not been exposed. There had been no fall from grace. On the contrary, from her central position, surrounded by her disciples, she seemed to have gained strength. She was elevated. She was calling it a miracle.

'You should have seen her, Ella, she was magnificent,' said Dizzy, in favour once again.

'Sister Gagnier was in tears when Mhairi described Our Lady's face, wasn't she Theresa?' said Bernie.

Ella swallowed. 'They know?' she said, slowly. 'About the Visitation? About Mhairi's Vision?'

Bells answered. 'They do. Yes.'

'And they… believe her?' She could sense Catriona's alarm at her comment and sure enough, like an attack dog, Tibby jumped in. 'Of course they believe her!'

Mhairi tilted her head to one side and regarded Ella through a curl that had slipped forward. 'Why wouldn't they?' she said, flicking back her hair. Smiling.

Ella took a step back, a deep flush rising up her neck. 'I

don't know. I just thought, maybe, they would need some sort of proof?'

Mhairi stretched out her arms and draped them around Bells' and Dizzy's shoulders. 'Proof? The Sisters have faith. They don't need proof. It's enough for us to have told them the truth.'

Ella shook her head, trying to ignore the signals flashing from Catriona's frightened eyes. 'It's just that…' She shrugged.

Bells pursed her lips and leaned forward in her seat; her blue eyes were trained on Ella. 'It seems we have a Doubting Thomas in our midst.'

Mhairi waited, absolutely still, controlling the silence that followed, while Ella shifted her weight from one hip to the other and pulled at the loose stitching on the pocket of her satchel.

'Is Bells right Ella? Do you have doubts? Do you need proof? Even if the Sisters don't?'

Ella ran her fingers through her cropped, choppy hair. Fatigue swept through her body. She hated how Mhairi did this to her. Made her feel pathetic, tongue-tied, weak.

But who the hell was Mhairi to make her feel like this? She was just some jumped-up, posh, fantasist. Ella was done with this shit.

She straightened her back and stood up straight. She knew the truth. Her hand was strong. But she would keep it to her chest for now, until she had her trump card –proof. She looked Mhairi squarely in the eye and smiled. 'I'm a Cecilian. Your word is enough,' she lied.

CHAPTER 28
I'm a Believer (The Monkees)

The fervour spread through the school like a fever. From the Bubbers to the Upper Sixth, girls had begun to bless themselves when Mhairi passed by. Some even reached out to touch her – her arm, her hair, the hem of her tunic. They wanted to make contact with the girl who had spoken to the Virgin Mary – as if Mhairi was a portal that could connect them too. The atmosphere was so intense that sometimes Ella almost forgot it was a sham.

Every morning during Mass, she stood with the Cecilians in the front pew, feeling the eyes of the congregation boring into her back. During the *Hail Mary*, right on the beat, Mhairi would fall into the same trance-like state. She reached out her hands to the altar, her eyes fixed on something remote, a vision no-one else could perceive. And while she knelt, her face shining in ecstasy, the girls all around her craned their necks to see.

Morning Mass had never been so well attended: pupils arrived earlier and earlier to get closer to Mhairi and jostled to be seated at the aisle ends of the pews. Some girls began to say they too could see a light, a shimmering luminescence up by the altar, and one or two fell to their knees to show their devotion too. Their gullibility made Ella gag.

Catriona had begged her to sit on their secret. 'It's too late to come clean now. It's our word against the entire school. Even the nuns believe them,' she had said. And Ella had promised to stay quiet. She was biding her time, waiting for proof. But in the meantime a bit of her couldn't help being enthralled by Mhairi's story. Like everybody else, she wanted to know what was going to happen next.

It didn't take long before word spread beyond Saint Cecilia's. A few Third Formers told their mothers on the phone and by Thursday there was a steady stream of parents, driving up to school to check on their daughters. And others, not connected to the school, turned up just to gawp. The front gates were locked, and a nun, of the fiercer variety, was stationed in the lodge-house to keep intruders out. John, the caretaker, had reportedly chased a bunch of local journalists he'd caught peeping over the boundary wall. The story was gathering momentum.

***

On Thursday evening Tibby informed the Cecilians that the nuns were in conclave in the lecture theatre.

'They'll be meeting behind closed doors to decide how to proceed,' explained Theresa.

'There's rules about this sort of thing,' Bernie chipped in.

'Yah. And if they're going to prove that Saint C's is the site of a new miracle, they'd better follow those rules to the letter.' Bells had been reading up on the catechism. 'Believe me, it'll be in their interest if all goes to plan. They'll be rolling in it, if this place becomes a shrine.'

'But until they've spoken to the priests, they won't want outsiders butting in on our business,' said Dizzy. 'First things first. The priest needs to decide if we're the right sort of girls.'

'Right sort of girls? What the hell does that mean?' Ella scoffed.

Mhairi looked at Ella with a smirk of false pity. 'The Virgin only comes to those with pure hearts and blameless characters. Such a pity you weren't with us that night, Ella.'

***

On Friday morning after breakfast, Sister Gagnier was waiting for them outside the dining room. She gathered them around her. 'Mes chères filles, you look exhausted.' She put her hand on Mhairi's cheek. 'The roses, they have gone.' She paused for a moment, drawing them in with the warmth of her gaze. 'But I have good news. There will be no lessons for you this morning. Sister Hanrahan has asked me to take you to the parlour where you can unwind. The fire has been lit.'

Dizzy clapped. 'The parlour! Fabby!'

Ella cringed. Sometimes they were such a bunch of losers. *How the fuck did I end up here?*

Sister Gagnier continued. 'In an hour or so, Father Di Pono will be arriving. He wants to talk to you about recent events.' She glanced over to Ella and Catriona at the edge of the group. 'Since you two were not present on the night of the visitation, there will be no need for you to attend. You should go to classes as usual.'

Ella was disappointed. She preferred to see things unfolding first hand. And Mhairi looked upset too. 'Oh but Sister, our friends have been such a support. They may not have been with us on the night, but they were with us in spirit. Couldn't they come too?'

'The rules are strict I am afraid. Only those who witnessed the apparition are permitted in the interview. Even Sister Hanrahan is not allowed to attend. We cannot risk compromising the statements.'

Immediately the Cecilians gathered round Ella and Catriona, reluctant, it seemed, to have their numbers reduced. Their sympathetic murmuring made Sister Gagnier think again.

'Well, I suppose Father is not arriving for a while. Why don't you enjoy some time together in the parlour.' She looked over at Ella and Catriona. 'Just make sure you go back to your classes by ten.'

'Oh, thank you Sister,' said Mhairi. 'You've no idea how comforting it is to have the support of our friends.'

'You have the support of all of us, my dear child.' Sister Gagnier took Mhairi's hands and kissed them. And Mhairi glanced over the top of the nun's head and fixed Ella with the brightest of smiles.

***

The parlour. Ella had heard about this place. When parents visited their girls, they were permitted to make use of it. But she'd never been inside. It was decorated like a drawing room in a stately home. Like the ones they had visited in Bath, that summer before Mom died. Beneath a huge mantelpiece, a fire had been lit and above it, an enormous painting overshadowed the room. Three rather stiff sofas formed a 'U' around a coffee table and Ella wondered if she'd ever been anywhere quite so grand.

'Wowzer!' said Dizzy. 'I've never been in here before.'

'I saw Daddy here once when he popped in after a business trip to Inverness,' said Catriona. 'He didn't have time to take me out for tea, but it was nice to see him. Sister Cobb brought us some of her famous scones.' The girls wandered round, wittering. None of them – even Mhairi – knew what was coming next. What should they say? What would the priest ask them when he arrived?

'Let's all sit down,' said Mhairi.

Ella was expecting her to get started on the prayers, to whip them up into a lather as usual, but instead she took her position in the centre of the sofa and listened while the rest of the girls talked. Sister Gagnier was right, Mhairi did look tired. Perhaps the strain of keeping up the pretence was finally starting to show.

'At last, it's just us,' said Theresa, throwing herself down onto the sofa. 'I feel like everyone is watching us all the time.'

'I know, it's like being a celebrity,' said Dizzy. 'Everywhere I look there are people staring.'

'One of the Bubbers even asked for my autograph yesterday,' said Theresa, and Tibby gave a little whoop.

Ella noted that Mhairi looked less comfortable at this turn in the conversation. 'Sisters,' the Queen Bee said finally, stiffening her frame and putting out a hand to stop them. 'This isn't about fame, or celebrity. It's about devotion to Our Lady and we must be humble and dignified in her service. This is not about us. It's about her.'

The girls looked embarrassed. 'Of course, Mhairi. Sorry, Mhairi,' they mumbled.

Mhairi stood up and walked over to the fireplace. '*The*

Assumption of the Virgin. Hm,' she said, looking up at the painting. 'We have been given a great responsibility. Father Di Pono may speak to us all together or he may want to speak to us separately, but whatever we say, there can be no contradictions. It's important that we are consistent.'

Tibby was on it, staring at each girl in turn, waiting for a nod of agreement.

Mhairi turned back to face them. 'And you must understand that our secrets stay secret. We will reveal nothing about our society or our rituals. They are between us and the blessed Lady. They go no further.'

'Yes, Mhairi.' They sounded like robots and Ella shuddered to find herself joining in.

'And the message – that stays between us too. Our Lady wanted me to pass it on to you, my sisters. But it's not for the unworthy, they wouldn't understand. We must keep it a secret. We must take it to the grave.'

Flipping right, thought Ella. *That Hallmark bullshit won't convince anyone. Only the brainwashed will fall for that crap.*

Mhairi was about to continue, reassured by their nodding heads, when Theresa broke in, 'But Mhairi...'

'...No, buts. You heard.' Tibby silenced her.

'The message is ours and ours alone.'

'And when does Our Lady want to see you again?' whispered Bernie.

'Tomorrow night. For a final visit.' Mhairi paused and lowered her eyes. 'And that stays between us too. Not Sister Hanrahan, Sister Gagnier, Father Di Pono. None of them must know. I'll walk alone, and in secret.'

There was a knock on the door and Sister Gagnier came in holding a tray of cakes and a jug of Ribena. 'Just a little snack before Father gets here, and then,' she turned to where Ella and Catriona were standing, 'it's time for you two to be on your way.'

***

It was suppertime before Ella and Catriona saw the Cecilians again. They had spent the day quietly. Their exclusion from the interview with Father Di Pono had quickly become common knowledge and their celebrity status had plummeted. They were waiting outside the dining room when a surge of excitement spread through the assembled girls.

Mhairi had appeared at the top of the steps, the Cecilians in close ranks behind her. She paused, and Ella wondered for a moment if she was going to make a speech. Instead, she scanned the crowd until she found Ella. She shook back her hair, relieved, it seemed, to have located her.

Ella smiled up at her. Mhairi might be cold-blooded and slithery, but she seemed to need Ella by her side. And despite herself, she felt a flutter of pleasure. It was good to be wanted once more.

As the crowd pushed into the dining hall, Tibby made her way over to them. 'You two. Meet us in the log store after supper.'

There was no denying it, she was dying to know what had gone on with the priest.

***

As they gathered round the oil drum, passing round a Marlboro Light, the story of their long day spilled out.

'He's a sweetheart really, Father Di Pono,' said Dizzy who had

259

tilted her head back to maximise the impact of her smoke-ring-blowing skills. 'I mean you could see he was squirming being shut in a room, unchaperoned, with all of us girls.'

'Yah, he had to keep wiping his forehead with his handkerchief,' said Bells, taking the cigarette. 'Mhairi was really making him sweat.'

They all laughed, still charged up by the events of the day.

'What did he ask you?' said Catriona, carefully. 'Did he already know what had happened?'

Bells answered. 'It was pretty obvious that the nuns had filled him in. He spoke to us all together at first. And then we saw him individually.'

'You were gone such a long time,' said Ella. 'You must be exhausted.'

'The church has a procedure and he has to follow it. We all do.' Mhairi's voice was quiet, weary. She was leaning against the wall.

'A procedure?' asked Ella, intrigued.

It was Bells who answered again, speaking for Mhairi. 'Yah. There's a process to decide whether apparitions are genuine.'

'And who decides that?'

'Well, first of all, it's Father Di Pono. He chooses whether the Bishop – Bishop Joseph – should be involved. If he thinks we're faking, it won't go any further. But if he believes us, it goes to the Bishop. Then after the Bishop it's straight to the Pope.'

'The Pope? Bloody Hell!' said Catriona. Ella could tell her astonishment was real.

'Let's not get ahead of ourselves. We're a long way from the Vatican,' said Bells, frowning at Catriona.

'And what did Father Di Pono do to test whether it's true? Did he bring some kind of holy lie detector?' asked Ella.

Mhairi pulled herself straight. 'This isn't a joke, Ella. First, he had to decide whether we were describing a vision or an apparition. They're different. I've been having visions in Mass. Those are spiritual and personal. But the apparition – that was physical. We all saw it, and our stories matched up perfectly.' Her voice might betray tiredness, but she was still slick and well-rehearsed.

'What else did he do?' asked Catriona.

Bells took over once again. 'He wrote down our testimony and ran through some questions to see if we matched the negative or positive criteria.'

'What are the negative criteria?' asked Ella.

Dizzy chipped in this time. 'He needs to be sure we're not trying to make money out of this, or that we're not all crackers. Girls' schools – they can be full of hysterics, you know.' She rolled her eyes, miming madness in a way that made the others laugh. It was all Ella could do to stop herself from butting in.

You're not kidding. Dancing naked round a fire and calling to some goddess that lives on the moon? That sounds pretty crackers from where I'm standing. And that was before you all started hanging out with the Mother of God.

Dizzy continued. 'The people that see the apparition. They have to be good people. You know, devoted Catholics, not rebels or troublemakers. The right sort. No crackpots or fanatics.'

'And do you know whether Father Di Pono thinks you're the right sort?' Ella asked.

'Well, obviously we are, *Ella*,' Mhairi emphasised her name with the faintest hint of derision and gestured to Bells to carry on.

'He's going to get in touch with Bishop Joseph, who will launch an official investigation. There will be doctors and psychologists, you know, to check out that we're not mad, bad and dangerous to know. And theologians to make sure that the message is doctrinally sound.'

'The message? The *If you love something let it go* message?'

'No, *Ella*.' Mhairi stressed her name once again, the subtlest of threats in the repetition. 'As I said, that message is *our* secret. It stays with us and goes no further. The message I'm talking about is the one that will be revealed in the final visitation.'

She's squirming, thought Ella. *She knows there's got to be a message, and it had better be a good one. I'm pretty sure a slogan from an Athena poster won't cut the mustard with the Pope.*

'And when is that going to be?' asked Catriona.

'Tomorrow. Tomorrow night. But not a word to anybody. Got it?'

CHAPTER 29
Nobody's Scared (Subway Sect)

On the low tables that skirted the edges of the foyer, newspapers were displayed every morning for the girls to read after breakfast. Ordinarily they remained untouched until breaktime, when a few serious sorts flicked through the pages while they sipped their soup. Most girls ignored the papers, happier, it seemed to Ella, to bob about in a Saint Cecilian bubble, cut off from anything as real as news. But the next morning, as Ella and Catriona headed into breakfast, a swarm had formed around one of the tables and girls were clambering over each other to get a better look.

'Alright, alright.' A Purple Ribbon clapped her hands, calling the girls to order. 'Stand back. Give it to me and I'll read it to you all.' She flicked the paper wide in front of her. It wasn't front-page news, but from somewhere near the middle of the *Saturday Recorder* she read out the headline, *Virgin Sighted at Top Scottish School.*

As Ella and Catriona moved closer, the Purple Ribbon continued. 'Schoolgirls at top boarding school have reported sightings of the Virgin Mary.'

The girls surrounding the purple ribbon gasped then shouted out questions, braying for details. Ella wondered if the pupils would be named and held her breath.

'Quiet. Quiet, or I won't carry on,' the Purple Ribbon shouted, and the group dutifully hushed.

'The exclusive Convent of Saint Cecilia's, in the village of Belgaddie, north of Inverness, has long been a favourite with Scotland's rich and famous families.'

A titter travelled through the crowd, and the Purple Ribbon looked up, her lips pursed, as she waited for silence.

'The Mother of God first appeared to the group last Saturday, while they prayed at the school's 'holy tree'. Since then, The Virgin Mary has been visiting one of the pupils every day.'

'Girls, girls.' The nun on breakfast duty, a bespectacled garden-nun with rough red hands and a habit that was rolled up to the elbows, shook a small golden bell energetically from the doorway. 'Enough of that now. It's time for breakfast. In you come.'

***

The atmosphere around school continued to be febrile. As they moved between lessons, girls called Mhairi's name, hoping she would look at them. Groups lurked in doorways, waiting to catch a glimpse. And everyone wanted to touch her. Hands reached out, waving, grasping, hoping to make contact with any part of her, and if they couldn't touch her, they grabbed at the rest of the Cecilians instead. Ella recoiled, shutting her eyes, pulling herself away, longing for the safety of the next classroom, where at least the girls in their own form would grant them some respite.

Pupils who had missed out on the paper at breakfast made a

beeline for the foyer at the start of break. But the papers had already been removed and there was a strong nun presence outside the dining room. Before anyone had a chance to get their soup, Sister Hanrahan called an unscheduled assembly.

Catriona and Ella stood together by the doors as the Bulldog climbed up the steps of the rostrum.

'Settle down. Settle down.' She spread her hands on either side of the wooden pulpit and leant forward so that her massive bosom cleared the edge, her crucifix swinging. 'You'll all know from your catechism that when the last Apostle, Saint John the Evangelist, died, the time of public revelation came to an end.'

Ella looked at Catriona and raised her eyebrows to show that she hadn't the faintest idea what the nun was on about, and Catriona, equally confused, shrugged back, trying not to smile too broadly.

'From that point onward, Sacred Scripture was complete. And perfect.' The Bulldog stopped to bless herself, maximising the drama as she always did. She flung her hand straight out in front of her until her elbow clicked, then, pausing for a fraction of a second, swung it back to dab the top of her head. In an arc she brought her hand down to a spot in the middle of the massive mono-breast, then sailed it out to the left and back to the right in a vigorous callisthenics display. The girls, Ella included, copied her automatically.

In front of the rostrum, her hands together as if in prayer, Ella could see Mhairi gazing up at the Bulldog.

'But over the centuries Our Lord has continued to make private revelations.' She paused and leaned forward. 'From time to time, exceptional individuals have been visited by the Lord, and by his Mother, the Blessed Virgin Mary.' She dropped her voice so that the girls had to shuffle forwards to hear. 'These visitations have shown us how to be better Catholics. Saint Francis, Saint Bernadette, Saint Bridget, to name but a few, all had private revelations.'

At the mention of Saint Bernadette, the twins, who were standing right in front of Ella, clutched each other's hands.

'While we are a long way from calling this a miracle, I can tell you that something very special is happening in our little school. I'm sure you've all heard the rumours that some of our girls have been graced with a revelation of the Holy Mother's presence – a visitation. And one of our girls has been specially blessed. We should all pray for Mhairi Campbell.'

Ella lowered her head. *Holy crap.* The Bulldog had bought it lock, stock and barrel. And by the look of the girls who jostled to get a better look at Mhairi, they had bought it too. And why wouldn't they? Mhairi looked perfect, completely still, her eyes fixed unblinking on the headmistress. For a second Ella wondered whether even Mhairi now believed it was true.

'Now girls, you'll know about the newspaper report. In due course, the community will respond with a statement. But if you yourselves are approached by a member of the press, you're to reply, 'No comment.' Let me make that clear. No girl from Saint Cecilia's is permitted to speak to the papers.'

The Bulldog was enjoying this. Saint Cecilia's would really be something now. Not just a school, but a centre of pilgrimage. She was Mother Superior of her own Scottish Lourdes.

Shame surged in Ella's belly. Mhairi was feeding them lie after lie. And she herself was standing back and letting it happen. If she wanted to stop this appalling charade, she had to find some proof. And quickly.

The Bulldog continued. 'There are many on the outside who will wish to share our blessing, but until we know a little more, we must keep this within the family of Saint Cecilia's.'

The girls were bursting to talk about what they'd heard and shuffled towards the door, ready to bolt. The Bulldog knew she was losing her audience, but she carried on, her voice louder now. 'Dignity and decorum, girls. Dignity and decorum. Don't be phoning all your friends and family to tell them all about it. No show-offs now, you hear. Let us join our hands in prayer.'

Catriona caught Ella's sleeve as she turned to leave. 'Not yet,' she whispered. 'Not yet.'

***

Although security had been stepped up, matches were going ahead as planned that afternoon, and while Mhairi and the Cecilians headed out to the hockey pitches, Ella tightened the laces of her trainers and slotted Mikey's Mix Tape number 2, *Punk: – the Origins*, into her Walkman. The combination of a run and Mikey's music would, she hoped, clear her head and remove the filthy taste from her mouth.

She set off at pace on the now familiar Pilgrimage circuit, hammering through the puddles, the cold wind nibbling the tops of her ears. Bob Dylan wasn't making her feel any better but she was down to her last pack of batteries and didn't want to waste any juice forwarding the tape. It didn't matter anyway, the words in her head were louder than the music. They were thumping in time with her feet. *This is wrong. It's a lie. This whole sham is a lie. This is wrong. It's a lie. It's a warped and twisted lie.*

Waves of self-loathing engulfed her. She was a coward, a weakling. What was her problem? Did she think that holding back the truth gave her some kind of power over Mhairi? Who was she kidding? The reaction at assembly had made it clear that Mhairi's power was multiplying with every minute that passed. And it all felt so big now. So much bigger than before. She couldn't confront her about Magda unless she had some proof. And she had nothing.

Blitzkrieg Bop. Hey ho, let's go! Ella pictured Mikey pogo-ing and a rush of energy recharged her. It steadied her raggedy breathing and soon she was pounding her way along the boundary wall towards the furthest reaches of the estate, glad to be putting space between her and Mhairi.

And then she spotted a figure in the distance. As she got closer, she saw it was a man and that he was holding binoculars that seemed to be trained on her. He jumped over the wall and stood in her path, a camera with a long lens swinging around his neck. He wasn't old, late 20s at most, and good-looking in a greasy sort of way.

She ran on the spot for a few seconds, wondering if she should turn around and head back the long way, but curiosity – and a delight in disobeying the Bulldog's orders – got the better of her. She ran towards him.

He thrust out a hand as if he expected her to shake it. 'Ella, it's Ella, isn't it?'

How does he know that? She ignored him and side-stepped to get past, but he jogged alongside her, fit enough to keep up.

'Ella, I want to talk to you. I think you know why.'

She stopped and bent from the waist, her hands on her thighs, catching her breath.

'OK…' She scanned the landscape, checking she hadn't been followed and that she couldn't be overheard. There was nobody out on the muddy fringes but them. She slipped the headphones around her neck and pressed the off button. 'Who are you? And how do you know my name?'

He fished in the pocket of his long wax jacket and pulled out a stack of business cards held together with an elastic band. 'Jack Trentham,' he said, peeling one from the top of the pile. 'I'm a reporter. My editor's Hector McBlane. His daughter's in your year. She told him what was going on.'

She gave a weary laugh. Noids. It was Noids who'd blabbed. She should've guessed.

Jack Trentham carried on. 'Let's keep that between us though. Hector wouldn't want it to be common knowledge.'

Neither would Noids. That's for sure.

Confident he had her attention he gave her a creepy smile and looked her up and down. 'You must be like a fish out of water out here with these Hooray Harriets. You don't belong here at all, do you?'

'Not exactly my choice,' she said. Was she supposed to be grateful for his observation? She stared him down.

'Anyway, McBlane's daughter told him all about Mhairi and her little band of acolytes. I think they've made her life pretty miserable over the years, to be honest. And she said that one of the gang, a tall girl with a nose ring and cropped black hair, was a runner. She said you knew things. That you might want to talk. I didn't have to be Sherlock Holmes to track you down. Not many girls here look like you. You're kind of... cool.'

'Forget it. I'm not interested,' she said and put her headphones back on.

'Wait. Give me a minute. I've been here for a while, getting the lie of the land, you know. I saw you out here on Thursday.'

'You wanna to be careful. Hanging about near a girls' school. People will take you for a pervert.'

He laughed briefly. 'Ha. You're a smart one. I can see that. But seriously, Ella. There's more to this story, I'm sure of it. A bright girl like you, I bet you know what's going on. I want to know all about it, from an insider's perspective. I want details. Pictures.' He pulled a pack of cigarettes from his pocket and flicked open the lid, offering her one. A whole cigarette to herself. She nodded and he lit up, taking a slow drag before passing it to her.

'There's quite a press pack assembling. Especially after my report in today's *Recorder*. I tried to get in for an interview but there's a snappy little nun on the front gates. She wouldn't let me within a mile of the place, even when I said I wanted to take my niece out for tea.'

She took another drag, working hard to stop herself from spluttering, slowly exhaling the smoke. 'I think they might have heard that one before. They're nuns, not morons.'

'Like I said, smart cookie.' He made a clicking sound with the side of his mouth and twitched his head, as if he was geeing a horse. 'Look, Ella.' She wished he would stop using her name. 'There are loads of girls willing to sell me their story. Honestly, they'd sing like canaries for fifteen minutes of fame. But those airheads can't tell me anything worth listening to. You, on the other hand, you're an observer – I can tell – and I bet you see *everything*.' He let that hang in the air for a second. 'I'd make it worth your while.'

Ella thought about the Bulldog forbidding them to speak to the press. 'What exactly do you want?' she asked.

He lifted the camera from his neck. 'Not much. A couple of pictures. It's loaded up with film. 1600 ASA so it'll be good in the dark. You can just lean it on a branch. Leave the shutter speed where it is. Point and shoot.' He tapped a dial on the top of the camera. 'See if you can get a shot of The Virgin Mary. We'd pay good money for that.'

She laughed. Was he serious? She could blow this story wide open if she wanted to. This could be her chance.

'Look. I think, deep down, you want to tell me what happened at your school. Why don't you just take the camera and have a little think. I'll be back tomorrow at the same time. And if there's anything you'd like to tell me, anything at all, I'll be right here. I'll bring a flask, some biscuits. We can have a proper chat.' He smiled at her. She guessed he considered it a winning smile. It gave her the creeps.

'You don't belong here with these posh girls and those dried up old witches. I bet there's quite a lot you'd like to get off your chest. And there'd be something in it for you. A nice fat cheque with your name on it. Fifty quid. That'd come in handy, wouldn't it? See you here tomorrow?'

She reached out and took the silver camera from his hand. 'I'll think about it,' she said and looped the strap around her neck.

***

The camera bounced off her bony chest as she ran back across the pitches, and she pulled it close, her hands cold on the metal.

She wanted the truth to come out, didn't she? She needed the truth to come out. Maybe this could be the way. Mhairi was walking again, tonight. She could follow her to the tree. If that was where she was going. If Jack Trentham thought she was going to get a picture of the Virgin Mary, though, he was going to be disappointed. But if Mhairi wasn't going to speak to the Virgin, what exactly was she planning? And why was she so insistent that she walk alone? Maybe she was going to do the whole weird ritual thing by herself. That would make a good photograph.

Turning the volume up to max she ran so fast she fought for breath. She pushed until her legs screamed, *Subway Sect*, clashing in her ears. But still the argument in her head did not die down. She wanted Mhairi exposed. Yes. But in the last few weeks she had felt more connected with the world than she had felt in years. She'd been part of something. Something that had nothing to do with her past, with Mom, with Dad. And she'd been lonely for so long. But if she snitched it would be the end for her. If she blew this whole fragile world of hers to smithereens by telling the truth, she might not survive it.

And then it struck her. Why did she have to be the one to break the story? The thought stopped her in her tracks. There was somebody else, a real, live person, who could clear this up. Magda. She could tell the truth. She could tell Sister Hanrahan that it wasn't the Virgin Mary the girls had seen. They'd seen Magda and jumped to conclusions. It was a fanciful mistake. Just a mistake that they'd taken a little bit far. They could stop this before it went any further. Mhairi would be expelled – Ella wouldn't lose much sleep over that – and this nonsense would stop. Everyone would be better off. Why hadn't she thought of it before?

Ella ran straight to the Chapel, her muddy feet leaving size eight footprints all the way down the aisle. Magda was usually there at this time, but today The Lady Chapel was empty, no sound but silence filled the air.

Ella leaned on a prie-dieu while she caught her breath, inhaling the emptiness, letting the disappointment settle. On the altar, votive candles burned on a wrought iron holder, each one a hope, a wish, a prayer. She thought of her statue buried under her pillow, and knelt for a second, writing an invisible scrap in invisible Biro. Whispering the words. 'Help me, Mom. This is too big for me to sort out on my own.'

Pushing open the door reserved for visitors, she sprinted out into the gloaming of the late winter afternoon. She ran down the side of the Mansion House and turned onto the gravel of Front Drive. She ran past the entrance to the dormitories on her right and the forest on her left, all the way up to the Steading where she'd seen the light flickering on that first night at Saint C's. That's where Magda would be. She was sure of it.

It was dusk and the courtyard was in darkness. There was nothing to indicate that in this tumbledown collection of farm buildings people had made a home, not even a glimmer of light. But as she approached the door in the far corner of the courtyard, she detected the faintest smell of woodsmoke. A fire was burning somewhere inside. She knocked and waited, but no answer came.

Just as she was about to leave, she saw a curtain flicker and knocked again, leaning in to listen. There was no sound of movement, just the leaves swirling in the corner of the courtyard, but she was as sure as she could be that Magda was in there. Why wasn't she answering? She reached out for the doorknob but just as her hand touched the metal, the door swung open and a woman stepped into the frame. She was wearing a headscarf, her hands lost in knitted mittens.

The woman didn't speak but stepped to one side and gestured for Ella to follow her down a dark corridor, into a windowless room. The light came from one solitary, shaded bulb that dangled from the ceiling and a fire which smouldered in the grate. Ella's eyes took a minute to adapt to the gloom. Now that she was here, she wasn't quite sure what she was going to say.

The camera lay cold against her chest and she shivered, pulling down the arms of her tracksuit to cover her hands. The room smelled of onions, wet wool, damp earth. The walls were bare and the only pieces of furniture were a small moquette settee and an outsized sideboard, surplus from the big house, she suspected. Draped over the back of the settee lay a cream shawl, embroidered in threads of palest blue. Ella couldn't take her eyes off it. It was the only beautiful thing in this miserable place.

The woman left her alone, and from somewhere nearby, Ella heard quiet voices speaking a language she didn't understand. Magda had told her she was Hungarian, hadn't she? Was Hungarian even a language? Dad would know.

Ella stepped closer to the fire, her footsteps echoing in the emptiness. And then she caught sight of the lyre on the sideboard, its strings flashing in the firelight like gossamer in the dew. A second beautiful thing.

'Ella.' Magda appeared in the doorway, her black hair loose around her shoulders and her white face luminous in the gloom.

'I need your help.' Ella's voice was fast and urgent. 'I need you to come with me to talk to Sister Hanrahan. The girls – Mhairi's girls – they believe they've seen the Virgin Mary.'

'Yes. Sister Cobb, she brings us food. She likes to talk.'

'I know it sounds crazy, but the nuns believe it. Everyone believes it. But it's not true. It's a lie. And we've got to tell someone.'

Magda sat down on the sofa, her movement gentle, her voice low and steadying. 'How wonderful to have such faith.'

Ella stood between Magda and the fire. 'But it's not true. They didn't see the Virgin Mary. They saw you. You told me that yourself in the Chapel.'

Magda's long face dipped low, and she hesitated for a moment before replying, 'They saw what they wanted to see. They saw, and they believed.'

'But they're wrong. And facts are facts.' She needed Magda to act. To help her put this right. But Magda said nothing. She just sat there. Ella wanted to shake her.

'Okay, okay. Maybe the crazy dancing and the vodka got them so whooped up that when they saw you, they really believed you were Mary. I can buy that… But everything that has happened since then… it's bullshit, Magda. Can't you see that?' The words were spilling out of her now. 'She's twisted… all she cares about is power. And this crap about the visions – the shaking, and the voices – that's just her way of grabbing attention.'

Ella was kneeling in front of Magda now, willing her to get up off of the sofa. 'Can't you see that she's just laughing at us? She says she saw Mary again on Monday… But it's not true, is it? Were you at the tree on Monday?'

'No. I was not.'

'So she's making it all up.' Ella slowed down, emphasising the words so that there could be no confusion. 'She's lying. And we have to tell the truth. Please, Magda, come with me.'

'Is there only one truth?' Magda looked towards the fire. 'I cannot go with you, Ella.'

Ella's voice was loud now, out of place in this house of whispers. 'I don't understand you.'

'There is much, I think, that you do not understand. I have my reasons for staying in the shadows.'

Ella dropped Magda's hands and jumped to her feet. 'Who are you? Sneaking around in the middle of the night. Who does that?' She was shouting now.

Magda rose and stepped over to the sideboard. She ran a finger slowly over the strings of her lyre. The noise filled the dark room and reverberated through Ella. 'I don't sleep well. I have bad dreams. And sometimes it helps to walk. I walk to the tree and then onto the spring. It lightens the darkness.'

'Why? What's out there?'

Magda paused. 'Hope. I think. Hope for the future. For goodness. My mother always tells me, hope deferred makes the heart sick, but desire fulfilled is a tree of life. I have to hope.' Magda turned away from her. She was talking in riddles. She would not help.

The fire guttered in the grate and the cold sank into Ella's bones. She shut her eyes and she was standing on the roadside once again, the rain was soaking her Guide uniform, and the sirens filled her head and her heart with fear. She was a leaf in the floodwater that rushed down the side of the road, she was swept away by a force she could not control.

Ella ran out of the Steading and all the way back to the dormitory. She was not allowed to be in there at this time of day, but she no longer cared about anything like that. There was nowhere in this terrible place that was hers, not a corner of it, not a breath of its air, and she needed to be far from people. She had to find somewhere to hide.

She chucked the camera into the bottom of the wardrobe and throwing herself onto the bed she spread the patchwork quilt over her legs. She was trembling with cold, and as she pulled it around her, her freezing fingers tracing its seams, she wanted to split into hexagons and fuse with its pieces.

And then from nowhere the Wasp-Witch was upon her, bearing down. 'What are you doing in the dormitory at this time of the day? Lying on your bed, you bold child.' The nun tugged at the quilt. 'Girls are permitted one regulation tartan travel rug, as per the uniform list. So I'll be having this tatty thing, thank you very much.' The Wasp-Witch hauled the patchwork quilt off the bed and rustled out of the dormitory.

Anger coursed through Ella. She leapt from the bed and ran after the wizened woman. Grabbing her by the shoulder, she pivoted her round so they were standing face-to-face. 'Give that to me. You can't take it!'

The nun's gaze was steely. 'I think you'll find, young lady, that here in Saint Cecilia's I can do exactly as I please. And you, you wicked girl, have lost your Note.'

'Get off it! It's mine!' Ella shouted. She grabbed for the quilt, but the Wasp-Witch's grip was strong. She tugged and the nun tugged back.

And suddenly Ella heard a sound that sickened her to her stomach. The precious stitches ripped. And as something so beloved was wrenched from her hands she felt a rending, like the rending that had happened once before.

'Ella Richardson. Go to your cubicle this instant.' It was the Bulldog. 'You will stay there with no supper and think about your behaviour. Sister Cullen, I'll take that thank you.' She tucked the patchwork quilt under her arm and swivelled, gliding off along the corridor with a rustle of her habit and a clatter of her beads.

While the other girls went to supper, Ella lay on her bed and scraped her muddy trainers down the yellow gloss walls, marking tally lines, like the stitches on the quilt that now lay on the floor of the Bulldog's study, crumpled, eviscerated, destroyed.

She hated this fucking place and all the fucking people in it.

CHAPTER 30
Rhiannon (Fleetwood Mac)

When Catriona came to find her for the Saturday night film show, Ella was stretched out on the bed still in her muddy games kit.

'What happened? Where have you been all afternoon?'

'Cullen's put me on early bed.'

'Why? What did you do wrong?'

Ella rolled over and faced the wall. 'Nothing. I don't wanna talk about it.'

'I'll stay here if you like. I don't care about the stupid film. There's only so many times I need to see 'The Sound of Music' in one lifetime. I've still got some tuck left; I can bring it up.'

'No. You should go.'

'I don't mind staying with you.'

She sat up. 'Just go will you. Just leave me alone.'

Catriona's face crumpled behind her glasses, and she turned away.

Ella fell back on the bed and hid her eyes in the crook of her elbow. *Who are you?* she thought. *What kind of person treats someone like shit when all they've ever done is be kind? A person who doesn't have the courage to stand up to the baddies and kicks the goodies instead. That's who does that. The worst kind. The worst kind of person.*

***

After the film, Catriona appeared in the doorway of the cube once again. 'Night. I hope you're alright. Sleep well.' But Ella kept her eyes shut and pretended she was asleep.

She didn't get out of bed for prayers and when the Wasp-Witch came in with the holy water, she turned her face to the wall.

'You're a bold girl, Ella Richardson, and if you carry on down this road you're headed straight for hell.'

***

An hour or so after lights out, Tibby shook her awake, shining the flashlight in her eyes. 'Mhairi's room. Now.'

'Piss off.'

'What did you say?'

'I said "Piss. Off."' In the eerie glow of the flashlight, Tibby's spotty face was open-mouthed, like a gargoyle. 'If Mhairi wants me, she knows where to find me.'

Unaccustomed to insubordination, the ginger terrier wasn't sure how to respond and carried on regardless. 'She's walking tonight. Half-past midnight. No need to do the lights, she doesn't need to hide. But we're all planning to be there when she gets back. This isn't easy for her, you know.'

'It isn't easy for anybody. Tell them I'm sick.'

Tibby kicked the metal bedframe, turned on her heel, and left.

***

She lay on her bunk, the tiny statue of Mary in her hands. As she traced the smooth curvature of the mantle with her fingers the afternoon looped in her mind. The journalist. The offer of money. The silver camera that was hidden in the bottom of the wardrobe. And Magda. Why, when she really needed them, did people let her down? If there was one thing in life she could rely on, it was that. People were fucking useless.

The clock beneath the fire exit sign glowed green. It was just after midnight. Soon Mhairi would be walking, creating her mythology, weaving the fabric of her lie, while the rest of them lay in their beds, spineless and immobilised, like puppets in their boxes. Mhairi had them where she wanted them. And it was time for that to change.

Still in her tracksuit Ella pulled on both her jumpers, a hat, and her gloves. She grabbed the camera from the wardrobe and waited. She kept her body still and listened: the wet rumble of Noids' breathing two cubes down, the frigging rhythm of the pipes, and outside, somewhere, a vixen, howling like a baby at the defilement of her sex.

And then, she heard the faintest creak of the door at the end of Mhairi's corridor, the soft suck of trainers on the smooth wooden floor. Ella counted Mhairi's steps, mapping her movement, anticipating the metallic *voosh* of the fire door. And once she was sure that Mhairi was at a safe distance, she followed her out.

***

Mhairi was wearing a long Victorian nightgown beneath an outsized tweed coat. Soft pink socks slouched round the top of her wellies and a cashmere scarf coiled around her neck. She walked in the middle of the footpath, hips thrust forward, gait swinging and relaxed, in the full glare of the security light. She was unassailable.

Ella crouched low, clinging to the wall, hugging the shadows. At the corner of the Mansion House, Mhairi crossed the drive and walked into the forest.

But Ella didn't follow. She had no torch, but the waning moon was still big in the sky and the stars were bright. Besides, she knew the route of the Pilgrimage well enough by now. She used to be afraid of the dark, but not tonight. There was nothing out here that could scare her now. She traced the route in reverse, running over the playing fields, along the edge of the wood until she came to the narrow path that led into the glade from the west, the route she had taken on that first run. She was there well before Mhairi with plenty of time to set up the camera. She got ready to take pictures of nothing. To record her proof.

Using a branch as a makeshift tripod, she balanced the camera, took off the lens cap and found Our Lady's Tree through the viewfinder. Jack Trentham had set the shutter speed, now all she had to do was focus and shoot. She pressed her eye to the cold metal and turned the lens until the tree became sharp.

She took a practice shot, and as she was adjusting the focus a woman stepped into the frame. It was Magda. She hadn't come from the direction of the Steading like last time, she had come out of the woods on the other side of the glade. Wrapped in a long, embroidered shawl, her head was covered by the now familiar mantilla. She shone in the darkness, just as before.

Magda turned to the statue on the tree, her hands held together in prayer. And Ella fingered the cold metal of the camera.

Blessing herself, Magda straightened the tiny crosses and placed something, an envelope perhaps, on the little shelf below the Virgin's feet. Her hand lingered on the tiny foot that firmly crushed the serpent's head and Ella pressed the shutter. She jolted at the whirr of component parts and the volume of the click. But if Magda heard, she did not react; she blessed herself once more, crossed the glade and disappeared into the woods, back towards the Steading.

Moments later, Mhairi came out of the trees, her torch blazing, a travel rug over her shoulders, a cloth bag across her chest. She walked straight to Our Lady's Tree and made the sign of the cross, then on her knees, she prayed. Ella hadn't expected this. She was so sure the whole visitation thing was a fabrication, a power game. But here was Mhairi, head bowed and worshipping. Could she be genuine? Was Ella wrong about this girl?

As she listened to the low rumbling of the incantations, something in the sincerity of the sound made her want to join in with the prayer. Mhairi was out here, alone, as Magda had been, offering her devotion to her Blessed Mother. Maybe she had consecrated herself to the Virgin after all.

With her prayers complete, Mhairi rose and stretched up to the statue to touch the tiny foot. Seeing Magda's letter, she plucked it down and read.

Ella held the camera steady and took a shot. Mhairi was stationary, her eyes lingering on the statue until finally she tucked the letter into her bag. But rather than heading back towards school, as Ella expected, Mhairi kicked off her wellies, spread the travel rug on the ground and sat down with her back against the towering redwood tree.

Suddenly, from the direction of the playing fields, Ella heard a disturbance in the woods. Heavy footsteps were approaching, branches were breaking, and she grabbed the camera, getting ready to run.

'Mhairi, where the fuck are you?' Somebody blundered out of the bushes in a shambolic flurry of leaves, brandishing a torch – a man, not much more than a boy really. He was handsome, she could see that as he pulled twigs out of his floppy blonde hair and straightened his combat jacket.

Now it all makes sense! She covered her mouth to stop herself laughing. *This is why she needs to be alone!*

'Here, Toby. I'm over by the tree.' Mhairi stood up and waved her flashlight. 'Keep the noise down. The penguins will be on high alert tonight.'

'Oh yah, I can just see them stumbling through the bushes with their habits tucked into their gym-knickers.' His voice was posh. 'But who wants to think about the penguins? I'm dying to get my hands on that miraculous bod.'

Ella stiffened. *Shit.* She should go. She knew she should go.

'Oh, Toby. You're so wicked.' It didn't sound like Mhairi at all. Her voice was high and girly. Reduced somehow.

'And you, my angel, are a very clever girl.' He pulled a hipflask from his pocket and poured the liquid into Mhairi's open mouth. 'You're going to be untouchable after this.'

Mhairi dropped her torch onto the blanket and leaned against the tree, her arms reaching up towards the branches, her body a sinuous curve. 'Except by you.' She giggled, like some nauseating coquette.

Ella thought about Bernie and the Bulldog, the hysteria back at school and suddenly she was raging. *What a hypocrite! What a piece of work! What a cheap and nasty liar!*

She tasted acid on her tongue as she zoomed in through the viewfinder. Her breath caught in her throat as Toby pushed Mhairi against the tree. She watched, as he took off Mhairi's coat and unbuttoned the neck of her Victorian nightgown, one pearly button at a time. She watched as Mhairi pulled his head down to her breast, grasping the thatch of his hair. She heard the clink of his belt unbuckling, saw it land in a coil on the tartan rug. Watched, as Toby, one palm against the tree trunk, pulled up Mhairi's nightdress and slipped his hand inside. Listened as Mhairi groaned, head thrown back against the tree, losing herself in the warm, living flesh of another person's fucking body.

From behind the camera, Ella watched it all. Like a dirty peeping Tom, who stood on the outside while the real people got on with living. She heard the animal grunts, felt the jolt as he lifted Mhairi from the ground, the hand gripping the back of the neck. They were real and alive and breathing and now Ella was living too. Through them she felt the wetness between her legs, her nipples hard on the rough white aertex. She felt each thrust of Toby's hips and gripped at the branch to keep her legs from trembling. Desire burned hot and hard, eating her from the inside out. It built and built until finally she exploded into fractals, leaving her full of nothing but shame. Breathless now, Ella zoomed in to take the shot. Then another. Shot the hipflask on the tartan rug. Shot the bare buttocks, thrusting in the moonlight. Shot the long legs that curled around his back and the feet in their soft pink socks.

CHAPTER 31

Do You Really Want to Hurt Me?
(Culture Club)

'Come on, Ella. They're starting to wonder what's up. I've told them it's your time of the month, but they're not buying it. Please come.' Catriona was waiting in the doorway to Ella's cube. 'We'll be in so much trouble if we skive Mass. They're waiting for us in the corridor.'

Ella had skipped breakfast and had been lying on her bed ever since. She had every intention of staying there all day, but the pleading tone in Catriona's voice was too much to bear and she threw her feet onto the floor and straightened down her crumpled kilt. 'Okay, okay. I just wanted to be on my own for a while.'

At the far end of the corridor, by the statue of Saint Anthony, the Cecilians were waiting. 'Get a move on,' shouted Tibby, 'It's gone eleven!'

'Calm down. We're all together now, and that's what matters. She's just a little overwhelmed, aren't you, Ella? We've all felt that way at some point this week, haven't we?' Mhairi reached out a hand, but Ella drew back, images from the night before flashing in her mind. The Queen Bee, however, was insistent and grabbed her arm, pulling her in. 'We'll walk together, you and me.'

The corridors were ominously empty, and their footsteps echoed as they approached the Chapel. The Mass had begun. 'Don't worry,' whispered Mhairi, 'they'll have kept our seats.'

They'd missed the opening hymn and the congregation was seated, listening to the first reading. The Chapel was completely full and Mhairi paused at the back, her arm linked through Ella's, waiting for the others to fall into formation behind her.

'It's packed,' Ella whispered. 'Where have all these people come from?' There was standing room only. On a normal Sunday there might be ten or twenty visitors. Today there were perhaps two hundred.

'They've come to see the girl who's seen the Virgin, of course.' Mhairi caught herself. 'Whoops. I mean, the *girls* who've seen the Virgin.' She turned round to the line of Cecilians behind her. 'Now let's give the people what they want.'

The reader stopped as they processed down the aisle, two by two, like bridesmaids at a wedding. The schoolgirls in the pews turned to stare as they passed, and over in the Lady Chapel some of the visitors stood to get a better view. The Cecilians filed into the front row, Ella next to Mhairi, in the position of honour. Keep your friends close, and your enemies closer.

Ella felt the peripheral heat of the collective eye that was fixed on Mhairi, and she hunched her shoulders and slid her bottom to the edge of the bench in an attempt to shrink herself. She dreaded the inevitable moment when Mhairi would slip into her visionary reverie and begin to speak in tongues. But the more she longed for time to slow down the more it hurtled forward. She desperately wanted to make a run for it, to push past Mhairi and sprint out of the Chapel, but her legs were iron and the ground a magnet.

When the congregation stood to say the *Hail Mary*, Mhairi stepped into the aisle and prostrated herself in front of the altar, arms outstretched as if she was making a snow angel, face down in the snow. There was a collective gasp from the congregation and from the Lady Chapel a photographer pushed forward, snapping pictures. A protective rush of congregants threw themselves between Mhairi and the camera while a father in a Barbour jacket grabbed the reporter and dragged him out the visitors' door.

Ella turned around and saw the nuns on the balcony leaning over the balustrade, craning to get a better look. This was a circus, a freakshow, a total fucking mess and she could not stand it for one second more. While all eyes were on Mhairi, she took a deep breath and bolted out of the Chapel. She sprinted all the way to the dormitory without looking back and picking up the camera, she belted out of the double doors and headed straight for the fields. Her boots squelched in thick mud and rain soaked her jumper as she ran, kilt flying, to the boundary wall.

Jack Trentham was already there, hunched under a red umbrella. 'You'll freeze to death, Ella. Come and sit in the car. I've got a flask of hot chocolate and some caramel wafers. I'll put the heater on.'

'One of you lot got into Mass. I think he got a picture of Mhairi before someone threw him out,' she said, as she climbed into the front of the red Escort.

He handed her a thermos mug and she clutched it with both hands. 'That will be Billy Thompson. He works for us.'

She was quiet for a moment and then the story came pouring out. The sham of it. The secrets and the lies. She told him about the Cecilians and their rituals and Mhairi: the Queen Bee, the top dog, the high priestess, herself. And she told him all about the losers who followed blindly in her wake.

She told him about the naked dancing, the vodka and the fags, the fires and the fir switches, the whipping, the drumming, and the speaking in tongues. And Jack lapped it up like a kitten drinking milk. He filled page after page of his reporter's notebook.

She was there, she told him, she had seen what they'd seen. And the woman was no more the Virgin Mary than she was. She was a flesh and blood refugee who lived in a barn, a gardener who was fed on scraps. Just a woman, called Magda.

And finally, handing him the camera, she told him about last night. About the man-boy. And Mhairi. The tree, the hipflask and the sex. And when she had nothing left to tell him, she named them, one by one. Mhairi. Bells. Dizzy. Theresa. Bernadette. Tibby. And Catriona. She named them all, one by one.

By the time she was finished, the windows had steamed up and condensation dripped onto her elbow. There was nothing left. It was all out.

He took the camera from her and with a thumbnail flipped out a little crank in the bottom. He wound the film, took out the reel, dropped it into a little tub and sealed it with a plastic lid. 'Not expecting too much from these. But at least it's proof.'

'Proof?' she whispered.

'Yes. If you've got what you say you have on film, I'd say it's conclusive proof that this visitation story is a hoax. You've done a good job, Ella. You'll make a great reporter one day. Not everyone has the strength of character to stand apart from the crowd and speak the truth.'

Was that really what she'd done?

He fumbled in a leather satchel and took out a cheque book. 'How do you spell your surname again?'

She told him.

'Fifty pounds. That should come in pretty handy. Put it in the bank. Save it for a rainy day.'

She took the cheque from him, but having no coat and no pocket, she slid a cold hand down the front of her blouse and stashed it in her bra. Then, without even saying goodbye, she opened the door of the car and stepped out into the rain.

CHAPTER 32
Take a Message to Mary (Everly Brothers)

It was mid-afternoon when she got back to the dorm. Dripping and shivering she took ten pence from her satchel and walked down to the phone box near the cloakrooms. The cold made her hands shake as she dialled the number.

'Hello, Perth 298,' the voice said. Dad. Same as ever. Deep and steady.

The phone pipped and she pushed the ten pence piece into the slot.

'Hello? Ella? Is that you?'

A raindrop trickled from her bare head, down her forehead to the bridge of her nose, and she wiped it away with the back of her hand. She didn't know what to say to him. She wanted him to rescue her before the shit really hit the fan. She wanted him to take her home. But she had asked him to do that once before and she didn't think she could bear it if he said no a second time.

'Ella? Who's there? Hello?'

'Hi, Dad,' she whispered eventually.

'Oh Sweetheart, it is you? The line's very faint. I can hardly hear. But it's so good to hear from you. I thought you must be so busy that you hadn't had time to call. How's it all going?'

'Fine Dad. It's all fine. I just wanted... I just wanted to hear your voice.'

He hesitated. She heard him swallow. 'Brilliant. That's brilliant. I'm so glad it's going well. I knew that all you needed was a fresh start. A fresh start with some nice girls.'

The pips went again. Their time was up.

'Have you got enough money, Ella? I can't wait to...' *Pip. Pip. Pip.* The line went dead.

Yeah Dad. It's fine. Lovely girls. I'm having a blast.

***

Half an hour later she was standing outside the San. She couldn't stay in the dormitory, she didn't want to be in the Chapel, and the Form Room was full of people she couldn't bear to see. There was nowhere left but here.

Sister Forsyth put a cool hand on her forehead. 'Temperature seems normal.'

'It's my time of the month, sister, and I'm in a lot of pain. I need to lie down and there's nowhere I can go.' It wasn't entirely a lie.

'Well, ordinarily we don't admit girls to sick bay for the curse, but you've had quite a week of it. And you look totally exhausted. Why don't you go and have a little lie down and we'll see how you're feeling a bit later on?'

'Thank you, Sister.'

The nurse nun opened a door in the side of the surgery that led into the sick bay. 'It's empty at the moment, so you'll get a bit of peace. Mind you take off those tackety-boots before you get into bed, though. They're completely caked in mud.'

The big bay window was right at the front of the school, with views out over the playing fields. Ella could see the drive on the left, winding through a tree-lined avenue all the way to the enormous front gates. On the right, the gravel drive swept up towards the Steading, passing the forest. Our Lady's Tree was somewhere in the middle of it, out of sight, desecrated. Straight ahead she saw the playing fields, the little stream, the tennis courts on the left, and beyond – the river and the hills. She put her hands on the sash window and watched the glass steam up around them. When she took them away an imprint was left, a negative, inside gloves of white.

On the sofa in front of the empty fireplace she untied her boots. She was alone. Nobody but Sister Forsyth knew she was here. She didn't know what was going on outside of these walls but something had been set in motion, and she would hide here until it had passed.

There were about ten single beds arranged around the large room. Crisp white sheets, cellular blankets, like a hospital. Her mind raced back to the squat, that night before Christmas. Her fingers had stretched out like light towards the black-haired woman, draped in white. It was Mom. She had heard her. Mom had called her name.

When she shut her eyes she was in that other hospital. The one where Mom had lain so still. Her face white, her hair black. Her skin so cold.

Ella didn't like hospitals.

But she was weary and picked the bed in the darkest corner, far away from the door. She didn't lie on the bed, she burrowed right into it and pulled the blanket over her head. Within seconds she was fast asleep.

***

It was dark when she woke up and Catriona was sitting on a chair by the side of her bed. Ella blinked to make sure she was awake. 'How did you know where to find me?'

Catriona put her finger to her lips. 'Shhh. Sister Forsyth doesn't know I'm here. When you ran out of Mass, I didn't know where you'd gone. And then, when you didn't turn up for lunch, I looked everywhere. I thought you'd run away. This was the only place I hadn't checked. I crept in about an hour ago. I've just been sitting here since then. I hope you don't think it's creepy, me sitting here, while you were asleep.'

Ella laughed, 'You little weirdo!'

Catriona laughed too, 'I've been wondering whether I should wake you up, but you looked so peaceful.'

'I'm sorry I've been so horrible. I just needed to escape.'

'I get that. It's been crazy while you've been gone. After you ran out of Chapel, Sister Gagnier knelt by Mhairi's side while we all filed out. I don't know how long they stayed in Chapel but they were both in the Parlour when we were summoned there after lunch. Sister Hanrahan too. Sister Gagnier wanted you to be there, but nobody knew where you were.'

'I went for a run.'

Catriona looked at her, clocking the white Sunday shirt. It was obvious that she was lying.

'Anyway. Mhairi told us about last night. She said she'd had another visitation.'

Ella snorted. 'Well, I suppose you could call it that. And the nuns believe her?'

'Yeah. She's pretty convincing. I nearly believed her myself.'

'And…'

'She said that the Virgin appeared again. In the same place as before. She described it and everything, and she said Our Lady left her a final message. A secret message. Only for the Cecilians. Sister Hanrahan was pretty pissed off about that, but Theresa reminded her about the secrets of Fatima – you know when the children had secret messages that they weren't allowed to share – and that soon that shut her up.'

'So, what happened then?'

'Well, the nuns left – you could see it was killing them – and Mhairi pulled this envelope out from her pocket. She went all dreamy, you know like she does when she's faking the visions, and she put on that voice, you know the one.'

'*My dear sisters, we are so blessed…* that one?'

'Yes! That's the one. Don't make me laugh, Ella, Sister Forsyth will hear us. Then she made us pray for what felt like ages. Bernie was crying as usual, Dizzy was crying too, it was all pretty tense and then, when she felt we were all holy enough or something, we all held hands and she read us the message.'

Catriona pulled out a piece of paper from her pocket and flicked it open. 'So, imagine you're listening to the Virgin Mary. I'll do my best Virgin Mary voice.'

Ella laughed at Catriona's face – pious, lips pursed.

Catriona stood up to maximise the performance. 'Ok, shut

your eyes. Picture it. She's all dazzling white and standing right in front of you. Here goes. *"My blessed child, consecrated to my Immaculate Heart…"* I don't know what that means. Do you?'

Ella shook her head.

Catriona made her voice all wobbly and pompous. *"I come to you tonight as the Queen of Peace. Peace is the only hope for the salvation of the world. But you will never find Peace unless you are Reconciled. Tell your sisters this: Be Reconciled with God and with one another. But begin with yourself. Be Reconciled and learn to Trust. It starts with you."* She ended with a bow, as if she'd finished a poetry recital at school.

Ella laughed and took the paper from Catriona, reading it through once again.

'I don't really understand it. You can keep it,' said Catriona.

Ella wasn't sure what it meant, either; it sounded like a load of old baloney. 'Did she tell you where she got it from?'

'She said Our Lady gave it to her, out by the tree.'

'So the Virgin Mary left a letter in an envelope? The Blessed Mother uses Biro?'

'Ha. This is just my copy. Mhairi dictated it to us so we'd each have our own. She didn't let us see her version.'

'She's such a liar. She got it from Magda. Magda left the message on the tree.' Everything made sense now. 'Trust me. The two of them are in this together.'

'But how do you know?'

Ella took a deep breath. 'I was there. I followed her last night.'

CHAPTER 33
God Save the Queen (The Sex Pistols)

Sister Forsyth brought supper on a tray. Not the slop that they provided in the dining room – Sunday night was cauliflower cheese that tasted like sick – this was real food made with care. Scrambled eggs and toast. Butter, not margarine. Salty. It tasted better than anything she'd eaten for weeks and Ella wolfed it down. There was even a cup of tea.

'Why don't you just settle down for the night. I'll get somebody to bring up your nightdress and your washbag. Anything else you need?'

'Thanks, Sister. My satchel maybe? It's got my book in it.' Her Walkman was in the bag too, though the batteries were almost dead.

'Who shall I ask?'

'Catriona, maybe?'

'Catriona Bentley? Lovely girl. Good choice. I'll speak to Sister Cullen; she'll send her up with your things.'

***

An hour or so later, Catriona appeared, on a sanctioned visit this time, and handed Ella the satchel.

'I miss you, Ella. It's so much harder without you. Honestly, they've all gone bonkers out there!' Catriona kicked off her shoes and sat down on the end of the bed. 'Sister Hanrahan talked to the whole school at supper. There's going to be a candlelit pilgrimage tomorrow night. Everyone's processing. We're going to lay lilies at the tree. And it won't just be us, visitors are coming from all over the place, apparently. She said people will be sleeping in their cars, because all the local places are full.'

Ella thought about the condensation on the windscreen of Jack Trentham's Escort and her stomach constricted.

Catriona continued, 'The tree's going to become a shrine. Can you imagine? It's bonkers. And Mhairi is loving it, obviously.' She pulled her feet up onto the bed and pushed a finger into a hole in the toe of her tights. 'When is this going to be over?'

'I have a feeling it's going to be over quite soon.'

'Really? But how?'

'Oh, I don't know. I just feel like the truth has a way of rising to the surface.'

Catriona, her eyes wide and trusting, reached over and took Ella's hand. 'I hope so. I really do.'

***

When Catriona was gone, Ella drew her satchel from the foot of the bed and pulled out her nightshirt. Something was wrapped inside. Catriona had taken the small statue of the Virgin from under Ella's pillow and swaddled it carefully in the cloth. Ella held it in her hand for a minute or two. It was cool and weighty, familiar and reassuring.

Mom had taught her to speak the truth, to stand up for the underdog, to do the right thing. And she had done the right thing, hadn't she? Soon Mhairi would be exposed and that had to be good. But why then did the thought of it make her feel so sick?

She shivered, and her thumbs twitched as she stroked the statue in her hands. If the truth had a way of surfacing then it wouldn't be long before someone figured out that it was she who had spilled the beans, told the tale, sold the story for thirty pieces of silver. What had she done?

She thought about Catriona sitting on her bed. It had been a long time since she'd got this close to having a friend – or being a friend. Mikey and Cass liked her, and she liked them, but it wasn't the same. Nicola was different – they had been friends, best friends, blood-sisters. They had sliced their thumbs with the breadknife and squeezed out drops of darkest red, pressed the pads together, until the slippy became sticky, then dried to a rust-brown stain. Best Friends Forever. Ha. It turned out that forever hadn't lasted very long. And now, when she had a chance of making a proper friend again… what had she done? She had sold Catriona to Jack Trentham, along with all the rest.

She pulled her knees into her chest and wrapped her arms around them, making herself as small as she could. What was the matter with her? She had stuffed everything up. Again.

***

She was watching the white sunrise spread like a droplet in a watercolour when Sister Forsyth brought in the breakfast tray. She had a newspaper tucked under her arm.

'Morning, Sister,' said Ella.

'Hmmm,' came the reply. Sister Forsyth, usually so sunny, didn't make eye contact. She put the tray and the paper down on the table in the centre of the room and turned to go, then stopped at the door as if reconsidering something. 'I expect Catriona told you about the procession. It's been cancelled. Once you've had your breakfast, you should have a bath, then take yourself off to lessons.' Sister Forsyth smoothed her starched cotton apron and slipped through the side door into the surgery.

She left the door ajar, and Ella overheard her talking to someone. 'It seems like this nonsense is finally over.'

'And not before time. I warned her to be cautious.' It was Sister Fraser, Ella recognised the voice. 'I said, wait a while and see what happens, but no, she rushed in, stoking the fire. She was desperate for it to be true. For us to have our own little miracle.'

'Thank the Lord it's not on the front page, that's all I can say. That would have finished us.'

Ella slumped back against her pillow. So, it had happened. The story was out. And so soon. Her stomach clenched. The newspaper was on the table. She didn't want to look at it, but she had to see it all the same so she climbed out of bed.

Her fingers were too dry on the smooth paper and she fumbled through the pages, looking for the right article. And there it was – a double page spread. *'Virgin Mary': Girls' School in Pagan Sex Romp* the headline screamed at her. With the palms of both hands, she flattened out the paper. Holding her breath, she took in the photographs – one of Mhairi prostrate before the altar, another of her pressed against a tree, blurred, her face obscured by Toby. And a third picture of Magda, a hand on the Virgin's foot. The backs of Ella's knees buckled, and she sat down at the table. Her photos were in the paper. She read:

> **GIRLS at one of Scotland's most exclusive private schools have been taking part in pagan sex rituals, it can be revealed.**
>
> Saint Cecilia's Convent, where many of the country's Roman Catholic elite send their daughters, is at the centre of wild claims that the Virgin Mary has been sighted.

Shit. Was the Bulldog reading this? It would take more than dignity and decorum to brazen this one out.

> But, as roads around the boarding school are blocked by the cars of the faithful, the *Daily Recorder* has learned that sex romps involving underage pupils are taking place under cover of darkness beneath a 'Holy Tree' in the convent grounds.
>
> Sources at the school and our exclusive pictures reveal that the Virgin sightings are a sham, concealing a web of depravity and lies.
>
> The schoolgirl at the centre of the scandal (16) cannot be named for legal reasons. Daughter of a wealthy landowner and benefactor of the school, claims that she…

They hadn't named Mhairi. But it wouldn't take a genius to work out who she was. Ella felt sick. Actually sick. The porridge was congealing in the bowl and she pushed the tray to the back of the table.

> … claims that she, along with a group of other girls, first saw The Virgin in the early hours of Sunday 5th March. The schoolgirl says she's been experiencing daily visions ever since. 'The Virgin Mary appears to me and gives me messages,' she said to our source.

'The source' – that was her. She was the source!

> The insider revealed that at the time when the girl says she was consorting with The Virgin Mary, she was in fact engaged in an alcohol fuelled sex romp with an unnamed officer from the nearby Belgaddie Barracks.
>
> During Sunday Mass, she appeared to be experiencing some kind of religious transfiguration, but recent revelations have exposed her as a fraud.

A source in the school told us that the schoolgirl is the self-appointed High Priestess of a secret sect, known as the Cecilians. Although they claim to be devoted to The Virgin Mary, the girls tank up with booze before dancing naked around a fire and whipping each other with branches. The girls claim to have first seen the Virgin during one of their kinky romps.

Our source revealed that the woman who appeared to the girls, was not in fact the Virgin Mary but an illegal immigrant who has been hiding out with her mother in a derelict stable block on school property. The Home Office is certain to be interested.

Ella's hands flew to her mouth. She hadn't thought. That was why Magda was so keen to keep a low profile. She was in the country illegally. How could Ella have been so stupid?

The high priestess's acolytes cannot be named for legal reasons, but we can reveal that the daughters of prominent aristocrats, advocates, hoteliers and industrialists are all tangled up in this dangerous sex cult.

They hadn't named Catriona. At least they hadn't done that.

The Bishop was due to visit the school to take statements about the Virgin Mary sightings. Perhaps, in light of these revelations, he will be taking statements on a very different matter.

Ella put her head in her hands. Here was the proof she had wanted so badly. So why did it all feel so wrong?

***

It was breaktime when Ella left the San and her heart was pounding as she walked to the dining room. The foyer was crowded with girls standing in tight clusters and she hovered on the edge, looking for Catriona. But Catriona wasn't there. The noise was so intense it seemed to be hurting her and she had to fight against an instinct to put her hands over her ears.

Before she could escape, a group of girls over on the stairs spotted her and for a second the room was quiet. And then sound exploded again as the crowd surged forwards, towards her.

'Ella! Ella! is it true?'

'Did you know?'

'Where is she, Ella?'

Urgent voices overwhelmed her and she bolted.

'No running in Silent Corridor!' a Purple Ribbon shouted, but Ella carried on, panic rising in her chest. She was stuck in this place, there was no way out. The only way to survive was to keep playing the game.

She needed to keep her head. They need never know that she was the source, not if she stayed cool. They would be up at the log shed, she was sure of it, and she had to be with them now. The longer she stayed away, the more suspicious she would look. They mustn't guess that she was the grass. She had to keep her secret safe, it was a matter of survival now.

In the log shed the girls were knotted together, their arms entwined, in a ball around their queen. Ella ran inside and put her arms around the outside of the knot, tentatively laying her head on Dizzy's back, wondering if they would smell it on her, the betrayal.

From somewhere in the dark centre, a low keening came. Minutes passed and finally Mhairi was silent. She raised her head and the girls stepped back. Then, standing in the centre of the circle she began to turn slowly, pausing to look at each one of them in turn, scrutinising their faces, reading their eyes. While Tibby twitched and Bells flicked back her long blonde fringe, Ella held her breath and waited.

Mhairi's face was wet with tears. 'I don't know the name of the traitor,' she whispered, 'the one so eaten up with jealousy that she would betray us; the one who would seek to shame me, to shame the Virgin herself with her lies. I don't know her name yet, but whoever she is, when I find her, I will crush her.' Mhairi stamped her foot on the ground, the flat heel of her pump grinding the bare earth.

When Mhairi's eyes finally locked onto hers, heat swept up Ella's neck and prickled her cheeks in a scarlet admission of her guilt. It felt as clear as if she had blurted out the words, as evident as if it were tattooed on her forehead. It took every bit of her strength not to break eye-contact first. But it was Mhairi who turned away, her eyes locking onto Bernie's. And Bernie flushed too, paralysed and terrified in the face of such rage.

Tibby spoke next. 'Sister Hanrahan's going to call us in within the next few hours. We need to stick to our story. Okay?'

The girls nodded in agreement but Mhairi glared. 'It's not a story, *Tibby*. The truth is the truth.'

The girls looked down, embarrassed by Tibby.

'Sorry, Mhairi. Of course. I only meant that we need to stick together. Stay strong. We know the newspaper was full of lies, don't we?'

The Cecilians hesitated, waiting until Mhairi nodded before they added their agreement. Ella caught Catriona's eye and they followed suit.

Tibby was determined to rally them. 'There is a traitor in our midst. And we need to know who it is.'

'Yeah!' the girls brayed.

Ella was immobilised, frozen. Yesterday, in Jack Trentham's car, Mhairi's power had seemed impossible and Ella had told herself that she could resist, but up close it was mesmerising, terrifying, and she was disarmed. She no longer cared about the truth, or the underdog, or doing the right thing. In that moment all she cared about was saving her own skin. Her absence had detached her from the group and she needed to find a way back into the centre. She'd been silent for too long. 'Who knows the secrets of the Cecilians? Who else has been to a ritual?' she said.

'Good point. I like your thinking,' said Dizzy.

The fear on the faces of the others left Ella in no doubt that they were too scared to speak, to incriminate themselves by saying the wrong thing.

'There have been a few 'visitors' over the years. The ceremonies have…' Mhairi reached for the right word, '*developed* as we matured.' She shut her eyes as if recalling the rituals. 'Noids. She's been to a few. She's always been jealous.'

Ella nodded. She could drop Noids in it. It would only be half a lie.

'And there was that New Bug, Jo, who was here for a while,' said Bells.

'It was a mistake to invite her,' Mhairi spat. 'She was nobody.'

Ella jumped in. This 'nobody' might get her off the hook. 'Maybe it was her!' The enthusiasm in her voice was barely hidden and on the opposite side of the circle, Catriona jolted to attention.

'Maybe…' said Mhairi. 'I suppose.'

'Yah, I know that she stayed in touch with a few of the girls from the front row. She was at a party in Edinburgh over Christmas,' said Bells.

Mhairi nodded, apparently unsurprised. 'Yes, it could be her.' Her eyes flicked to Catriona. 'You're awfully quiet, little Kit-Cat. You liked her, didn't you? I don't suppose you've spoken to her recently, have you?'

Catriona blinked and pushed her glasses up her nose. Her eyes looked puffy and the lenses were smeared. 'No, Mhairi,' she replied hurriedly. 'I haven't spoken to her in ages. Honestly, I haven't.'

Ella winced at Catriona's tone. She was talking too fast. She sounded guilty.

'I didn't see her at Christmas, we were staying at my Dad's house. You know because of the new baby and everything. I didn't see anybody.' The colour had drained from Catriona's face and she looked freezing cold. Her arms were crossed, and she had tucked her hands under her armpits for warmth, but she was shivering and her voice trembled. She lowered her eyes, refusing to meet Ella's.

'Methinks the lady doth protest too much,' said Bells.

And as the huddle turned on Catriona, Ella felt only relief that it wasn't turning upon her.

CHAPTER 34

Break on Through (to the Other Side)
(The Doors)

Catriona was sitting on the steps outside the pet shed, a rabbit in her arms, when Ella found her. She was red-eyed, and her breathing shuddered.

Catriona had cowered like a pecked hen while the accusations flew at her. And with neither the strength nor the voice to defend herself her silence had finally damned her. And Ella had not stepped in to help her friend; she had stepped back and watched.

Ella sat down, fiddling with her nose ring, sick with shame while Catriona stroked the rabbit in the soft spot between its ears. And Ella could think of nothing to say – she could never make this right.

Catriona had not deserved the names they had heaped upon her. It was Ella who deserved them. *Tattletale. Snitch. Grass. Tattletale. Snitch. Grass.* The words hissed in her head, searing her from the inside.

'It wasn't me,' said Catriona eventually, more to the rabbit than to Ella.

'I know.'

'Well, why didn't you say something?'

'I don't know. I just couldn't.' And that much, at least, was true.

Catriona took a deep breath. 'Don't worry. I don't blame you. She's terrifying.'

'She's with The Bulldog now. Maybe this will be the end of it.'

'Don't count on it. Not after last time. Sister Hanrahan will take her side. She'll think Mhairi's the victim and that the journalist's report's all just lies.' Catriona twiddled the rabbit's lopping ears in her fingers.

'Really?'

'Oh yes. That article doesn't prove anything. And the photo of the couple in the woods – it could be anyone.'

Ella nodded. She was right. The photos proved nothing to anyone but her.

'But you saw her, Ella. Did you see her with the man they wrote about in the papers?'

The bell went, and Ella used it as an excuse not to answer.

'You go on ahead. I'll catch up with you,' Catriona said, heading into the shed to put the rabbit back in the hutch. 'Best not get into any more trouble.'

Ella walked fast, her head down to avoid the stares of the girls in the corridors. In the Form Room the front two rows were deep in conversation but when Ella arrived, they broke apart, pelting her with questions. The Cecilians, and Sister Gagnier, were missing.

'Where is everyone?'

'Have you seen the papers?'

'What did Mhairi say?'

'Stop!' Ella put her hand out as if she was halting traffic. 'I don't know anything, okay? I have no idea where they are.' She took her seat at the end of the empty third row and lifted the lid of the desk to shield herself.

She glanced up at the clock: Sister Gagnier was never late. It had been ages since the bell went, and Catriona still wasn't there. Something wasn't right.

The chatter quelled and a strange silence replaced it, tight and arrested, like a pause between breaths. No-one was moving very much, except to check their watches or flick their eyes to the door. Ella's mouth was so dry that swallowing was difficult.

And then it started – a ruckus, angry voices, running feet. She heard the mob tearing down the corridor.

Sister Gagnier pushed past, beads of sweat dripping at the edge of her wimple. She stretched her arms wide, putting herself between the mob and the classroom. Fierce and vicious, the fury rose off them like heatwaves round a fire.

Ella was in no doubt it was her they had come for. The nun wouldn't hold them back for long. Dropping the desk lid with a clatter she drew herself up to her full height, shoulders back, chin out.

Mhairi surged forward, followed by the Cecilians, pushing Sister Gagnier out of the way.

'Ella Richardson!'

'You piece of shit!'

'You lying bitch!'

Sister Gagnier gasped, her black sleeves flapping like wings. 'Girls. Girls. Control yourselves. Let us be calm.' But no-one was listening.

Mhairi grabbed a rectangle of paper from Theresa's hand,

waving it in the air. 'Look what we found in the bottom of your wardrobe. Anything you want to tell us, *Ella*?'

The room shifted. She glugged air. They had found the cheque! The game was up.

Mhairi jabbed a long finger at the name on the bottom of the cheque. '*The Daily Recorder*. Your thirty pieces of silver. Judas!'

And then they were all shouting.

'Judas!'

'Judas!'

'Judas!'

'Judas!'

Over by the blackboard, Catriona stood on her own, not shouting, just looking, the hurt scorched in the wheals on her cheeks, flaring hot and raw.

***

An hour later, Ella stood in The Bulldog's office on the other side of a wide wooden desk. The lights were off and the heavy sky on the other side of the window did little to brighten the room.

The nun sat immobile, her eyes fixed on Ella, her hands gripping a crucifix as if warding off sin. On the mantelpiece behind her a black clock chimed three. 'Tell me, girlie, are you ashamed of your lies?'

Ella looked down at her thumbnail and picked at a bit of skin with her index finger. Nothing she could say would make any difference so there was no point in wasting her breath.

'The photographs prove nothing. In fact I'm quite sure they've been staged. It would be easy enough for someone with friends on the outside. People who might be greedy enough to profit from their lies. Am I right? Am I?'

Ella turned and stared out of the rain-streaked window at the playing fields beyond.

'You are a deeply troubled young woman. But to tell such lies about the girls who welcomed you, who opened their hearts, who tried to be your friends. . . What made you do it?'

What did she think? That Lucifer himself had appeared to her in a vision and tempted her to lie about Mhairi? She pictured him behind the Bulldog – bright red, pointed tail slung over his arm, trident poking the nun's oversized arse. Ella snorted.

'I thought as much. Wickedness. Pure and simple.' The headmistress pulled a pad of paper towards her and, taking a pen from a holder, began to write. Then she stopped. 'If you were just spinning a story, that might be forgivable – your childish desire to be the centre of attention. Mhairi's told us about your envy and your jealousy. We could forgive that. But to take money from these gossipmongers. To sell your lies and profit from the blackness in your heart. That's a whole different ball game.'

What a hypocrite. The Bulldog had calculated exactly how much money they could make from Mhairi's stories. Pilgrimages. Candles for sale. There would have been plastic statues of Our Lady of Belgaddie before the month was out. The nun's anger was as much about loss of income as the humiliation of a double page tabloid spread.

'Have you nothing to say for yourself, you ungrateful child?'

Ella stayed silent. And the insults shot so fast out of the Bulldog's mouth that soon they became arrows. Ella drew them in Biro in her mind. Wooden arrows with rubber suckers, like the ones she and Nicola had played with in their Cowboys and Indians phase. She ducked when they flew at her, spit flicking as they soared by. She was quick and nimble, but the Bulldog was relentless. What if one got her right between the eyes? Hideous and slimy on her bare skin. No. It was time to run to safety. To get back into her covered wagon and wait till the coast was clear.

'I don't think you're even listening.' The Bulldog continued. 'We thought we were doing a kindness offering a place to a troubled girl like you. But I see now that my judgement was faulty. I've called your father. He'll be here to pick you up in an hour or so. In the meantime, collect your trunk from the Steading and pack up your belongings. I don't want you upsetting the girls any more than you already have. They've been warned to steer clear of you.'

Ella turned and headed for the door. But as she reached for the handle something bright caught her peripheral vision, like a kingfisher's wing. It was her quilt, draped over the edge of a box labelled *Contraband*. She pulled it out, spilling forbidden fruit across the floor: a Walkman, a Jackie Collins' paperback, an assortment of lip-gloss.

'Put that back. Who gave you permission?…'

But Ella was already gone.

***

In the cobwebby damp of the trunk room, Ella sat on the floor and drew circles in the dust. For weeks she had been craving solitude, but now that she had it, she felt like a particle lost in space.

Rows of trunks were stacked on the metal shelves in front of her and somewhere in the middle of them was hers. Shiny and new, just a few months old. Most of the trunks were neatly labelled. Hers, she knew, was not.

She was scanning the rows for something that might distinguish it when her eye stopped at a deep steamer trunk. It looked old. The leather was worn but the brass tacks still had some of their lustre. Peeling luggage labels looked tea-stained like a treasure map she'd once made, and a list of names had been professionally painted down the centre of the short end. She read:

Miss Evangeline Scott,
St Cecilia's Convent of the Sacred Mysteries,
Belgaddie.

Miss Harriet Hamilton,
As above.

Miss Belinda Fraser,
As above.

Miss Iona Campbell,
As above.

Miss Mhairi Campbell,
As above.

Five generations of Mhairi's family had been here, in this place. The names chimed – the Campbell Laboratory, the Fraser Hall, the Scott Library. The family practically owned the place, their dust was in the floorboards, their money was in the walls. No wonder the nuns would do anything rather than upset Mhairi.

Ella considered the list. If they had been boys, there would be no need for these name changes. A single surname would suffice. Girls were not named for life, they were named for now, placeholder names until some man gave them a new one. There was nothing in these words to show the blood bond that ran through these women. She looked again. The surname before Mhairi's was also Campbell. Not her mother, she must have been Belinda Fraser. Iona Campbell must be her sister. But she'd never heard mention of a sister before.

Ella kicked a metal trunk on the row nearest the ground and dust, unsettled, fell from the rafters. Why was she wasting her time thinking about Mhairi? She sneezed and wiped her nose with the back of her hand. She was finally getting out of this place. But if this was what she wanted, why did she feel so shit?

On the top shelf, sandwiched between Bernie and Theresa's red and green trunks, she spotted her own, and hauling it out, let it crash to the ground.

Behind her, the door creaked open. 'Hello, Ella.'

She stared. It was Magda.

'Sister Cobb has shown us the newspaper.'

Ella's palms prickled with sweat. 'Magda. . . I didn't mean for them to print that stuff. The stuff about you. I just wanted everyone to know Mhairi was lying. You wouldn't help me. And I wanted to do the right thing, to tell the truth.'

'You told your truth. And has it made you happy?'

Ella shook her head. 'It's all such a mess. I've hurt Catriona. And you.'

Magda clutched her hands together, a thumb worrying her bony white knuckles.

Ella swallowed, ashamed of herself. 'Why didn't you tell me? If I'd known you were here illegally, I would never have said anything. I would have kept your secret.'

'Oh, Ella.' Magda smiled. 'We are not here illegally. My father had connections. He secured our passage before the revolution and made sure we reached a place of safety. Though he did not follow us, in the end.'

'What?' Ella frowned. 'I don't understand. If you're not in

314

hiding, why didn't you help me?'

'Did I not help you? I asked Our Lady for guidance. I am an instrument of her peace.'

'I knew it! You and Mhairi are in this together, aren't you? I saw her pick up your letter!"

Magda nodded. 'But there is still much you do not understand.'

Ella was done with this. She was too tired for Magda's riddles, and she sat on the trunk and put her head in her hands. 'I can't handle this right now. Just leave me alone.'

Magda took an envelope from her pocket and placed it on top of the trunk. 'This is for you.' Crouching, she took Ella's hands in hers and kissed them gently. 'Be kind to yourself, Ella. I will miss you.'

Ella sat a while after Magda had gone, turning the envelope over and over in her hands. She wouldn't read it. Not now. Instead she put it in the pocket of her tunic and lifted up one end of the trunk. She dragged it across the cobbles, over the gravel and down the drive, the stones scraping the blue paintwork, the metallic ting grating the nerves of her teeth, the marrow of her bones.

***

Later, back in her cube, she was throwing her things into the trunk when she heard a familiar voice from the other side of the partition wall. 'Packing has never been one of my strong points either. But how about I give you a bit of a hand?'

All she wanted to do was fall into his arms, to smell the safe, grassy scent of him and let go. But if she did, if she shrugged off that armour which was holding her together, she knew she would evaporate into the bone-dry air and disappear forever. Instead, she pulled in her stomach and held her breath. She wanted to be stiff and solid, and as long as she didn't move or breathe everything would be just fine.

'I can manage. I'll see you in the car.'

'Ella…'

'Go Dad, I'll manage.'

***

As the clapped-out 2CV ground its way over the gravel, Ella looked across to the woods, then back at the Mansion House that squatted heavy as a toad. She watched in the wing mirror as the granite building receded, and the rain streaked the last of it from view. She thought about the Cecilians cheering her home from her run, film-night, midnight escapades, and Catriona, sitting on the end of her bed. Catriona. Her friend. For a minute there, it had been the nearest thing to good.

CHAPTER 35
All the Time in the World
(Louis Armstrong)

Ella curled up on the front seat, twisting her body away from her father, and soothed herself with the rhythm of the wipers. She traced the jagged path of the raindrops as they made their way down the window, raced them like she'd done as a child.

At first, Dad tried to make conversation, but she deadened his efforts with grunted replies, and the next two hours passed in silence. He stopped for petrol in Dunkeld, and when he returned to the car he threw a bag of liquorice toffees onto her lap. 'We're going to have to talk about this sometime. I need to know what's been going on.'

The scream inside her head scared her. She wanted to swing open the car door and jump from the moving vehicle, tumble onto the verge like she'd seen them do in movies, roll into the long grass and burrow somewhere until the coast was clear. She could emerge as somebody new. No mistakes. No tragic past clinging to her shoulders, dragging behind her, like some anti-magic cape where all the stars had been nibbled off by mice. She could be nobody.

'Ella… can you hear me?'

'Yeah,' she mumbled, her right arm over her face, clinging onto the seatbelt, holding the words in. 'I hear you.'

***

It was dark by the time they pulled into the drive. The lights were all off and she sat in the car for a moment, looking at the house.

Dad had gone in ahead of her and was waiting for her in the kitchen. 'I didn't have time to get anything for supper. Why don't we take your trunk upstairs and I'll pop along to Errol for some fish and chips?'

Errol. Where she'd gone to Guides. Where it had happened. Blinking, she saw blue lights and rainfall, ambulances and starched white sheets, headlines, photographs and the Mini, crumpled like tinfoil under the truck. She blinked again, and they were gone.

'No, Dad. I'm not hungry. Please don't go there.'

She watched his face as he realised what he'd done. What he'd said. His brow knotted and that worried look returned to his face. She felt almost sorry for him. How could he get it right when he didn't know her anymore? She was just some stranger who kept turning up, no matter how hard he tried to get rid of her.

He laid a hand on her shoulder. 'Come on, let's get this bloody trunk inside and I'll see what's in the fridge. I think there's some bread. And eggs. How about scrambled eggs on toast?'

They struggled up the stairs and dropped the trunk on the floor in the middle of her bedroom. She flicked on the light. It was just as she had left it. If she'd put a hair in the door before she'd gone, it would still have been there. Her desk, bare since her grandmother's pre-Christmas visit, was thinly layered with dust and the bed was unmade, as it had been the day she left for Saint C's.

'I wasn't expecting you back, or I would've changed the sheets.'

'Don't worry. It's luxury compared to St. Cecilia's. I didn't even have a door there.'

He laughed. 'Well, I'll leave you to it. I'll make some tea. Come down when you're ready.'

Was this home? Was this the place where she belonged? It couldn't be. All she felt here was sadness, even the memories of happiness made her sad.

She went over to the desk and picked up the small, framed photograph. Ella, aged about six, and Mom. They were smiling, laughing, the wind in their hair and their eyes wet with the cold. 'Love'. It said it on the frame. Mom, laughing. As if they had all the time in the world. Tricking her into believing there were things she could count on, that there would be forever, that love was enough.

Nobody else had a Mom like her. One who smelled of sunshine and soil, whose hands were always covered with paint, whose hair was wild and full of fresh air. She could bury her face in Mom's hair and everything would be all right again. She was never in a rush, there was always enough time. And now there was no time at all. How could somebody love her so much and go? With no goodbye. And no sorry. Just go.

Trust and hope – where did that get her?

'How could you leave me? When I don't even know who I am?' Ella's voice seemed to come from somewhere old and distant. She barely recognised it as her own. 'I wasn't ready. You weren't finished. I needed you to be here.'

She hurled the photograph across the room and it shattered on the wall above her bed, splintering onto the pillows and the crumpled sheets below.

Ella slipped to the ground and pulled her knees to her chest. Everything she cared about was gone – her mother, her friends, her home. She belonged nowhere and nothing belonged to her. She was nothing, after all.

***

Days passed, nights passed, and Ella drifted in and out of time. If she shut her eyes for too long, she was back in the glade, at Our Lady's Tree, watching the rituals and the sex, and the lady. But when they were open, the loneliness was too real for her to bear.

Dad was at work and she moped about the house watching *Bod* and *Fingerbobs*, *Pebble Mill at One*. She didn't want to hear music. She couldn't read. Her room was a disaster. The trunk blocked the route from the door to her desk, immovable as a megalith, its contents ignored.

She ate toast and drank tea until her body was awash, swilling with a wateriness that made it hard for her to stand. Lying on her bed, on the sofa, on the living room floor, she buried herself in the quilt until she gasped for air. On the rug in front of the empty fireplace she worked her way into the pile with her toes, rifled through it with her fingers, searching for traces of the past. She dug deep beneath the cushions of the sofa, burrowing until her fingernails were black.

And all the while she couldn't shake Catriona from her mind: Catriona, who had reached out a hand to show her the way back, who had risked so much to stand by her side. Ella was a coward. She could point her finger and call the Cecilians fakes, but in the end, she had turned out to be the biggest fraud of them all.

And Magda saw it. She, who knew what it was to survive on the scraps of a life, seemed to see into the darkness of Ella's damaged heart. She had spoken in riddles, but her words, which had been swirling formless, began to arrange themselves in Ella's mind. *Hope deferred makes the heart sick, but desire fulfilled is a tree of life.*

It made no sense, but she wanted to hold onto it before it disappeared. Taking a sketchbook from the desk drawer she scribbled Magda's words across the middle of the page. She stared at them for some time, going over them with her Biro, until the proverb pushed through the surface of the paper, turning it into a rippling relief map. And then she began illustrating the words with dark, hard sketches. She drew a withered heart, black and elongated, the arteries branching out like vines, twisting round the words, choking the message. Putting her hand to her chest, she felt the ravaged pulse of her own heart. And in the corner of the page she drew a single cypselae from a dandelion clock, the tiny seed carried by a parachute of feathery hope. And as she drew, something shifted. *The first message*, she thought.

Words kept coming, and on the next page she wrote: 'If you love something, set it free. If it comes back to you, it's yours; if it doesn't, it was never meant to be.' She called this second message, *Hallmark Bullshit.* It almost made her smile. The title bounced across the top of the page like candyfloss clouds. And then she drew a black horse with huge powerful flanks leaping over a gate. The horse, mane tossing in the wind, left behind a meadow of love-hearts and kiddie flowers. It soared headlong into a blackness which covered the right side of the page.

The third message, she had to retrieve from her satchel. The fake letter from The Virgin – or Magda as it turned out – that Catriona had read to her in the San. Ella read it again.

Two words stood out and she wrote them across the middle of the next page. *Trust* and *Reconciliation*. Around the word *Trust*, she drew two hands reaching out towards each other. And *Reconciliation*? What did that even mean? Forgiveness? Maybe. But it was more than that. Mobilised now, she ran downstairs and into Dad's study where the two volume *Shorter Oxford Dictionary* always stood, on the shelf by the desk.

Reconciliation: Being at one with others. Making one's belief compatible with others. The end of an estrangement, between God and man. A father and his children.

She thought about that for a long time while she sat in Dad's swivel chair, spinning round from one side to another, as she'd done as a child. Sitting on his lap.

She looked at the two words she had written on the paper, the hands reaching out around the word *Trust*. She pictured Catriona at the bottom of the bed, reading the letter in her best 'Virgin Mary' voice. It was pretty good for a fake letter. Sitting at Dad's desk she drew hands around the word *Reconciliation* too. Reaching out, willing themselves to touch in the middle, the fingertips not quite making contact.

The final message was the card from Magda. She knew where it was. But she wasn't ready to look at it just yet.

CHAPTER 36

Yes Sir, I can Boogie (Baccara)

Ella had been avoiding mirrors. But when she did catch sight of herself, she did not like what she saw. Her hair stuck up straight all round her head, as if she had her hands on a Van der Graff generator, and not in a cool way. It was too long over her ears and although it had grown down the back of her neck, it wasn't long enough on the top. But who gave a shit about her hair? All she did was read, lie on the sofa and watch telly. She re-read childhood favourites – *The Secret Garden, Charlotte Sometimes, Flambards*. She watched crap TV. No-one would see her anyway. She was never going to leave the house again.

But one night, a few weeks after she'd left Saint C's, there was a knock on the back door while she and Dad were eating supper. She kept her head down. He knew better than to expect she would go to the door.

'Hello, Nicola. It's good to see you. It's been a while.' He didn't sound surprised.

Ella swallowed hard. Nicola hadn't stood in that doorway for years. Why the fuck was she standing there now?

'Hi, Dr Richardson.' Nicola's voice was quiet, reticent, as if she wasn't entirely sure what she was doing there either. 'I... I just wanted to see how Ella was getting on.' She paused. 'Mum said she was back.'

Ella knew Nicola could see her from the doorway, but she didn't look up, she kept squashing the peas into the Smash with the back of her fork.

'Come in, come in. We're just finishing supper.' Dad picked up his unfinished plate from the table. 'I'll leave you to it. Why don't you make Nicola a cup of tea? There might be some Digestives in the cupboard, though they're probably a bit soft.' He pulled the door shut behind him.

She sensed Nicola hovering, waiting for the silence to break.

A minute or more passed. 'Can I sit down?' Nicola said.

Ella looked up. In the last year or so Nicola had changed. She had taken on the shape of her mother – ample hips, sturdy legs, arms folded across her chest. Standing on the opposite side of the table she looked well-planted, rooted, as if she wasn't going anywhere. 'Do what you like,' Ella said.

Nicola put her hands on her hips. 'I won't stay if you don't want me to.' She was always like that – putting on a good show – but Ella knew her. There was apprehension in her voice. 'Mum said I should come round to see you.'

Ella wished that her table book wasn't *The Secret Garden*, but she picked it up anyway. 'Yeah, well. You've done that now. You've seen me. I'm fine. Bye.' She opened the book and pretended to read. But there was no sound of movement.

'Come on. G'me a break. I'm tryin', Okay?' Nicola said.

She didn't look up. 'Forget it. It's too late.'

'Is it?' Look, I've been thinkin' about you lately...'

'Oh yea? Seen the papers?'

'No, not that. I've been thinking about you and me. Us.' She pulled out Dad's chair and sat down.

Ella straightened herself up and spread her hands out on the table, looking at her square on. She had known that face so well. They had been opposites and they'd liked that. Nicola was fair and rosy, while she was dark and pale: Rose Red and Snow White. They had seen each other every day. The had been best friends forever. Ha.

'Has my dad put you up to this?' Ella asked.

'No, it's not that. He has been speakin' to my mum though. He's worried about you. We all are.'

'Bullshit.' Ella turned away.

'No. It's true. Look, I'm no good at explaining things. You were always the one who was good wi' words. But I wanted to say sorry.' She paused. 'I am sorry. I really am.'

'I don't know what you're talking about.'

'Yeah, you do. Look at me, please look at me. I'm sorry about what happened to your Mum. It was terrible. Really terrible. And I'm sorry that when you came back from America, nothin' was the same. You were different. I was different. I didn't know how to be around you anymore.' She had lost her swagger. 'I was scared I'd say the wrong thing. That I'd make things worse.'

Ella scoffed. She *must* have known that she certainly *had* made things worse.

'D'you remember when we started at The Leven? We got such a hard time from the Dundee crowd. Callin' us teuchtars and all that. But at least we were together. And then your mum died, and you

325

stopped comin' to school. And I was on my own. I missed you.' Nicola sniffed, biting the side of her mouth. 'I mean, I'm not lookin' for sympathy – obviously it was much worse for you – but you were away for such a long time. I was lonely. I had to make new friends.' Her voice broke and a big tear plopped onto the table.

Ella frowned. She didn't want to hear this, but she couldn't turn away.

'And then, when you finally did come back, you were so... different... You weren't the same Ella that I knew before. And that kinda' freaked me out. They used to give me stick for even speakin' to you. And after that you just got, well, y' know, weirder and weirder, until it was too late and I didn't know how to talk to you anymore.'

'Weirder and weirder? Thanks. That makes me feel a lot better.'

'You know what I mean – you started hangin' out with the punks – that lot – they're weirdos. Or at least I thought they were.'

'Changed your mind, have you?' Ella narrowed her eyes.

'Yeah. I suppose so. I got speakin' to Mikey at the bus stop a few weeks ago.'

The mention of Mikey's name caught Ella off-guard and her hand went to her hair instinctively.

Nicola smiled. 'He's pretty cool, actually. He was in the village visiting his mum. Tappin' her for cash probably. He's passed his drivin' test, wants to get a car – a banger, y'know. Anyway, he asked me if I'd heard from you. He didn't seem to know that we weren't friends anymore. He told me about the stuff that had happened at your new school. He'd read it in the papers. It sounded crazy, Ella.'

Heat flushed up Ella's neck. She'd been so sure that Mikey would have forgotten about her. To hear that he'd been thinking about her, asking about her even, reminded her how much she liked him. But she needed to play this cool. 'Yeah, it was crazy.'

'Did you know those girls?'

Ella took a deep breath. 'You could say that.'

'And did you see that stuff? Was it true?'

Ella stood up from the table and took her plate over to the sink. 'Look, if you're just here for the gossip, maybe you should go.'

'Sorry, no. I don't care about that shit. It sounded pretty screwed up. I'm just here to see if maybe we could… you know… hang out sometime. I mean, I understand if you don't want to. It's just that, well, I've kind of missed you.' Nicola moved to where Ella was standing and stretched out a hand along the counter-top, almost as if she expected her to take it.

'What about Craig? He looked like a pretty full-time job to me.'

'He dumped me. Got with Elaine at Jane's party.'

Ella turned to face her. 'Ha! So, now that you're sad and lonely, you're running back to me?'

'No! Well… actually… if you think about it, yeah!' She laughed at her own transparency. 'Typical of you to see right through me. You always could. We didn't have any secrets, did we?'

And Ella couldn't help smiling. Her mind flashed back to the hot summer of 1977. The radio was on and they were dancing in the kitchen. Nicola was pretending to smooch with an invisible boy, her hands wrapped round her back, squeezing her own bum. They were laughing.

Nicola wiped her face with the back of her hand, smearing kingfisher eyeliner down the side of her cheeks. 'So, now that I'm young, free and single, I wondered if you fancied comin' with me into town?' She looked at her watch. 'There's a bus in half an hour. That should be enough time to get out of your pyjamas and put on a bit of slap.'

Ella hesitated. 'Oh, I don't know. I'm not really in the mood.'

'I'm going to Mikey's. Aye. I thought that might surprise you. He said I could come over anytime. He's havin' a party tonight and I told his sister Sheila I'd be there.'

Adrenalin shot through Ella's body making her fingertips tingle and her tongue fizz. During those crazy months at Saint C's, she'd given up any hope of ever seeing him again. But since she'd been home she could hardly get off the sofa, let alone get herself into town. Maybe going to the squat with somebody else, even if it was Nicola, was less terrifying than going there alone. 'I'll go and get changed,' she said.

Uninvited, Nicola followed her upstairs and stood in the doorway of her bedroom while Ella squeezed past the trunk to get to her wardrobe.

'Jeezy-peeps, it's a midden in here. How can you find anything?'

The floor was covered with towels, cereal bowls, crusts of toast and mugs that were growing discs of mould. The desk was the only clear surface. The bed was still bare after she'd stripped it to get rid of the broken glass. The ticking of the mattress was stained. She had been sleeping on it all week and barely noticed, but now that she saw it through Nicola's eyes she pinked with embarrassment.

'Why don't I come round tomorrow and help you sort it out? Remember how we used to do bedroom make-overs? That time you made a tent with your Mum's old tablecloths from India and we made a den with all the cushions from the living room. And your Mum brought us up brownies. We had torches and everything. 'Member?'

'Na, not really. I don't have much of a memory,' Ella lied.

Nicola's forehead crinkled; she wasn't falling for that. 'See if you can remember where your clothes are in all this mess, you cannae go out in your jammies! We need to get our skates on if we're gonna make the bus.'

Ella sprayed her armpits with deodorant, threw on an out-sized jumper and pulled on black jeans.

'What about a bit of make-up?' Nicola asked, not unkindly.

'Nah. I'm going for the natural look.'

'Then maybe do something with your hair?'

Ella went into the bathroom, took a long deep breath and looked at herself in the mirror. *Shit.* It was worse than she thought.

She grabbed a pair of curved nail scissors from the cabinet and started snipping around her ears. She chopped into the top and reached round the back of her neck, nicking the hair into some sort of shape. Then squeezing the last of the gel from an old VO5 tube she mushed her hair, scrunching it into choppy tufts.

Nicola chapped on the door. 'Come on, we'll miss the bus.'

Ella dusted the black hair from her shoulders and took a last look in the mirror. Not too bad. Not too bad at all.

At the front door Nicola gave her a double thumbs up and called out in a voice so familiar it was almost as if the last four years hadn't happened. 'Bye, Dr Richardson. We're just going down to my house to watch a video. I'll make sure she's back before eleven.'

Ella grinned and pulled the door shut behind her.

CHAPTER 37

You Can't Always Get What You Want
(The Rolling Stones)

They sat side-by-side at the back of the bus. 'You look like a ghost. Let me give you a wee bit of colour. It'll warm you up.' Nicola took out a lipstick and drew rosy circles on Ella's cheeks. Her cool, busy hands blended the lipstick into the hollows under Ella's cheekbones. And with the excess she rouged Ella's lips. 'There, better already.'

Nicola's easy chatter made her think of Catriona. Saturday night. It would be film night. She'd be hunched on a bench trying to stay awake, watching *Escape to Witch Mountain*, or worse. It was an image she couldn't quite shake as Nicola ran through the gossip from The Leven like Ella was part of it. Like she cared.

***

On the street below the squat, Ella stopped for a moment and listened to the pounding music. She looked at the puddle under the broken drainpipe and her hand instinctively went to the long scar on the back of her cranium. The wound had healed some time ago, but no hair grew along the stripe. She fingered its baldness.

'Come on, what are you waiting for? It's pure Baltic out here.' Nicola ran into the dark close and Ella followed her up the stairs to the squat. The door was open and the party was spilling out onto the landing. When she had been there before Christmas, there had been groups of people, milling and drinking, but now there were crowds.

Nicola dragged her in. The living room was steamy. The smell of beer, damp bodies and cigarettes was visible, a grey-green haze that wrapped itself round everything and everyone. And as she went deeper into the crowd, Ella scanned the room for familiar faces. But she recognised nobody. It was like a punch in the gut. She shouldn't have come. She needed to go. And then, from behind, two plump arms grabbed her round the waist.

She could see by the nails that it was Cass. 'Snow White! Oor Snowy's back!'

Nicola, mouthing that she had spotted Sheila, disappeared into the mass of people, and Cass pulled Ella into the kitchen. 'Let me get a look at ye. Fuck me, that boarding school's no agreed wi you! No one wee bit. Look at you! The nose ring's still cool but yer a bag o' bones. And whit the fuck's happened t'yer hair!'

'It's good to see you too!' Ella laughed, relief flooding through her, delighted by the genuine pleasure on Cass's face.

'Eh wiz so gutted when you disappeared. It took Stan ages tae come clean aboot the 'shrooms. Whit a twat. He'd been after you fir ages, but he kept his distance when Eh wiz aboot. He's far too old for you!'

'I don't think it was his *age* that was the problem,' said Ella.

Stan was the same age as Mikey after all. 'More that… well… he's not exactly a looker.'

'Stan! Ha! Ye ken he got that nickname 'cause he looks like Stan fae Laurel and Hardy? If ye ask me, he looks more like Shane McGowan fae the *Nipple Erectors* – gadgey bastard. Anyway, y'had a lucky escape. Knockin' yersel oot tae get awa was a bit extreme though!'

'Yeah. And I've got the scar to prove it.' Ella turned to show Cass the back of her head.

'Nasty! And as if that wisnae bad enough, it was Mikey's mum heard fae Nicola's mum, who heard from yer Da, that he'd sent you to a boarding school in ooter bloody bumfuck. What a total freakin' nightmare!'

'Yeah. Nightmare.'

'And whit a place! A' that shite aboot the Virgin Mary! We saw it in the papers. Then it turns oot the hale thing wiz made up. Just so they girls could sneak intae the woods to hae a shag. Maybe it wisnae sae bad after all!' Cas gave a hearty chuckle and elbowed Ella in the ribs. 'Whit was it like, Ella? Did you see her? The Virgin Mary? Or were you just there for the voddy?' She laughed again.

It seemed unreal now. All of it. 'Ha, Cass. You make it sound like a laugh. But I don't know… it was all a bit hard really…'

'Aw, Ella. Ya big soaftie. Come here,' Cass pulled her into a big hug, her head somewhere around Ella's belly button.

'Is everyone else here?' Ella said, itching to see Mikey.

'Aye, Ah think so. No Stan, you'll be pleased tae hear. He's got an apprenticeship at Holo-Krome. He's no goin' oot as much as he used tae. But abody else is here. Ah left Dek over on the mattress and Mikey's aboot somewhere. He'll be pure chuffed that you're here. He speaks aboot you a lot, 'specially when a' that stuff wiz in the papers!'

'I'll go find him.'

'Just one thing…' Cass called after her, but Ella was already off.

The Goths were gathered over by the mural. It seemed to Ella as if they hadn't moved since the last time she was there. The tall guy with the Lady Di fringe was leaning on the mantelpiece with a bottle of Grolsch in his hand. He was flicking the ceramic cap back and forward with his thumbnail, a look of boredom carefully fixed on his beautiful, thin face. He caught Ella's eye from behind the bleached fringe and in pulling himself up a little taller, his elbow slipped off the fireplace. Scrabbling to save his dignity, he turned the slippage into a wave. Ella smiled and waved back.

Where was Mikey? She rubbed her fingers through her hair, spiking it up a bit, and licked her lips. People were looking at her. People who might be interested. But Mikey was here. Somewhere. She thought of his face and the feel of it in her hand the last time she'd seen him, when she'd tasted excitement on her tongue. She scanned the crowd. He wouldn't be dancing this early in the evening. He was far too cool for that.

And then she saw him. The back of him. He was entangled with Goth Girl, the one with the spider-web make-up. Ella stopped, frozen. He was flattening the girl against the wall. Her arms were all over him and one leg was hooked around his hip. Ella's stomach lurched. Their heads were gyrating, their mouths working on each other as if they were trying to swallow each other whole. She wanted to look away but she couldn't. She couldn't even blink. The muscles in his arse clenched tight in his bondage trousers, and he thrust forward, the Goth's leg twitching, working its way higher. *Fuck!* She was such an idiot. Why had she come? Had she honestly thought he'd come running and take her in his arms?

The music was banging, the heat unbearable and she stood in the centre of the crowd, the whole wild jumble spinning about her. And then, suddenly Nicola was in front of her. She put both her hands Ella's shoulders and looked at her straight in the eye. 'I wondered where you'd got to.'

Ella's eyes flicked back to Mikey and Nicola followed her gaze. 'Ah. Okay. Seems like Mikey is otherwise engaged. Look. Why don't we blow this taco joint sky high? Let's get out of here. Take my hand.' She hauled Ella through the crowd, out of the flat and down the stairs onto the street.

All the time they waited for the bus, Nicola never let go of Ella's hand. 'You like him, don't you? I hadn't realised quite how much.'

Ella nodded. 'I'm a mug. I know I am.'

'Ha. You're way too good for him. And he knows it. He spoke about you non-stop though, when I met him on the bus. He thinks you're cool. Like a wee sister.' Nicola reached up and threw an arm round Ella's shoulder. 'Actually, you are pretty cool. I've always known that; I just forgot it for a while. Sorry 'bout that.'

They stood like that in silence. And it felt easy. Ella no longer felt awkward, or tentative. She felt comfortable and familiar. She was recalibrating. And the pain of realising that Mikey didn't want her, was never going to want her, vanished, like a drop of ink in water.

Nicola suddenly laughed and punched Ella's arm. 'But did you see that Goth boy checking you out? I mean seriously, he didn't take his eyes off you.'

CHAPTER 38

Running Bear (Johnny Preston)

The next morning, Ella was still asleep when Nicola burst into her bedroom. 'Wakey, wakey, rise and shine. Your Dad let me in. Time to get out of your lazy bed and get this midden sorted.'

Ella pulled the bare pillow over her head. 'Didn't anybody tell you it's polite to knock? Get lost. It's too early.'

'It's eleven o'clock! The day's a'wastin'.' Nicola pulled off the blanket and Ella groaned, blinking in the bright light.

'Here,' Nicola handed her a steaming mug. 'I've made you a brew. Shift yer bum.' Emerging from the fog of sleepiness, Ella shuffled over, and Nicola stretched out beside her on the bed. They sat for a while in silence, sipping their tea. Then Nicola stood up and pulled a string of binbags out of her back pocket like a magician conjuring silk handkerchiefs. 'Right. Let's start with the floor.'

She gathered up crockery and cutlery and scraped the waste into a binbag, while Ella picked up the clothes and sorted them into two piles – clean and dirty. They worked their way around the room until, from beneath a mound of mildewed towels, they unearthed the record player. Small and made of brown plastic, it was still plugged in.

'Great. Let's get some tunes on. That'll get us going. Your records in the usual place?'

Bums in the air, they rootled around under the bed.

'Do you remember this one?' Ella asked, pulling herself out. Dust billowed as she waved the lurid album cover: *Rock and Roll Hits: The Jukebox Collection.*

'Oh, bloody hell, yes! How many times did we listen to that? Remember our dancing? And those rock and roll skirts your mum made us out o' the curtains?'

Ella blew on the vinyl and put it on the turntable. She lifted the needle and placed it carefully in a selected groove. Practised. She'd done this before.

'Oh. My. God!' shouted Nicola as soon as she heard the *hooga-wooga, hooga-wooga* chanting at the start of the track. 'Running Bear! That one was our absolute favourite. 'Member the dance! We had it all worked out.'

Ella jumped into her Running Bear position, feet planted, legs wide, hands on her knees, bouncing up and down in time to the beat.

He couldn't swim, the raging river
Cause the river was too wide,
He couldn't reach, Little White Dove,
Waiting on the other side.

She scanned the river of clothes between them, miming the breaststroke, shaking her head, reaching out to Little White Dove (Nicola), who jumped from foot to foot, waving to her Brave.

They were having fun. She didn't care how stupid she looked or what anyone thought about her, she was laughing and happy and actually having fun.

When they finally turned their attention back to the bedroom, Nicola assigned them more tasks. 'We need to get all your clothes out and see what you should keep and what you should dump. You get the stuff from the chest of drawers and I'll get stuck into the wardrobe.'

They sorted through piles of stuff, stopping every now and again to reminisce. Ella held up a summer dress that she had worn at primary school. 'I swear there are things here that haven't fitted since I was about ten.' She looked over just as Nicola grabbed an old shoe box from the back of a shelf in the now empty wardrobe. 'Leave that!' she shouted, and Nicola pulled her hands back as if the cardboard was hot. 'Sorry. I mean, just leave the box. It's nothing… just leave it there.'

'No worries.' Nicola pushed the box back and sat down on the bed. 'I don't want to be an interfering old busybody. Hey, remember this one!' Johnny B. Goode was playing on the record player, and she did a little shimmy on the bed to reassure Ella that they were good. 'Right, now for the trunk. What the hell have you got in there? A dead body?'

'I don't know. Maybe. I've been too scared to look.' Ella snapped open the metal catches and flipped the top of the trunk back so that it rested on the wall behind it.

'Bloody hell, Ella. Did you just fling it all in?'

'Something like that. I was in a bit of a rush to get out of there.'

'Do you want to… you know… talk about it? What happened at the school?'

'Nah, not really. Crazy fuckers. I'm just glad I'm out of there.' Catriona's face appeared again. She blinked. Catriona disappeared.

Nicola seemed happy enough with Ella's response. 'There's so much stuff. What are you going to do with it all? You're not going back there are you?'

'I don't know. I don't think so. They pretty much kicked me out.' Ella didn't know if she was ever going back to Saint Cs.

'What the fuck! Please tell me you didn't have to wear this!' Nicola held a pinafore up in front of her. It practically reached the floor and it was wide enough to fit both of them inside.

'Bad, eh?' Ella pulled out a blue aertex and saw the name tape on the inside of the collar, the tiny, regular stitches that the Wasp-Witch had made. She remembered the pursed mouth, felt the spit and the resentment contained in every single stitch and shivered. 'Give me a binbag. There's a second-hand uniform shop at the school. Maybe Dad could hand it in there and get some money back?'

They emptied the trunk, folding what felt like hundreds of items of uniform. At the bottom was the quilt. And rolled inside it was the small statue of the Virgin. Ella had left it there deliberately. What good had it done her? But when she unwrapped it from the quilt it felt smooth and solid, cool and comforting in her hand. She placed it on the desk, on top of the black and white photograph, frameless now.

'What's this?' asked Nicola, holding up an envelope that she found in the pocket of the tunic. 'Letter from one of your friends?'

'I didn't have any friends in that place,' she said. But even as she said it, she knew that wasn't true. She took the letter and put it under the statue, on top of the photograph.

When the trunk was empty, they carried it down the stairs and through the kitchen. Dad was making a pot of coffee and some ham sandwiches. 'I thought you two might be hungry. Sounds like you've been having a great time up there. It's been a long time since I've heard that kind of music from your room, Ella-Bella. Usually your music makes my ears bleed.'

It had been a long time since he had called her Ella-Bella.

After lunch they finished off the room, making the bed with fresh sheets and spreading out the quilt. All that was left were the records. Nicola scooped them out from under the bed. 'Your dad's right, you've got some right shit here. Bauhaus? Kill me now!' She groaned and faked her own death on the carpet that she'd just hoovered.

But there wasn't just the new stuff, all the old records were here too. Mom's records. Ella spread them out on the floor. *Let it Bleed. Blood on the Tracks. The Doors.* Mikey knew these. There were songs on his mix tapes from all of them. She ran her fingers over the album covers. This was the music she had grown up with. She took James Taylor's *Gorilla* out of its sleeve and put it onto the turntable. Track 3. *How Sweet It Is (To Be Loved by You).*

When the light started to fade, Ella lit the lamp on her desk, sat on her bed with her legs curled up under her and smiled. 'Thanks. I really appreciate all you've done.'

'What are friends for, hey?' said Nicola. Ella felt a weight in her chest as she thought about the question, and Catriona's face flashed into view.

'I'll need to get home. I've got Biology revision and an essay on the suffragettes.' Nicola looked around the room, satisfied with their work. 'Looks good, hey? Hang on a wee minute. It just needs one more thing.'

She ran downstairs and Ella heard cupboard doors banging, the backdoor opening, taps. And then her heavy footsteps on the stairs again. She returned with five jam jars full of daffodils and dotted them about the room, filling the space with colour. 'Doesn't take much to brighten things up.'

CHAPTER 39

Redemption Song
(Bob Marley and the Wailers)

When Nicola was gone, Ella swapped the James Taylor for a Bob Marley album. It had been one of Mom's favourites. With the lamp on and the bed made, her room didn't look that bad. She felt loose, unwound, a little bit brave, and from the top shelf of the wardrobe she took down the shoebox. She wiped a flat hand across the dusty lid.

What would happen if she opened it? Would things fly out? Would she be sucked in? With one hand on the lid and one hand underneath, she nursed the box and its contents, drawing it closer, feeling its push and its pull.

She knew roughly what was inside. She had watched while the Boston Grampies had packed things away. *For safekeeping*, they had said. *One day you'll be glad we saved all this. Someday, you'll be ready to open it up.*

Was she ready now?

And then the door opened. No knock, just a gentle opening.

And Dad was standing there, like an oak tree, in his brown cords and green jumper. 'Hey Ella, it looks fantastic in here. You and Nicola have done wonders. I can take all that stuff to the charity shop in my lunch hour tomorrow and...' He stopped, his eyes settling on the box in her hand.

Her legs dangled over the edge of the bed, and she looked up at him, feeling suddenly small.

'Hey, honey.' He sat down on the bed beside her.

She couldn't talk. But she didn't want him to go, so she shrugged and leaned into him, a little. It was the tiniest of gestures but it seemed to her that he had been waiting for it. He breathed in deeply and put his arm around her shoulder. 'Shall we look at this together?' he said.

And he waited.

The voice in her head was loud and hard to ignore. *Tell him to back off*, it said. *You're better off without him. Be safe.* But somewhere in the dark interior something voiceless was unfurling. Something fragile and scared that needed him to stay. So she nodded, and he put his big hand over hers and held it there for a moment.

She opened the box.

Tightly bound with a hair ribbon, the bundle inside was just as she remembered it. She spread the contents over the bed between them: letters, photographs, lunchbox notes, homemade cards, pressed flowers. She touched things tentatively at first, fearful that they might hurt her. But Dad was bolder, opening up the cards, reading the messages aloud. Soon she was joining in.

'Look at this one,' Ella laughed, her finger tracing the unsteady handwriting: *You is a bad mommy for making me go to bed wen the sun is shinning. Hate, Ella.*

Dad smiled. 'You were such a funny little girl. You used to make us laugh every single day.' He picked up a message written in green crayon. 'Look at this one: *Dear Mommy, I love you more than ketchup.*'

Ella remembered writing it. As if it were yesterday. Sitting at the kitchen table. They were having hotdogs for lunch. Mom had stuck the note to the fridge with a magnet shaped like the Statue of Liberty and kissed her on the top of the head.

The pain in the box was the love in the box. It flowed through her fingertips, and into her veins, all the way to her wilted heart, pumping it until it was full again, so full it felt like it might burst. And tears which had been held back for so long, flowed at last. And Dad sat with her, holding her close. He sat with her until there were no more tears and then he sat with her in the silence.

'I'm sorry, Ella,' he whispered finally. 'I let you down. You were so little… and you needed me. But without her… I was lost.' He picked up a small square photo of Mom, dancing in bare feet, her long hair spinning. 'She'd have known what to do.'

Ella looked up at his wet face, tears were running into his beard. His glasses were steaming up. She took them off his face and put her hands on his cheeks. 'I'm the one who should be sorry, Dad.'

'No.' He said, emphatic, and squeezed her hand. 'You have nothing to be sorry for.'

She shook her head. 'I do.' At the worst moment of their life she'd made it worse. Her words had broken him. She knew it. And how could she ever be forgiven for that? 'I didn't mean it. When I told you that I wished it was you and not her. I didn't mean it, Dad.'

He looked at her with surprise, his eyebrows raised. 'When? When did you say that?'

'That night in the hospital.'

He pulled her closer and she rested her head on his chest. She felt his warm breath on the top of her head, his hand on the side of her cheek. 'I don't remember much about that night. I certainly don't remember that. But if you did say it, it was only what I was thinking. Oh Ella, my Ella-Bella, there's nothing to forgive.'

She crumpled onto the bed and he lifted her head onto his lap and stroked her spiky hair. He loved her. She loved him. She was connected to him through every cell of her body, her pain was his. But now, it was not stifled and smothered. It had oxygen; they could name it. Their grief came from love, and the love was out of the box.

'Contra mundum. Like the old days?' she said.

'Contra mundum,' he replied.

CHAPTER 40
Brand New Cadillac (The Clash)

It was almost 8am and the sun was up as Ella walked to the bottom of the village to catch the bus for school. As she approached the shelter, Craig, his arm proprietorially around Elaine's shoulder, shrugged a kind of reluctant greeting and Nicola stepped out of the bus shelter to stand by her side.

She had been back at the Leven for a few months now, and Nicola had hardly let her out of her sight. On the bus they occupied Ella's old double seat at the front because Nicola said she didn't want to see Craig snogging the face off Elaine. And that seemed fair enough.

***

Before she'd gone back to school, Dad had taken a few days off work and they'd hung out together. Nothing special. Just ordinary stuff. They'd stocked up at the supermarket, watched TV, and on a bright spring morning, spur of the moment, they drove up to the Braes of Foss and climbed Schiehallion. There was a sharp breeze and not a cloud in the sky. Ella's eyes glistened in the wind, and her cheeks glowed like plums.

On the way back down the mountain, she told Dad everything that had happened at Saint C's. He knew the story, of course. Or bits of it. According to the Bulldog, it was simple. Ella had sold a false story to the papers, she had broken the code of conduct, she was no longer welcome at Saint Cecilia's. And he'd read the papers, just like everybody else. But he knew nothing really.

She had thought he would take an anthropologist's interest in the Cecilians, their rituals, Our Lady's Tree. But he didn't seem to give a stuff about that. Instead, as he listened to her story, he seemed to waken up. Like a bear coming out of winter hibernation. And his anger surprised her.

As soon as they got home, he phoned the Grandparents. She sat at the top of the stairs, listening. 'You were wrong,' Dad said, his voice strong and resolute. 'What Ella needed, what she needs, is to be at home. With me.'

'Go, Dad!' Ella whispered.

He wrote to the Editor in Chief of the Recorder Group. He showed her the letter. In it he accused the paper of exploiting vulnerable children and complained about Jack Trentham and his unscrupulous tactics. Ella hadn't felt exploited, she was more than a match for Trentham, but she was pretty impressed with Dad's incandescent rant.

The full force of his rage, however, he reserved for the nuns. She heard him on the phone to the Bulldog, expressing his outrage at her handling of the situation and his incredulity that they had believed Mhairi and the Cecilians over her.

And when his anger abated, the two of them sat at the kitchen table, eating a Chinese take-away and talked about her choices. She had to go back to school, there was no question about that.

But Perth Academy or The Leven? The decision was hers. One thing was certain though, wherever she went it wasn't going to be Saint C's. Dad made that quite clear. 'I sent you away twice before. I'm not letting go of you again.'

Starting fresh at Perth Academy might have been easier in some ways. But much as she had hated her old school, Nicola was there, and that made the choice easy. They'd seen each other every day since the bedroom make-over.

Dad had a meeting with Mr Kelman. It took a bit of persuading to convince him that Ella would be less trouble this time around. He had assured him there would be no more chopping and changing – Ella was on an even keel; she would be coming back for good.

And when she started back at the Leven, in some ways, nothing was different. She could find her way round, knew the routines and the teachers. It was reassuringly boring to be back. But in other ways, everything had changed. She'd been something of a minor celebrity once before, when she arrived in the village as a cute seven-year-old, fresh off the plane from Boston. And now she was a minor celebrity again. At first it was all anyone had wanted to talk about, and they'd buzzed about her like wasps around a spoonful of jam.

'Whit did she look like?'

'Wir ye fashin' yersel?'

'Is it true what those posh girls were up to?'

'Did they really pay you £10,000 for yer story?'

Part of her enjoyed all the attention. She wasn't invisible anymore. And she could walk away from it whenever she wanted. With Nicola right by her side.

On the bus they talked about Saturday. They were going to Quick Burger, a new place that had just opened at the bottom of the Nethergate. It was 'American-style', and the closest thing to a McDonald's they were going to get in Dundee. They were meeting up with Cass and Dek in the afternoon and Mikey was joining them after work. They had become quite a unit. Cass was never off the phone. They'd already decided what they were going to order, now they were just figuring out what to wear.

But something was still not quite right. As she lay in bed, unable to sleep, her thoughts switched from Catriona to Magda and back again. In the dead quiet of the night she knew it was time to put things right. She was done with running away. Done with waiting for someone to sort things for her. This was a mess she had to fix herself.

***

The leaves were out on the trees and the nights were shorter by the time she came up with a plan.

'You must be boilin' in those Docs,' said Nicola. She had pulled her skirt up over her thighs and rolled her socks down to her ankles.

There were only a couple of days left before the summer holidays and they were sitting on a low wall at breaktime, with their legs stretched out in front of them. Ella had replaced the hoop in her nose with a sparkling stud and it glinted in the sunlight. 'I've been thinking. Do you fancy taking a road trip at the weekend?'

'A road trip?' Nicola looked at her like she was off her head.

'Yeah, I'm thinking we could persuade Mikey to drive us. Maybe Cass would come too.'

'Where?'

'Saint Cecilia's.'

'Are you off your head? Why would you want to go back there again? They're all as mad as –'

'Yeah. They are. But this one girl, Catriona, I've told you about her, she was nice. And I feel like there's unfinished business, y'know.'

'Could you not just write her a nice wee letter? You're good at writing.'

'Nah, I think this needs to be done in person.'

'When were you thinkin'?'

'Saturday. Saint Cecilia's follows the English holidays, and they don't break up for a few weeks. We could camp. Dad's got all the gear.'

'Could be a laugh, I suppose. If my mum would let me. Which I doubt. Let's run it by Mikey after school.'

***

'No way. It's out of the question,' said Dad as he ladled out the chilli con carne. The atmosphere in the kitchen might be better these days but the same could not be said about his cooking.

'Wait. Hear me out. We need to give back all that uniform. It's hardly been worn and the bin bags have been sitting on the landing for months now.'

'Yes. That's true. But why don't I drive you up? I'd like to sit down with Sister Hanrahan. There's still plenty I've got to say to that woman.'

'No, that's exactly what I don't want. If anyone's going to say anything it should be me. I've had enough of letting everyone else do the talking.'

He looked at her with that expression he always had when he was thinking *you remind me so much of your mother*. But he knew better now than to say the words out loud.

'I'm sure there are things you want to say, but she's a formidable woman, and I'm not comfortable with the idea of you facing her alone. She left you in pieces last time.'

'It's not her I want to see. It's Catriona. The friend I told you about. I need to put things right with her. It has to be face to face.'

'I'm all for that. But I'm not too happy about Mikey driving you all that way. The boy's off his head most of the time, and that car's a banger.'

'Seriously Dad? You're having a go at his car? Have you seen the state of ours?'

Dad smiled. 'You have a point. But is he a safe driver?'

'He passed first time. And the car's passed its MOT. He's not as daft as he looks. He's been promoted to deputy manager in Bruce's. He's growing up, Dad. We all are.'

Dad paused. He was much more chilled these days, but his forehead was crinkled and his mouth was tight. 'Would it be just the two of you?'

She screwed up her nose. 'Ew! No! Cass and Nicola are coming too. We thought it would be a great way to start the summer holidays.'

'And Nicola's mum's happy with this?'

'Oh, yeah,' she said. It wasn't exactly a lie. Mrs Stout *had* agreed. Eventually. 'She's buying the sausages.'

'Well, I suppose… if Mrs Stout is happy…'

Dad stopped talking and ate a forkful of rice.

'Let me think about it overnight.'

She knew not to push it.

In the morning at breakfast, he was sitting at the table surrounded by Ordnance Survey maps.

'I've given your proposal a good deal of thought. I can't say I feel easy about it, but I trust you.' He nodded, as if he was still trying to persuade himself.

'Thanks, Dad. I won't let you down. I promise.' And she meant that. She really did.

'But if you're going to camp, at least let me get all the gear ready.' He wagged his forefinger at her. 'And I'll pack the car when Mikey picks you up.'

And so it was decided.

***

On Saturday morning they heard the music pounding before they saw the green Cortina. *Highway to Hell.* Mikey was having a laugh.

'This mix tape is fuckin' epic!' Mikey leaned out of the window, reversing up the drive. 'Sorry Mr Richardson, I mean Dr Richardson...'

Cass and Mikey piled out of the car just as Nicola arrived with her holdall and two bulging Tesco carriers. The binbags full of school uniform, the tent and the sleeping bags were piled up in front of the garage. Dad had found a camp stove, pots and pans, filled jerry cans and washed out the old tin mugs. And he packed it all into the boot while Ella and the others looked at the tiny play list on the tape in Mikey's hands.

'Ella knows how to put the tent up. We used to go camping a lot when she was small,' Dad said.

'Quite the Girl Guide, weren't you Ella?' said Cass.

Ella jolted, but when she looked across at Dad he was smiling reassuringly. He knew she could do this. She knew it too.

'Dib Dib Dib, Dob Dob Dob. You can rely on me,' laughed Ella.

***

Cass sat up front with Mikey and Ella and Nicola sat in the back. They sang along to the mix tape with their heads stuck out of the window. Ella's hair had grown. It was now a choppy bob and the wind blew it back from her face, catching her eyes till tears streamed down her cheeks, smudging her black eyeliner. They could hardly hear themselves as the car rattled along the A9 and Saturday drivers, out to enjoy the countryside, honked their horns in disapproval as *Holiday in Cambodia* blasted out of the windows.

They had a pee stop after a couple of hours and she used the money Dad had given her to buy Spangles, Opal Fruits, Munchies and Irn-Bru.

'You should sit in the front, Ella. Eh dinnae hae a clue whar the fuck we're goin',' said Cass.

Dad had written instructions and paper-clipped it onto the right page of the AA Roadmap he'd left on the dashboard. Ella was a decent map-reader and although she had only done this drive once before, she had no trouble directing them to Belgaddie.

The campsite was on the far side of the village, past the pub. 'I used to run around here,' she told them as they drew up.

'When you were trying to escape from they nut-jobs?' said Mikey.

'Something like that.'

But for a few sheep, the campsite was empty. At Cass's insistence, they chose a pitch close to the shower block. 'In case

Eh need a wee in the middle o' the night. That sheep has a right beady look in its eyes. Eh wouldnae trust it as far as Eh could spit.'

They unpacked the car and Ella and Nicola got to work on the tent, while Cass and Mikey unfolded the camping chairs and made sandwiches for lunch. 'Not exactly rock and roll, but comfy,' said Mikey as they settled down to eat.

'Once we've had wir lunch, we'll come wi you to drap aff they clothes,' said Cass.

'It's okay. I can go on my own,' said Ella.

'No way,' said Mikey, 'We've no come a' this way no tae get a look at they mad bitches. And anyroad, you cannae carry a that on yer ain.'

He had a point. There were three binbags full of clothes.

'Before we go though, I need tae dae something wi yer hair,' said Cass.

She sprayed Ella's short black bob and backcombed it within an inch of its life. 'Great. Ye look like thon lassie fae Bananarama.'

Ella laughed. 'Just the look I was going for.' She was wearing a black T-shirt and black jeans and what she lacked in colour, Cass made up for in spades. She was in a fluorescent pink tutu that her mum had made, black fishnets and yellow patent stilettos. 'They're crackin', but they're no great in a' this mud,' she laughed and Ella and Mikey took an arm each and lifted her out of the field.

Mikey looked hot. His bleached hair was spiked solid and his tartan bondage trousers were tight on his thighs. The belts that strapped his legs together made it hard for him to take big steps, but he looked cool, so who gave a shit. They didn't make quick progress, what with the bin bags and the stilettos and the bondage trousers, but Nicola was in her trainers. She took one bin bag and Ella carried the other two.

Two old men who were on their way into the pub for an afternoon pint, stopped in their tracks as they walked past.

Cass blew them a kiss. 'Shut your gobs, old timers. Yer drooling!'

'I'm not sure Belgaddie has seen anything quite like us before,' said Nicola and the four of them strutted, slowly, wobblily, down the main street of the village towards the gates of the school.

CHAPTER 41

Once in a Lifetime (Talking Heads)

As they walked between the pillars of the giant wrought iron gates, Ella swallowed hard, trying to control the nervous laughter that bubbled in her throat.

Most of the Saint C's girls were outside, playing rounders or tennis, or cheering on their friends, and the gravel driveway in front of the school was full of parents clustered around their Range Rovers, drinking tea from tartan flasks.

'Fuck me sideways! It's like Buckingham Bloody Palace!' gasped Cass, teetering in her towering heels while Mikey, leather jacket slipping off one shoulder, surveyed the scene.

'You okay?' asked Nicola, who was staying close.

'I'll be better when we get rid of these bags.'

Pupils were banned from using the wide staircase at the front of the building. But Ella was no longer a pupil. 'This way,' she said. 'Follow me.'

From somewhere on the gravel, a familiar voice called after them. 'Stop right there, young lady!' The Bulldog heading towards them.

Ella's stomach clenched. 'Hurry!' she called as she and Nicola bounded up the stairs. But the other two were not so fast. Cass, wobbling in her heels, clutched Mikey's elbow. He was laughing like a hyena, struggling to move his legs wide enough apart to get up the steps with any speed. And by the time they got to the top, the Bulldog was at the bottom.

Ella threw open the doors into the Great Hall.

'Bloody Hell!' shouted Nicola as they stepped inside. 'This is not exactly The Leven!'

All four of them looked up at the great glass dome.

'Ella Richardson. Is that you?' The Bulldog was standing in the open doorway, panting. She blinked her stony eyes, dazzled by Cass and Mikey.

Ella turned. 'Yes, Sister. It's me. I'm back. But don't panic, I'm not staying. We're just dropping off these bags at the uniform shop – Dad's arranged it with Mrs Short – and then we'll be on our way. I'm glad we ran into you. I wanted to say thanks.'

The Bulldog shook her head, her wattly jowls flapping under her wimple. Ella's words had thrown her off guard. 'To say thanks?'

'Yes. I was a bit lost before I came to Saint Cecilia's. Confused. And you were right – I *was* troubled, maybe even jealous like you said. I still don't know *exactly* who I am, but at least I know now what *I'm not*. I'm not cruel or wicked. I'm not a hypocrite like you.' The Bulldog clutched the banister of the great, wide staircase as Ella continued. 'But hey, we both know that nothing's as straightforward as all that. So, yeah. Thanks. Thanks for all you've done.'

The Bulldog's mouth flapped open, but no words came out.

'Great outfit,' Mikey piped up. 'I've got a spare ticket for a *Sisters of Mercy* gig down in Leeds if ye fancy it?'

'Come on, let's go,' said Ella, and her friends followed her out of the Hall, leaving Sister Hanrahan slack-jawed, and temporarily immobilised.

'We've gotta move quick,' she called over her shoulder. 'She'll call out the dogs. We don't have long.'

They followed her through the maze of corridors until they arrived at the uniform shop and dropped the heavy binbags. Ella stretched her arms above her heads, glad to be free of the dead weight.

'Right,' said Nicola, 'time for the grand tour. Show us where you used to sleep and all that. This place is bonkers.'

Like a game of cops and robbers they listened for the swish of nun-robes at every corner, then sneaked on tiptoes down the passageways. Mikey was hamming it up, pointing his toes and bringing his knees up as high as the leather straps would allow.

She showed them the dorms and led them up the narrow staircase to the bathrooms with the ancient claw-footed baths. She took them to the shed with the pets and the empty dining room, where Mikey sang *If you don't want to fuck me baby, baby fuck off.* And spotting a posse of nuns, she pulled them down Silent Corridor and into the Chapel where the group grew uncharacteristically still.

When the coast was clear they sneaked up the back stairs to the San and standing in the big, bay window Ella pointed out the woods, the glade, the top of Our Lady's Tree. All across the pitches groups of girls were walking back towards the school where parents, full of afternoon tea, were packing up their hampers.

Finally, Ella walked her friends down the main staircase and out through the double doors to the front drive. It was time to go it alone.

'I'll see you back at the campsite,' she said. 'There's something I have to do.'

She watched the colourful trio make their way back down the drive. Heads turned as they passed by. Mikey pointed at a cluster of women in fancy headscarves, and punched the air with a fist, poking his middle finger straight up towards the sky. Cass wiggled her bum and blew a kiss at a nun. They had come all this way for her.

Alone, Ella made her way to the Form Room. And there, at the far end of the front row was Catriona. Ella watched her for a while. Catriona had been in that same position when she first saw her, using a ruler to cross off the words in a word-search. She was still dressed in her games kit and must have come straight here while the others went to change. She often did that. Ella guessed it was her way of finding some peace. That and the rabbits.

Maybe a floorboard creaked or maybe she just felt her presence, but Catriona looked up, her face rosy from the afternoon sunshine. 'Ella,' she said.

'Hi there.'

'You're back.'

'Not for long. I just wanted to see you.'

'You did?'

Ella squeezed along the row to the desk beside Catriona. 'I've been thinking about you such a lot. About everything that happened. I tried to write to you. I started dozens of letters.'

'Me too,' said Catriona.

Ella looked down at her hands. 'I needed to see you. To tell you.' She shut her eyes and images flashed through her mind – Catriona's face, bleached white as they watched the ritual, her tiny frame cowed in the log store.

'To tell me what?'

'That I'm sorry,' her voice broke. 'I'm so sorry… that I let you down. I know this doesn't make it any better, but I need you to know that I never meant to hurt you. I only ever wanted to hurt them.'

'Them?'

'Well, Mhairi, really. She was the one I wanted to suffer.'

Catriona straightened her ruler. 'I don't understand her.'

'Me neither. When I was here it seemed pretty simple – she had everything, and I had nothing.' She felt embarrassed saying it. It sounded pathetic. Spoilt. But it was true. She had been jealous.

Catriona scrunched up her nose, wiggling her glasses back into place. 'Yeah. I know it seems like she has it all, but if her life is so fantastic, would she have made up all that stuff? About the visions and everything?'

Ella thought about that for a second. 'You're right. It doesn't make sense. Do you think everything that happened was just to get attention?'

'Maybe.' Her eyes darted to the door, as if she wasn't sure whether she should go on.

'Please. I want to understand.'

Catriona put her pencil in the little groove that ran along the top of the desk. She was whispering now. 'I don't know for sure. It's just gossip really. I mean it's true that she's rich and her family are powerful. But I don't think they give a shit about her.'

She rolled her eyes. *Poor little rich girl.*

'Don't be like that. Apparently, her big sister, Iona, was the golden child, the one they all adored. And she went off the rails. Disappeared or something.'

She shifted in her seat. She didn't want to feel sorry for Mhairi, not when she'd got so used to hating her.

'And maybe she's not that complicated. As long as you're loyal, she stands up for you. That's all she needs.' Catriona seemed battle-weary, her voice strangely flat. 'And we were disloyal – you and me. And she found that out.' She raised her eyebrows a little and looked at Ella over the top of her glasses. 'I was loyal to you though. And you still fed me to the wolves.'

The words hit Ella like a sound wave, their truth reverberated. She felt the shame of it and they sat in silence for a minute or two, Catriona rolling the pencil round and round in the groove.

'I wish I'd done things differently,' said Ella, eventually.

'You can't change the past.' Catriona shrugged. 'You're just like everybody else. You just wanted to fit in.'

Was she? Was she just like everybody else?

Catriona smiled. 'But you also wanted to be different.'

She laughed. Her friend saw right through her, just like Nicola. But this was no joke. She took a deep breath. 'What was it like after I left?' she asked.

'Pretty bad. They sent me to Coventry for three weeks. Nobody spoke to me, nobody, even some of the nuns wouldn't look at me. Your name was banned, obviously. The stories about the Virgin Mary just sort of fizzled out and the pilgrims stopped coming. There haven't been any rituals since then. Not that I know of anyway. Though I don't suppose they'd tell me.' She sounded so matter-of-fact.

'Three weeks of not speaking to a soul – how did you survive?'

'Oh, it wasn't so bad. I quite like it when it's quiet. I took up walking, and I copied you – I went to the Lady Chapel. I even got friendly with Magda. She spoke to me when nobody else would.'

'Magda?'

'Yes. Your old friend. You were right, she's not creepy. Just a bit weird.'

'Yeah, I suppose she is pretty weird.'

'But she sort of knows stuff, doesn't she? She could tell I was sad anyway. And she knows about the Cecilians.'

'Yeah. I asked her to tell Sister Hanrahan that she was the figure in the woods. I thought she would help me. But she wouldn't.'

'Why not?'

'I dunno.' Ella paused. 'Didn't you say once that she and Mhairi go way back?'

'Did I? Wait... Yes, that rings a bell. What was it again?... Gardening Club! When Mhairi was a Bubber.'

She pictured nine-year-old Mhairi, out in the garden planting seedlings with Magda. 'You'll probably think I'm crazy, after everything that's happened. But there were times when Mhairi was praying, or speaking in tongues or whatever, when it really seemed like she believed it.'

'I know what you mean,' said Catriona.

'And I don't think there's anything fake about Magda. Not anymore.'

There was a lot to think about.

'Magda thinks I should forgive you. But I don't know if you want to be forgiven.'

'I do,' said Ella. 'I want to make it right.' She opened her arms and Catriona threw herself at her, hugging her so tightly that she let out a squeal.

'Of course I forgive you,' said Catriona. 'You're my friend.'

'I don't know why I let them treat you like that.'

'You were probably scared – I know I was. And you were sad. It's hard to understand stuff when you're sad.'

They stood for a while, neither one wanting to let go.

'It's supper soon,' said Catriona. 'And then, of course, it's the Saturday Night Film. Something riveting I'm sure, like…'

'The Sound of Music!' they said in unison.

'I need to get going too. We're staying in the campsite in Belgaddie and Cass is doing a sausage sizzle.'

'Walk back to Silent Corridor with me? One last time?'

'Of course.'

They walked arm in arm, relaxed and easy in one another's company again.

'I thought you might want to see Mhairi,' said Catriona, 'that you'd come back to tell everyone about her lies.'

'Nah. That's not important anymore.'

Catriona looked relieved and smiled. 'I miss you, Ella.'

'Me too. I'll write. And you could come and stay in the summer? You can meet my crazy Dad. You'll like him. Everybody does.'

As they hugged goodbye Ella caught sight of a group of girls passing the wide opening at the opposite end of the passageway. Six of them. In formation. Mhairi out front. Bells and Dizzy behind, and in the third row, Theresa, Bernie and Tibbs. Nothing had changed really, except that Mhairi looked a little ashen, her hair had lost its bounce.

Mhairi saw Ella and hesitated, as if Ella – hair grown, in her jeans and t-shirt – was someone from her past who she vaguely recognised but couldn't quite place. But it was nobody. Nobody she knew. And correcting her posture she turned and walked away.

CHAPTER 42

The Kick Inside (Kate Bush)

By the time Ella reached the campsite, the others had got the fire going and Cass was leaning over the frying pan. The sausages were spitting and Mikey was cradling a six-pack of Tennent's that he had hidden under the passenger seat of his car.

'Hey, look who's back!' he said. 'Sit doon and tell us aboot it.'

'Did you get that Mhairi telt?' said Cass, turning the bangers. 'You were fair something wi' thon big nun.'

'Nah. I didn't see Mhairi, just Catriona – my friend.'

'You should've sneaked her oot for a wee sausage and a tinnie,' said Mikey, pulling a can from the plastic ring.

'Not sure that would've been her thing. She's quite quiet really, and there's a film on in the gym tonight. She wouldn't wanna miss that.'

They sat by the fire and ate their supper. Mikey played the road trip tape on the battery-powered tape recorder he had borrowed from his sister and they sang along to *2-4-6-8 Motorway*, *The Passenger*, *Truckin'* by the Grateful Dead and other travel-related tracks that Mikey had illegally recorded onto a blank tape in the staffroom at Bruce's. When *Mustang Sally* came on the girls all got up to dance around the campfire and Mikey pulled his leather jacket up over his ears and pretended he wasn't enjoying himself.

'If any o' youz ever tells a'body that I'm listening tae this shite I'll send the boys roon t'gie you a hidin'.'

Everything that evening seemed funny. Cass pulled a jumper over her head like it was a headscarf and tugged on an imaginary Labrador. 'Oh Mr Tibbles, come away from those nasty people. They look… unwashed.'

Nicola did an impression of the Bulldog, mouth open, shaking her head, like a dog shaking off rain. Everybody joined in, their lips wobbled and spit flew, and they didn't care. They laughed until their eyes were streaming. Ella's body was loose, her movements were assured. She was happy.

And as the fire started to die down, they began to tell stories from their childhoods. The mood got quieter and more reflective and everyone pulled their chairs closer to the embers. By eleven o'clock it was almost dark and Mikey was sleeping in his chair. But Ella had one last thing on her mind.

She grabbed the torch from the tent and pulled the envelope that Magda had given her from the front pocket of her satchel. There was only one place she could read it.

'I'm going for a walk,' she said.

'Fuckin' weirdo,' said Cass, who had drunk the best part of a quarter bottle of vodka. 'Wha goes for a walk at this time o' night?'

'I'll come with you,' said Nicola, standing up and pulling on her jacket.

'Thanks, but I wanna be on my own. I'll be okay.'

'Y'say that, but Eh'm tellin' you, them sheep are pure evil. That one over there has had his beady eye on me a' night. Eh'm no goin' tae the lavvy on ma oan. C'mon, Nicola, gonna chum me?'

And while the two girls stumbled to the toilet block, Ella crossed the field and stepped onto the main street of the village. She began to jog and soon she was running full tilt, breathing hard, the smell of the campfire and the fatty sausages still clinging to her hair. It wasn't as cold as it had been at the start of the year, and she soon warmed up, sweating under Dad's big Aran jumper.

Rather than run down the drive, she turned left before the gates and followed the wall around the outside of the estate. She ran along the country road that skirted the bottom of the hill, to the place where she had sat in the red Escort. Here she jumped over the wall into the grounds of Saint Cecilia's.

She was following the route of the Pilgrimage now, and she knew it well. It took her down the side of the pitches, to the edge of the wood. But soon, she slipped off the track and into the trees. It was a cloudy night and the moon broke through infrequently, her path was mostly dark. As she approached the glade, she remembered the last time she had been here. She had stood and watched Mhairi. Seen her with that man-boy. Ella had wanted the feel of hands on her own body, the closeness of his touch. She flushed at the memory.

Up ahead, the glade opened out. In the distance, Our Lady's Tree stood tall, its thick red trunk straight and true, its roots splayed like a skirt on the mossy ground. And there was the statue of the Virgin, pearlescent in the darkness, luminous almost. Ella made her way to the tree and reached up to touch Mary's tiny foot. She held her breath for a moment and shut her eyes. Something *had* happened here that first night. She had felt it.

From her back pocket she slipped out Magda's letter and tore it open.

Inside there was a Mass card with a picture of the Virgin. She was dressed in white, a long cloak draped over her shoulders, a mantle covering her head. A halo of tiny stars girdled her, and light emanated from her hands, pouring down from her perch on a crescent moon. It looked just like the statue in front of Ella. The Virgin's eyes were cast down with a motherly tenderness, just as the Virgin on the tree looked at Ella. Our Lady of Grace. A small silver medal was attached to the card. It was the medal she had seen round Mhairi's neck. It was the medal all the Cecilans wore.

Ella read Magda's letter.

> *Dearest Ella,*
>
> *I have let you down. And for that I am truly sorry. You asked for answers and I have not given them to you. But I have seen your pain and felt your struggle. Perhaps because I know something of it.*
>
> *I was a child when we escaped from Hungary. While we crossed the border into Austria, Soviet Troops quashed the uprising with absolute brutality — tanks, lynchings, public executions. Though I do not know how my father died, pictures haunt me nonetheless. But when I walk, I find my peace. I pray that you will find yours too. Perhaps the only answers worth having are the ones we find ourselves.*
>
> *Once I spoke to you of hope. But before we can hope we must understand our need. And you need your mother, no?*

Ella – your mother is in the faces of all those who
show you kindness. She is in the cells of your body
and the air that you breathe. She is the soil beneath
you and the rain on your face. Let her in. She has not
gone.

    Open your heart, Ella, as I open mine to you,
I am ever your friend,

        Magda

She leaned her back on the tree and slid to the ground, weeping. Her mother. Her mother. Her mother. There was nothing else now.

***

She did not know how long she sat there, the tree supporting her, giving her its strength, but the moon was right over the centre of the glade by the time she got to her feet. Her fingers were clumsy as she turned over the silver medal on her palm.

She put it in her pocket and began her slow walk back to the campsite. The air had a kind of clarity, as if a watery veil had lifted, and there was no need for the torch anymore. She crossed the glade and stepped into the woods, meaning to make her way back to the playing fields. Soon though, she realised she was lost. The trees became thicker, the roots denser. The smell of moss and damp soil seemed close, and she imagined for a moment that she was a creature burrowing through the undergrowth.

And then a flash of iridescence caught her peripheral vision. She turned. It moved like a firefly and she followed it through the trees, into the deepest, densest part of the forest. She pushed through the branches, keeping her eye on the spark of light, tracking it, until, at last, it settled on a rock. A boulder really, as tall as Ella.

She was afraid that if she got too close the light might vanish, and everything in her wanted it to stay, so she crouched low behind a tree, and watched. The light-source unfurled, grew, until it seemed like the moon had settled on the rock. And then Ella saw water – crystal clear, glinting in the white light, and pouring over the surface of the stone. It cascaded, like a waterfall, into a pool below. And there, kneeling before the water, her hands clasped in prayer, was Magda.

This was her spring. Her head was draped in a white shawl, as it had been that first night, her face was illuminated and serene. Ella watched as her lips moved silently. She seemed to be in conversation with the light. And then she stopped and smiled as if listening to a response. Magda bowed her head, her rosary in her fingers, her lips now whispering a prayer.

Before Ella's eyes, Magda became the water, her whole being was liquid and flowing, crystalline, a mirage. And for a moment she longed to join her in the water, to be here and not here, to leave the weight of her mortal body behind. But this was Magda's place. And she was not invited. It was time for Ella to go home.

***

Ella walked across the playing fields, pulling her jumper down over her hands, feeling the warmth of the wool. A light flicked on in the Bulldog's cell and one by one the attic windows illuminated, like a bad Mexican Wave. The first prayers of the morning. Lauds, Bernie had called it.

New spotlights had been installed all along the front of the building, but Ella didn't plan to sneak out the back way to avoid them. She would walk down the drive and out of the gates. She could see her breath. She was outlined in silver.

POSTSCRIPT
Let it Be (The Beatles)

6 months later

Ella sat in the kitchen scooping up a blob of ketchup with the last of her bacon roll while Dad poured himself a coffee from a large cafetière. It was Sunday morning and the papers were spread all over the table. Gregorian Chant droned out from the stereo and Ella was reading the joke page in the *Sunday Post*. Every now and then she read one out to Dad.

'"A teenage girl phones her dad at midnight and says: "Can you come and get me? Eh've missed the last bus and it's pouring wi' rain."

"Okay," says her dad. "Where are you ringing from?"

The girl replies: "From the tap o' my heid right doon tae ma knickers."'

Dad laughed.

She knew she was good at accents. She had Dundonian down pat. 'Have I ever told you this music really sucks, Dad?'

'I think you may have. Once or twice.'

She rifled through a drawer in the pine dresser and pulled out a mix tape. The handwriting was Mom's. 'Songs for Sunday Morning,' she read.

Ella slipped it into the tape deck and when the music began, she started to sing.

'When I find myself in times of trouble…'

And Dad joined in. 'Mother Mary comes to me, speaking words of wisdom, let it be.'

ACKNOWLEDGEMENTS

Visitation has been willed into being by a great many people. Without their love, support and encouragement it wouldn't have made it out of the notebook. Special thanks to Cordelia Dobb, who has helped me reimagine myself as an author.

I wrote a first draft of this novel at the University of Surrey and am indebted to my wonderful tutors Liz Bahs and Carl Thompson. I thank them, and my fabulous cohort for workshopping the first sketchy chapters with such sensitivity and insight. Julie Evans, Trevor Datsun, Jane Puddicombe, Emma Wood, Hannah Nathan, Flo Corr, Celina Wilde and Evan Cook – thank you, you gave me the confidence to keep going.

I am hugely grateful to my agent, Lindsay Fraser, of Fraser Ross Associates who worked so tirelessly with me on the early drafts of this novel.

I was fortunate to find a willing group of early readers and I am enormously thankful to Alice Tarbuck, Julie Evans, Trevor Datsun, Rachel Parsons, Liz Rumbold, Laura Macdonald, Lily Parkes, Florence Gill, Alyssa Gillespie-Muzyk, Clemency and Romily Gillespie and Mary Took for such perceptive and constructive feedback.

I am grateful to my fabulous Creative Writing teacher, Melanie Whipman, and would like to thank her and the brilliant 'Thursday Group' for all their encouragement and invaluable advice. Julie, Charles, Emmanuel, Bill, Susan, Cassey, Mary, Lisa, Laura, Danielle, Emily, Claire, Philippa and Jacky – I couldn't have done it without you!

Big thankyous (youz) to Katie McAlinden and Mandy Keir for

the expert Dundonian dialect coaching and to Laura Macdonald for all her help with the nuns. I am hugely indebted to Brian Gill and Claire Davies for their careful proofreading of the final MS – I am in awe of their superhuman attention to detail. Thanks to Brian and Jacky Power for their assistance with the dreaded blurb and to Gregor McAlinden for his immaculate design input. And heartfelt thanks to Catia Riva for her help with the marketing and for the stunning cover art – her incredible vision has turned my words into beautiful images.

Writing is a solitary pursuit, but I would be nowhere without the fellowship of my writing buddies. Julie Evans has read this manuscript more times than I would care to mention and her steadfast support means the world to me. Trevor Datsun has rescued me with coffee and technical expertise on numerous occasions. Danielle Simpson has gently set me back on the path with wise counsel, and Laura Macdonald is a constant source of inspiration and encouragement. What would I do without you?

I am constantly in awe of the vast creative potential of emerging adult women. Thank you to all the girls who survived boarding school alongside me, and to all the girls with whom I have had the privilege of working over the years. You are the beating heart of this story.

The biggest thank you, however, is reserved for my lovely husband David and our beautiful children – Alexander, Constance and Joss. Your support has never wavered. I love you all with my whole heart. And now I want to make you as proud as you have always made me.

Originally from Scotland, Kari now lives in the South of England. A short career in publishing was followed by a longer career as an English teacher. She has a first degree in English from Oxford University and an MFA in Creative Writing from the University of Surrey. Her first book, Pilgrim, is a best-selling memoir of a very long walk. She has won the Wells International Poetry Prize and has been shortlisted in the Soutar and Fish poetry competitions. She has been a panellist at the Guildford new Writers Festival, is a mentor at Ministry of Stories and occasionally runs creative writing workshops for children. Carolyn is married with three grown-up children. She is currently fighting a losing battle to gain control over her unruly garden and Bernard, her fox-red labrador.

Instagram: @carolyngillespiewrites
Facebook: Kari Gillespie
TikTok: WriterCarolynGillespie
The Visitation playlist is available on the author's website:
www.carolyngillespie.co.uk

www.ingramcontent.com/pod-product-compliance
Lightning Source LLC
Chambersburg PA
CBHW010815250626
47156CB00011B/3076